Augland

AUGLAND

ERIN CARROUGHER

AN AUGLAND NOVEL

NEW YORK

LONDON • NASHVILLE • MELBOURNE • VANCOUVER

Augland

an Augland Novel

Published in New York, New York, by Morgan James Publishing. Morgan James is a trademark of Morgan James, LLC. www.MorganJamesPublishing.com

Proudly distributed by Ingram Publisher Services.

Publisher's Note: This novel is a work of fiction. Names, characters, places, and incidents are either products of the author's imagination or used fictitiously. All characters are fictional, and any similarity to people living or dead is purely coincidental.

Morgan James BOGO™

A **FREE** ebook edition is available for you or a friend with the purchase of this print book.

CLEARLY SIGN YOUR NAME ABOVE

Instructions to claim your free ebook edition:
1. Visit MorganJamesBOGO.com
2. Sign your name CLEARLY in the space above
3. Complete the form and submit a photo of this entire page
4. You or your friend can download the ebook to your preferred device

ISBN 9781631959257 paperback
ISBN 9781631959264 ebook
Library of Congress Control Number: 2022935954

Cover Design by:
Megan Dillon
megan@creativeninjadesigns.com

Interior Design by:
Christopher Kirk
www.GFSstudio.com

Morgan James PUBLISHING Builds with... **Habitat for Humanity** Peninsula and Greater Williamsburg

Morgan James is a proud partner of Habitat for Humanity Peninsula and Greater Williamsburg. Partners in building since 2006.

Get involved today! Visit MorganJamesPublishing.com/giving-back

*To Mom and Dad. Thank you for always believing
and encouraging me to follow my dreams.
To my husband, Joe, for the continued love and support.
And finally, to my entire family. I love you all so much.*

ACKNOWLEDGMENTS

When I had the crazy idea to write a book, I didn't realize the hours upon hours of writing, rewriting, and editing that would go into it. The amount of support I've received has been incredible and I'm eternally grateful for all those who have helped me on my writing journey.

Dad and Mom—you've always been my biggest advocates. You inspire me to be the best version of myself and always follow my dreams. Dad, thank you for your countless hours of reading my drafts and giving me ideas. I don't think I could have done it without you.

Joe—thank you for being my rock. Days and nights that I was writing, you gave me feedback, encouragement, understanding, and love.

Michelle, Lisa, Thomas, Willie, Gavin, Wyatt, and Annabelle—the best family I could ever ask for.

Chelsea—my amazing friend who gave me feedback and help on this journey.

Kerry Wade and the team at Inspira Literary Solutions, my editors: I couldn't have done this without you.

To all my friends and family—I wish I had an entire book for just acknowledgments. I'm a firm believer that you never do anything alone. Manifest positivity to reach your dreams. There is nothing you can't accomplish.

WELCOME TO AUGLAND

Because you deserve to live a great life.

All of us here at Augland 54 welcome you and your loved ones to the Pacific Northwest's most extravagant Augland park! Choose the life of your dreams from one of our seven parks, fitted with the most up-to-date technology and customized to your needs and the specifications of your Artificial Existence Being.

Let our Atlantis Park take you to the depths of your underwater fantasy or, if the city is more your scene, live in the sky-high towers on Hollywood Boulevard. Walk amongst nature's most beautiful creatures at Predator's Biome or spend your days lounging at our Maya Bay luxury resorts. Stroll the past at Victorian or party in outer space in Venus, where every variation of person is celebrated.

Coming Soon!

Augland 54 will soon be the first Augland to present Land of Legends, an interactive park like you have never experienced before! Have you ever wanted to be a king? Be in the midst of battle? Our Battle of the British Isles simulation is what you've been waiting for.

At Augland 54 you can live your dreams as the person of your dreams! Because you deserve to live a great life.

Augland 54

An Augland Park
Artificial Existence Center

PART 1

CHAPTER 1

Ashton

Ashton looked into the brilliant sunset reflected across the water on the distant horizon. She knew the enhanced colors weren't real (the outside climate was far too cold and drizzly for this manufactured beach paradise), but she liked to pretend, even for a moment, that the heat, the sunset, and the perfect specimens walking past her were authentic.

Even after three years of working at Maya Bay, Ashton was still in awe of its artificial beauty. White sand and crystal-blue water stretched out for miles. Lush green trees and staggering cliffs created a sheltered cove around the restaurant where she worked as a server, and she daily admired the manufactured beauty. Down on the beach, crowds of Suits were headed toward one of several Maya Bay Resorts or to the Suit Transit Station, which would take them back to the parks where they lived. Their perfect artificial bodies set against the flawless landscape almost made Ashton believe that Augland was a real paradise.

Behind her in the restaurant, Marius was wiping down the bar, scrubbing the counter vigorously. He didn't look up at Ashton as she passed him to clear off a recently vacated table. He had his favorite servers, and Ashton was not one of them.

They had worked together since Ashton first arrived at Maya Bay. They quickly became friends, a relationship that lasted even after Marius was promoted to manager. A few months earlier, however, their friendship had taken a turn for the worse when Marius revealed his romantic intentions. Ashton wasn't one to continue anything under false pretenses. Suffice it to say, Marius hadn't taken the rejection well.

"Ashton," he said curtly, not looking up from the already spotless counter he was still wiping. He was short, with sandy blond hair that swept to the right and large, coke-bottle glasses that made him strangely intimidating. "I still see water marks."

Marius pointed with his towel toward the table Ashton had just cleaned. She followed the damp rag with her eyes to the empty table between the bar and patio full of Suits. Ashton nodded, acknowledging his request, and continued carrying her full tray to the kitchen.

"Now, Ashton," he said with a stern voice. Ashton jumped at his sudden spike in volume. It wasn't uncommon for Marius to act in a controlling manner; it was how he liked to lead the staff, to find their weakness and exploit it to show his authority. He was fond of power plays and testing boundaries. Ashton turned and headed toward the table she had just cleared.

"No problem," she said, turning back to the table and wiping harder than she normally would. Marius hovered around her for a while as she worked and then made his way back to his office. Ashton sighed in relief as he rounded the corner past the kitchen and out of sight.

Nearby, Niall spoke to a Suit sitting alone at a patio table. "Oh, Sandra, you get me every time!" he flirted. Sandra came in each evening at 8:30 p.m. on the dot. She ordered the same meal—a tropical mai tai, macadamia-encrusted sea bass, and mashed potatoes—while looking over the beautiful view of the beach.

Just like the sky and the Suits, the food wasn't real either. It certainly looked like real food but was, in reality, a similar-looking substance that allowed Suits to "eat" while sending taste codes via transmitters to their taste buds back in the pods. That was one of the privileges of living in a Suit: you could eat and drink whatever you wanted and never gain a single pound.

Sometimes, Ashton imagined the real human bodies of the Suits, overweight and ugly inside their pods. Niall said she was just jealous. But Ashton didn't think that was it; the thought of her body submerged in goo in a pod while her Suit traipsed around an Augland park being served by the underprivileged Suit-less workers didn't appeal to her.

Sandra's Suit was gorgeous: dark skin, brown eyes, and in great shape. She didn't wear a shirt, only a bikini top. Most of the Suits in Maya Bay looked like models: tall and thin with no blemishes. Some Suits kept their own faces, but most designed their artificial bodies to increasingly outrageous perfection.

"All right, you ready for another one, Niall?" crooned Sandra.

Since their days training at Victorian, Ashton and Niall had been inseparable. Victorian was a historic theme park in Augland 54 where workers trained before heading out to their final posts in other Augland 54 parks. There, the workers lived with Suits in their Victorian mansions, waiting on them day and night.

Before Niall had been placed in her mansion, Ashton was considered a "wild child" with little regard for authority and always getting into trouble. Niall helped her understand the way of Victorian, Augland 54, and the Artificial Existence Center (AEC) as a whole. *Work hard, blend in, keep your head down, make your way up the system.* If you were really lucky, you could end up in the Executive Office, where you would get a Suit of your own. Niall knew how it worked and played the system well. He took Ashton under his wing and became like a brother to her. Every day, Ashton thought about how lucky she was that, after Victorian, they had been placed in the same park, Maya Bay. Besides Sheva, who kept her company on the train each day, Niall was her only real friend.

"Oh, of course, Sandra," Niall responded coquettishly to the Suit.

He leaned in closer as he started telling her another joke, probably dirty. Sandra erupted in a short giggle attack and tapped Niall lightly on the shoulder. Ashton shook her head and smiled. Niall was such a flirt. Sandra grinned widely and chuckled along with him. Her hand squeezed Niall's shoulder, and his black shirt started to stretch under her hand.

Maya Bay was one of the few parks that programmed Suits to be able to touch workers. At the entrance of each park, tall scanners programmed the capabilities of the Suits for each park, dictating how they could engage with workers. Maya Bay was less of a threat due to the clientele and less-hostile Suits who lived there. Other parks, like Hollywood Boulevard, were party areas and had restrictions for worker safety. It had been rumored that the Executive Office was considering turning off certain transmitter restrictions for a better customer experience, which wouldn't be good news for workers.

Niall slowly made his way away from Sandra, carrying a large tray of untouched food to another table. Ashton followed behind him.

"What was your pickup line today?"

He turned and made a puking motion. Niall was quite good-looking and almost blended in with the overly perfect Suits who lived in Maya Bay. He used this to his advantage.

"You're up," Niall chuckled as he saw a few Suits enter and seat themselves in Ashton's section. She rolled her eyes, and Niall pushed her toward her tables.

"How are you fine folks doing? My name is Ashton, and I'm going to be your waitress today." Ashton knew how to flip the customer service switch to full force. Since the day she was born, she had lived and breathed customer service. Her ability to read people and adjust her manner came in handy as a waitress but never seemed to help when it came to her relationship with managers.

Time passed slowly and exhaustion started to set in around midnight. Maya Bay was a prime vacation spot for some and a retirement spot for others, meaning it was always busy. Ashton could feel her brain shutting down as she tried to stay awake. A new table had just arrived. She cranked her neck from side to side, stretched her arms above her head, and hoped blood flow would wake her up enough to finish this last table.

"Hello there!" Ashton greeted her new guests warmly. It was Randy and his wife Susie, two Suits who came by the restaurant every so often. Unlike most Suits, Randy and Susie were kind and appreciative of the workers at Augland. Both always asked Ashton about her day and knew most of the staff at the restaurant by name, something that could not be said about most other Suits.

"Hello, Ashton, and how are you this evening?" Randy asked her.

"Just peachy, Randy. It's a beautiful night out there." She smiled. "What can I get you?"

"Susie, what are you thinking, dear?" Randy asked his wife as he took her unrealistically young hand into his.

"You know, the coconut shrimp and Hawaiian pineapple fried rice sound amazing. I haven't had that recently. The rice comes in a pineapple still, right?" Ashton nodded to indicate it hadn't changed.

6

"That sounds great," her husband agreed. "Ashton, let's get two of those with some champagne. We are celebrating our anniversary." Randy smiled.

Ashton forced a surprised look. "How many years?" she asked with as much enthusiasm as she could muster.

"It's our fortieth! Can you believe it?" Ashton really couldn't, as their Suits didn't look a day over twenty-five years old.

As the night grew late, Niall stopped by the countertop Ashton was clearing. He gave her his famous heart-melting grin. Ashton smiled back.

"Go okay today?" she asked.

"Yeah. You? Heard you had attitude with Marius." He put his chin on the palm of his hand and placed his elbow on the countertop.

"I did not," Ashton said defensively. Marius always seemed to complain about her.

Niall laughed as he picked up a rag and began cleaning the next table. Then his face grew serious. "You really should try harder. Marius isn't that bad, and all you have to do is be nice to him."

Ashton knew that Niall had a point; he was always looking out for her. She struggled with giving into authority—always had, even during training at Aug-land Center, before she even came to Victorian. If it hadn't been for Niall, she probably would have been transferred already. There were parks that offered what were considered higher-end jobs and those were where the Trainers sent the more "troubled" workers. They were rarely heard from again. There were only rumors about the sick and twisted entertainment they were forced to provide.

"You remember the dairy farm?" Niall asked while she picked up a couple of glasses from a nearby table.

"Yes, why?" Ashton asked, looking perplexed at the sudden change in topic.

Victorian didn't compare to the beauty of the Maya Bay, but it did have aspects that Niall and Ashton both missed. It had radiant blue skies that unfurled across large, rolling hills with flawless green pastures and farming land. There were fields on the outskirts of town that had cows, chickens, horses, and goats. When they worked at a dairy farm, Suits could come and milk the cows. Ashton had loved working with the animals.

Niall hopped up on the counter he had just cleaned. "Wonder if it's changed? I feel like it's been forever since we've been there—what, almost three years now?"

Ashton didn't feel like going down memory lane with Niall today. He had a different perception—a more rose-colored-glasses perspective of Augland 54. Ashton viewed it differently. What she remembered was torment. Long hours, even longer days, working away at the mercy of the Suits and the Executive Office. Suits at Victorian had outrageous demands, from bathing and dressing them to entertainment at the workers' expense. Some would even bet on who would win fistfights or be able to hold their breath underwater the longest before passing out. To most, working in an Augland was like a prison, where the only way out was in a body bag. Others, like Niall, saw it all as a competition and worked hard to make their way to the Executive Offices.

"I think about it from time to time. I would go back there if I ever got a Suit for myself." That statement surprised Ashton.

"That place? C'mon, Niall." Ashton sprayed her table and began wiping it again. "Besides, we'll never get one. Not in this lifetime."

Niall constantly talked about getting a Suit of his own, and it frustrated Ashton. Augland didn't pay workers, so it was unlikely that any of them would get a Suit unless they made it to the Executive Offices, which was next to impossible. Their payment was a dingy dormitory, a small amount of food, and protection from the outside world beyond the walls. That was it.

"Someday, I'll be able to do it, and I'll be super buff with brown hair and big muscles like that Suit, Walter." Niall flexed his own muscles, trying to make Ashton laugh.

"You're already good-looking; why would you of all people want to change that?" Ashton threw her towel down. They had engaged in this conversation countless times.

"You're telling me, if you had the opportunity to live forever in one of those Suits, you wouldn't take it?" he snapped back.

Ashton was about to answer but saw Marius heading their way. Niall quickly slid off the counter, picked up his serving tray, and headed toward the back. Ashton turned around to the already clean table and began wiping it down again. She hoped that Marius hadn't seen them talking and pretended like she didn't notice him standing behind her.

Marius drew so close that she could feel his breath on her neck. "Thought you should know, I've submitted my quarterly report on you, and it's not good. If I catch you again talking with Niall and not working, you won't like the outcome." Ashton stared ahead, frowning, and nodded. She'd heard his threat loud and clear. "Now, let's not have another mistake like that, shall we? I think I've been very lenient with you, and my patience is wearing thin." Marius took a few steps away from her and gave a disapproving look. Ashton hid her anger. Niall never seemed to get into trouble for talking to her.

Ashton remained silent for the rest of her shift, staying away from both Niall and Marius. When the time came to catch the train, she ripped off her apron and stuffed it into her locker for when she returned tomorrow. Before she shut the locker door, she grabbed her notepad and opened it to the last page where she had scribbled almost illegible notes the night before. Ashton had only been able to write a few strokes on the train before it made a sudden, lurching movement. Glancing down at the last page, she tried to memorize the words she had written: *Reactive Power: The portion of something, something the electric and magnetic fields of* . . . She couldn't make out the rest of the sentence. *Measured in VARS.*

What is VARS again? She started flipping back through the pages as she hurried out the back of the restaurant toward the train station.

As soon as she entered the train car, she saw Sheva waving at her. Ashton pushed her way through the already crowded train full of tired workers until she was close enough to give Sheva a hug. Mornings and evenings on the train with Sheva were the best part of Ashton's day.

Each morning, she took notes, while Sheva—who had been an engineer before the war, before Auglands, and way before Ashton was born—taught her about engineering. Her conversation with Marius made it even more clear that she needed to find a different position here in Augland 54 if she was going to survive. Sheva had been teaching Ashton on the train for the last two years in hopes of helping her get into the engineer training program in Augland Center. Ashton was realizing she might need a new position sooner rather than later if Marius kept looking for reasons to fire her.

The train started to move, and Sheva began quizzing Ashton. As Ashton took notes, she had no idea this would be her last train ride with Sheva.

CHAPTER 2

Ashton

"Don't tell me. I know this!" Ashton was determined to get the answer. Sheva smiled at Ashton's shut eyes and scrunched-up face. It was an easy question, something Ashton should have known.

"An electrical current that is routed to the . . ." Ashton repeated the question. "The . . . electrical voltage divider?"

"You're right, but you're guessing." Sheva knew her well and was disappointed how little Ashton had practiced beyond their train lessons. She knew studying, on top of long, hard workdays, was exhausting and affecting Ashton's quality of customer service. While Sheva did not want Ashton to be in a precarious position at work, she knew Ashton needed to understand this material to make herself more useful, and therefore valuable, in Augland 54.

The two swayed together as the train made a short turn to the right, and Sheva reached out to Ashton to regain her balance. Ashton's hand dug deeply into her older friend's arm, the color and texture contrasting against Sheva's dark, crepe-like skin.

"Oof, I can't take those corners like I used to," Sheva half-joked as she flicked back her grey braid and pulled herself upright with Ashton's help.

Ashton turned to Sheva. "I'm exhausted; could we pick this up tomorrow?"

Sheva shook her head and smiled. "Sure, sweetie." She reached down and grabbed Ashton's hand. "Oh! I almost forgot; I got you something." Ashton looked down at the hands cupped between hers. "You didn't think I would forget your birthday!"

Ashton was surprised. She hadn't even remembered what day it was. Tears stung her eyes at Sheva's thoughtfulness as she looked down at a copper wire swirling around a white stone. The stringlike wire came up to make a loop that allowed it to be worn as a necklace. She gave a wide smile.

"Shev . . ." was all she could say as she studied the only gift she had ever received.

"I found the stone at Venus Park last week and thought it would make a pretty necklace. It's not much—just wanted you to have something." Ashton's eyes watered as Sheva pulled her closer. Her head rested right below Sheva's chin. "You're welcome, darling," Sheva whispered, recognizing Ashton's unspoken appreciation as she stroked the younger girl's dark brown hair, her hand weighing down the curly mess.

"Okay, I'll ask one more question, and we will pick it up again tomorrow. Sound good?"

Ashton exhaled, visibly protesting but not so much that she would refuse to give into Sheva's twinkling eyes. "Sure, one more," she agreed begrudgingly.

Sheva looked around at the train, trying to remember her training from before she had sought shelter in Augland 54 thirty-five years earlier. She had traded work for refuge, like everyone else, but as an engineer, she was considered a valuable asset to the parks.

The train stopped and workers shifted toward the exit, each pushing their way through until most people had departed the train. Ashton's dormitory stop was next and Sheva's after that. Before the doors closed, however, three individuals entered the car, dressed all in black with white badges, scanning the train with steely eyes. Ashton froze; security was never a good sign. One tall security guard led the other two toward them. Ashton quickly grabbed Sheva's hand in fear, stepping back until they were up against the barred window of the train car. The tall man took several strides toward them, keeping his eyes on Sheva. Ashton could feel the trembling of Sheva's hands as they approached, and she squeezed them tightly to give Sheva comfort. The man glanced down at a sheet of paper he held then back up toward them.

11

"Are you Sheva?"

"Y-y-yes," Sheva replied, looking confused.

"What is this about?" Ashton butted in, pulling Sheva behind her and situating her body between Sheva and the security guards.

"You'll need to come with us." The man reached behind Ashton and grabbed Sheva's arm, yanking her forward. Ashton still had her hand laced around Sheva and tightened her grip as the guard tried to rip Sheva away.

"No, you can't!" Ashton yelled, with panic draped across her face. The man didn't pay any attention to her. Instead of moving aside, Ashton grabbed the man with her free hand and started pushing them apart. The two other guards stepped in and grabbed Ashton by her hair and arm.

Ashton didn't let go. "Stop it, you can't take her away. Stop it!" she yelled frantically. Sheva was being pulled away and tears started to roll down her face as they were separated.

"Stand down!" The first security guard yelled sharply as Ashton's nails dug into his skin. Ashton didn't listen. She was now fighting off the two guards who were holding her as the third was pulling Sheva away. "Silence her; she's making a scene!"

Sheva tossed and turned in the security guard's grasp. Ashton screamed as they slowly dragged her friend away. There were only a few others left on the train who were watching the commotion, standing still and silent as they witnessed the scene. They had seen this kind of activity all too often. The guard holding Ashton lifted his hand, and it came down swiftly on her head. She instantly collapsed against him, and he let her fall to the ground with a loud thud. Almost at the door, Sheva cried out hysterically.

"Shut up. Just shut up!" the man shouted at Sheva as he pulled her out the train door. Sheva couldn't take her eyes off Ashton's limp body, laying sprawled out on the train floor.

"No!" she screamed as the doors closed and the train disappeared into the darkness.

It was dark. Ashton squinted as she looked up at her dorm room. The area was no larger than a closet and had black mold creeping down from the ceiling. She sat upright in bed and gave a heavy sigh as bits and pieces of last night's train ride came barreling into her mind. She relived Sheva being taken away screaming and the security guard's unexpected force. Her eyes shifted to the puke, her puke, on the floor beside the bed, and she recoiled in disgust. *What happened? How did I get home?* She put her hand up to her face and winced in pain. As memories flooded in, her eyes began to water.

She knew what had happened to Sheva, and the thought sent sharp daggers through her body. While she hadn't seen a take-away firsthand, she had heard stories of old workers randomly being seized by Augland security guards. Where they went or what happened to them, no one knew. Ashton had her theory: they were tossed out beyond the outer walls to starve, or worse, be killed by whatever roamed there.

Augland protected them from the outside world, and the workers paid for that safety with servitude. For most workers, the unknown was scarier than the horrors they faced inside Augland. Even if they wanted to escape, the walls were meant to keep whatever was outside out, and inside in.

Ashton tried to look over at her alarm clock but couldn't quite squint her eyes enough to make out the time. Her eyes adjusted and went wide: 7:00 a.m. She jumped out of bed and stood in front of her cracked mirror. She was still in her uniform: black shirt and pants from the night before, still covered in dried food-like substance from yesterday's shift. As she moved closer to the mirror, she checked out her swollen eye and the black and blue bruise forming on the side of her face. She winced in pain as she touched it. There wasn't enough time to fix anything about her appearance, even if she could, as she was already late for work. She was going to regret leaving the puke mess beside her bed later tonight but getting to work was the top priority.

It took her fifteen minutes to walk to the train, and she used it to tame her curly dark hair and smooth out some of the wrinkles in her shirt. "Crap," she muttered as she tried to scratch off most of the goo on her black pants.

The train approached, and the door opened to an empty car. The image of Sheva reaching out as she was carried away flashed before Ashton's eyes as if it were happening all over again. Sheva's scream as Ashton lost consciousness rattled in her head, then faded.

The train started moving, and she glanced out of the window toward the dark, grey walls she saw every morning. In her shadow reflection on the window, Ashton stared at her big blue eyes surrounded by puffiness and the dark shades that covered half her face. On instinct, she reached down to the necklace Sheva had given her moments before she was taken. Ashton didn't look down at it but rather examined it in the reflection. A tear trickled down her face, and she wiped it away, knowing she had to pull herself together. The black and blue face alone would get her in trouble, but being late and crying would draw too much attention, and that was the last thing she needed.

The train went underground, and the car darkened. Most of the infrastructure had been here before Augland 54, the specific Augland where Ashton worked, was built. Before, this area had been called "Seattle." Very little of the old train system had changed since then, except for some expansions as the park grew. The train emerged aboveground, and Ashton stared at the tall needle in the distance, where she knew the Executive Offices sat and Suits looked down over the park. Ashton shuddered in anger.

Ashton exited the train in a hurry and ran through the sinking sand toward the restaurant stairs. When she entered, she saw Marius working alongside Niall, serving Suits crowding the tables on the large patio facing the beach. Marius hadn't seen her yet, and she tried to keep it that way. There was a part of Ashton that wanted to get the conversation over with and another that hoped to go the entire day without having to deal with him at all.

Marius turned around and stopped in his tracks when he saw her.

"What the . . ." was all he could muster as he stared at her face. Ashton said nothing and turned to walk away from him.

"Don't walk away from me," he hissed, walking toward her. She looked up to find his beady eyes behind his oversized binocular glasses staring down at her.

"Bad night."

"Ashton, really?" He was always being overly dramatic. "What in the world is going on with you?"

Ashton tried to ignore him as she went to her locker and pulled out her apron. She situated it so it hid some of the stains from last night and quickly dragged her hands through her hair. It was no use; her shoulder-length hair had a mind of its own.

Marius stared at her, looking her up and down. He threw up his arms in disbelief and stormed off toward his office in the far back corner of the restaurant. Once Marius was out of sight, Ashton rested her head on the cool steel of her locker door.

"Whoa, you okay?" she heard Niall say. "You look awful." He cupped her chin and moved her head to the side to see the deepening purple on the side of her face. "What did you do?" Even Niall was accusing her. Ashton's expression changed, and she pulled her face from his grasp.

"I didn't do anything," she said as tears started to form again. Ashton fiddled with her apron to keep her gaze away from Niall's, and her attention distant from the words swimming through her mind.

"Ash," he started.

"They took her, Niall. They took Sheva, and she's gone," she said, breaking down.

"Shhh, shhh," Niall responded quietly, not out of comfort, but out of fear that a Suit, or Marius, would hear her cries. He pulled her into his arms. He was significantly taller than Ashton, not like that was uncommon. Ashton was short but had a strong physique. "It happens, you know that. She was old." He stroked her hair. "It was only a matter of time." She pulled away from him, giving him a frown at his remark.

"What?" he returned defensively. Ashton turned and wiped the tears away. Niall was not known for his comforting ways, but he was right, and Ashton knew it.

"Pull yourself together. I know you're sad, but you can't give Marius another reason. You don't know what will happen if you are fired." Ashton just nodded, understanding that he was looking out for her. He gave her a quick kiss on the cheek and left. While Ashton loved Niall like a brother, he had no idea how to be supportive. On top of everything, he still hadn't said happy birthday to her. Ashton always looked for his approval, but she sometimes questioned whether Niall truly cared for her the way she cared for him. But she wouldn't get a chance to find out if she didn't get to work.

CHAPTER 3

Ashton

Niall's last comment rattled in Ashton's head. *Don't give Marius another reason.* Don't give him a reason to fire her. She didn't know what would happen if she lost her job, but especially after this morning, she knew it wouldn't be anything good.

If she was sent back to Victorian, that would alienate her from everyone she knew. She would live in a mansion, serving Suits twenty-four hours a day. She would be among young, new workers, graduates from Augland Center.

A brothel would be the next worst-case scenario. The thought made a shiver run down Ashton's spine. To think of a Suit's rubber-like fingers even close to her made Ashton want to puke. What creeped her out more was not knowing who they truly were or what they looked like behind the mask they wore. A young female Suit could be an old man in a pod. The genderless, tattooed, bright-haired Suits could be anyone, of any age. But most in the pods were old. Back in the old days, before Auglands, Suits and pods had been marketed as a retirement solution: give all your money to the AEC and live forever in a pod, in any body you want. Become ageless.

After the war, the Auglands weren't so bad at first. The amusement park-like Auglands, built as retirement communities for Suits, were quickly walled in and became sanctuaries from the destruction of the war. Those who were lucky enough to make it inside an Augland traded work for safety, shelter, and food. All Ashton knew was that after the war, people had had no choice but to be in the AEC, in an Augland.

However, over the years, the conditions at the Auglands had grown worse for the workers. They were no longer safe havens but instead prisons, where workers lived and died within the walls. At Augland 54, under the current leadership of CEO Warren, the treatment of workers had become almost unbearable.

Ashton had accepted the fact that Marius would never let her go to a top-tier park like Atlantis or Venus, not with her track record. So she focused on the worst he could do. The thought of Sheva flashed in her mind and she reached up to the stone that hung just below her collarbone. She grasped the stone and tried to breathe.

But maybe she would be demoted to Predator's Biome. Most workers in Predator's Biome supported the exotic live animals in the park. They made sure the animals stayed fed and didn't attack the Suits. It was the least popular park in Augland 54 and most Suits only stayed overnight in the bungalows or visited for a day. *That wouldn't be half-bad. If only she could convince Marius to send her there.*

She took a deep breath preparing herself to head out toward her tables. Right as she turned, Marius slid in front of her, stopping any more movement.

"Oh no, no, no," he said. Ashton looked confused. "You aren't going in front of customers looking like that." He swirled a finger around her face and grabbed her arm with his other hand. "You're on beach duty for the rest of the day." His eyes were small but they grew twice their size behind his glasses as he spoke to her. "You know there need to be consequences for . . . this."

Ashton felt the pressure of his grasp against her arm and it took all her self-control not to rip herself away from him. There were many things she wanted to say, but she knew that wouldn't go over well. Instead, she gritted her teeth. *At least I wasn't fired.*

"Okay."

Beach duty meant a miserable shift in the blustery beach weather of the Northwest. The day would go by slowly and Niall would have to work all the tables himself, which would be exhausting. The artificial yellow sun and the temperature control for the machines made it feel like a tropical, warm water beach to the Suits. But for Ashton, it was still a cold, windy, upper Northwest Coast day. Ashton shivered. Marius did not care that Suits saw her like this on the beach; he wanted to make an example of her.

She walked down the steps to the sand. The restaurant was located on a man-made beach that spanned Maya Bay. On either side, large resorts towered over-head, with oasis-like pools situated in front and genuine waves crashing onto the sand. Augland 54 had built Maya Beach on the shores of the Puget Sound so they wouldn't have to manufacture an ocean. They had simply left an opening for the natural water to flow into Maya Bay and a gate for Augland supply boats to enter.

Ashton spent the day traveling around the beach picking up trash and other objects that didn't match the Maya Bay aesthetic. Her back ached and she grew so cold she could barely feel her body. She felt like she would never fully straighten or feel warm again.

Finally, Ashton slowly made her way up the stairs to the restaurant, wincing with pain and exhaustion. Niall stopped in his tracks and watched her slowly hobble into the back room.

"Oh, Ash," he said sympathetically. Ashton rubbed her hands together to try and get warm. Her body felt like ice and her face felt like fire from all the seawater and wind that had repeatedly pelted her chapped skin. Niall didn't touch her; instead, he stood beside her as she washed her hands in the sink beside the dish pit. Marius rounded the corner, coming from his office, and stared wide-eyed. Ashton's wild hair, black and blue face, and now-bloodshot eyes made her almost unrecognizable.

"Well, I think you are done for the day," Marius started, shifting in his shoes. If he felt bad about her current state, he didn't show it. He knew she would be cold, chapped, and that her eyes would burn in the wind: that was part of the punishment, but he hadn't expected her to look this bad. "I hope you learned your lesson." He briskly exited the dish area and headed out toward the now-empty restaurant.

"What a sack," Niall cursed toward Marius once he was out of earshot.

"I'm going home," Ashton said. All the energy had drained from her and she had no desire to hear Niall's empty threats to defend her honor.

"Want me to walk you to the station?" Niall asked.

18

"No." Normally, she would have welcomed the company, but the thought of another train ride without Sheva was too much to bear, and explaining her sadness to an unsympathetic Niall would be worse.

"See you tomorrow."

A few days later, Ashton's eye and face had faded from purple and blue to green and yellow, which was almost as off-putting. Marius kept her in the back, washing dishes while her face healed. Today was the first day she would be back in front of Suits and she welcomed the shift back to normalcy.

She took a deep breath and headed toward the tables near Niall's section, where a group of Suits had been sitting for quite some time. Before Ashton could say anything, a Suit with long, blond dreadlocks and deep brown skin interrupted her.

"We will start with four bottles of champagne and fresh-squeezed orange juice."

Typical, Ashton thought. "Right away!" she answered quickly. "Is there anything else I can get you started with?" But the Suits had already gone back to talking. She turned and walked toward the bar to grab what they had requested. Niall was behind her and shuffled closer.

"Right away, Suit," Niall mimicked her, trying to make her laugh. He liked to make fun of her customer service voice.

"Stop it with that already." Ashton threw one of the rags; he of course caught it before it had the opportunity to hit his face.

"You have the worst table; I had them yesterday," Niall remarked as he looked over at the table she had just served. He always knew everything about everyone, even the Suits. When they had lived in the same mansion at Victorian, he had fallen into trouble a couple of times for his gossip. Still, Ashton found it hard not to love him for the person he was. Niall could be intrusive and lacked empathy, but he had a heart of gold. She was glad to still have someone now that Sheva was gone.

"Thanks, I noticed." Ashton rolled her eyes. First customer of the day, and she could tell it was going to be a long one. Ashton pulled the computer close to her while she put in the order, but flashes of Sheva kept creeping into her mind.

It had been like this all week. She closed her eyes and shook her head back and forth, trying to stop the thoughts from appearing. Instead, she tried to focus on submitting her table's order.

"Alrighty, all! I've got your champagne and orange juice right here! Anything else I can grab for you?" She attempted to win over her annoying guests with her sweet charm. Again, no one answered as they chatted amongst themselves. After placing the drinks in front of the oblivious guests, Ashton walked away. She was only a few steps away when she heard one of the Suits she had just served dramatically spit out his drink. With a concerned look on her face, she rushed back to him.

"Oh! Everything all right?"

"Uh, does it look okay? This isn't orange juice . . . it's . . . it's . . ." He paused as he smacked his manufactured lips together. "Carrot?" He looked at her with total disgust. "How hard is it to get one thing right?" he asked the others while Ashton patted the table dry with her rag.

"I, I—" Ashton panicked. If Marius found out about this, it could mean the end of her employment in Maya Bay. Customer satisfaction was the number-one priority for management and the Executive Office.

"Pathetic," the Suit scowled.

Ashton turned and walked away to grab orange juice. Ashton never made mistakes like this and didn't know why it had happened. She went over to the computer and looked over the order she had placed for Table 4: champagne and carrot juice.

Ashton edited it quickly, deleting the carrot and opening to drinks, then down to orange juice. Of course, it was right next to the button for carrot juice. She bit her lip in frustration instead of cursing as she tried to correct the mistake without causing further damage. If she served them well from now on, maybe they would be less likely to speak to Marius. Ashton put her fist down in frustration, then grabbed the bottles of champagne and the newly poured glass of orange juice. She stopped dead in her tracks when she saw Marius bobbing his head over at the table, listening to a yelling Suit while he profusely apologized.

Ashton's mouth opened and she backed up against the counter. *Calm down, Ash; it will be fine, just breathe*, she told herself.

Marius shook his head as he turned from the table toward Ashton. Her mustard-yellow bruise became more prominent as all the blood left her face.

"Ashton, a word, my office," he hissed while he passed her near the bar. Marius didn't even look at her; instead walked briskly to the back. She silently delivered the drinks and then followed Marius to his office. She looked down, knowing this was not going to be good.

As she entered his hole-in-the-wall office, she noted that everything was clean and orderly, very Marius. Ashton took a seat; she'd been here twice before and knew the drill. She wasn't a troublemaker per se, but between the appearance problems, tardiness, and now this . . . Ashton knew she was in a dangerous position.

"So what happened?" he asked as he folded his hands and gave her a disapproving frown. He looked almost sympathetic for a moment. "Ashton, focus!" Marius scolded. He snapped his fingers in her face. "Why don't you tell me why you think you are here." His large bottle cap glasses slowly slid down his face but he didn't break eye contact with Ashton.

"It's been rough the last few days. I lost . . ." Ashton began.

Marius interrupted, "I don't want excuses; I want to know why we are here. From you." He studied Ashton as she carefully thought about what to say next. "You know, that's your problem, Ashton; you live in this fantasy land. There are so many people that would kill to be in this position; you have it good and you go and get yourself into trouble constantly and hang out with Niall all day. All you have to do is make our customers happy, that's it."

Ashton's fingers intertwined. This mean side of Marius was why she had rejected his advances.

"I was late to work."

"And . . ." There was a long pause.

"My face."

"And . . ."

"The . . ." Ashton started but couldn't find the words.

"Lack of professionalism? Customer service problems? Need I go on?" Marius took his time naming all of Ashton's infractions. "And what does that mean?" he continued.

"That means that . . ." Ashton paused, hoping that Marius would finish the sentence. They both sat staring at each other for what felt like an eternity. "I—I . . ." she started, but Marius cut her off.

"What are my options, Ash? I have to show that I won't let this happen in my team."

Ashton's fears rose to her face.

"Ah, I have your attention now," Marius said as he leaned back in his chair. "With the past infractions and now this . . ." He shook his head. "I just don't know what to do with you anymore." He crossed his arms and sat back in his chair. "But I can't have you here at the restaurant, or at Maya Bay for that matter." Marius emphasized the end of his sentence and shook his head, frustrated by the situation. She ignored him while she digested what he was saying. She had known it was a possibility, but was waiting for the third, or fourth, chance. Ashton thought about the many years they had worked together. She thought that would amount to something.

"Marius." Ashton wasn't opposed to begging at this point. "Please, I got sick and had a really tough time the last few days. I'm so sorry and it won't happen again. It really was an honest mistake. Last week, I got sick and there was puke when I woke up and . . ." She was grasping at straws at this point and knew it. Marius would not change his mind but she had to try. She had lost the only person who resembled a mother in her life, and now she was about to lose her job, her home, and her only best friend, the only person who'd been with her since Victorian.

"You can't come up with a good excuse this time, Ashton. My hands are tied and we do not tolerate your lack of professionalism in Augland 54. Executive Offices have requested that those who need more . . . rehabilitation, as you will, are to be brought to the new park that is being built."

It took Ashton a second to hear what Marius was saying.

"Rehabilitation?" she said out loud without intending to.

"Yes." The look on Marius's face was all business. He picked up a pen and started writing something down. "You are to move out of the dorm today and bring all of your belongings to the new dormitory assigned to you. Here." He handed Ashton the paper with instructions on where to take her things. "It's in the northern-area Augland 54, where they are building out a new amusement park, 'Legends,' or something like that. Officials will be expecting you there within the hour so you only have limited time to gather your things and head out."

Ashton didn't move. She didn't say anything.

"Ashton. Did you hear me?"

She stared off into the distance, thoughts swimming in her head. In a way, she was thankful that she wasn't going to a brothel, but the uncertainty of a new park that she hadn't heard of shook her more. Finally, Ashton nodded.

"Good. Since you are no longer associated with the restaurant, you can empty your locker and leave through the back door."

Ashton made eye contact. "Can't I say goodbye?" she asked desperately, thinking of Niall.

"I think it would be best if you didn't."

Ashton didn't move; the shock of it all stung deeply. Marius stood from his chair and motioned for Ashton to exit. He walked her to her locker and then opened the door to the beach sand in the back of the restaurant. It all happened so fast.

"Best of luck to you; you'll need it."

Ashton walked out of the restaurant for the last time and Marius shut the door behind her. She stared at the closed door and tried to wrap her mind around what had just happened.

CHAPTER 4

Ashton

The train stopped and Ashton sprinted out the doors before they had completely opened. Marius had given her exactly an hour to grab her belongings and take the train from the southwest end of the park to the northern side of Augland, which was at least a forty-five-minute train ride.

When she arrived at the new park, the train doors opened to a long, empty corridor with rows of pillars. She looked around frantically until she came to a dimly lit foyer. Doors lined on either side of the hallway, each labeled with a number. Theater 1. Theater 2. Theater 3. There were more but she didn't notice how many.

Long, red velvet drapes matched the plush crimson carpet. A few men ushered her toward a door, behind which she heard the muffled sounds of chattering voices. She swung the doors open to a large room lined with chairs and workers. It seemed she had made it just in time.

"Your attention, please." In a moment it was dead silent. A thin, blonde Suit stood in front of the dark auditorium, dressed professionally in a white pencil skirt and matching blazer. The echo of her high-pitched voice sent waves around the tall walls of the spacious room. "Welcome, all. My name is Wintefred Shozler and I am Head of Development here at Augland 54. We are so very pleased to have you here with us today.

"I know most of you may be confused as to what you will be doing here at this brand-new park, Land of Legends." She paused and shifted in her high heels. "But first, I want to take us through a presentation that will shed light on our new park. We at the Executive Office are thrilled about this new attraction for our customers." Wintefred walked to the side of the stage and the room went dark. A bright light emanating from a large projector engulfed the front of the stage, and the film began.

Ashton stared in her seat at the images of muscled men, dressed in fur and leather with long, braided hair, screaming as they ran across the scene. "Hello, fellow Vikings!" they roared. Today we fight the Saxons! Today we decide who we are and who will bow down to us! Today, we fight for our land!" Following their leader, the band of men turned and ran across a field to a large castle, where there ensued a battle between them and a group of unidentified pre-medieval-era opponents dressed in metal armor. While the video continued, snickers could be heard all around the room and Wintefred gave scrutinizing stares at the crowd. The movie stopped and the lights came back on.

"Well, that was just a taste of what our new storyline will be—action-packed to help our customers feel like they are true kings," she said, grinning from ear to ear. "We want to bring the stories of war, passion, and victory to our guests, so they can experience what it truly feels like to be in the legends of old." Wintefred pointed her remote toward the projector and changed the video to a slide show.

The first image showed Augland 54 in the background, a large compound with high walls and a globe top. Below the domed glass, there was a saucer-shaped building with a needle pointing toward the sky. "We have created an experience for our guests that provides them with the body they have always wanted and the luxury of living the lifestyle they have only dreamed of. Now . . ." she waved her finger for dramatic effect, "now we are transforming from just a place of relaxation, adventure, and happiness to interactive storylines. This is a pivotal moment for you all. You are about to become part of history.

"Augland 54 is the first of Auglands given this privilege. You should be honored to be part of something new." Wintefred finished with Augland's original slogan: "Because our customers deserve to live a great life!"

The slide changed to happy Suit-less workers at the various six other parks in Augland 54: Victorian, Maya Bay, Predator Biome, Hollywood

Boulevard, Atlantis, and Venus. There were even pictures of smiling children in the Augland Center.

"You won't be just characters—actors in this world to help turn this vision into a reality for our guests. You will become their friends and family and be a part of this adventure with them. We will teach you scripts and you all will play a vital role in our guests' experiences. You will be alongside them through the beginning, middle, and end of their journey." A moment of silence passed. Ashton was still not clear what this all meant.

"I can tell this is sinking in for all of you, and while you may think this is some sort of punishment, it is actually a chance of redemption for you all. This is your opportunity to advance!" she shouted. The staff around her started cheering and slowly the crowd started to clap. She smiled. "We will assess your skills and where to best place you in the storyline. I'll pass things over to Jorgeon, one of your producers." An older man with salt-and-pepper hair came up to the podium next to her.

"Pleasure to meet you all, and thank you, Wintefred." Jorgeon clapped alone. "We will begin with roll call, please make your way to the far-left side of the auditorium once your number is called." The workers filled only half of the space available.

"HB223, Y4718 . . ." Jorgeon rattled off other worker identification numbers. "JR105." Ashton lifted her head at her worker identification number. She saw people all around her get up, pick up their bags, and head toward the far-left side of the large room lined with chairs and separated by an aisle. She picked up her own bag, the standard duffle issued to all workers when they left the Augland Center, and began working. Everything they owned had to fit inside the duffle. Ashton walked across the room to where other workers mingled. She stood against the wall, out of the way, as the group became larger with workers.

"I was at the Predator Biome for about two years before they sent me over there," one of the girls sitting near Ashton was saying. Ashton didn't mean to eavesdrop, but the people were talking so loudly she couldn't help herself. She glanced around, hoping to recognize someone, to see some sort of familiar or even friendly face.

"What did you do to get here?" a man behind Ashton asked. She swung her head around, nearly hitting him in the face. "I slept in too many times," he said, flashing a flirtatious grin.

"How many times is too much?" she asked, honestly curious.

"Three," he said with a smile. "I'm Hunter."

"Ashton, but people mostly call me Ash." She didn't say anything else to him and instead turned her head in the opposite direction to watch what was happening around her.

"You look nervous," Hunter continued, apparently wanting to continue the conversation.

"A little," Ashton admitted. "I just don't know what to expect."

"Yeah, that's what they want. It gives them more power to hold all the information." Ashton nodded. She knew there had to be some sort of catch to this program. Everyone had been kicked out or in trouble in some way; no way they would receive this opportunity "just because." Ashton needed to focus on how to get back to Maya Bay. That was all that mattered to her at that moment. Back to Niall.

The man who had yelled out Ashton's worker identification number came toward the large group of workers that had now formed. "Hello, all! I'm thrilled to have you all here as part of this amazing opportunity. I'm Jorgeon, your acting instructor and mentor through this incredible process. What we are going to do is to head over to the room across the hall." He pointed through the doors. "There we'll examine each one of you and identify your character for our upcoming project. Once we have figured out each of your roles, we will start reading through some scripts. We have a limited time to perfect our performance, so we'll be working day in and day out for the next two weeks."

A tall girl with short, light-gold hair, seated to the left of Ashton and Hunter, raised her hand. Jorgeon noticed but chose to ignore her. "You will be living here and will find your rooms on the third floor. Directions will be provided when our work is done for the day."

"Excuse me." The young woman spoke again, standing so she was a head-length above the crowd.

Jorgeon turned his head suddenly to her, looking offended by her interruption. His face tilted to the side and he changed his expression, a forced smile passing across his face. "What was your name? I'm sorry, I missed it when you rudely interrupted me." Jorgeon quickly went from perky and upbeat to stern and accusatory.

The girl recoiled back a step.

"Your name?" he asked again, impatiently.

"Ingred," she replied uncertainly, obviously regretting her previous assertiveness.

"Well, Ingred, if you had waited to hear the entire instructions, you would have heard that I was about to inform you of everything you need to know. That will be your strike one." He wrote down what must have been her name on the clipboard he held. "To be absolutely clear, Augland 54 takes disobedience and lack of work ethic very seriously. We want to provide the best experience for our guests and are very intolerant of behavior that does not exceed the expectations set forth. Therefore, in this probation period, if you will, you all will be given three strikes. It is up to me and my team to administer these strikes, and once you have received three you will be terminated, immediately. Do I make myself clear?"

What does he mean, "terminated"? Despite all the upbeat language, Ashton had been waiting for the other shoe to drop, and it seemed like it was beginning to.

"Now, follow me and we will start the audition process," he said in a more playful tone.

The workers followed Jorgeon through a door and down a large corridor.

The blonde girl who had just been scolded now made her way to the front of the pack, most likely trying to receive some extra points to compensate for her failed first impression.

"So where'd you come from?" a very high-pitched voice asked. A thin, tall girl with brown hair and big brown eyes was staring down at Ashton.

"Umm, Maya Bay?" Ashton said.

"Is that a question?" she chuckled.

"Oh, sorry. No, I definitely came from Maya Bay; I worked at the restaurant there. What about you?" she asked.

"Hollywood Boulevard. I was a waitress at a nightclub there," the girl said.

"No way!" Ashton had never met anyone who had worked at Hollywood Boulevard and was very interested to find out what the other parks were really like.

Just then, another girl appeared. "I heard that it's like a party there twenty-four-seven. I'm Haven, by the way."

"Versal," the tall girl said. They both looked at Ashton.

"Oh. Ash."

"So is Hollywood like what people say? I hear they have gambling, parties, and lights." Haven was clearly curious.

"Yeah, I mean, for the most part, all I ever saw was the club, but I'm pretty sure there was much more outside of that. It was popular, though; I mean, there were some days it was completely packed from ten at night to five in the morning."

"Wow," Ashton said admiringly. "My restaurant at Maya Bay would get hectic, but most people came in in the morning and we slowed down toward the end of the night."

"That's because that's where all the old folks go," Haven interrupted. "I heard that they all migrate there as some sort of retirement dream or something. It seems like an easy place to work," Haven scoffed. Ashton tried to ignore it. She could already tell Haven was someone she didn't care to know.

The herd of workers made their way into another room lit by fluorescent lights and filled with cushioned chairs almost identical to the previous auditorium. Ashton's body sunk into the soft material.

"As you all know, I am Jorgeon, and I would like to introduce you to Wolfgang, the head producer and trainer for our storyline. There will be several different tiers to the performances. Some of you will play vital roles in this production and some will play more supportive, background roles. Each and every performer is vital to the success of this show, which will go live in about two weeks." Jorgeon stared at everyone, making a note to point his pen down at the clipboard.

Ashton looked around and could tell by the wide eyes of her silent companions that they all felt the same. Whatever they were meant to do, two weeks could not possibly be enough time.

"We will start promptly at four every morning in theater room five and go to eleven at night. You will perform at least three rehearsals a day. Questions?" He paused and no one spoke. He motioned to Wolfgang, who walked toward the microphone and brought up his clipboard. Wolfe, as he preferred to be called, wore the uniform of Executive Office management. He was not a Suit, but he stood tall as he walked past Jorgeon, his large frame minimizing the man beside him. Wolfe walked off the stage toward them.

"We will get started, then."

They entered their new dormitory after a long first day. It was a large room filled with bunk beds arranged in a mazelike format. Ashton, Haven, and Versal made their way toward the middle of the room. Versal picked a bed and turned toward Ashton. "Bottom okay for you?" Ashton nodded her head yes and set her bag beside the bottom bunk, relieved that Versal wanted to bunk with her. It would be awkward to walk around the maze looking for an open bed.

After putting her bag on the top bunk, Versal wandered off toward Haven and two other girls who had taken bunks near them. Ashton slumped onto her bed, but before she had a moment of peace, Hunter came by and leaned against her bunk. "Good choice," he said as he looked around. "I think it's quieter on the bottom." Ashton just shrugged.

"Where were you before?" she asked Hunter as the other girls continued to talk amongst themselves. Ashton and Hunter were clearly not included in their group.

"I was an engineer. I did most of my work on the back end of things. So I didn't work in front of them." Hunter emphasized the word "them."

Ashton sat up straighter. Suddenly, she was very interested in Hunter's profession. He may not have known Sheva, but maybe he could help her get out of here and into that engineering program. A glimmer of hope lit within her.

CHAPTER 5

Ashton

Ashton sat next to Versal in the same auditorium as the day before. The entire building was a large cement structure with fluorescent lights. Ashton hadn't been outside or even seen a window since arriving. While she knew it was early in the morning, she seemed to have lost all concept of time. Wolfe cleared his throat and Ashton forced herself to stay alert and focused.

"Good morning," Wolfe said loudly. "You will be professional and on point every moment you are with Jorgeon and me. I do not have patience for anything less than perfection when it comes to this project. My expectations are high, but you will find, if you follow the rules, this will be a smooth and fun experience for our guests."

"We will be performing the Battle of the British Isles, the battle between the Vikings and the Anglo Saxons." The auditorium went silent.

"Like a real battle?" Ashton whispered to Versal, trying to keep the panic out of her voice. Versal just shook her head as Wolfe kept talking. Wolfe was stern and his very presence demanded respect. He acted more like a drill sergeant than a manager, which was fitting as he would be leading the charge of this battle.

"This morning we will evaluate your strengths and weaknesses. This storyline requires a lot of cardio. You will be either fighting or running for long periods. After these two weeks, you will be in top physical condition. And the process won't be easy." Ashton had thought a day picking up trash at the beach was long, but it would be nothing compared to the next couple of weeks. Besides running to and from the train, Ashton hadn't needed to exercise a lot for the jobs she had had since Augland Center. From what she could tell, Wolfe looked in great shape, which made her nervous about the extent of exercise she would need to do for this park. Combat training sounded hard.

"I'd let him teach me a few things." Versal winked over at Ashton and the girls sitting in their row. Ashton shook her head in disbelief that Versal could be thinking something so trivial at a time like this. "C'mon, lighten up, he's cute!" Versal nodded in Wolfe's direction. Ashton hadn't really taken time to look at the man directing their group. She had to admit, there was something about him that caught her eye.

Versal, Hunter, Ashton, and the others around them stood up and followed the line making its way out of the auditorium.

"What they wouldn't do for those Suits . . ." Hunter said to Ashton.

She looked up at him, confused.

"Executive Office doesn't do it for the Suits. They do it all for power. And money." Ashton looked around, making sure they were out of earshot from Jorgeon or Wolfe. It wouldn't be a good first impression to be speaking ill of Augland in front of management.

"I wouldn't say that too loud," Ashton whispered to Hunter.

"What, you scared?"

"No, just don't want to get in trouble."

"We're already in trouble. Don't let that big Executive Office hotshot make you think any different. They want us to think everything is sunshine and rainbows." Hunter huffed. "Acting and storylines, there's got to be a catch and it's not going to be in our favor." Hunter was right. As they waited for their number to be called, most of the workers slumped against the wall or sat on the cold floor. They might as well take advantage of this still moment to lean against the hard cement wall in the auditorium hallway.

The silence spoke volumes as to what was on the minds of each worker, especially the older ones. Augland wasn't known for its great company perks and upward mobility, so the Executive's perky explanation of this new park didn't make any sense. Ashton knew Hunter had a point and as she stared at the older workers all she saw was fear. Older workers, like Sheva, knew life before Augland. It was forbidden to even discuss time before Augland, so there was little information Ashton knew. The young children didn't seem to mind being here, and that scared her even more.

In the hallway outside the auditorium, Ashton heard her name and looked up toward Jorgeon. She straightened up and headed to the auditorium door.

"Good luck!" Ashton turned to see Hunter with a big smile on his face. Versal echoed him.

"Yeah, good luck!"

Ashton's palms were cold and damp, and she could feel her heart beating too fast in her chest. She tried to take a deep breath to calm her nerves. *Just breathe*, she thought to herself. *All you have to do is go in there and get this done. One step at a time.* Who knew what doing well meant or didn't mean? The only thing they were told was that they were auditioning. What happened if she didn't do well? Would they get rid of her? Thinking of all the possibilities made her anxiety worse.

Ashton pushed the door that separated the workers lined up outside the auditorium and the silhouettes sitting at a long desk in the audience. As Ashton came closer, she realized there were only four people in the room besides herself, two of whom were Jorgeon and Wolfe; the other two, she had never seen before. Ashton walked up to Jorgeon, whose hand was outstretched and holding a script. The four Executive Office members talked amongst themselves as Ashton made it to the center of the stage. No one was paying any attention to her. She stared at them trying to make out their conversation but was too far away to hear anything but mumbles. One laughed at something the other said. Ashton's heart beat out of her chest, and it was all she could hear.

Taking her mind off her audience, she looked at the first few lines of the script: *Chieftain Bjorn! The Saxons are bound to make their way to us. We must attack now, while we have the element of surprise!*

Jorgeon began speaking. "Please say your name and where you came from, and then read the lines."

"Try to put some character into it," another man said sardonically. "So we have an idea of your skills."

From the distance, Ashton could see he held a piece of paper with her face and name on it. It was a profile picture she'd had taken when she started at the restaurant at Maya Bay. Ashton hadn't realized it would be dispersed to other departments in Augland.

"We don't have all day." Wolfe leaned back in his chair, visibly irritated at her delay.

Her hands shook and she tried to compose herself before reading the lines. Clearing her throat, she began. "Chieftain Bjorn!" Ashton said with as much authority as she could muster. "The Saxons . . ."

"Your name, where you came from, and then the lines," Jorgeon repeated.

"Sorry," she mumbled, becoming more nervous by the minute. "JR105, Maya Bay." She looked at the piece of paper again. "Chieftain Bjorn! The Saxons are bound to make their way to us. We must attack now, while we have the element of surprise!" This time she tried to put more effort into it.

"Next paragraph, please." It sounded like Wolfe again. She looked down at the piece of paper.

"King, the invaders are on the shore! They mean to dethrone you and conquer our land! Sir, we must defend our country!"

"All right, turn around so we can get a view of you." Ashton didn't see who made the request. She hesitated, not sure if she had heard correctly.

"Turn around."

She quickly turned around to the back of the stage and then back, staring at the white lights above her. Awkwardly, she raised herself up onto the balls of her feet and rocked back and forth. The silence was overwhelming as Ashton teetered between making conversation or just standing there. The four judges, sitting behind their desk, scribbled notes as they assessed her.

They didn't know her; they didn't know any of them, really. All they had were notes of disciplinary action, face, name, age—none of which defined Ashton. While she'd had problems in the past, she was a good person, caring for others, warm—but they wouldn't see that on their notes, or Marius's notes if they were there. She was sure they were.

34

"You may go," Jorgeon said, without giving any indication about how she had done. Ashton made her way down the stairs and handed the script, which was now a little damp from her sweat, back to Jorgeon. She sighed in relief as she started to walk farther away from the stage, feeling better with each step.

As she walked, the next person in line came down the long aisle past Ashton. The young girl looked down at her feet as if to make sure she was putting her left foot in front of her right. Ashton tried to look at her, to give her any reassurance that it wasn't so bad, but the girl just walked past her. As Ashton exited the auditorium and back into the hallway, she replayed her audition over and over again in her head. *Maybe I did okay?* she asked herself. Her inner thoughts didn't reply.

"Up! Up!" A voice rang through the dormitory. The noise bounced around in Ashton's brain as she awoke. She squinted at the bright artificial lights above her bunk; it felt like she had been asleep for two minutes. Ashton winced, her body unbelievably sore from sleeping on a flimsy mattress. Blinking felt like sandpaper on her eyeballs. Unlike her small, personal room at the old dormitory, this room was a large echo chamber that amplified the sounds of her sixty roommates. Ashton had hardly slept.

"What time is it?" groaned Versal. Ashton didn't say anything and instead rubbed her eyes to help wake herself up. Rolling over, she sat upright on her bed while others around her started undressing and putting on new black clothing. It was the same uniform she had worn at Maya Bay. Versal jumped down and miraculously was already dressed. Ashton opened her duffle bag to bring out a clean pair of pants and shirt and quickly put them on as people started walking toward the exit. It wasn't long before everyone was out the door and heading down the stairwell toward the auditorium.

"Good morning. I presume you all slept well," Jorgeon started as workers made their way to the chairs in front of him. "I bet you all are very curious about the Battle of the British Isles show you will be performing. You will be our soldiers. You will be put into two groups today, Vikings and Anglo-Saxons, how exciting. During our two weeks together, we will be rehearsing the battle scenes, which are the crux of this project. Wolfe and I have decided on the leading and the supporting roles in each group but show us a good performance and that can always change." The suspense in the air was chilling. Ashton was sure the other workers around her were nervous as well.

Wolfe stepped down from the stage and started separating workers into several groups, according to his clipboard notes.

"Byron, Roach, Hunter, Scar, and Versal, you are the main characters on the Saxon side. Versal will be the queen of the Anglo-Saxons." Versal shrieked gleefully and turned to hug Hunter, who looked stunned, but soon had a big grin on his face. Ashton waited patiently for her name to be called; she desperately wanted to be on the side with her new friends. If they were going to go through grueling physical training, she would rather be with people she knew.

"Miaka, Pais, Zeel, and Ashton: Vikings. Miaka will be the Viking princess." Ashton let out a breath as she heard her name cast as one of the main roles. She hadn't met any of the people named.

Others around the auditorium were placed in groups: Viking extras, storekeepers, cooks, animal tenders, castle court, blacksmiths, and everything else that would make the world of the Viking camp and Saxon castle come alive. The room exploded into frantic movement with people moving left and right to make their way to their respective areas. Ashton was overwhelmed by the commotion, still shocked that she would be in the battle, and one of the main characters. Niall would have praised her, but all Ashton wanted to do was keep her head down and get through this. It didn't look like that was going to happen. It probably would have been better to be cast as an extra or a maiden, two parts that were given to many individuals. Ashton looked around at the two groups that had formed— Vikings and Saxons. The groups began to separate and soon it was only nine of them left in the auditorium.

The Saxon and Viking lead characters headed toward Wolfe, who stood on the stage to the left of Jorgeon. Ashton was one of the last to make her way up to the front of the stage where Miaka, Byron, Roach, and Pais had already introduced themselves to Wolfe.

"Thanks for joining us. I'd appreciate more of a hustle next time." Wolfe looked straight at Ashton and her face flushed pink.

"I'm sorry," she said, looking away. It was day two and she had already made a bad impression.

"Don't apologize, just be better," Wolfe remarked, not looking at her. "Now that we are all here, let's get started. Miaka and Roach, you will be my stars here so we will begin first . . ." Wolfe had paired them all together, one Viking for one Saxon character. Byron and Pais would be the right-hand men for the Suits who would be participating in this simulation and would work together during the combat training. It seemed fitting, as they were of similar size and stature. Pais seemed more put together with short, blond hair and distinct caveman-like facial features, while Byron had messy black hair and crooked teeth. Byron was larger and much more intimidating.

Next, Wolfe aligned Hunter and Ashton, who would be counterparts on the Anglo-Saxons and Viking sides. Ashton thought it was odd she was placed with him but seeing as they didn't have another girl fighting on the Anglo-Saxon side, she understood. Wolfe mentioned that her role would be Miaka's maiden. Finally, Scar and Zeel were paired together.

"So Miaka, as the Viking princess, I'll be working with you closely as you will be in the middle of the battle with the customer. It is your responsibility to be with the customer at all times."

Miaka looked up and nodded. Ashton could see why they chose Miaka; she was well-built and strong and had beautiful, long, curly hair. She did look like a Viking princess. Ashton could tell just by looking at her that most people found her threatening. Ashton certainly did.

"This first week of training will most likely be the hardest you have ever worked in your life. I want you in top shape, to look as though you can fight with expert precision. I have high standards for this position specifically, understood?" Wolfe looked directly at Miaka as he spoke.

She nodded and said, "Yes."

Wolfe looked around. "This goes for the rest of you as well. Now, watch as I demonstrate with Miaka. Get into fighting pairs. Ashton and Hunter, Miaka and Roach, Byron and Pais, and Zeel and Scar." Ashton looked over at Hunter, who was smiling at her.

"What about me?" Versal asked.

"You are considered the queen of the Anglo-Saxons and will not be partici-pating in the actual fighting." Versal sat behind the group as they began training.

Versal was skinny and delicate. She didn't look like a fighter, but then neither did Ashton. Ashton was small but strong, and she hoped that would be enough.

"Best of luck. You guys have the worst two weeks of your lives ahead of you. I expect perfection, or you're out." Wolfe warned. The group knew he was serious, too. If Ashton wanted to succeed, she'd have to work very, very hard.

CHAPTER 6

Ashton

Wolfe sat in front of the cast members with a large whiteboard, drawing out the battle scene.

"Vikings run up to England's castle." He put little dots on the board to indicate where each of them would be standing relative to the Suit with whom they would be interacting. "Saxon group sees they are about to be invaded. Saxon group comes out and meets the Vikings in the middle of the battlefield."

Wolfe drew arrows as he tried to mimic the scene. "You will first battle your opponent, making a show of the battle scene, and then you will fight the customer. The choreography has to be perfect: believable enough for the customer to enjoy but practiced enough so no one gets hurt."

Wolfe continued, "First Miaka will go up against Roach. Roach then transfers and goes up against the customer. We will let you know the scene beforehand, whether Vikings or Saxons will win the battle." Wolfe put down his pen and looked at the group. "Questions?"

Ashton didn't want to say anything, but she was confused. Wolfe had run through the play so quickly she hadn't had time to process her role in the midst of everything.

Sitting beside her, Roach studied the drawings on the whiteboard intently. If he was confused, he tried hard not to show it and shook his head no when Wolfe

39

looked at him. He had a similar build to Wolfe; they had obviously been looking for strong individuals to enact the battle fantasy.

"Wolfgang, how will we know what the Suit is going to do?" Roach asked after a long pause. Everyone was surprised to hear him speak. "I mean customer," Roach quickly corrected himself. Management never called them Suits.

Wolfe didn't comment on Roach's mistake. "When the customers enter the park, they will be programmed against making contact with the workers. Rest assured this will not be a park that has no boundaries. They know this is a reenactment, but we do want to make it as believable as possible. Through training, we will teach you to read the reaction of the customer, follow their movements, and act based on that. It is important to react to every hit, as they do believe they are hitting you," Wolfe answered. "That's why this training is so important: I want you to be able to understand the fundamentals of fighting. We want this believable and safe. We want perfection." Wolfe paused. "And it's Wolfe, not Wolfgang."

A sigh of relief swept across them. The programming stations were their safety net against an unstoppable and dangerous customer. Wolfe looked around to see if any additional questions came up, but no one said anything.

"Great. Well, we will go ahead and get started then. I need Miaka and Roach front and center."

Wolfe walked the two through a slow-motion fight sequence. His actions made it look easier than it was going to be. Ashton watched as Miaka and Roach worked through the beginning of the sequence. It didn't look graceful, but she could see it coming together as Wolfe slowed down the choreography. He continued to interrupt them and adjust their positions. To Wolfe, the movements looked second nature. Ashton wondered how long it would take them to learn to move like that, or if any of them would even come close.

The room looked like a time warp as the pairs worked through the fight sequence slowly.

They had spent the past hour practicing the individual movements and it was time to put it together. Ashton squared off against Hunter.

"Okay, Ashton, like this." Wolfe stepped forward with his right foot and then swung with his right hand toward Hunter. "I need you to move right first, then swing left. Remember, you will have the weight of an ax in your hand."

Ashton squared off in front of Hunter. She tried her best to follow exactly what Wolfe had said. Hunter was much taller than she was so when she swung, she had to reach up higher than Wolfe had to.

"Good. Once you've done that, you will step back and push with your left hand toward Hunter, like so." Wolfe showed her step by step what she needed to do. After making sure she had it, he moved on to the next pair.

"You're not doing it quite right," Hunter said as Ashton practiced her right swing.

"What do you mean? I'm doing what he said!" she snapped more than she had intended. After three hours, Ashton was getting tired.

"I mean you aren't swinging up high enough; you look like you are ducking too far down and it's weird." Ashton repeated the move and realized she was crouching down to the point that she was well below Hunter's waist.

"I'm just trying to do what he did," Ashton said defensively.

"I get it; just try and stand up a little and I'll crouch lower. That should make it better." Ashton could work with this compromise. While she could tell Hunter was arrogant, he was smart and that was something she respected.

Wolfe told the group after their exhausting day, "It was a good first rehearsal, but this was easy compared to the tricks you'll have to complete. It's late, so go to bed. I want you all here first thing in the morning and you will practice before I get here. Understood?"

"Yes," the group said, almost in unison. Wolfe then turned and walked away from them. The Viking and Saxon crews stood up. Moans echoed across the room as the day's activities finally caught up with their bodies. Following Wolfe's orders, they all headed down toward the large dorm room for bed, completely exhausted.

"Well, that was fun," Hunter said sarcastically as he stretched out his sore arm muscles. Versal had just returned to the dorms and made her way to the bunks where Hunter, Byron, Pais, and Ashton were sitting.

"Versal! How was your day, my queen?" Hunter bowed down as she came over to the group. Versal made a proper face and tiptoed over, mimicking her interpretation of royalty.

"My loyal subject."

He grinned as she started laughing at herself. It was comical, and everyone chuckled watching them interact. It was nice to have some fun. This was new to Ashton and made her feel at ease, so she welcomed it. Hunter and Versal went along with their flirtatious game for a while but soon made their way to their respective bunk areas for bed. Ashton crawled under her covers when Versal jumped up into her bed.

"You know, today was not all that bad," Ashton whispered to Versal from the bottom bunk. "To be honest, I thought when Marius sent me here that it was going to be horrible, but this might actually be fun." Versal didn't say anything but rather hummed in acknowledgment. For the first time in a long time, Ashton felt like she was making friends. *Maybe this won't be so bad*, Ashton thought to herself as she dozed off to sleep. But she couldn't have been more mistaken.

"Ashton! Do you have two left feet or something?" Hunter screamed. For the fourth time in a row, she had forgotten the last part of the fight scene and accidentally collided heads with Hunter. Ashton breathed heavily. They had been training twelve hours a day for the past week, but each day seemed to get harder, not easier. There were so many fighting sequences to memorize and moves to learn. The auditorium now felt like a prison. Everyone had been starved of the outdoors and any privacy since the park wasn't yet ready for them to rehearse in. Until next week, they would be in the same two rooms with the same people, day in and day out. People had started to turn on one another and the comradery they had originally felt was beginning to fade.

"I can't believe you can't get this." Hunter stormed off. Ashton had found out quickly he had a short temper, specifically with her. She didn't respond and returned to her position. Hunter went over toward Byron and Pais, whom he had grown close to—besides Versal, of course, who could do no wrong in Hunter's eyes. Byron and Pais shook their heads as they looked at Ashton. She slightly blushed but pretended she couldn't see them and continued to practice without Hunter next to her.

"Ashton, show me your steps." Wolfe had been evaluating the other pair next to her and had obviously overheard Hunter's remark.

Ashton nodded, took a deep breath, and went through the fighting scene she had been practicing. *One, then two, three, four, five, six.* She said the numbers in her head as she swung and ducked, then hit with her left, right, then left hand again. She was thankful she was able to get through it without messing up this time. Wolfe smiled and was about to say something when Miaka shouted at Roach.

"This is ridiculous; the last part of this just doesn't look good, Wolfe!" Miaka had found her temper as well during the course of this, and she and Wolfe were butting heads. Ashton watched Wolfe's expression change from pride to frustration as he turned to Miaka.

"I don't care, Miaka. You don't look relaxed and it doesn't look natural, so the problem might not be the steps," Wolfe snapped back at her. Miaka was about to say something when Wolfe interrupted. "Think long and hard whether or not you want to say something right now."

Miaka didn't say anything, but she also did not back down. She stared Wolfe straight in the eyes until he turned away.

"Jerk," she muttered under her breath, loud enough for most of the workers to hear. Ashton looked at Wolfe, but he didn't acknowledge her and kept his glare straight ahead. He paused and looked around the room.

"We'll work until midnight tonight, thanks to Miaka," Wolfe said. Everyone erupted with frustrated sighs and went back to practicing their moves. It was nearing ten o'clock and they should have been done. Miaka didn't say a word. Ashton could tell that she was tempted to come back at him with another comment but didn't want another punishment for the rest of the group.

"Great, thanks, Miaka," Hunter said. "Not that Ashton here can't use the extra practice, but now we all have to suffer." Ashton winced at the quick jab and attention put on her. Miaka scoffed and went back to Roach, who was in position as they prepared to go over their routine again.

Ashton went back to her position and practiced without Hunter. She seemed to do much better when he wasn't with her. Hunter had been kind, even fun, in the very beginning and was quite patient while Ashton tried to pick up the moves. She hadn't realized how out of shape she was until she started working out all day long. A week in, Ashton wasn't sure if her muscles and bones would ever feel normal again. Her entire body was sore. When Hunter and Ashton missed their steps, she would end up hitting him or him hitting her. Those hits hurt.

"How are you able to make the moves when Wolfe is here, but when you practice with me you seem to forget everything?" Hunter asked as he approached Ashton.

"I don't know," Ashton said honestly. She wasn't sure why she wasn't able to get the moves down with Hunter.

"Part of me thinks she's doing this on purpose to make me look bad. Might as well go to Wolfe and let him know I can't work with her." He turned to Miaka, speaking as if Ashton weren't right beside him.

Ashton stopped what she was doing to look at him. She couldn't believe he wanted to take it to Wolfe. It wasn't intentional on her part. Still, she couldn't quite understand why she wasn't able to get things right when they practiced.

Ashton was about to retort when she noticed Wolfe beside him. She had quickly realized there were two sides to Wolfe. Most of the time he was very strict and emotionless, but other times he was sensitive and empathetic. Now was not one of those times.

"Stop standing around and go through it again!" Wolfe demanded as he saw them all talking instead of practicing. Ashton quickly drew back into position and Hunter followed suit.

"Ready?" Hunter asked.

"Ye—" Ashton was about to affirm she was ready when she saw Hunter's right arm come swinging around. She quickly put up her arm to defend herself and he came around with his left fist to her side and made contact. Ashton's breath left as his hand struck her rib cage. She could feel a sharp pain radiate through her left side. Her body sank to one knee to compose herself and she gasped for air.

"Stop!" Wolfe came running and stopped short, face-to-face with Hunter. "What happened?"

Hunter shook his head innocently. "She can't seem to remember the steps, and I accidentally hit her in the side." Wolfe looked at Hunter. He was angry, but he let it go and turned his attention to Ashton.

"You okay?" Wolfe asked as he leaned down toward her.

Ashton narrowed her eyes at Hunter, who had a smirk on his face. She nodded her head yes. Wolfe stood back up.

"I see. Well, Hunter, why don't you take twenty and get some water; I'll work with Ashton." She couldn't tell if Wolfe was upset with her or giving her a break from Hunter and his bullying tactics.

"All right, Ashton, get back up and do it again, from the start." Wolfe took Hunter's position. Ashton stood up and took a deep breath, the pain in her side making her lean to the left.

"Ready?" he asked, and again she nodded her head.

Ashton stepped forward with her right foot and swung her arm up, blocking Wolfe's right forearm. She stepped back and pushed with her left fist forward and Wolfe's right arm came back up toward her. They continued the routine. Wolfe was much easier to work with; he was patient and slowed down when she needed and picked up the pace when she found her rhythm.

"It's not that you don't get the steps, you just don't have the rhythm. You move too slowly at times and too quickly at others. It's hard for Hunter to keep up," Wolfe commented after they completed the routine. "I would say try to make it a song to keep you on track. That's what I did when I first learned how to fight."

"Where did you learn?" she asked as she caught her breath.

"I worked security before this, and we were all trained in combat." Wolfe drank some water from a bottle he had brought with him and looked around at the others, who were still practicing. "Keep practicing; you'll get it." Wolfe turned to head toward Miaka, who was currently yelling at Roach.

Ashton appreciated Wolfe's patience with her and wished she could work with him instead of Hunter, who was sitting in the back with Byron. Hunter and Ashton seemed to be at odds at this point.

"Ah!" Miaka gave a high-pitched scream and Ashton turned toward her, Roach, and Wolfe. Miaka was laying on the ground, holding her ankle and crying. Wolfe was looking down at her leg. Miaka pulled up her sweats to expose her ankle and a few of the onlookers gasped and took a step back. Her foot was limp and twisted to the right side.

"Stay still, Miaka," Wolfe said as he looked at her ankle. "It's broken; we have to get you to the doctor. Roach, take her up to Jorgeon and tell him to keep me posted." Roach, the silent giant, just nodded, scooped Miaka up, and started heading toward the exit.

45

"What happened?" Pais asked.

"Roach stepped too far forward and landed on her ankle," Wolfe said. "This just goes to show that we need to be careful and learn the steps with precision." Wolfe looked over at Ashton and she couldn't help but feel like he was talking directly to her. "Go back to the dormitories; we are done for the evening." Wolfe finished speaking and walked toward the exit where Roach had just taken Miaka.

As Ashton walked to the dormitory, she began to wonder what would happen to Miaka. One thing Augland 54 had made clear was that you needed to be useful to them to survive. Miaka's sobs were not just pain, but the realization that she was no longer useful, and that had scared her. It scared Ashton too. Then it hit Ashton: they would need to replace Miaka with someone. There was little to no chance that she would be able to perform in under a week, not with a broken ankle. So whom would they replace her with?

CHAPTER 7

Ashton

"Incompetent. This isn't rocket science!" Jorgeon's voice rose as he watched Wolfe and Ashton go through each step in the fight scene. To Ashton's dismay and horror, Wolfe had picked her to replace Miaka as Freya, the Viking princess. This meant more attention on Ashton, one-on-one interaction with the Suit, and worse, new moves to learn.

Ashton knew she had forgotten them once she had swung her leg at Wolfe and his arm had gone up in a blocking motion, which wasn't the scheduled routine. Ashton hated all the attention she was getting from management. Jorgeon didn't seem to leave Wolfe and Ashton alone at all, micromanaging every single detail of her performance.

"All right, chill, Jorgeon," Wolfe said. His patience with Jorgeon was wearing thin as well. He walked around, catching his breath as they took a quick break. Jorgeon stepped back.

"Chill? We go live in three days and you think this is sufficient enough for the Executives to see?" Jorgeon turned to Wolfe with a heat that could have burned holes into the ground.

"You focus on your side and I'll focus on the fight scenes, okay?" Wolfe had his own expectations of workers, but Jorgeon was constantly coming over to give feedback. Wolfe had passed along the management of scenes, scriptwriting, and overall customer experience to Jorgeon, which allowed Wolfe to focus on the main battle. He regretted that decision now. The divide-and-conquer method hadn't gone as well as he had expected, and the extra responsibility seemed to have an adverse effect on Jorgeon.

"This is a pathetic excuse for a fight scene. I hope they shut us down; this is embarrassing." Jorgeon stormed back through the room, throwing his clipboard at the wall. It landed as he exited. Jorgeon's attitude was getting worse the closer they were to showcasing in front of the Executives.

"You do have to be better about remembering the different steps or I think Jorgeon is going to have a heart attack." Wolfe half-joked. Ashton smiled and chuckled under her breath now that Jorgeon was nowhere to be seen.

Since Jorgeon and Wolfe had decided to replace Miaka with Ashton, it had been day and night training to get her skilled enough to play the Viking princess, Freya. Wolfe had been spending all his time working through each scene with Ashton. They had bonded over their mutual distaste for Jorgeon.

Wolfe tossed Ashton a bottle of water and bent down to pick one up for himself. Ashton fiddled with the lid of her water bottle as she built up the courage to ask Wolfe about his past working security. All she could imagine were the guards who had dragged Sheva off the train. She dreamed about the attack almost every night.

"You said you worked security?" Ashton spoke as casually as she could about the subject.

"Yes. Why?" Wolfe asked as he finished gulping down the last of his water.

"Just curious," Ashton said defensively.

"Yes, I worked security, for the last six or so years." Wolfe came back into position, indicating to Ashton that they were to start practicing the fight scene again.

"So you worked out in the parks?"

Right-hand punch, miss, left-hand block, left-leg kick, stumble, and get up. Ashton had learned this routine the day they had started practicing for Miaka's character and could practically do it in her sleep.

"No, Executive Offices." Wolfe started to sense that she was prying and he stopped. "Why do you want to know?"

"I . . ." Ashton wasn't sure she should ask or even if she wanted to know the answer. If he told her what had really happened to Sheva, it wouldn't mean the nightmares would go away. But maybe it would give her closure.

"Why are you curious about security?" Wolfe pressed further and took a step closer to Ashton. The air around her became thin as he came close. Even with his constant shifts between sweet and stern, she found herself growing close to him, even fond.

"No reason," she said, deciding to keep it to herself.

"There's a reason. You want to know about something?" Wolfe studied her. "No, not something. Someone?" Ashton's eyes shifted and Wolfe slightly smiled. He prided himself on being able to read people. It made him good at his job.

"Never mind, forget I asked." Ashton came back into position to fight, not making eye contact with Wolfe as he gazed intently at her but followed her lead and went to his position.

"Someone near to you then. You want to know what happened to them and you think I would know," Wolfe said while they reenacted the second phase of their routine. "You know I can't tell you that."

Ashton's next hit toward him was a little harder than she intended. If he noticed, he didn't show it.

"No, that's not it. I was just making conversation." Ashton's heart beat fast, as he had called her out.

"You're a bad liar." Wolfe laughed at her and she furrowed her brow. Ashton moved closer to repeat the same phase they had just done and quickly moved toward Wolfe as he backed up from her quick movements. She was putting more force into each blow and could tell that Wolfe sensed that he had hit a nerve. "All right, calm down, Ash."

Ashton hadn't realized that she was almost out of breath. She stopped and bent over to calm her nerves.

"Oh, yeah, thanks, I'll calm down just because you asked so nicely," Ashton said sarcastically. Wolfe was taken aback by her attitude.

"Watch how you speak to me. I'm still your manager, Ashton."

Ashton knew that and instantly regretted her tone. "Sorry," she started, trying to deflect the direction of the conversation, "just tired and wanted to make conversation, that is all."

"You think I'm not? You think I'm not working as hard as you, but it's all of you who choose to complain. It's a weakness." Things had escalated quickly.

"Weak? That's what you think of us, huh?" Ashton scoffed. She put her knee into his side stopping right before it made contact. Wolfe then used her leg to swing her down and hopped to roll over the top of her. She had lost count, but she knew the different steps for this particular part of the fight scene by heart. Ashton could feel her blood start to boil. The fact that he thought she was weak, workers were weak, just because they were tired, angered her. This was probably the hardest thing she had ever done. He stayed there, pinning her down on the ground.

"What would you call it then?" he said after a while, rolling back up into his fight stance. She had paused and hadn't finished her thought. One last punch and miss, then a punch to the face in this phase of the fight.

Ashton caught her breath while trying to get out all the emotions she was feeling.

"Anger, fear, anxiety, panic, exhaustion, but not weakness."

"Well, then, use that. You don't have the luxury to take a back seat and hope that everything will turn out okay," Ashton was taken aback by his comment. Wolfe didn't pity them; he was upset that they had let this happen.

"Sounds easy coming from someone like you."

"You think life has been easy for me? You don't know me well enough to make that judgment."

"So what happens to us if we fail?" Ashton blurted before she had time to think. It was the tension that loomed over them all, but it was rarely ever talked about, especially with someone in management.

Wolfe paused and took his gaze away from hers. Stunned.

Ashton quickly realized that she shouldn't have asked that. Not only was Wolfe in management, but he was her direct manager.

"Wolfe, I'm sorry, I shouldn't have asked that," Ashton said. He was part of the system and not one of them, and she needed to remember that.

He sighed and shook his head, his tone much softer as he spoke to her. "You know what happens, so let's try and make it through this okay? Next choreography, begin." Wolfe's demeanor changed and Ashton knew that she had dug too deep. But he wasn't upset. He looked discontent, maybe even empathetic.

"I can assume," she said quietly. The Executives kept their secrets to keep workers at bay, and afraid. *Maybe Wolfe was right, maybe it is weakness.*

With that, Wolfe took his position again. Ashton and Wolfe didn't say another word after that, but she completed the next round with only one mistake. He made them go again and again until she had effectively completed all scenes without a mistake.

"That is enough for today." Wolfe wouldn't make eye contact with Ashton. Instead, he grabbed his bag and headed out the door. "Good work." He said not another word as he exited the room into Theater 3, where the other cast members rehearsed.

Ashton was exhausted. She could barely move, and her muscles felt like jelly. She had worked countless hours trying to figure out the steps while memorizing the different play-by-plays for Freya. The left side of her hip felt like it could swing out of its socket at any moment. She recalled the moment she had twisted too early when Wolfe swung her around and onto the ground. He had then given another lecture on how she needed to be careful and learn the steps to avoid getting hurt. Her anxiety made it hard to sleep, and her dreams of Sheva still woke her up at night. As the days went by, she grew more nervous about the moment they would present in front of the Executive Board. What would happen to them if Land of Legends failed? If the Suits didn't like their performance?

"Ah, Ashton, how goes our little Viking princess?" Hunter came over and jumped on her bed.

"Could you leave it for today, Hunter?" She didn't have the mental capacity to deal with him right now. Hunter hadn't liked the fact that she had been given the Freya part. He chuckled as she winced in pain, trying to lift her body to make room for him on her bed. She wished he would just leave her alone.

"Oh c'mon, you're the star of the show! Wolfe's golden girl." He was making fun of her and spoke loudly enough so his clique, Byron and Pais, could hear and laugh at what he had said. "Oh, there it is, your crimson is showing. What they saw in you is beyond me."

With that, Ashton could feel her face getting warmer; the redness grew worse whenever someone pointed it out.

"Shut it, Hunter," Versal said, coming up behind Hunter. His eyes grew wide as he was taken aback by her defense of Ashton.

"What? When we partnered, she was the worst. I took so many hits to the gut because of her screwups and now she has the leading part? This show doesn't stand a chance and now we are all screwed." Hunter emphasized the last of the sentence loudly enough for everyone around to hear.

Ashton slouched down into her bunk. There was a growing invisible divide between her and the other workers. Fear was an evil poison. She felt herself drifting away by herself in a cold dark room. She wanted to scream out and confide in someone, anyone, but she had no one. No Niall. No Sheva. She grasped the stone that hung high on her chest. At times like these, Sheva's gift brought her comfort.

Her body slept, but her mind stayed wide awake. In her dreams, she saw herself from Sheva's point of view, as if she were watching herself lie down on the floor of the train car, frightened and alone as she was dragged away by Augland guards. Before the doors closed, she awoke, panting and out of breath.

"All right! Please everyone to your designated areas to start rehearsal! As you all are aware, we only have a few days to nail down the specifics before the first pilot starts. And I want a perfect performance," Jorgeon screamed over the chattering voices. "Tomorrow morning, we have a special event for you all."

The Viking and Saxon cast members, the castle residents, and the fighters stood in the auditorium, stretching. Jorgeon looked excited and could hardly contain it. The workers, however, paid little attention to him as they stretched and rubbed their sore bodies. The only person seemingly not affected was Versal, who laid her head down on Hunter's lap. She had only needed to practice lines during the time the other workers were training.

Living in Augland 54 made switching reality on and off easy so it was no surprise to anyone that Versal was able to pick up the character so well. She also had similarities to her character—delicate, sophisticated, and poised. Ashton wished she had the same luck with her character. Freya was so different from her own personality—strong, intimidating, and daring. Ashton was scared and anxious. Jorgeon had told Ashton that she needed to bring out "the leader in herself" for it to be believable. Freya was a battle warrior during the Viking reign and was instrumental in the success of the Norsemen's takeover of the Anglo-Saxons. There was a part of Ashton that envied her character's fierceness.

"Ready?" Wolfe came from the left side of the auditorium toward Ashton.

She nodded, picked up her small bag of protein snacks Augland had given her for lunch and dinner, and followed Wolfe to the spot where they had been rehearsing the last couple of days.

The Viking and Saxon smaller parts stayed in the other auditorium, typically running through lines and practicing the different routines they had when it was their turn to be in front of a Suit. Jorgeon and Wolfe had thought of every angle. Each segment of the story was broken out into several different versions depending on how the Suit wanted to proceed. For the most part, everything remained the same, like the fighting scenes and the play lines, but it was dependent on the Suit's course of action during the play. Depending on which side the Suit wanted to be on, Anglo-Saxon or Viking, they would have a chance to fight, and the side the Suit was on would win.

"Okay, so we did okay last night. Hopefully, it wasn't just dumb luck and the moves actually stuck this time," Wolfe said in a condescending tone.

Ashton just shook her head and smirked. Mornings weren't Wolfe's strong suit, as he tended to be more aggressive and hostile. During the day, he would warm up and it would be easier to deal with his mood swings. A lot of the workers feared him, but Ashton had grown close to Wolfe and didn't find him as threatening as the others did.

"Look on the bright side, Wolfe. I can't be any worse than I was a week ago," Ashton tried to joke, hoping last night's argument wasn't still lingering in his mind. He gave her a half-smile as he walked past her toward the Viking group that was practicing wielding their weapons.

Ashton noticed Wolfe's attention was suddenly drawn to something at his hip. He picked up the small communication device he kept at his side and looked at it. His face was emotionless as he stared at it for some time before pressing a button and putting it back to his side. Wolfe's back straightened and he took a moment to himself before proceeding.

"Roach, Hunter, Scar, and Byron, I want you over here and practicing part of the initial run-up to the clash of Vikings and Saxons. I will play the role of the Suit. Ashton and I will be on the other side running toward you. I want this to feel realistic, so come hard, but remember once we make contact, the steps become imperative. If you miss one step, that is how people get hurt. You got that, Ashton?" She was listening but guessed he thought she wasn't paying attention.

"Uh, yes. I—"

Wolfe interrupted: "Good. Now take positions." He made his way to the other end of the auditorium, farthest away from the England crew.

"We will do this all night until we get it right," Wolfe yelled as he trotted away from them. *Something is wrong*, Ashton thought to herself. *One minute, he seemed fine, then the next . . . it was like a light switch.*

Ashton hurried to catch up with Wolfe but decided to stay a few feet back.

"It will be much different having the Suits here and to be moving forward instead of staying in one spot. Don't forget that," he said looking forward, but obviously to Ashton.

"I got this."

"Just don't screw this up, Ash," he said. The look on his face was uncharacteristically vulnerable for a moment before he straightened his expression to its normal impassivity. "Please, I don't need Jorgeon's lecture again today." They by now had reached the farthest point of the auditorium and turned toward the Saxon crew, standing opposite of them.

"I'll try." Ashton took her position to start running toward the four teammates on the other side of the large room. Her job was to stay as close to Wolfe, the Suit, as possible.

"All right, go!" Wolfe yelled and that was their cue to start the rehearsal. He ran so much faster than Ashton, and with her sore body, it made it even harder to keep up. He kept looking over his shoulder, and she could tell that he was already disappointed. It didn't help that Wolfe was built for speed, and she had two very short legs that made one full leg rotation for every one of his steps. She had to work twice as hard to keep pace with him. It wasn't long until they made it to the Saxon soldiers. Ashton drew her ax and went to battle.

CHAPTER 8

Ashton

Ashton stepped forward and swung her ax toward Roach's right side and he blocked, just like she had practiced with Wolfe. They collided again and this time he took her arm and swung Ashton behind him. She crashed hard to the ground. Ashton coughed at the sensation of a boulder sitting on her stomach, making it nearly impossible to breathe. She rocked into a ball as she tried to release the tension that twisted her gut and resist the dizziness she felt from hitting her head on the ground.

"Stop!" Wolfe shouted. "You trying to cause a concussion? What is wrong with you!" he screamed at Roach, pushing him away from Ashton.

"I didn't mean to; she came at me pretty hard."

"So what? You're like three times her size!" Wolfe was almost nose to nose with him now. Ashton sat up and touched the back of her head; she knew it was going to be sore tomorrow, but she'd manage.

"I'm fine, Wolfe, really." She tried to diffuse the situation.

"It's not—" Wolfe turned his head, obviously irritated. "Do it again. This time, Ashton, don't come into this with such force, and run faster."

"Oh! Okay," Ashton said and immediately regretted it. She slowly stood up and started running back to the end of the large room, to where they had originally started. She could already tell this was going to be a long day.

"Excuse me?" Wolfe shouted at her. He followed behind and she could hear him catching up to her. Ashton tried to run faster, hoping he would just let it go.

"Hey! I was talking to you, Ashton," he yelled as he put his arm on her shoulder to slow her down. "What was that?" he asked.

Ashton's fingertips were tingling as she was both angry and astonished by her own reaction. Her motto had always been *Don't make waves*, but she kept lashing out. Ashton stopped once he grabbed her, knowing full well she would have to explain herself.

"I'm sorry." Ashton still spoke more sarcastically than she would have liked.

"If you have something to say, then say it," he shouted. They were far enough down the long auditorium where the others couldn't hear them.

"Forget I said anything; I'm just tired," she lied.

"This was exactly what I was talking about yesterday."

"Weak, again with the weak. You know you push us day in and day out. First, I'm going too slow, then I'm pushing too hard. Now I can't run fast enough, jump high enough. I don't know how much more I can give. I give and give and give. And still, you all don't . . ." Ashton's temper was rising, and she could feel her rage setting in. "You think just because we are low on the totem pole of importance that it somehow justifies treating us this way. And the fact that you, you push us this hard for what? Them? The Suits? You don't give a crap about us." Ashton paced there and for a moment forgot she was talking to someone above her. Wolfe stood there, dumbfounded.

Ashton came back from her rant and couldn't believe the words that had come out of her mouth. Instead of waiting for a response, she sprinted to her post. She knew he would have something to say to that, something that would put her in her place. She could hear Niall's reaction to what had happened over the last two days and he scolded her in her mind.

Wolfe didn't catch up to her. Instead, he walked toward his post next to her.

"Don't do that again," he said, low and hoarse.

Ashton took in several deep breaths, her anger simmering down. "I won't."

He was giving her yet another chance, and she wasn't going to take that for granted. He should have given her a strike for that. Jorgeon would have wasted no time at all. She didn't know why. Maybe he just didn't want to have to replace her so close to the grand opening in front of the Executives. For whatever reason, she was grateful.

"I know you are all very tired, but good work today. Wolfe and I are proud of how far you've all come in such a short amount of time," Jorgeon announced as he gathered all the workers, Saxon and Viking, together after rehearsal. "I know it's late and you will need your rest before our big debut. Tomorrow, you will wake up bright and early and go straight into wardrobe." Everyone started chattering amongst themselves, and many showed a new burst of energy.

Jorgeon put his hands up in the air. "Settle down, settle down; yes, it is very exciting." He was smiling from ear to ear. "Tomorrow is a very important day, very important. I can't stress that enough. So go back, get a few hours of sleep, and let's make this happen." Jorgeon motioned them away. Ashton rose from their circle on the floor, feeling every bone in her body creak. She started heading back to the dormitory. As she left, she saw Versal in her periphery catching up to her.

"Hey, Ashton; you'll never guess what," Versal started.

"What?" Ashton said, curious.

"So Jorgeon came to me and started talking about the different shows we could be performing if this went well." She lit up with excitement as she walked beside her. "He's thinking I could be, like, a production star, maybe even famous."

"That's great, Versal." It was all Ashton could muster as she hobbled alongside her.

"I know, right; can you imagine?" Versal couldn't contain herself. "Like Suits wanting to meet me and know who I am." Ashton wanted to shake her head, as that seemed too unrealistic, but she didn't want to say that to her. "I mean, you could, too, now that you are a star." Ashton didn't say anything, just nodded as she tried to smile. Versal wrapped her arm around Ashton's. It was good to see her so happy.

She smiled and broke the silence between them. "So you and Wolfe are getting a lot more time together."

"It's not like that." Ashton started to turn red and she was sure Versal noticed.

"Oh, come on! You're seriously going to deny that you like him?" She said it louder than Ashton would have liked.

"He's management, Versal," Ashton said, trying to diffuse the girl's curiosity. She pulled her arm away and looked around to make sure no one had heard them talking.

"C'mon, just tell me," Versal pressed further, giving Ashton a big grin. Versal reminded her of Niall; they had similar outlooks on their life at Augland. Positivity and acceptance seemed to be their strongest character traits.

Ashton smiled. Wolfe was stubborn and hotheaded, but Ashton found him charming sometimes.

"Ah! See! I knew it. Knew it," Versal burst with excitement. If Versal was good at something, it was talking. She could have an entire conversation by herself. Hunter stopped by and took her away from Ashton and she began chatting with the others, mostly about the wardrobe happening the next day.

Ashton was just happy to get some quiet in her bed. Tomorrow was going to be a big day. Not only were they getting fitted; they were going to see the new park and their first-ever pilot of the new series.

The large auditorium was now filled with rows of tents. Each worker was directed toward a tent to receive his or her costume and props.

"Come in, this won't take long, my dear." One of the stylists went behind Ashton and closed the curtain-like shade across the tent opening. "Please, go ahead and get fully undressed, then take a seat." Ashton slowly took off her clothes, thankful at least it was a woman and she wasn't undressing in front of a man. Ashton did as she was asked, sat down, and rested her head against the back of the chair that stood in the middle of the tent. The woman stood behind Ashton, combing out her dark brown hair. Ashton widened her eyes as she looked up toward the mirror on the wall, noting with alarm that the woman now had scissors in her hand. Suddenly, Ashton felt the weight leave the top of her head. She didn't move; she just sat there while large chunks of hair fell to the ground. Ashton could feel her heart beating out of her chest. It wasn't losing her hair; she knew that would grow back. It was giving away yet another layer of herself to Augland. Ashton's eyes swelled with tears.

"Where ya from, dear?" the woman asked as she traded the scissors for a razor. Ashton didn't have the words to answer as her mind went numb.

"I used to work for the Suit design team, working on the synthetic hair," she continued as she put water, then soap, across Ashton's head and dragged the sharp blade across, creating a smooth foundation. "You know it's a good line of work. They've got a teaching group now at the Center. Great young talent there." The lady didn't seem to mind that she was talking to herself.

For all that Augland had done, taken, and demanded, Ashton had always felt like herself. In this moment, she sensed them taking something that defined her.

"There, all done. Not so bad, huh? For what it's worth, you had beautiful hair."

Ashton brushed her fingers across her now-bare head. She felt like screaming. Beating the tent down to pieces. Instead, she stayed still and followed the woman out the tent doors toward a large array of clothes.

"All right, grab these and follow me; we will take you to the dressing area." She handed Ashton a large pile of clothes. Ashton followed her toward the exit to the large hallway and across the hall to another auditorium. Ashton saw the others shaved and wearing the same thing she was—undergarments. Some didn't seem bothered by it, mostly the men, but the women were visibly saddened as they touched their bald heads and hid away from others.

"Right this way, Ashton." Ashton followed the stylist down the walkway into another room and another tent.

"Let's go ahead and try this on." She laid out a red wig on the chair and motioned for Ashton to get dressed. "We may need to do some alterations, but it should fit you just right."

Ashton touched the distressed marbled leather garment with soft fur outlining its perimeter and for a moment forgot all about her new appearance. She had never really worn anything that felt like this before. It had long fur and was covered with both white and black spots. There was a tiny leather thread through the center that kept the entire two pieces of the material together around her midsection. The lady came over and started to undo the strings to bring the two materials apart.

"Here, step into this." She brought the outfit down toward Ashton. She stepped into it and stood still while her body was wrapped in the lavish garment. It didn't take the wardrobe stylist long to assemble everything and, just before she laced up the boots, she placed the red wig on Ashton's head. Ashton turned to the front and straightened out the new hair. She was gone and Freya had taken her place.

The worry left as Ashton glanced at a strong version of herself. She hadn't seen herself since her days in the dorm and could now see what the last two weeks of constant exercise had done to her body. She looked strong, with new definition accentuating her arms and legs. The red hair contrasted nicely against her fair skin and made her eyes glisten a new shade of icy ocean blue. The leather and fur made her feel the fierceness that only Freya would know. She now understood why she was a warrior, and, for the first time, Ashton felt connected to her character. She felt strong.

PART 2

CHAPTER 9

Wolfe

Wolfe and Jorgeon stood waiting in a bright white room on the top level of the Executive Offices. They had both been summoned to speak in front of the board to showcase the new program details and report their progress so far. It was Jorgeon's first time in the high globe overlooking the parks, but Wolfe had been here countless times before. He hated it. It was too clean, too perfect. White and black marble floors with dark wood splashed as accents across them. Large vases full of exotic white flowers, most likely grown somewhere in Predator's Biome.

"The Executive Board and CEO Warren are in there. I can't believe how nervous I am," said Jorgeon, fidgeting with his clipboard full of notes.

"You're fine; just cool it." Wolfe was unsympathetic.

"The message said they needed to talk to us? Anything more?" Jorgeon asked. Wolfe remembered the message from the beeper he carried, only telling him that his presence was requested by the Executives. He knew what it would be about, though. Warren had been requesting updates from him almost daily. Wolfe had been dreading this day.

"Yes, same as what I told you before. It said that we have an appointment with the board to talk about the program."

"It's a great view of Augland from up here—beautiful." Jorgeon looked out toward the parks that divided Augland as it spanned across the surrounding territory for miles. Each park had its unique place in time and history. The circular sphere in which they sat rotated slowly. Wolfe looked in the other direction from Jorgeon, toward the outer walls. He thought it was beautiful outside the walls of Augland 54.

It was a cloudy November day and the rain—real rain—beat down on the glass around them. Wolfe appreciated the outside world because of its authenticity. It wasn't manufactured, manicured, or maintained. It was natural in its beauty. Jorgeon didn't see it the same way. He ate up whatever Augland spoon-fed him to believe.

"You can come this way," a Suit said. The Suit turned and motioned for the two of them to walk with her. She was very tall and thin and wore a business pencil skirt with a jacket. It was easy to tell the difference between real people and Suits. While they had nearly perfected the small details of the human body—it was Augland's mission to create flawless imitations—real people had flaws, blemishes, scars. Suits had almost a shine to them. Wolfe and Jorgeon looked at each other. Without hesitation or a word to each other, they followed the Suit down a long hallway with glass surrounding each one of the conference rooms. As they approached a large room, the foggy glass shifted to clear. Inside were several men and women, some Suits, some not, all looking toward them.

"Gentlemen!" said a smartly dressed Executive. He was tall and had brown hair and a salt-and-pepper goatee. He came forward and shook hands with both Wolfe and Jorgeon as they entered the room.

"Everyone, you know Wolfgang and this is Jorgeon, the two men who have spearheaded the recent amusement park being presented tomorrow to the board: Land of Legends." He introduced himself to Jorgeon. "I'm Warren, CEO of Augland 54; it's a pleasure to meet you, Jorgeon. Wolfgang has said great things." That wasn't true. Wolfe had complained to Warren about Jorgeon plenty of times.

Jorgeon cleared his throat. "Hello, my name is Jorgeon." He gave a nervous laugh. "I mean, as the CEO just said." He paused. "Uh, okay. Uh, well. We . . ."

"We have recently gone through the new recruits from the various areas of Augland. Most workers are in this as a reform program," Wintefred, the Head of Development, interrupted. "After careful evaluation of each individual, we are committed to delivering high-quality, real-life experiences. Jorgeon and Wolfe spearheaded the Battle of the British Isles—a battle scenario where our customers are able to experience war just like the Norsemen and Anglo-Saxons did years ago."

"And it is very realistic." Jorgeon cleared his throat. Wolfe gave him a side glare and shook his head.

"Today," continued Wintefred, "you will witness a profitable storyline that gives our customers exactly what they are looking for: history, romance, and action, all packed into one experience."

Each Executive in the room gave a small clap as Wintefred finished. She smiled at Warren, looking pleased with herself.

"Are our customers given a script to follow along with?" A woman Suit in the seat adjacent to CEO Warren spoke up with the question.

"Uh, no. Well, they are given a backstory, which will help them understand what is about to happen," Jorgeon answered.

"For example," said Wintefred, "the Vikings are about to head into battle, so they understand they are up against the Saxon cavalry. Everything else is up to the customer to decide. Our workers are ready for any scenario; they try to keep the customer to the storyline by talking to them and giving them clues on what to do next."

"How realistic is this?" another board member spoke up.

"Uh, very realistic, Wolfe and Jorgeon have done a great job training the workers to make it look like they are fighting for real."

"Well, that doesn't make it realistic," a Suit with bright blonde hair and a pristine black dress said. "I mean, if we are suggesting this is realistic, shouldn't it be real fighting?"

"It can still be realistic without causing harm to them, we—" Wolfe started.

"What Wolfgang is saying is that we have weeded out the weak, to have the strongest workers out on the field. Many of them have been training day in and day out for this. They will be ready for anything," Wintefred added and Wolfe glared at her.

"Well, then, let's let them do that," said Warren. "If they are as strong as you have indicated, they should be able to handle this. I mean, they are workers who have already had their three strikes. This serves the purpose of teaching a lesson and giving a profitable performance."

"We—" Wolfe was about to interject when Warren stood up. The others in the room followed suit and stood up as well.

"Well, I believe that is all the time we have today; we will vote after we see the performance later this afternoon on whether or not this will be available to our customers. Thank you, Wolfgang and Jorgeon, for your time today; great work and we look forward to seeing you later."

Jorgeon took a bow, obviously very happy with the outcome of the meeting.

"I'll walk you both out," Warren said to them as he motioned for the door.

The Suit assistant was waiting as the three of them made their way out.

"Thank you, Maggie, but I will see them out."

"Yes, Warren." Maggie turned around and walked back to her desk. Warren smiled.

"Wolfgang, a word?" Wolfe turned to face him, and Warren motioned to Jorgeon to head out to the front lobby. He watched to see that Jorgeon was out of earshot.

"Walk with me for a minute."

"Yes, sir." Wolfe followed Warren around the office along the windows that looked out toward Land of Legends, where workers were putting the final touches on the new park.

"It looks like this new addition is going well for you, and that is good to see," Warren started. "I hope you know how important this is for you, and your position here at Augland 54."

"I do, sir," Wolfe said.

"This is the last opportunity I can give you. I can't stress the importance of this. I saw the hesitancy you showed in there when they mentioned turning off the restrictions and allowing real fighting. You don't have an issue with this, do you, Wolfgang?"

Wolfe looked down. "It isn't right. We shouldn't hurt them, and, honestly, if they get hurt, we won't be able to do the project. I'll run out of workers."

Warren didn't seem fazed by Wolfe's remark. "That won't be an issue. There will always be workers to replace them. Somehow they keep multiplying." Warren chuckled. "Things aren't the same now as they were back thirty years ago; these days we have more than enough bodies to use."

Before the war, the Artificial Existence Center had hired workers like any other company. Its success had been virtually instantaneous as families paid everything they had to put their elderly loved ones into a Suit so they could live in an Augland park. The AEC's goal had been to monopolize the vacation and retirement market, and they did.

People clamored to work for the AEC as the company offered retirement plans that could lead to getting a Suit of their own. Whether this ever actually happened or not, the lure of the Suits kept people working and buying, and the customer base seemed ever-expanding.

Then energy efficiency came along, discovered by NeuroEnergy, outpacing conventional energy companies and ultimately shaping the future of energy usage. The innovation harnessed sunlight to create fusion in glowing crystals of polymerized metals. Tiny grains of these polymers could run robots for days on minimal sunlight exposure. The energy was safe, clean, endless, and tremendously powerful. Soon NeuroEnergy developed software to direct the boundless energy to run artificial neurons that could animate synthetic biologic material, thus enabling the AEC to produce amazing synthetic organic beings that could be biologically programmed. Human memory and thought could be reproduced and transferred to biological units. The Suits were born and perfected. Wealthy companies and individuals started sheltering money in lifetime investments in AEC memberships that acted like annuities. This began a cascade of redirecting tax revenue away from the government to enrich the AEC and progressed to involve most of the wealthy. The economic power of the AEC grew rapidly.

A new President came to power who sought to regain authority, but the AEC would not give up control and suggested the people rise up against them. They convinced the people that the government could not be trusted and wanted to control them. Citizens rose against the government using the Suits, a powerful army that could not be killed.

Since NeuroEnergy was a utility company and relied heavily on government regulation, the AEC created its own generators to hold energy. NeuroEnergy, who still controlled some resources within the power grid, recognized the danger in the AEC expansion and began developing secret subdivisions of energy technology and weaponry and offered to assist the new President in returning power to the national government. They joined with the government and, in retaliation, shut off the power to many major cities, including those that held many of the AEC offices, which were filled with pods, Augland parks, and Suits. It was a civil war like no one had ever seen. Both sides hit harder and harder as they engaged each other. With each Suit the government was able to destroy, ten more were there to replace it. Then, each AEC location slowly began losing energy—their generators depleting. NeuroEnergy plants were taken over by indestructible Suits, creating a monopoly. The war lasted only a year before both sides ran out of essentials and the government toppled. But the AEC had the people and money. The government fell and NeuroEnergy became a subsidiary of the very company they'd competed against.

Infrastructure and resources were destroyed, and the AEC offered its parks as sanctuaries for those who had survived the war. Those in Suits held the power and the rest exchanged their freedom for life in the aftermath of the war. But after thirty years, Auglands were no longer the sanctuaries they promised their workers. Wolfe was one of the only people he knew under thirty who knew the whole story. He could see the Executive Office was needing to crack down harder and harder to keep things under control. They needed workers within their walls to keep everything running.

"We have been looking for a rehabilitation program that works. Instead of the old process, this new one will give those who rebel a fighting chance. You see? Just discarding them below doesn't give us any use for them and takes valuable resources." Wolfe was silent as Warren spoke. "Listen, you do well. If this goes well, you have secured your spot in Augland as Head of Security. You'll be able to come home." Warren placed his hands on Wolfe's shoulders. "You will fully be a part of the family business. I'm hoping someday I can pass this along to you, son." He looked out across the large bubble that overlooked Augland. "I just need you to step up here. I'd hate to be disappointed." Warren squeezed Wolfe's shoulders hard. Warren's Suit was tall and thin with a chiseled jawline and his grip hurt Wolfe's shoulder muscles.

"Yes, sir," Wolfe said softly.

"Good. Now, I'll see you this afternoon, and if it is everything you and Jorgeon have said it is, I can imagine this is going to go very well for you. Do not let me down."

"I won't . . . Father." With that, Wolfe turned and headed down the hall of glass toward the lobby.

Wolfe left Jorgeon and made his way to his office, which also happened to be his home. He had set up a small cot and a lamp off to the side. He preferred his secluded area to the deluxe suites his family received. He loosened his tie and sat down rubbing his head.

Wolfe hated getting dressed up for the Executive Board. They had been harping on him to choose his Suit for when he received his promotion. That was, if he could get the promotion. It all depended on how the day went and if the board liked the new park.

When his father had given him this responsibility, he'd wanted it. It had seemed a noble mission to find a better way to rehabilitate workers, better than the alternative they faced, anyway. He did not want to return to his security role where he had to handle rogue employees, down in the cages.

The workers at the new park had no idea what would happen today if it didn't go well, but they also didn't know what would happen to them if they succeeded. Wolfe felt torn. His father's approval would make his career here at Augland. But at what cost?

CHAPTER 10

Ashton

"Out this way, everyone. Please! Go and explore our new Land of Legends!" Jorgeon motioned the workers through the large concrete opening of the train station. Augland had finished creating the park for the Viking-Saxon battle. The bright lights shone above Ashton as she put her feet on the grass and looked out toward the vast rolling hills near an imposing stone castle. It was the first time any of the workers had felt the fake wind and touch of grass since starting their war training. Across the perimeter, tall trees located just beyond the structure and fields of grass swept from one end of the park to the other. On the other side of the rolling green hills was a small town full of pitched brown yurts: the Viking camp. Smoke from campfires swarmed around the large tents. There were little paths that wove amongst the yurts connecting them in the middle to a path that led up the long hill toward the castle. It was magical.

Ashton first noticed the silence. The constant chaos and echoes of the building fell away, and it felt peaceful to hear her own thoughts for once. While many workers wandered toward the castle, Ashton made her way down a long hill that sat just west of the Viking camp. The area was so vast that it took a while for her to be out of view of anyone else in the park.

Farther down a hill she walked until she was between the short grass and the tall, wooded area. It was where the park ended, just beyond the tree line. Ashton walked along the grass, touching the tree trunks as she walked by them. She admired the beauty and details Augland put into their parks. Each tree looked strong with rich colors. Pine and dirt, that was what she smelled.

Distant whispers briefly interrupted her tranquility, though not loudly enough to make out what they were saying, and she didn't mind it. She tried to block it out while she listened to the wind howl around her. *How did they do wind?* She stopped as she came across a large rock and sat down across it. It felt warm, and she was sure the lights had warmed its surface. She laid her head against the hard stone and looked up at the artificial clouds slowly making their way across the ceiling-sky. Ashton felt peace pouring over her. For the first time in two weeks, she felt more herself. She liked being alone. Every day felt as though she was pulled in every direction. *Do this better, be stronger, work harder, do this differently.* It was constant criticism. She took a deep breath in, letting the purified air flow through her body, then exhaled, hoping the anxiety would leave along with her breath. For a moment it did help. There were echoes in the wind as she could presume others were on their way to the Viking camp. She hoped they wouldn't come near her. Closing her eyes, she just relaxed. She wanted to get as much of this time to herself as possible before she was called back again, like sheep being summoned by their shepherd.

A whistle blew and Ashton could hear Jorgeon speaking, pulling her out of her time to herself. It meant that they needed to start rehearsal. Sighing heavily, she pulled herself up and fixed her Viking outfit before heading out toward the castle. It would be running exercises and stretching to prepare for the first show.

"First show today! How are you all feeling?" Jorgeon approached Ashton, Roach, Hunter, Byron, Pais, Zeel, and Scar. The group stretched and grabbed water after running the Viking drills for the last hour or so. Ashton panted and tried to keep air flowing in and out of her body. The leather was unforgiving and tight around her waist. The rest of the group did the same as they recuperated from the vigorous running drill.

"C'mon! Where is the excitement? This is going to be a great day." Jorgeon was alone in his enthusiasm. The rest of them only stared at him, some even shaking their heads. Jorgeon had been vocal about the importance of this pilot going well. He had insisted that their careers in Augland were at stake. All this work didn't guarantee that any of them would be there tomorrow. None of them talked about it.

Hunter tossed his water aside. "Where's Wolfe? Shouldn't he be here?" Hunter had asked several times during practice where Wolfe was. It bothered him that he wasn't there to practice with them. Since the beginning, Wolfe had been playing the Suit, which helped them visualize what it would be like during the real production. Out of the entire group, Hunter seemed the most anxious today.

"Wolfe will be by later this morning . . . all right, up, up, up. We will run through it a couple more times and then we will break before our customer gets here. Great work, everyone. Wolfe and I are proud of the work you've all done. It is really up to you all if this show is a success. Make us proud."

The group slowly stood up, saying nothing to one another. Whether it was anxiety for the first show, the pressure they all felt, or exhaustion from two weeks of brutal, nonstop work, they were all tired. Only a few more run-throughs and it would all be over.

Finally, they were able to break and Ashton took that time to seclude herself. She returned to her rock and pulled back part of the leather that rested between her arm and shoulder, wincing in pain as it exposed a patch of red, raw skin. Her costume had rubbed against her while she was running drills, and it was causing some areas to become bare and bloody.

"Ouch, looks painful," Wolfe said as he approached the rock where Ashton was sitting. She hadn't heard or seen him coming. He wore a tie that he had obviously loosened and his sleeves were rolled up right past the elbow. If his appearance didn't give it away, his facial expression would have done the trick. He looked miserable.

"Yeah, doesn't feel so great," she said, wincing. Wolfe came and sat down next to her. "Where were you this morning?" she asked curiously. Wolfe picked up a piece of grass and started playing with it.

"We had a meeting with the Executives to brief them on today."

"Did it go well?"

"Not bad," he said. She couldn't necessarily tell whether that was a relief or not.

"Good." There was a long pause while they both just sat there, looking out to the grass in front of them.

"This is actually really peaceful," Wolfe said, breaking the silence.

"Yeah, I like coming over here. No one tends to bother me. Not that anyone really talks to me anyway, but it's been nice to get away from it all." She grinned. "Well, except for you." Wolfe didn't laugh or say anything, which made things awkward.

"Are you nervous about today?"

"Yes and no."

"Why not? I am."

Wolfe didn't respond right away; instead, he intently worked on the small piece of grass between his fingers. He was ripping it apart piece by piece. "I guess that is a lie." Wolfe paused. "There's a lot of pressure to make sure this goes well . . ." Ashton could tell he wanted to say more but wouldn't. Instead, he changed the subject. "How do you like the red hair?" Wolfe asked as he took a piece of it and ran it through his fingers. The sudden closeness took them both by surprise. His intent was to change the subject, but instead, he created tension.

"It's growing on me. Not sure how I like the shaved head." She turned her head away from him.

He chuckled. "I know, but we needed to make it easy to make quick changes with you all. This seemed like the easiest method."

"Ah, I see." She just shook her head. Typical for Augland to think of what would be easiest for them.

"Well, for what it is worth, it looks good on you. I know it doesn't seem fair, but easier than trying to put your hair up for all changes."

"You wouldn't understand," Ashton murmured quietly.

"Oh, come on Ash, are you seriously upset about it?" Wolfe lashed out, but it wasn't all directed at Ashton. She could feel that anger bellowed behind his eyes like a volcano waiting to erupt. She felt it too.

Ashton thought about what he'd asked. It wasn't the hair. They moved so quickly in Augland 54 that they didn't have a chance to really feel, but when she stopped for even a moment, she was angry. Angry at Marius for taking her away from Niall. She was angry at Wolfe for putting her through torture the last two weeks. She was angry at Sheva for leaving her, and at Augland for taking her away.

73

The realization hit her as if she had plunged into freezing water. She had been trained. Just like everyone else in this place. Like an animal, she didn't step out of bounds for fear of what might happen, so she obeyed. Held everything deep inside her and pretended that this was all fair. All around her, workers had been convinced that this treatment was normal. She knew it wasn't.

Sheva had told her of the days before Augland, or at least some of it. The war that divided government and people. AEC and Augland were supposed to help the people, be their savior. Instead, it manipulated and conquered. They had supplied people with Suits to wage war against the tyrannical government and when they had won, there was a cost. The economy broke down—no laws, rules, or regulations. The AEC had capitalized on it, seizing power, and the people had no choice but to let it happen.

"Why, yes, I am, Wolfe. You don't tell us anything, just have us go into this whole thing blind. It keeps us on edge, not sure what to expect next, and then, you strip us of our . . . our . . . individuality. It's messed up."

Ashton was shocked that she had said that and for a moment wished that she had just said it to herself. There were times she forgot that Wolfe wasn't one of them, because of their closeness. She thought they knew each other, or at least she hoped. Wolfe was still a mystery to her. There was a long pause and Ashton wasn't sure he knew what to say. If she had learned anything about Wolfe, it was that he was better than most at turning off his emotions. One minute he was sitting there having a good conversation and the next it was all business.

She was getting ready to hear the lecture, for him to tell her that she couldn't talk to him like that. She could get away with that kind of talk once, but not twice. *What's gotten into me?* she berated herself.

"You're right."

"What?"

Wolfe shrugged. "It is unfair, but this is how it is. You can't change it. You can try but that will just get you into more trouble. And it does get worse, trust me . . ." Wolfe looked down at his hands.

Ashton looked stunned as Wolfe admitted it. She had never heard management admit to the treatment of workers.

"How much worse . . ." Ashton pushed. She thought of Sheva and her heart beat out of her chest. Then she thought of her peers and the burden of this new park. She didn't want to think of alternatives because it would lead her down a path from which she couldn't return. Wolfe didn't answer; instead, he hung his head down and took a deep breath. He had done it again, switched back to the stern Wolfe she had grown used to.

"Okay, are you ready for this?"

"Sure," Ashton said, disappointed she hadn't learned more from Wolfe. She knew better than to keep trying.

"You are going to do great, Ashton. I know it. Just try to make a connection with the Suit; show him who you are and how strong you are. They will like that." He smiled and put out his hand to help her up. She took it and noticed the rough fingers against her soft skin. That didn't surprise her; he was tough.

"Everyone to your stations!" Jorgeon's voice rang out over a loudspeaker, interrupting Wolfe and Ashton as he still had a grip on her hand. Ashton stared at him intently, trying to read his feelings.

"Come on, let's go to the Viking camp." He pulled his hand away from hers and strode briskly toward the camp. They walked in silence. Ashton was nervous. Wolfe must have sensed it because he put his hand on her shoulder and quickly turned her so she was facing him.

"Ashton, it will be okay. I promise," he said.

She lifted her shoulder to brush him off. She didn't need his words of heroism. If she didn't have a bad feeling about the production before, she did now. He had to promise her she would be okay. Ashton wasn't dumb; she knew she didn't have the full story and he was keeping things from her. He didn't owe her anything, not in her position, but she hated it nonetheless.

CHAPTER 11

Ashton

The show began and Ashton feared the worst. If this wasn't a success, if the Suit didn't enjoy his time, it would mean the end of Land of Legends. What would happen then?

The Suit, who was playing the role of Chieftain Bjorn, looked around at the Executives to make sure they were paying attention to him. Warren and Jorgeon looked like dogs waiting to be fed, hungry for any scrap of approval. This Suit was from the AEC headquarters, all the way from Washington, D.C. He would determine the outcome of this park, and that had everyone falling over themselves.

Ashton made her way to the Suit's side. "Chieftain Bjorn, it will be an honor to serve you in the upcoming battle with the Saxons." As Ashton spoke, her face turned red and she glanced at Wolfe. He nodded his head and mouthed to her, "Keep going."

Ashton had practiced this moment with Wolfe every day for the last two weeks and knew that once she was at the Suit's side, she didn't leave it.

"Please, feel free to roam around and browse your Viking camp with your fellow Norsemen." Ashton's voice sounded rehearsed and robotic. An awkward silence ensued as they all waited to hear what the Suit would say.

Jorgeon stepped over and intervened. "When you are ready, the battleground is located on the other side. Freya will be able to guide you there. You are going to have a great time, sir," he said, trying to alleviate any confusion the Suit might have on the next steps.

Ashton was sure Jorgeon was hoping she would say something, but at the moment, she couldn't think of what to say next. The Suit looked over at Jorgeon and then back at the Viking camp and stepped forward.

The workers in the Viking camp visibly tensed, returning to their tasks with an unrealistic enthusiasm. While they had practiced their busywork countless times, to be in the moment seemed so foreign to them all. Each worker had a specific skill and role to play outside of fighting. Some worked in the pubs, while others made bread or worked at the metalsmith. Each building in the Viking camp was fully functional, with smoke coming out of every rooftop. It felt like stepping back in time. Some practiced fighting each other, others tended to meat over a fire, and everyone else walked back and forth from one end of the camp to the other, pretending to have conversations amongst themselves. Ashton walked with the Suit across the grass of the battlefield and onto the dirt street leading to the Viking camp.

For the next two hours, they all waited on "Chieftain Bjorn" hand and foot. He went to the local pub and played the various bar activities available to him. He drank and told long stories to the Viking warriors, who pretended to adore him.

Then, as planned, two crew members dressed in Viking combat gear appeared in the dining area and informed him that Anglo-Saxons had started advancing. This was Jorgeon and Wolfe's way of letting him know to move this along. It worked and the Suit stood up.

"All right, we go now." The Suit was speaking in shorter, more abrupt sentences. He raised his glass and the hall erupted in cheers. Ashton jumped from the long wooden table and guided the Suit toward the exit and down the path that would lead them to the battlefield.

While she stood by, he gawked at the area around him, obviously loving the detail of the park. He wasn't wrong to admire its beauty; the Augland park designers had thought through every detail. A stone path resembled tree roots as it meandered through the small huts and centers of commerce in the Viking camp. As the warriors filled in behind him, forming the Viking army, the Suit played perfectly into their plan. Amidst the leaders' screaming battle chants, he proceeded through the camp toward the green field that lay between it and the castle. The sun shone bright and the wind blew behind them, almost pushing them toward their destination.

"Chieftain Bjorn, what should we do?" Ashton felt silly pretending, and the lines she had been given felt forced and awkward on her tongue. The crowd behind them, now geared up for war, waited for his response.

"I believe we should just go up and start killing them," he said with forced bravado, looking at Ashton awkwardly.

"Excellent plan. Lead the way, Chieftain Bjorn!" Ashton motioned for him to go forward. Out of the corner of her eye, she glanced at the rock to her left at the edge of the forest she and Wolfe had claimed as their sanctuary. While they walked side by side, the Suit bent down toward Ashton.

"So are you supposed to be my wife?"

"I'm—I'm Freya, I mean the warrior, Freya. I have led many battles."

"But, like, we are together, right?" he asked, a little more emphatically this time. He gave a sly smile as he touched her hand. Ashton looked down, not fully prepared for this. Jorgeon had warned her and Versal about this sort of affection. They were women in battle and would be seen as consolation prizes. Ashton had prepared herself, but now she didn't know how to react. She had flirted with Suits before, and this wasn't any different. *Just act*, Ashton told herself.

When Niall and Ashton had lived in Victorian, she had heard about Suits fraternizing in some of the other parks. Of course, Augland forbade this behavior and, when it happened, the workers, not the Suits, were punished. It was never a good sign when the Suits were persistent with their affections, and it was a constant worry, especially among the female workers. Ashton had heard of a girl in Victorian who denied a Suit's advances and was sent away to the brothel, or at least that was the rumor. If Suits ever complained about a worker, it was immediate dismissal.

"I could be if you survive the battle and conquer the Saxons," Ashton said, thinking quickly on her feet. If he was victorious, which he would be, the show would be over and her role done. She couldn't help the small smile that crept across her face. It was a small victory. He would leave once this was over, and she wouldn't have to deal with his flirtatious bravado toward her.

"I'll win this for you then, Freya, my love." He brought her hand toward his face and kissed it. She laughed at the pathetic gesture and pretended to be flattered.

"Thank you, my Chieftain," she said demurely. The Suit grinned wide and turned toward the Saxon army assembling on the other side of the grassy hill.

Rows of Viking cast members made their way to the top of the hill at the edge of the camp with a view of the large grey castle in the distance. The castle town was guarded by a five-foot stone wall. The entire Viking army stood on the ridge where the battle would take place, just like they had rehearsed so many times. The Saxon crew was on the other side, ready for the show to begin.

"Should we begin?" Ashton asked. This was part of the rehearsal she was most comfortable with and prepared for.

"Yes!"

"Raise your weapon and charge your men toward the Saxon territory. We will win this battle and take over!" Ashton yelled.

The Suit raised his ax and started running. The entire Viking clan followed in his wake. Ashton stayed close as instructed during training. He was much faster than her, but that was to be expected as he could program his Suit to whatever athletic propensity he desired.

As they made their way toward the Saxon army and clashed with the front line, Roach was there to fight her. Jab. Step back. Duck. Right hook. She went through the routine. Hunter was ready and Ashton watched the Suit approach him out of her peripheral vision. The Suit crashed into Hunter; colliding with such force that Hunter's body contorted backward and lifted off the ground. The Suit took a large swing and struck him hard as Hunter fell to the ground. What was going on? Hunter recoiled in pain and Ashton could see a visible dent in his armor. She stopped, fighting every instinct she had to go over and help him. This shouldn't be happening. The Suit should not be allowed to hit like this, right?

Wolfe said they had taken precautions. That Land of Legends would not be a park that would allow forceful contact between those with Suits and those without. This was a mock battle, a show. Hits and jabs were to be expected but not this: this was real war. The Suit lifted his weapon again and again it came down on Hunter with full force. Hunter followed the weapon with his eyes and quickly moved to get out of the way of the blow. Fear was written all over Hunter's face—he was in more shock than Ashton. He backed up quickly, putting his hand up. He had lost his sword after the first blow and just scooted on the ground in surrender. The boy who had always seemed so confident suddenly cowered and begged for help.

"Get up, you heathen!" the Suit yelled and let out a harsh belly laugh. Hunter looked around, but when he saw no one was coming to his aid, he stood up. Hunter took a sword from another Saxon and looked visibly confused as he slowly brought up his sword toward the Suit.

"Ashton, come on!" Roach yelled at her. She couldn't peel her eyes away from Hunter. While she didn't like Hunter, she didn't want to see him get hurt.

"Ashton!" Roach yelled again. Ashton ignored him again. It didn't take long for the Suit to overthrow Hunter, who was now not getting up from the ground. The Suit moved on to his next victim. He went from one person to the next, swinging left and right and leaving a trail of battered fighters in his wake. Workers were rocking back and forth on the ground; some didn't move at all. The ax was dripping blood from its tip.

Ashton needed to get to the Suit; it was her job to stay with him. Yet she couldn't keep up; he was going through each person faster than she anticipated. Ashton had to skip two or three fight scenes just to keep up with him. All she could do was watch as he dove into each person like he was swatting flies. Ashton felt sick to her stomach. A girl lay on the ground with her face split open, her nose bleeding and blood pooling around the flaky flesh pulling from the bone. Before long, workers were backing away, afraid to run and even more afraid to move forward. Cries of desperation swarmed around Ashton as defeat fell behind her and surrender in front of her.

It wasn't just the hits that shocked her. It was the violence caused by the bodiless Suit, controlled by a man suspended in a pod somewhere far away. It was the look of despair and fear on each face she knew. Ashton glanced behind her and saw Hunter still lying on the ground groaning in pain. He was still alive.

Workers lay sprawled out, some too frightened to get up and go through another round of fighting just in case he came back, and others trying to keep a distance so they wouldn't get hurt. Everything felt like it was in slow motion and rushed at the same time. So many things ran through Ashton's mind; she couldn't believe no one was stopping this. *Where is Wolfe?* No one intervened, not the Executives or Wolfe or Jorgeon or anyone else. Workers froze in a bizarre rhythm, too scared to go on and too scared to recoil for fear of what might happen to them later.

"Victory!" The Suit's roar broke her thoughts as he yelled at the top of his lungs to his surrounding Vikings. She quickly ran up to him. "Freya, my princess, we won!" He was laughing as he turned around in triumph. He put his hand around her waist and brought her up to eye level. Ashton squirmed as he held her tight and put his fake lips to her face. The kiss was rough as he forced her toward him. He pulled away and yelled again toward the Vikings, shaking his ax. The workers raised their weapons and yelled back in victory cries. It wasn't as enthusiastic as she was sure Jorgeon would have liked, but they were all too stunned to do much else.

Versal came out as the queen of the Saxons and handed the crown to the Suit, her fingers shaking. "You fought well and for that, you have conquered the Saxons." She made her way toward the Suit, who just laughed. Versal looked confused. He quickly grabbed her and placed her over his shoulder like a doll. She was his trophy.

"Do we return to our camp?" he turned and asked Ashton, with the terrified Versal dangling over his shoulder.

"Uh, y-yes. Yes, we go back now." That wasn't her exact line.

When they came back to the Viking camp, the show over, the Suit dropped Versal roughly to the ground and walked toward the area where Wolfe and Jorgeon stood. Once the Suit was out of sight, Ashton went over to Versal and helped her up.

"You okay?" she asked as she pulled Versal to her feet.

"I think so." Versal brushed off her beautiful purple dress, which now had dirt spots from where she had been thrown to the ground. They both looked back at the battlefield and saw some workers tending to their wounds and some still not moving.

"What in the world was that?" Versal was hysterical.

"I don't know."

Versal turned and started getting sick. Ashton pulled her friend's wig back and rubbed her back as she finished dry heaving. Ashton looked behind them, even though she knew she shouldn't. There was so much blood on the ground. She looked forward and all she could do was stare at Wolfe.

CHAPTER 12

Wolfe

Hours before the first Viking and Saxon production, Wolfe was conflicted as he counted down the minutes until the show began. He hoped for an impressive performance, but was concerned about injuries that would undoubtably occur. Soon, the workers would finally know the truth about their destiny at Land of Legends. The camp had come together much better than Wolfe had anticipated, still, how could he be expected to keep the workers safe and meet Warren's impossible expectations. The Executive Office had given only a few weeks to prepare an entire two-mile park up to the highest Augland standards. Workers and supplies had been brought in to clear the land and build the Viking camp and castle structures. Everything had popped up overnight, it seemed. When Augland put its mind, and workers, to a task, the results were incredible.

But Wolfe could not enjoy this moment. The meeting with the Executives still rang in his mind. It hadn't gone exactly how he would have liked, and now, anxiety radiated through him. He loosened his tie.

He walked slowly toward the Viking camp and saw a beautiful figure with swaying red hair. It took him a moment to realize it was Ashton in her Viking costume.

He hadn't thought much of Ashton in the beginning. He found her short-tempered and stubborn. He also found her passionate, kindhearted, and fierce. She was strong-willed, and that was something Wolfe admired. He found himself enjoying the times he spent with her, which seemed the only times he wasn't analyzed for every decision he made.

He didn't tell any of the workers, or Jorgeon for that matter, that Warren, the CEO of Augland 54, was his father. He didn't want anyone to think he had achieved anything because of his name. Also, Wolfe didn't agree with the way Warren ran things. Wolfe wanted to use Land of Legends to give workers who struggled another chance. For too long, he'd handled the workers that Augland 54—his father—had decided no longer served a purpose. Begging cries and frantic faces down below the park flashed in his mind, and he quickly shut his eyes. The memory of those screams still bounced around in his head. Not even time seemed to help; he had been away from the cages below Augland 54 for at least a year, but he still thought about them every day. He couldn't shake the worst memory—the lifeless bodies he'd ordered to be carried through the tunnels to just outside the Augland walls.

He turned his focus to Ashton. She was beautiful, sitting there truly looking like a Viking warrior. Before he knew it, he was walking toward her and meeting her gaze. She smiled. Wolfe forced himself to remember that smile. Soon, she wouldn't want to look at him, not with what the Executives had in store.

Ashton, he thought, was performing well—a couple of hiccups here and there with her lines, but she acted the part beautifully. Her fierceness and strength had really come full force in just two weeks. Before, she had looked weak and delicate. Now, she had confidence, and to see her interact with a Suit would make this show.

"Ouch, looks painful," he said, staring at a bright red rash on Ashton's arm from the leather outfit she wore.

"Where were you this morning?" Ashton inquired, trying to come off as nonchalantly as possible. Wolfe picked up a piece of grass and started playing with it between his fingers. He had become good at lying.

"We had a meeting with the Executives to brief them on today." That was all the information he would give her. He wouldn't go deeper, couldn't give her any idea what it would be like for her in the coming hours. They made small talk as she tried to get more information about the program, and for a moment, he thought he would cave. She had that effect on him. He could be himself around her. But he caught himself and reminded himself of his mission—the only thing that mattered, that should matter.

Wolfe walked with Ashton all the way to the Viking camp. As he walked away, he took one last glance. *Poor girl.*

Wolfe slowly walked toward the small hill that overlooked the battlefield where he and the Executives would watch the show. His father and Jorgeon spoke between themselves, while Wolfe set his focus on the scene ahead. The anticipation for it to start and for it all to be over had his heart beating out of his chest. He couldn't even pay attention to the dialogue around him, even though he heard his name mentioned several times.

Then it began and Wolfe felt a small sharp pain in his chest. He almost grabbed his upper body but knew his father was standing nearby and would want to see his reaction, studying him and looking for ways to criticize Wolfe's empathy. He blamed Wolfe's mother, claiming she had made Wolfe soft.

The representative the AEC had sent over was Senator Cleveland, a ruthless man whose large appetites were reflected in his overly proportioned Suit. After the war, the AEC had been full of politicians who had turned against their government. The large AEC headquarters stood only a mile from the White House in Washington, DC, and by the time the war was over, it was clear who really held the power. Once the AEC held enough politicians in their pockets, the frail government could not stop them even if they tried. The government didn't know what had happened until it was too late. There was nothing they could do but take advantage of the current situation by joining the AEC efforts. Things turned rapidly after that, and the monopoly soon took over the entire country, leaving nothing but a puppet government.

Senator Cleveland was a man who believed the sole purpose of the AEC was to serve the Suits like himself. The workers were given protection within the Auglands from the war-ravaged country and NeuroEnergy, the company that had never quite come under the AEC's rule. He saw himself and the leaders of the AEC as benefactors to the workers. They had protection; why did they need rights as well?

As soon as the battle started, the senator had begun swinging his ax, coming down hard on the workers. It was effortless for him. Wolfe followed him as he staggered left to right, leaving no one out of his wake. The sharp steel came down heavy and hard, bodies stiff until they went limp and dropped to the ground. Wolfe stood frozen, silently watching as this artificial thing, controlled by a man resting safely in a pod somewhere, used his programmed strength to hurt real bodies and cause real pain.

Warren spoke. "Wow, Cleveland is really getting into this. Typical politician, though; they all love the power." Jorgeon chuckled. Wolfe just ignored him.

Wolfe frowned, shaking his head. He knew if his father saw him, he would see it as a sign of weakness. There would be a consequence for that. Warren had never differentiated between his role as a father and his role as an employer.

Wolfe stared ahead, looking at the faces he had watched for the last two weeks become whispers in the wind. The grass around them grew red as they lay there, motionless. He screamed inside.

"Wolfe," Jorgeon said, putting his hand on Wolfe's shoulder, "are you all right?" He asked as if he had been saying Wolfe's name with no response. Wolfe cleared his throat, not wanting to answer.

"It's fine. Warren says there are more workers. So it's going to be okay." Jorgeon misread Wolfe's disappointment, projecting his own thoughts of losing workers.

"Yeah, yeah it is." Wolfe looked ahead now, scanning the area for something familiar. He saw bright red hair only meters from the Suit. He could tell even from his vantage point that she was beyond scared. She hadn't done any of the rehearsed fight scenes; she just stared as the senator charged ahead. *Stop acting surprised; you knew this would happen.*

Before Senator Cleveland could even make it back to the Viking camp, Wolfe was heading toward the train station. After the show ended, he knew they would need to reconvene in the Executive Office and get a status report on whether the park would be implemented. He knew the answer already. He knew they would want to continue, and Wolfe had mixed feelings. This hadn't gone according to his plan. With each step, he tried to think about what he would say to his father. *Should he try to stop this? Should he try to protect the workers? What cost would that have?* This wasn't going to be easy.

Wolfe didn't stop at the front desk as he had when he was at the Executive lobby with Jorgeon; instead, he marched to Warren's office and opened the sliding glass doors. Warren saw him and motioned for him to be seated for a moment while he finished a phone conversation.

"Yes, you are going to love it, Chandler. I can tell you this will be the time of your life." Warren emphasized each word. "All right. I have to go, but we will see you later this week, Chandler . . . yes, yes, okay, goodbye." Warren hung up the phone and brought his attention to Wolfe. "Wonderful, Wolfgang. Just wonderful."

Warren came to Wolfe's side from behind his desk. Warren grinned from ear to ear, the wrinkles on his Suit looking almost realistic. He had created a Suit with silver hair and wrinkles on an unrealistically youthful body. The result was unnerving. He put his hand on Wolfe's shoulder.

"That was better than we expected! You have done well with the workers. It felt so real, like I could feel their bones crushing. Ha! What a rush!"

"Yes, sir," Wolfe said.

"This is the ticket! This is your way into the Executive's Suite," Warren said as he clapped in excitement and went to go pour himself and his son a drink. Wolfe ran his hands through his dark brown hair as he thought about what he was going to say to his father. They had vastly different perspectives on the "success" of the program today.

"We can't do that to them again," Wolfe almost whispered as he stared out toward the field where workers were still cleaning up the spotty blood that contrasted against the bright green grass.

"Oh, they are fine! We have plenty more where those came from," Warren said nonchalantly, almost mimicking Jorgeon's words from earlier.

Wolfe was about to say something when he was interrupted. Another Executive entered Warren's office. Dressed in all black with slicked-back hair, he walked toward Wolfe and Warren.

"Splendid performance, Wolfe!" the Executive remarked, placing his hand on Wolfe's shoulder and shaking it hard. "This is going to be the next big thing at this park, and we are on our way to being the premier park of the West. Senator Cleveland said he hadn't had that much fun in a very long time." Both older men started laughing. Wolfe gave a small, forced chuckle. Warren and the Executive brought him into their huddle and started recounting a few good hits the Suit was able to land on the workers. Wolfe tried to ignore them; he had no desire to relive anything that had happened earlier in the day.

"Wolfgang, my boy; let's have another go at it. I have another high-end client who would absolutely love this." Auglands lived and breathed for their top-tier customers, who had multiple Suits and sway within the AEC.

There was a pause as Wolfe tried to pull himself together. He looked up at his father and saw pride in his eyes for the first time. This is what Wolfe had always wanted, but he felt like he had betrayed everything to get it.

"Yes, sir." Wolfe stiffened as he answered and let the two men proceed.

The older man was not stupid and could feel his son's resistance. Warren clicked the glass in his hand. "Give me a moment; I want to talk to Wolfgang. I'll swing by your office for some celebratory drinks."

The Executive gave a salute and shifted his gaze from Wolfe to Warren. "Sure thing, Warren. And Wolfe, so happy to see you step up here. I'll see you soon." With that, the Suit turned around and walked out the glass door, leaving father and son alone.

"I'd like to speak to you about the workers again. I don't think we should be treating them as 'dispensable' as you think we should," Wolfe started.

"Nonsense," Warren said almost immediately, dismissing the notion. "What has gotten you so uptight about this? They are workers; we have plenty of them. Who cares if a few get hurt along the way? We will have replacements before the day is done." Warren looked down at a stack of paperwork on his desk.

"It's not that; we shouldn't be hurting them at all. It isn't . . . right." Wolfe knew he was being bold. Warren slowly looked up, and his face twisted toward a frown.

"Are you forgetting what is at stake here? You knew all this before we began this little adventure. This was your idea," Warren started. "You wanted us to do this and find a new way to rehabilitate workers. Now you don't like the way it is handled?"

"No, this new park will work, I promise you, but—" Wolfe started but Warren's hand went up to silence him.

"The only way I sold this to the board, who might I remind you have offered criticism about this park, was that it would be a way to show the workers what happens if they don't obey. We are losing their focus, and this was our way to put them back in their place."

Wolfe looked confused and Warren laughed. "There had to be something to hang my hat on here. My hands are tied; this is what you signed up for." He made his way toward Wolfe. "I won't have this conversation with you again, Wolfgang. You will be a part of this, and you will do what we ask. This will go on as planned." He gave Wolfe a stern look. "Yes, we will most likely lose lives, but it will go toward the better good of this Augland and the entire AEC, both financially and systemically." Warren paused and lowered his voice. "NeuroEnergy is gaining power, and we have to keep the parks in check. Right now, we need solidarity, unity. We need to be in control." Warren looked menacing as he glared at Wolfe, who hadn't said a word. Wolfe stood unflinchingly as he looked directly at his father.

"This is where you say, 'Yes, sir,'" he said in a low voice.

As Wolfe stared at his father, he wished his mother Anastasia were present. She had come from one of the East Coast Auglands to visit Augland 54 when she met Warren. They quickly fell in love, and she came out of her Suit to give birth to Wolfe. But to Warren's disapproval, she never returned to her Suit. Soon, Anastasia and Warren were nothing to each other but co-parents. She raised Wolfe alone in a small apartment they shared in the Executive Penthouse. He hardly saw his father growing up, even though they were only a few floors apart.

While his mother raised him, Warren worked alongside Wolfe's grandfather to run Augland 54. The position of CEO had become a family legacy, and Wolfe was expected to take over for Warren when the time came. This was the root of the constant criticism Wolfe faced from his father. Wolfe needed to be perfect, to follow the legacy the men in his family had paved for him. His father wasn't a loving type of man: he yelled, he disciplined, he forced his way until everyone around him caved. As Warren grew in power, Anastasia seemed to shrink. Wolfe's mother would sit in her room for days on end, hiding away from the menacing world in which her husband thrived.

Wolfe learned at a young age to turn off his emotions. Emotions were what caused trouble with his father and what had crippled his mother. When his mother became secluded, Wolfe blamed his father for ruining her life. The more Wolfe fought his father, the harder Warren was on him, and the rest of Augland 54. At the age of sixteen, Wolfe had disobeyed his father's request to pick a Suit of his own. He had sworn to his mother he would never go into one. Warren cast him out to Security, telling him it would make him a real man and not a "mama's boy." That was where he saw it, firsthand: the torture in the cages. Warren was right; it did harden him. But it had also made him angry.

Wolfe straightened up and his eyes turned dark.

"Yes, sir."

CHAPTER 13

Ashton

"Hunter?"

Ashton quietly approached Hunter's bunk, wincing as if she could feel his pain herself.

"What?" he croaked. He lay on the side of his bed in the fetal position.

"I just wanted to make sure you were okay. I mean, after today and all," Ashton said. Hunter shrank back in pain when she touched his side.

"Go. Away." Hunter snapped and refused to turn toward her.

"I—I'm sorry about what happened," she said, turning away. She kept having flashes of Hunter cowering and putting his hand up in defense. Ashton paused, indecisively. She wanted to sit at his side and talk about how horrible the production had been. But, seeing his distress, she sensed he wanted space.

She looked around at the many who were icing their bodies or rewrapping bandages. The dormitory was silent. Many had not returned. Ashton made her way to her bunk, thinking she would find Versal, but it was empty. Sliding into the sheets, she tried desperately to relax, but the day's events and her worries about those who hadn't returned consumed her. She rubbed her shaved head and tried to stop herself from crying.

They arrived on the field the next day sore and saddened, most of them bruised and exhausted from the day before. They looked far from the imposing Viking and Saxon armies they were supposed to represent.

"Hello everyone!" said Jorgeon. "Amazing job yesterday. I can't tell you how proud Wolfe and I are of you all. We are very excited to announce that due to our success, we have received the approval for the new amusement, and this week, we will be launching Battle of the British Isles from Land of Legends to the general public!" He looked smitten, and it made Ashton furious, but her real anger was directed toward Wolfe. He could have told her—or at least given her a heads-up—about what was going to happen when they sat together at the rock.

Ashton was curious if Jorgeon was going to bring up the fact that yesterday had, in fact, gone horribly for the workers and talk about what he was going to do about it. Part of her hoped he would come in today saying that it was a mistake, and it wouldn't happen again.

"I want to put your mind at ease. I know yesterday was . . . exhausting for you all. Wolfe and I have decided that we will be bringing in quite a few other people to substitute in when need be, so rest assured." He paused, looking sympathetic to the group of workers. "We understand how physically draining this process can be for all of you."

Workers looked around and started muttering. "Physically draining" was an understatement; half of their group was gone.

"Now, enough chatter!" Jorgeon clapped his hands. "We have work to do. Chop, chop! Twenty minutes until rehearsal. Everyone head to costumes and get ready." With that, Jorgeon walked off toward Wolfe as if it were just a typical day.

Once outfitted for the day in their uncomfortably hot and chafing leather costumes, the Viking group walked in silence toward the camp. They were in relatively good shape since the Suit had been fighting for their side. The silence was deep with subconscious guilt.

"That was brutal yesterday," Pais said. Ashton looked up to see him and Byron walking next to her. They were good friends with Hunter and Versal, but she didn't know them well herself.

"Yes, terrible," she said sullenly.

"You think it will always be like this?" Byron asked.

"Yeah, stupid," Pais said as he looked at Byron and shook his head. "They tricked us, making us think we would be in this grand, new park with all the fun and excitement. If you ask me, this is a death sentence."

"You think they planned this all along?" Ashton couldn't help but drift closer, interested in Pais's theory.

Pais lowered his voice and looked around to make sure no one was near them. "My guess? They beat us down bloody and then dispose of us when we've had enough. Squeeze as much as they can get out of us before tossing us aside for the next worker. Then keep us hidden to hide the truth from the rest of Augland." Pais pushed his hands together to resemble wringing out a wet shirt.

"But why?" Ashton had to ask. "Why go through all this trouble of creating a new amusement and then get rid of the people they've spent time training?" This was what Ashton couldn't figure out. It wasn't like Augland to invest in something just to get rid of it.

"Who knows. Maybe they got tired of locking us up," Pais added. Ashton was shocked. She had heard rumors of the cages but had never heard anyone say it outright with such confidence.

"Or maybe . . ." Byron started. There was a long pause before he just shook his head. "Got nothing."

"If you ask me, we have the best chance of sticking it out longer. It's us they need—the ones they trained in the village skills, made characters out of, made to memorize lines—not the workers who are only part of the war scene." Pais smiled halfheartedly, and Ashton knew he was right. As Freya, she was in a good position.

It didn't take long for them to gather near the Viking camp to begin preparing for the next show. Wolfe arrived as warriors were practicing their routines.

"All right team, come in," he shouted. "We are going to do something different today. I know you all already know your routines; I saw that yesterday. Ashton, don't forget to keep up with the customer." He shot a look over at her. "What we haven't covered is how to block and defend properly. I am going to show you. Byron, up here." Byron made his way up to the front. "Get in your stance," Wolfe directed. "Instead of focusing on routines, we will be focusing on how you can read the movement of your attacker and put yourself in the best way to avoid being hurt. It was a vital part of my training when I first started in security. I think it is important for you all to learn how to properly defend yourselves moving forward."

There was silence for a moment while both Wolfe and Byron stood in front of them. Wolfe referred to the Suit as the attacker. Did this mean he was on their side?

"Byron, I want you to try and hit me." Byron almost laughed, thinking Wolfe was joking. But Wolfe just stood there with a stern look on his face.

"Are you serious?" Byron asked. Byron was maybe an inch taller than Wolfe.

"Yes, very serious. Try and hit me," Wolfe said again. Byron threw a soft punch toward Wolfe that Wolfe didn't deflect at all.

"I'm serious. Don't worry—you won't get in trouble. I want you to really hit me," Wolfe said. It took Byron only a few minutes to see that Wolfe was serious before he wound up and threw his right fist in Wolfe's direction. Without hesitation, Wolfe moved quickly to the left, pushing Byron's arm out of the way. Byron stumbled as his arm flung through nothing but air.

"Try again." Byron returned to position, this time looking frustrated and determined. He wound up his right hand but instead turned around and tried to kick Wolfe. Wolfe moved back and swatted away his swinging foot.

"You see now why defense is just as important as offense? Half the battle is being able to read the body language of your opponent." Wolfe referred to the Suit not as a customer but as an opponent. "Today, we will go through the different body indicators to identify the move of your opponent and practice defending yourself against the attack." Wolfe turned back to Byron. "Thank you, Byron, for your help here. Now, get into pairs, and we will go through this together."

Ashton went up against Roach. He took a swing at her, and she quickly moved her body back, missing his punch. She smiled at the small victory, and Roach tried again swinging at her with his left hand. She quickly brought up her hand to push his arm away from her. It hurt, but she didn't get hit in the face. It felt good to pick up something quickly for once.

A few days later, Ashton made her way to the rock, the only place she felt she could be alone, even if for a few minutes. As she drew closer, she saw someone had taken her usual spot.

"What are you doing here?"

"Same as you," Wolfe responded playfully. Ashton hadn't had a one-on-one personal conversation with Wolfe since the last time they were at this rock together.

"What, you can't share?" Wolfe asked.

"I came here to be alone." Ashton crossed her arms, not budging as she stared him down. Finally, she gave up and plopped down next to him as they both looked over toward the castle. It was quiet for a moment.

"So why did you teach us that stuff?" she asked. No one had really had the nerve to ask during their sessions, but she was dying to know.

"I thought it was important."

"Me too," Ashton said, which was true. She just wished he would have taught them before they had gone up against the first customer. For the most part, those who were just slightly injured had made a full recovery, with just bruises left. Others hadn't been so fortunate. Versal had counted and they had lost six workers during the first customer event and the injured were too many to count. Those who had more serious injuries were taken away. Ashton could only guess what that meant.

"How are you doing? With everything, that is," Wolfe asked quietly.

"As good as you can imagine." She wasn't sure if she should say anything about how she really felt; she wasn't sure she could trust him. Augland relied on managers to be their eyes and ears. If Wolfe ever wanted to get rid of any of them, all he would have to do is give the word. He'd have to do more than just teach them defense to gain their trust now.

"I get it." Wolfe let a long pause hang between them for a while. "It's okay to be angry. You can even talk about it if you want," he said.

She looked over at Wolfe's sympathetic look. She didn't understand why he would offer that. Of course, she wanted to talk about it, but there was a reason why these things weren't brought up. She had to keep her feelings quiet; they all had to keep their mouths closed and do what they were told.

"You know I can't talk about that, especially to you."

Wolfe nodded. "You can trust me, though."

"Oh, like you are so open?" she snapped back at him.

"I'm just saying you can talk to me, that's all," he said defensively. "If you did want to talk about it."

Ashton let out a big sigh. Wolfe confused her because he had these two sides. Most days, she felt like they were complete strangers; on others, he wanted to act as though they were actually friends. He was strict, formal, and uptight one moment and someone who looked like he genuinely cared about her feelings the next. She wasn't sure even he completely understood who he was.

Ashton shook her head. "I'm fine, but thank you."

"For what?"

"You taught us the defensive moves and for that, we are all grateful," she said, shifting her weight on the rock and scooting away from Wolfe.

Wolfe smiled and then his smile turned to a frown. "It's the least I could do."

Ashton had blamed Wolfe for not saying anything, but she understood why he couldn't. Like Pais had deducted, they didn't want workers knowing about their plans. Part of her hoped he hadn't known, and that the violence had been a surprise to him as well. It was the Executives' fault. Wolfe sighed as they both sat there for what felt like forever, until he stood up and started to walk away.

"Thanks for sharing your rock with me. It's been nice to get away," Wolfe said, turning to her and walking backward toward the Viking camp.

Ashton stayed for a while longer, taking in the moment of peace and silence before heading to the Viking camp too. Tomorrow, they would receive their second customer and relive the nightmare again.

CHAPTER 14

Ashton

Land of Legends went through three full days of back-to-back shows. Each time, the winning side would rage in triumph, and either Versal or Ashton was claimed as the prize. While some proved to be easier than others, most Suits reveled in the idea of causing pain without feeling any. Each blow came harder than the last. Wolfe stayed away, seemingly disappearing overnight.

Ashton took a few hits here and there but nothing like some of the people on her team. She tried hard at night to help or even just talk with the others. Her attempts were met with disdain. Her privileged position as Freya made her unpopular and her overtures unwanted.

Hunter and his fan base seemed to be the culprits who had turned the others against her. They reasoned that she didn't understand their pain; as the privileged "princess," she hadn't endured the same beatings they had received.

They were losing more people every day. She could feel the ice starting to form deep within her—but also the fire and rage. She had a front-row seat to the brutality, to the horror of seeing her teammates' bodies fall to the ground, some lifeless.

On top of that, she was dealing with her own dilemma. While she hadn't received the physical beatings like the rest, she had dealt with the mental torture from the Suits themselves. With each new customer came some sort of touching, groping, or vulgar language. She tried not to recoil in disgust when they treated her like a prop. Jorgeon told her she needed to be more involved and "make the customer feel important," but she knew what that meant, whether or not he would say it. He wanted her to pretend like she wanted the attention, which she knew she would never be able to do.

None of the workers saw that or cared. She still seemed lucky in their eyes. Even Versal had pulled away from her and switched bunks. The bed above her was now empty. Ashton had no friends and felt more alone than she ever had in her life. Most nights, she cried herself to sleep, feeling the anxiety of what the next day might have in store.

Three weeks into Land of Legends, Ashton headed toward the rock to steal a few moments of solace before the day's show. She looked up to find Wolfe standing near the rock. Her anxiety turned to rage.

"I want you to leave," Ashton said as she stomped toward the rock. Wolfe put up his hands in defense.

"I know how hard this has to be, Ash," he started.

"Hard? Have you and I been watching the same thing? Oh, wait—no, you've been hiding away as people die. The first day, yes, that was bad, but this . . . this is torture."

She was almost out of breath as she walked right up to him and pushed him. He didn't budge. She started punching him. Her arms moved automatically, hitting him over and over. Wolfe allowed it, and after her fifth punch, he gently wrapped his arms around her shoulders as she collided with him. She hadn't noticed the tears that were rolling down her face.

"It's okay . . . shhh. You'll be okay," he said with uncharacteristic kindness. She was caught off-guard, feeling herself melting into his arms. She stiffened and tried to pull away.

"No, no it's not! Where were you?" Ashton cried, hysterical. She dug into him, debating between ripping him in two out of frustration or holding on for dear life, never wanting to let him go. It felt good to feel embraced, comforted. But that didn't take away from the pain and anger she felt.

"I just can't believe you. I thought, I thought you ca—" she stopped herself and wiped the tears away. He didn't deserve to see her like this. She had let her anger bubble over. She pushed herself away from him, and he let her go, surprised by her sudden movement.

"What, that I cared? I do care. I care a lot about you all. But you know what, Ashton? I also have a job to do, just like you do."

"I know we all have jobs, but you let them do this! You did."

"Oh, so let's go over the alternative, shall we? Remember, you asked me what happens? What happens if this fails? Let's go over what you would have me do instead."

She paused. He had stumped her; she didn't know what would happen, but it was easy to speculate. This was the last stop for all of them; some would just last longer than others. She didn't know which was worse: to be thrown out into the wilderness and face slow death with no food or water or face the park with a small chance of survival.

"You think I like this? I don't want to see you get hurt, any of you . . . especially you." He looked distraught, and she could see now that this was weighing heavily on him too. She felt her breath going back to normal as she calmed down. Wolfe looked tortured, and she was confused. He sat down and dropped his face into his hands and exhaled. Ashton sat down next to him on the rock.

"We can't keep this up; you know that," she said. She already knew the answer, but she wanted him to at least admit that to her.

"Yeah."

Ashton's heart started to ache as she now had the confirmation. "And they . . . they will just replace us if we . . ."

"Yes," he said with a heavy sigh.

Ashton took a deep breath. "They blame me, you know. All the workers in there. They think I get it easy because I'm Freya. They can't see that it's bad for me too," Ashton confessed, hoping Wolfe knew what she was talking about.

"They are scared—and afraid. Fear brings out the worst in all of us. It's how you rise above that fear that defines who you are." Wolfe looked at her.

"What do you fear?" she asked.

He took a long pause. "That's my secret."

Ashton and Wolfe sat in silence for a while, not saying anything to each other. Ashton guessed it had been wishful thinking on her part to think that

Augland would somehow give them a second chance. This wasn't a second chance for them; this was torture before the end. Was there any other option? All because Suits "deserve to live a great life." The Augland slogan was engrained in her brain like a charred brand.

"I hate Augland. I really hate it," Ashton confessed. She knew she shouldn't, but at this point, there wasn't much more they could do to her. The workers were all as good as dead. Wolfe turned to look at her. His eyes looked bright now, and she guessed she had never seen how blue they were before. He looked as though he had aged in the week he had been away. Abruptly, Wolfe took her by surprise by leaning toward her and wrapping his arms around her waist, bringing her into his embrace. She was taken aback but found herself digging into his shoulder and starting to cry again.

Ashton needed Wolfe's hug more than she thought. Seeing people she knew, bleeding, broken, and dead, tore at her soul. Wolfe hugged her tighter. Maybe he needed the embrace more than she did?

Wolfe pulled away and stared at her. Ashton hadn't been close to him before, not like this. She felt her cheeks redden. Wolfe sighed and came closer. He paused for a moment, an inch from her face, as if waiting for her approval. She hesitated for a moment, then pressed into him, kissing him on the lips. She pulled back slightly, startled by the sudden movement, and was surprised at how good it felt. It was nothing like the customers who had brought her in for a kiss. Those were forceful and hostile. Wolfe was warm and careful as he kissed her.

Wolfe pulled away. He stood up and looked confused. "I'm sorry, I shouldn't have done that." Ashton didn't understand.

"Oh, it's fine," is all she could say, shaking her head and trying to make it seem like it wasn't a big deal. It was a big deal to her, though. Against the odds, and perhaps her better judgment, she liked Wolfe. Knowing that he felt as helpless as she did about the situation made her feel close to him, despite their difference in station.

"I should go—actually, we should go." Wolfe looked toward the camp. "For the, you know, the—" he pinched his brow while he mumbled something.

"The show?" Ashton interjected, trying to help him conclude his sentence and end their awkward conversation.

"Yes." Wolfe walked past her and left Ashton sitting on the rock. Ashton stood up, still wondering what just happened. *And what did it mean?* She had felt a connection with Wolfe and thought he had too. Or maybe he didn't. He had acted like this was a mistake. Was it?

Wolfe made his way ahead of Ashton, and she followed at a distance behind. As they headed toward the Viking camp, she tried to block what had just happened from her mind and focus on getting through another heartbreaking show. It would be harder once she started seeing all the Viking crew out in front. Every face she passed told the same story, and it hurt her heart to see all the sullen looks laced with fear and anxiety. Ashton also saw faces that looked alive and well, nervous but not terrified. The new recruits—they had no idea what was about to happen.

In just the last week, Ashton had seen one person get hit so violently that he went unconscious as he slapped hard against the ground, blood streaming down his face. He didn't survive. Another worker had the wind knocked out of her so hard, she keeled over and vomited. Ashton shook her head, trying to shake the memories away.

"You will thoroughly enjoy this, Chandler; this has been Wolfe's pet project for the last few months, and he has really taken the experience to a new level," Warren said proudly. Ashton stood a few feet away in full costume, waiting to be introduced.

"Well, I'm very excited. Senator Cleveland said it was a highlight experience for him." Chandler's Suit turned toward Wolfe. "Wolfgang, I've heard great things from Warren on this experience. You think you'll follow in your father's footsteps?" the Suit asked Wolfe.

Father? Ashton bit her lip sharply to suppress a cry of surprise and shock. Hopefully, no one noticed her reaction. *Wolfe is the son of the CEO?*

"One can hope," answered Warren. "I don't know how much longer I have before retirement, so we have high hopes for Wolfgang." Warren looked smitten as he gave a side punch to Wolfe's shoulder. Wolfe looked up, smiling, and suddenly stopped when he saw Ashton within earshot.

Ashton was not sure what look she had on her face, but on the inside, she was stunned and outraged. So many things ran through her mind. *So he first pretends to be chummy with the workers and to be doing all of them a favor . . . only now we find out he was pulling the strings all along.* She looked away once they made eye contact and quickly approached the Suit. If she looked angry it was because she was, but she tried to conceal it and put on her customer service face. Wolfe had betrayed her. Had their time on the rock been simply a game to him? *Liar.*

As Ashton approached, she threw a lingering glare toward Wolfe, hoping he could hear every word going through her mind and feel the betrayal she felt. *You're a liar. A manipulator.*

"Hello, Chieftain Bjorn. I am Freya, warrior of the Norsemen," Ashton robotically said to the Suit.

"Oh, oh, oh! What do we have here?" the Suit commented jovially, walking around Ashton slowly. "Mm, very nice."

Ashton stayed still and glanced over at Wolfe, who stood watching next to his father. The older man whispered something to him. Wolfe's eyes suddenly shifted downward. Ashton looked away. *Why all this? What he said, the kiss?* It needed to have meaning. There was no time for that now. She needed to get back to work. *Just concentrate on surviving.*

"Chieftain Bjorn, the Saxons are bound to make their way to us, so we must attack now, while we have the element of surprise," Ashton said.

"We can wait. I'd like to feast first with my fellow Vikings," the Suit said, turning toward the Viking camp. As he entered the site, he bellowed greetings to the Viking warriors. Ashton started to follow when her arm was tugged, stopping her movement forward. She turned to see Wolfe.

"What do you want?" she whispered, pulling her arm away from him.

"I get it. I do," Wolfe said urgently, but she couldn't really see the remorse on his face.

"No, you don't get it. You really don't, and you know why? Because you are one of them, you are *them*," Ashton hissed in a volatile whisper.

"This wasn't my idea. I swear. I didn't want any of you to get hurt. You have to understand the position I am in. I was trying to help." Wolfe looked hurt, but she didn't care.

"Help? You call this helping? You know, I really don't understand the position you are in. What was all that back at the rock then? Is this funny to you? A twisted game you play?"

"Ashton, you need to listen to me." Wolfe was almost begging for her to hear him out; she could hear it in his voice. But she was tired of feeling lied to.

"Save it, Wolfe. From where I'm standing, you didn't make this any better, and to top it off, you've had the power this entire time to stop it. Let me know when I can start calling you 'CEO.'" It was a jab, and she knew she shouldn't be talking to him like this, but Ashton couldn't hold it in any longer. She could feel her cold exterior that was always good, always obeying, starting to crumble. She wasn't sure how much more she could take before she exploded. Ashton stormed off toward the Suit.

"I have to get to work so I don't get killed."

"Freya!" the Suit yelled as he swung his drink toward her. The dining hall was loud with warriors and filled with smoke from the cooking fires. Even though she was angry, there was work to do.

"Where were you?" he asked while she took her seat next to him.

"Oh, I was talking with a few of the warriors about our battle strategy. Should we make our way to the battlefield soon?"

"Soon, but until then, I'd like to get to know you more," he muttered suggestively, getting closer than she liked.

"Chieftain Bjorn, I am here to serve you and help you fight this war. There isn't much to learn about me," Ashton said coolly. This wasn't her first time trying to divert a Suit's attention.

"Oh, come on. You are a warrior princess; you must have many tales of great exhibitions," he laughed. Ashton looked away. She could tell he was making fun of her, clearly knowing this was fake.

He put his arm around Ashton and brought her in closer; Ashton's body instinctively tried to pull away. The last thing she wanted was him touching her. He brought his face close and pushed his lips against hers. It wasn't nice or soft. Ashton wanted to spit at him.

"You are pretty; you know that? I love red hair." He pulled Ashton's chin closer to his and stared intently into her eyes. While most Suits were forward, Chandler gave her a bad feeling, and she wanted nothing more than to get away from him. Chandler pulled her chin again abruptly, so hard it hurt. He must have seen the panic in her eyes because he gave a small chuckle and dropped his hand from her face. He turned toward the group of Viking workers. "Let's go kill those Saxons!" he yelled. Ashton sighed in relief.

"Let's go, sweet cheeks." He stood up from his chair and headed toward the exit of the dining hall.

"I tell you, my people! We will destroy the Saxons. We will destroy everything they hold dear. We will keep going until every one of them is dead!"

The Suit yelled arrogantly, strutting back and forth in front of the Viking clan. Many of the newcomers looked conspicuously clean and well kept. Others had black and blue eyes and bandages. The Suit turned toward the Saxons who rallied on the other side of the field near the castle.

"Go, now!" he shouted. The crowd around him devoured his words, roaring and raising their weapons high. The newcomers had more energy to give.

Ashton followed Chandler like she had done before with other Suits, counting down to when the horror would ensue. She could feel the anticipation when she saw him approach Hunter, who was leading the pack of Anglo-Saxons. He was going full speed, and Ashton had to squint her eyes and look away as Chandler barreled into Hunter and two more people behind him. It looked like he was going through a field of daisies as he rummaged through and plucked each one, his inhuman strength outmatching them all. Ashton did her part and started fake beating the man in front of her. Fake punch, low duck, punch. Then she moved on to where Roach was standing, and he came in to start their routine. Suddenly, he hit her.

Ashton recoiled. Roach came back full swing with a right hook, and she ducked. That was not something they had rehearsed. Ashton backed up and raised her hands in defense.

"What are you doing?!" Ashton screamed.

"What, you can watch, but you can't take it, is that it?" Roach asked menacingly. He came back swinging, striking her on the right side of her ribs with his leg, anger radiating through him.

"What is wrong with you?" she cried, wincing in pain.

"Doesn't feel good, does it?" he snarled as he stood tall, facing her. Ashton looked around for a quick escape and noticed the Suit at least fifty feet in front of her. She gave a side glance to Roach and, still writhing in pain, moved past him to catch up with the Suit.

"Chieftain Bjorn!" Ashton yelled, trying to distract him from attacking his next victim. "Chieftain Bjorn!" she yelled again. He turned and looked at her as she limped over to him.

"You're hurt," he said, looking down at her as she held her side.

"Oh, no, I am fine," Ashton said, trying to reassure him. She didn't want him to take it out on the workers. "I—I think we are good, and we can proclaim victory," Ashton offered with an attempted smile.

"Absolutely not, not 'til all of them pay!" said Chandler harshly, an angry look in his lifeless eyes. Then he went wild, completely reckless as he plowed through each person who came near him, swinging left and right with his sword.

That was when Ashton saw her. She found a familiar face amongst the new members on the Saxon side, and it took all of her breath away.

Sheva!

CHAPTER 15

Wolfe

Warren had requested that Wolfe be present in the upcoming production staring Senator Chandler, Warren's long-time friend. Before meeting Warren and Chandler, Wolfe made his way to the rock in hopes of seeing Ashton. Although he did not know what to say, he felt he owed her an explanation.

After the first show, Wolfe had stayed away from the workers. He was busy with corporate meetings and strategy sessions with Executives, and he was still working his security management position. If he was honest with himself, though, he drowned himself in meetings to keep from witnessing the horror of seeing the workers, his workers, hurt. Sometimes, he couldn't help it, though; he would go to the skybridge of the Executive Office and peek out toward the Land of Legends park. The guilt ate at him from the inside out.

He received a daily report from Jorgeon of the injured and dead. Every time the report was delivered, Wolfe sat in his office, poured a glass of whiskey, and read each name. Some he hadn't met before—actually, most of them. Sleeping at night was next to impossible.

Wolfe knew he couldn't pretend any longer. He had tried to give the workers the best shot of survival, teaching them to defend themselves, but it would do little good. Humans against Suits would never be a fair fight.

The doors opened and the train station wind blasted his face. He stepped out and turned toward the brightly lit sky and grassy hill. It was quiet, but the fear still lingered like fog. It had been a week since he had stepped foot into the park—a week since he had seen Ashton. He would have to face her one way or another.

His first stop was the rock. He knew Ashton would head there at some point. No one in Augland did anything without their every move being captured on camera, and Wolfe had access to those images. He wondered what he would say to her. How could he tell her everything but keep the things he needed to be kept secret from her? How could he explain himself?

Ashton hadn't been angry with him the last time the they saw each other, but he had been away a long time. A lot had happened to her, to all of them.

Wolfe walked down a small hill toward the empty rock that lay feet in front of a wall of trees that marked the beginning of the thick forest. The wind made the trees sway back and forth, creating background noise as he sat down on the hard stone and looked up the hill. Ashton was right; this place was peaceful.

He heard footsteps just above him and soon red hair became visible, contrasting against the green hill. Ashton looked defeated as she slowly walked toward her place of solitude. She glanced up. Her sadness disappeared and anger emerged. Her footsteps quickened as she targeted him.

"I want you to leave." Ashton's blue eyes raged with ice-cold daggers toward Wolfe. Wolfe put his hands up in defense, knowing that she had words for him. He understood.

"I know how hard this has to be, Ash."

Wolfe didn't know how else to say it. He wanted her to know that he didn't want this. This was the work of his father and the Executives. He wanted her to understand his life, the choices he had to make, and his reasons.

"Hard? Have you and I been watching the same thing? Oh, wait, no, you've been hiding away as people die. The first day, yes, that was bad—but this, this is torture." Ashton didn't realize that Wolfe had been watching. It was true, though—she called him out on not being able to witness it firsthand, and she was correct. He had taken the opportunity to separate himself from it all.

Wolfe saw Ashton's intention before she started. He could have immobilized her so she wouldn't be able to throw any punches, but this he deserved, and he knew it. He let her get her frustration out. Her punches were hard, but he knew what to expect with Ashton. During rehearsal, he had been hit by her mistakes too many times to count. One after another, she kept hitting him, tears rolling down her face. Reaching around her small figure, he pulled her into him, holding her tight against his chest.

He put his hand on her red hair and let her sob against him. He closed his eyes and felt emotions coming to his eyes as well, but he quickly shoved them away. Ashton couldn't see the pain he was in, not when she had such a burden herself. She needed this, but in a way, Wolfe needed this embrace as well. There was no one he could confide in, no one he could lean on. Wolfe guessed they had this in common.

Jorgeon had mentioned the conflicts in the dormitory with Ashton and the rest of the workers, even suggested they replace her. Wolfe had said no, of course. The last thing he wanted was to put her in one of the cages below Augland. He knew all too well that workers who went down there never came back to see the light. At least as Freya, Ashton's chances of getting killed were slim.

"I thought you ca—"

Wolfe was having a hard time keeping this one in. To think he didn't care. He wished he cared less. He wished he could bury his emotions away forever and never feel anything about anyone else again. It would be easier if he were like his father, but he was nothing like him.

He would tell her as much as he could. If honesty was what Ashton wanted, then she would get as much as he could tell her.

Ashton's strength during their conversation was mesmerizing to him. He was even envious of how she took all the bad that life had dealt her with grace, strength, and understanding. Wolfe couldn't imagine being in her position—knowing certain death was ahead and simply accepting it.

Before he knew it, he had pulled her into him again, wrapping her tightly in his arms. This time, it wasn't meant to console her; it was instinctual. He wanted to hold her, wanted to take her worries away. This was a new feeling for Wolfe. He hadn't been this close to anyone, ever.

Ashton and Wolfe pulled apart, and he looked down at her face, noticing for the first time the sprinkle of light brown freckles around her nose. He smiled slightly as she looked at him. He wanted to kiss her. His heart beat out of his chest, and he couldn't tear his gaze from her beautiful eyes; they drew him in. In there, he could see the hurt of the past week, the awful Suits who had looked at her as an object. It sickened him. All he wanted in this moment was to keep her safe.

He dropped his head toward her and paused, an inch away. She moved in. It felt beautiful, safe even. They both disappeared from their lives for that moment—just a moment to take away the pain they both felt so deeply.

Wolfe pulled away and Ashton smiled at him. It didn't take long until the headiness of the moment evaporated and he remembered where they were and what he had just done.

"I'm sorry, I shouldn't have done that."

As much as he wanted to run away with Ashton and save her, Wolfe knew he had a bigger mission. He had made his decision a long time ago. She had asked him what he feared, and he feared failure.

He had complicated this for her. His feelings for her were real, he knew that, but he needed to be strong right now. Weakness wouldn't help either of them. She had a destiny here, whether on the battlefield or in the cages. Those were her options for now, and there wasn't anything Wolfe could do about it. Ashton couldn't do anything either. If she was smart, she would stay away from him. There was so much she didn't know about him. If she knew, she wouldn't feel the same way. Knowing what he was doing, and had done, for Augland made him sick. She deserved better.

Wolfe approached his father and Chandler, whose Suit had already been decked out as a Viking. Chandler was a long-time friend of Warren's and a very well-known Suit to Augland 54. His broad shoulders were prominent, and he stood inches above Wolfe's tall frame. Long brown braided hair and striking tattoos made his appearance that much more intimidating. He looked every bit a warrior king.

"You will thoroughly enjoy this, Chandler; this has been Wolfgang's pet project for the last few months, and he has really taken the experience to a new level," Warren boasted. Wolfe cringed inwardly, knowing this hadn't been his idea at all.

Maybe it had been at first, but Warren had sunk his devil teeth in and changed it so much that it didn't even resemble Wolfe's original plan.

"Wolfgang, I've heard great things from Warren on this experience. You think you'll follow in your father's footsteps?" the Suit asked Wolfe. *Did he want to follow in his father's footsteps? Be like him? Be a tyrant who relished power and devoted his life to this place?* Wolfe did want his father's approval, yet feared his father's wrath, feared what the older man's need for power would do. He didn't even get time to answer before his father butted in to answer for him.

"One can hope. I don't know how much longer I have before retirement, so we have high hopes for Wolfgang." No one called him Wolfgang anymore, only his father. But he would play his part for now. As Warren said, it wasn't much longer until he was out of power. If everything played out right, Wolfe would take his father's spot, not one of the other Executives—who were just as bad as Warren.

Before he could speak, Wolfe saw red in his peripherals and turned to see Ashton staring at him. She had heard. Panic ricocheted inside him. He wasn't ready for Ashton to know the truth about who he was and where he had come from. It wouldn't make sense to her. He was about to go to her, try and explain himself, but his father was next to him. Ashton didn't have time either; it was her job to welcome Chandler. Again, Wolfe had to choose and Ashton couldn't be his choice.

Warren watched the production in awe. While the first show was a success, the team had really put all their effort into making it realistic for the Suits. That had to be Jorgeon; he cared about décor and aesthetics. Warren and Wolfe followed along as Chandler sat in the dining hall, surrounded by workers cheering and drinking colored water meant to resemble beer. The food was programmed to taste like a medieval feast for the Suit but was nutrition-less and tasteless to the workers. It was cheaper that way.

Wolfe looked over at Ashton, who put all her attention toward the Suit. She was captivating; no wonder the Suits felt so connected to her. Chandler caressed her face and Wolfe wanted to punch him. Instead, he looked away, feeling cowardly, balling his fists in frustration.

"Chandler is really getting into this," Warren smirked. Wolfe just nodded.

CHAPTER 16

Ashton

It took Ashton a moment to even recognize Sheva. The older woman was shaking in her steel armor, eyes full of fear. This was not the strong Sheva Ashton had known. This Sheva was frail and scared. In slow motion, Ashton saw the Suit barrel through a Saxon fighter and set his eyes on the cowering Sheva. One blow and Sheva would be out. Ashton would not let that happen.

Before she could think, Ashton took off straight toward Sheva. Mid-run, she picked up an ax discarded in battle. Her feet dug deep into the grass as she propelled herself forward, passing the Suit and heading full force toward her friend. Chandler, the Suit, was right behind her—only feet away. Ashton didn't have time to think; she lifted her ax, turned around, and with all her force swung it at him, hitting him square on his side. The brute force sent a vibration from her fingers all the way to her shoulders. The Suit recoiled from the force of it, but of course, his artificial body felt no pain. Chandler's real body was somewhere safe, stewing in a pod located in what Augland Executives called "the spa." His Suit shot a furious glance toward Ashton. It took her a moment to realize what she had just done.

With a loud shout of rage, he lunged toward her. Instinct raced through her veins. Ashton swung again, this time aiming higher, and hit his neck. The knees buckled, his long, brown braids swaying behind him; he now was staring at Ashton's shoulders, eyes twitching from side to side.

111

The adrenaline swimming up and down Ashton's muscles took over and, all of a sudden, she felt all her suppressed frustration come lunging out of her. Ashton lifted her ax again and came down, hard, on the Suit's head. She screamed at him, each hit releasing all the hurt, disgust, and fear she had accumulated over the course of the last month. She thought of Wolfe and how he had lied, the torture they had put Sheva through, Hunter's constant power trip and criticism of her, and Niall, the thought of how sorry she had been to leave him. Finally, she swung for every young and old worker that had died, been mistreated, or been shamed because of these Suits.

Chandler kept yelling until his voice cut off, "Do you know how expensive this Suit is? You will pay for this!" That was the last thing she heard.

She wasn't sure how many blows she had dealt before coming back to reality and seeing the damage she had done. The inside of the Suit was filled with a green glowing plasma that sparkled with energy as it oozed from the wounds. As the Suit twitched, she could see mangled flesh-like strands that served as nerve connections to the thousands of sensors throughout the Suit. There were also complex networks of bounded fiber-like material which functioned as muscles that contracted randomly as the Suit laid haplessly on the ground. The boney structure of the Suit was a shiny metal alloy that was now gruesomely exposed. There were no internal organs, just circuits and plasma. The Suit continued to spasm as Ashton watched it slowly lose power. Then it stopped.

Ashton had never seen the inside of a Suit before. As she looked at the torn Suit on the ground, she felt her body relax and a sense of calm washed over her. She wished he would get back up so she could do it again.

"Ashton." Sheva was beside her. Ashton looked up and saw the entire Viking and Saxon cast looking at her with surprise. She scanned each face and then looked down at the broken Suit at her feet.

"Ashton, we have to run. You have to run!" Sheva was tugging at her arm and pulling her away. Ashton knew she was right; in seconds, Augland security would be pouring down upon them. She had to get out of there.

"It's going to be all right. Just breathe. We have to go!" Sheva was yelling at Ashton, but she sounded far away, muffled. Ashton could hear herself breathing. It felt as if she was moving in slow motion. Sheva continued to speak, and Ashton could feel the full force of reality hitting her. *She had killed one. Well, not killed, but destroyed a Suit.*

"Please! You have to run!"

Sheva pulled Ashton toward the forest and away from the destroyed Suit. Ashton and Sheva ran uphill. They had a head start from Wolfe, Jorgeon, and whatever security was surely on its way, but Ashton was sure with Wolfe's speed, he would catch up soon.

It didn't take them long to get to the tree line. Sheva was considerably slower than Ashton, but Ashton tried to pull her along as fast as she could. The forest behind the rock, where she had kissed Wolfe just hours before, was dense and would be a great hiding spot. Slowly, the lights above them became hidden by the tall trees.

"Where do we go?" Sheva said in a whisper.

Ashton needed to concentrate. The deeper they went into the forest, the more concerned she became. At some point, they would run out of forest. They would come to the end, a wall that would stop them. This wasn't a great plan; they were searching for a way out of a prison. Ashton paused, hearing voices in the distance behind them. She pulled Sheva down to the ground and put her finger to her mouth, motioning Sheva to stay quiet.

"Ashton!" a whispered shout called out. Ashton knew that voice—and it wasn't Wolfe or Jorgeon.

"Ashton!" the whisper said again. There was more than one person there. A few figures came into view, and Ashton couldn't believe who she saw.

"Hunter?" Ashton asked incredulously.

"Yes! Ashton, where are you?" She stood up slightly to show herself and then saw the few others behind him—Hunter, Versal, Byron, and Pais.

"What are you doing here?" Ashton was nearly speechless with surprise.

"You were absolutely amazing!" Hunter shouted enthusiastically, running toward Sheva and Ashton. "I had no idea you planned on doing that. Genius. I wish you would have said something!" he continued.

"I—" Ashton was completely taken aback. For the past week, Hunter had been treating her as if she didn't exist. The entire group had been giving her the cold shoulder.

"Ashton, that was so great." Versal came close and hugged her.

"We have to hide!" Pais interrupted.

"What's the plan?" Versal asked, glancing at Ashton and walking with Pais as he led them farther into the forest.

"I don't know," Ashton admitted.

"What do you mean, you don't know?" Versal sounded stunned. "Hunter, I thought you said there was a plan."

"Well, there was a plan until Ashton over here decided to make our plans happen a little faster than we thought."

"You were planning on running?"

"Well, maybe not destroying a Suit and putting a bounty on our heads, but escaping—yes, something along those lines."

"Yeah. And Hunter heard about a village of people outside the walls," Versal interrupted. "There are rumors of another place to work as well. Hunter says that is why they won't let workers outside the wall, that they don't want them going to another place." Versal was looking at Hunter, who didn't say anything but only nodded in agreement.

It was hard for Ashton to wrap her brain around this. Her mind was trying hard to poke holes in this theory. Not that she didn't want it to be true, but how was she just now hearing about this? *How did Hunter know this stuff?*

"There's nothing outside the walls," Ashton said, which was the only thing she could think of to say. The group was slowly making their way through the forest, casting nervous glances behind them every few seconds.

"That's what I thought; that's what we've been told, right?" Pais chimed in. "But think about it—there has to be food and life outside these walls. They have ships coming and bringing things from outside. What if they've been lying so we don't try to escape?"

"There are rumors of a secret group right outside these walls. I've heard it a couple of times," Hunter said.

"From whom?" Ashton didn't trust Hunter.

"From people, okay, Ashton?"

"We would know if there were people outside the walls." Ashton couldn't believe this, and the fact he had roped others into this was beyond her.

"Why would Augland tell you that? Why would they admit that you have a choice?" Hunter argued. Ashton had to agree with that because some of their coworkers had taken quite a beating. If they had known there was something else, something better for them outside the walls, they would have done anything to leave. Ashton looked down at Sheva.

So much had happened in such a short amount of time that she hadn't been able to even process reuniting with her friend.

"You doing okay?" Ashton asked.

Sheva smiled, but she was already out of breath.

"You shouldn't have done that, Ash," she said quietly so the others wouldn't hear.

"I saw you, and he was heading your way. I couldn't let him do that to you, Sheva." It had been a knee-jerk reaction and not something Ashton had really thought out. But the thought of that massive Suit laying a finger on Sheva? Ashton was not sure she could have come back from that.

"Yes, you could have, and you should have," Sheva said quietly.

"Sheva, you have no idea what you mean to me. For the last month, I've thought about you, hoped you were okay. Once I saw you, I knew I couldn't lose you again."

Sheva shook her head and embraced Ashton tightly. When they came apart, tears in their eyes, Ashton pulled out the necklace she had never removed from her neck, all this time.

"I thought of you every day." The fear and anxiety that lived in Ashton's stomach left and, for just a moment, Ashton felt somewhat normal.

"We'd better catch up." Sheva nodded to the four ahead of them.

"Any chance your plan had an escape route?" Ashton asked as they caught up to the others. Hunter and Versal exchanged worried looks.

CHAPTER 17

Wolfe

Jorgeon and Wolfe had run straight to the mangled Suit and watched Ashton as she ran toward the castle with Sheva.

"What in the world does she think she's doing?" Jorgeon yelled.

Wolfe was speechless as he looked at the damage. The ax had hit several vital areas. One blow to the chest left the leather of the Suit's costume hanging loose, and the blow to the head had almost split the Suit in two. Those were just the worst hits. Ashton had swung several times.

Workers gathered around the carnage. Everyone was mesmerized by the sight of this superhuman Viking, now nothing more than a pile of lifeless biosynthetic material, alloy, and plasma. Wolfe couldn't peel his eyes away.

"Wolfe!" Jorgeon yelled.

Wolfe snapped back to reality. His body stiffened to an upright position. This was bad, but Wolfe couldn't help the small spark of pride he felt for Ashton. Ashton had used his training to protect herself and others. Unfortunately, her disruptive behavior has sabotaged his plan. The pride quickly turned to fury. All this work, lives lost, and for what?

"Get everyone back to the dorm!" he shouted. "And, Jorgeon," he said as he looked over at Jorgeon with fierce eyes, "make sure they stay there." Wolfe's sudden movement startled Jorgeon, but he nodded and slowly turned to the workers staring nearby. Before he was too far away, Jorgeon turned toward Wolfe.

"What are you going to do?" Jorgeon asked.

"I'm going to find her," Wolfe said as he looked up at the castle. The escapees were out of his view now, but he was sure they were heading to the train station. This was something Wolfe knew well. He had worked security for most his life. He knew all the parks in depth and could use this to his advantage. While he had never led a chase, it should not be too hard. He just didn't know what he was going to do if he found them. Warren most likely would have his own methods, but maybe if Wolfe reached them first, he could lessen the consequences.

Wolfe walked down to the Viking camp, where he could see Warren and two Executives in tow. Wolfe let out a sigh and headed toward him.

"You had better fix this, Wolfgang!" Warren was visibly steaming from each ear. His face turned a deep red as he walked fast up the small hill toward the castle where the Suit lay motionless.

"Sir, I understand—" Wolfe started.

"You have no idea the damage you have done, Wolfe. So help me, if that girl is not found by the end of the day—" Warren threatened.

"She will be; I'll find her," Wolfe said calmly as he approached his father.

"How did this happen?!" Warren furrowed his brow as he looked intently at Wolfe.

"She went rogue. We had no idea this was going to happen, sir. She had been doing great, playing the part. I don't know what happened."

"Chandler will be beside himself. We will have to give him a free unit for the remainder of the year. Do you know how much that will put us back with the AEC? Not only that, but he was a prestigious member of this community. You can imagine how this is going to play out for us."

"Sir—"

"Don't you dare! This is over, and you can kiss that promotion goodbye unless you find those kids and fix this! I don't care how, but I want it done, and I want it now. Understood?!" Warren was inches away from Wolfe's face, but Wolfe remained still.

There was a long pause before Wolfe spoke again. "Yes, sir."

"Good. I want to know the minute she is found. Take a few men from security with you. No one leaves this park. We don't need this getting out to the rest of the workers. I want this done quickly and without notice." Warren was panicked, but as he took charge, his rage was replaced with a quiet fury. "This doesn't get out. Whatever we have to do to buy Chandler's silence, we will do, and we will deal with the workers."

Warren took a deep breath and pulled his son away from the two men beside him. "Do you think this was an outside job?" he whispered conspiratorially. "The Colony? NeuroEnergy? Is there a way they infiltrated our borders with their propaganda?" Warren was trying to piece together the reason behind the sudden rebellion against a Suit.

For years, the Colony outside the walls of Augland had sustained a treaty with the Executives. They stayed hidden, away from Augland, and the Executives left them in peace. The treaty had been put in place years before Warren took power, and he felt it unnecessary goodwill on Augland's part. He had made his opinion known to the Colony's leadership. He thought this might be an act of retaliation.

Wolfe didn't have anything to say to Warren. He remained standing in front of his father, his hands behind his back.

"What are you still doing here? Gather your men and go find her!" Warren yelled. Wolfe quickly turned and headed toward the entrance of the train station. He would need to quickly get a team together before Ashton had any ideas of leaving Land of Legends.

As Wolfe walked away, he thought about what would happen to the fugitives if they were caught. Best case, he would catch them early enough, and they would be put in the cages. He could at least keep an eye on them and diffuse Warren's anger.

Wolfe walked into his office and pulled a blue folder from his desk, quickly opening it and running down a list of names he had on his security detail. If they needed this done fast, he would need his best guys with him. An AEC-issued interconnect was on his desk, one he used to communicate with his security team.

Wolfe played the game with the Executives, but he could be more himself with his team. He had some of the best people he knew working for him, those he would trust to do his bidding and not the Executives'. If he said Ashton and the renegades should not be harmed, that is what they would do. As long as he could get the workers into the cages, he could potentially salvage his plan and save their lives in the process. He would need to act quickly, though.

His side started to vibrate, and he looked down at the device on his hip. Warren was paging him, asking him to meet him in the conference room. *I don't have time for this*, Wolfe thought to himself. Once Ashton had dismantled Chandler's Viking Suit, his mind would have transferred back to his body and customer service would have him in a new unit.

The pods were contained in a large, heavily monitored area on the outskirts of Predator's Biome and acted more like a spa than a container for human bodies. There were customer service locations and health facilities that made the transition back and forth from pods and Suits comfortable and safe. All things needed for an enjoyable customer experience were provided.

The pods were baths of nutrient-rich plasma gels that were temperature controlled. The information was then detailed and compiled by computers that instantly conveyed the information to the Suit. Every smell, taste, sound, temperature, or visual information the Suit reviled was included. Pain was muted so the customer would not have any distasteful sensations.

Wolfe honored Warren's orders, quickly changed to his security attire, grabbed his interconnect, and headed toward his father.

"He wants what?! Absolutely not!" Wolfe spoke more loudly than he had intended and Warren's face grew to a new shade of red and purple.

"Don't test me, boy," Warren said through gritted teeth. "You will go in there and apologize to Chandler. That is what he wants, and that's what he'll get. He is a prestigious member of the AEC and has a lot of influence here."

Wolfe wanted to say something—he looked straight into his father's eyes with profanities in mind. After a while, his face relaxed and he calmly replied, "Yes, sir."

"More like it." Warren stiffened and went into the conference room.

Wolfe followed a few steps behind and stopped right before the room. He could hear Chandler shouting at others. He took a deep breath and walked into the room where more than one disgusted look welcomed him.

Chandler's new Suit, most likely one of his spares, looked over at him. Similar to the one he'd previously worn, Chandler's new Suit was significantly taller than Wolfe with muscles built to kill. He had sandy blond hair slicked back and a perfectly manicured blond beard.

"Unbelievable. You call that the best new amusement? I had my head nearly chopped off. So help me, I will ruin you and all of Augland 54 for this. You have something to say to me, and it had better be good." There was a long pause as Chandler waited for Wolfe to speak.

"I'm very sorry for what happened," Wolfe said in a monotone voice.

Chandler scoffed. "This is the apology I came all the way over here for, Warren? I tell you what, you've gone soft on these people. If it were up to me, I would have gotten rid of the bunch, just for what happened in that pet project of yours." Warren looked at Wolfe and gave a subtle hint to make it more believable.

"This will never happen again; we will reprimand Ash, the worker, appropriately. Please accept my deepest condolences for what happened to you today," Wolfe said with as much consideration as he could muster.

Chandler then stepped closer to Wolfe and crossed his arms around his chest.

"You're pathetic. And over my dead body you'll be the next CEO," he said looking down at Wolfe with a large smirk on his face. Wolfe's face remained impassive, still, and strong. But behind his eyes, his hatred for Chandler and Warren simmered. He hated their politics and power that had destroyed Auglands and the AEC.

"Very well. I will keep this under wraps, but I'll get what is promised to me. Two new Suits." Chandler pointed to Warren. Warren nodded and gave a large smile.

"Of course, Chandler."

Chandler lifted his hand and patted Wolfe on the cheek. "Good boy," he whispered in a patronizing manner. Wolfe's jaw tensed and his fists balled up. Chandler walked past Wolfe and out the door; Warren walked toward the door but stopped as he came close to Wolfe.

"Find her, and bring her to the cages. I will handle it from there," he said. Wolfe didn't say anything.

"If you don't find her, well, we don't need to go there because she will be found, right Wolfgang?" Warren had a menacing look on his face. Wolfe closed his eyes, as he knew exactly what would happen if he didn't find her.

CHAPTER 18

Ashton

"We asked around and we've gotten, well, sort of a map together of Augland," Pais said. He was still in his full metal costume without the steel helmet. He must have lost it when running through the woods. The wind howled around them as they gripped one another and huddled deep in the forest.

"Oh, okay, great. Do you have it?" Ashton sounded relieved. Both Hunter and Byron chuckled.

"We weren't even close to being ready, Ashton. You kind of rushed our plans." Hunter looked annoyed.

"You have to remember part of it, right?" Sheva intervened.

"We thought about taking the train, but that would be a trap. They would have people waiting for us when exiting, and they monitor the cameras constantly on that thing," Hunter started.

"Are you sure about the train?" Ashton asked. That would be their only escape out of the park.

"Positive. There is no way that we will be able to make it from here to the train entrance. It's way too risky," Pais piped into the conversation.

"Are we sure there is a way to get out?" Ashton asked.

"Well, see, that was still part of the plan that we were trying to figure out. We hadn't gotten that far in the development," Versal sighed.

There was a long pause as the realization of their current situation sunk in.

"I may have an idea," Sheva said softly. "Well, if you are looking for a way to get from here to another park, there are camouflage doors in the wall between parks. The park engineers use them."

"The train station isn't the only way in and out of the parks? There is a door we could go through?" Hunter asked.

"Yeah, it is all through a code or key card, I mean, if they haven't changed it. I . . . still have some of the codes memorized." Sheva continued, "The only problem is I have never been here and don't really know what the surrounding parks are or where the walls are."

Ashton stared at Sheva, seeing again the determined woman she had known. She wondered where Sheva had been all this time, where the security guards had taken her.

Hunter almost yelled, "That's it, then! That's how we are going to get out of here. Do you think you could find it?"

"Maybe if I knew where we were relative to the other parks."

"We do know that this is the north side of Augland; does that help?" Versal asked.

"Well then, that's good because I think in most directions, we will find a door that leads to another park. Once we know that park, I might be able to help. I typically worked in Predator's Biome and Hollywood Boulevard and could tell you exactly where those doors are."

"Then, that's it! We will just head away from where they will be looking for us, and we will run into the wall and can trace that to find the doors," Hunter said.

"What if we go back, just tell them that we are sorry, and then we can wait until we have more of a plan?" Pais almost pleaded with the group.

"Absolutely not," Versal and Hunter said in unison.

"You know what will happen if we do? We won't come back, ever. They will get rid of us, especially after what Ashton pulled." Hunter nodded in Ashton's direction.

"What if we leave her here and say we had nothing to do with her?" Pais continued as if Ashton wasn't two feet away from him.

"What if they saw us running after her? It's most likely they would notice four people running after Ashton," Versal said, again with no regard for the fact Ashton was in earshot.

"Well then, we can say that we went looking for her or something to bring her back. We could find a way. It is her they want." Byron looked scared and had decided this wasn't the best option for escape.

"Wait. You guys aren't serious, are you?" Ashton asked. "You'll turn us in? You were going to run anyway."

"This is our chance. We can't go back now; I mean, who is going to want to come to a place where a Suit got essentially dismembered? Who knows what the consequences of that will be." Hunter's proclamation shook through Ashton. She hadn't thought of the repercussions. She hadn't thought of anything up to this point. She had pretty much ruined the entire production.

A snapping noise brought Ashton back. She looked over at Hunter, who was wide-eyed, looking at her, bringing his fingers to his mouth to keep everyone quiet. Ashton heard the rustling near them, and they crouched low, almost lying against the ground. People were coming through the brush.

Sheva grabbed Ashton's hand. Ashton shut her eyes and tried to quiet her breathing.

"Come out!" a voice yelled. "You aren't going to make it out of here, might as well save us all the trouble and come out."

Ashton looked up at Hunter, who shook his head no.

"They obviously went toward the train station. I'm not sure what's the point of looking out here. If I were to bolt, that's the first place I would go," one of the men said to his counterpart.

"Wolfe told us to search everywhere, and that is what we are doing."

"This is ridiculous."

"Come out! We have you surrounded!" Ashton's heart stopped. They had been seen. But nothing happened.

The first voice chuckled, "Come on, you think that is going to work?"

"It might. Who knows? It's worth a shot."

The voices started to fade as they went farther into the forest in search of the runaways.

"This is our shot," Hunter mouthed to Byron, Pais, Versal, Sheva, and Ashton.

"Let's head toward the other side of the castle." Ashton couldn't deny that this was probably the best timing, seeing as the security guards were heading farther away.

Ashton nodded. They couldn't stay here. They had been lucky once, but Ashton didn't think it would happen again. Ashton could feel her heart race as she kept looking toward the woods behind her to see if the two men had turned around. It was silent.

Ducking and crawling through the brush, they headed through the woods in the direction they had originally come from. Ashton looked up and saw the others trailing not too far behind as she led the group through the thick bushes, her small stature making it easier to stay out of sight.

"Ashton, get your friend," Hunter whispered ahead to Ashton. Sheva had been right behind her but had fallen behind and was almost standing as she couldn't bend down far enough.

"You okay?" Ashton whispered as she grabbed Sheva's elbow to help her.

"Yeah, fine." But Ashton could tell she wasn't fine. She was nearly skin and bone and was already at the end of her energy.

Out of nowhere, they heard voices coming from behind them. Realizing the two men must have turned around triggered a panicked look on Hunter's face. His countenance said it all, and Ashton brought Sheva closer to her, pushing her to go a little faster.

It was their luck that Augland designers had surrounded the entire castle with trees, and it felt like they crawled through the forest for hours. The back of the castle was a tall cement wall that cast a shadow on the forest and hid them well.

"It has to be around here somewhere." Sheva seemed to know much more about this than any of them, which made Ashton happy. Sheva was slow, but she had value.

Hunter smiled and kept moving. "Sheva you should lead the way. Let us know what to look for."

"It will be well hidden. It's not meant to be found, but I will try." Sheva hobbled her way toward Hunter, who looked behind them to make sure no one was on their tail. They hadn't seen the two men or heard anything in a while. There was little commotion around the castle. Ashton guessed all the workers had been sent back to the dormitories and the only people around would be looking for her and her new team of escapees.

"They must have brought everyone back to the dorms," Versal whispered to Ashton. Ashton saw the terror in Versal's eyes as her eyes darted through the castle, looking for any of the workers she had known for the last few weeks. There was not a movement or sound. It looked deserted.

"Yeah, must have," Ashton whispered back. That was the best-case scenario; Ashton couldn't worry about the repercussions her actions might have on the workers they'd left behind.

Suddenly, they ran into a wall. It was almost completely blended with the forest, a 3D mural of sorts. Hope sparked through their fatigued bodies.

"Finally," Hunter said. "Now what?"

"We just need to follow the edge until we come up to the door," Sheva said.

"Great! Let's go, then," said Hunter.

"It's not going to be that simple," responded Sheva.

"What do you mean?" Pais sounded a bit more confrontational than he intended.

"This place has got to have cameras along the border here; we won't have a lot of time once they see us to get through."

"Of course, cameras," Versal sighed dramatically.

"It just means we need to be quick, right?" Pais said. "They can't catch up to us that quickly; all we need to do is get to the door, use Sheva's credentials, and be on our way." This plan was not solid enough for all of them to be comfortable, and Ashton couldn't help but think they should pause and really think this through.

"What happens if we aren't able to make it through? What if Sheva's credentials don't work?" Hunter asked.

No one said a word. If this didn't work, they had no chance of getting out of Augland, and most likely not even out of Land of Legends.

"We just have to see what happens." Ashton tried to stay strong. The panic that settled in was almost intoxicating and her voice cracked. They all knew what they were about to do. Their actions would let Augland know where they were and where they are going, but the group of renegades didn't have another option.

Ashton waited in silence for a minute as she mentally prepared herself, and the minute felt both too short and too long at the same time. Hunter looked around, making sure no one had followed them. She could feel the anxiety start to overwhelm her.

"We don't really have a choice. We either stay here and ride this out and hope they don't find us, or we take a shot at going," Versal said, and she was right. There wasn't any sense in waiting around. The longer they waited, the greater the probability of getting caught.

"All right, let's make a run for it and find the door as quickly as we possibly can." Hunter started shedding his costume down to his black sweater underneath his heavy armor. Sheva, Byron, and Pais did the same. Ashton removed her fur.

Ashton turned to Sheva, who had panic written all over her face.

"You've got this," she said. Sheva started getting rid of her armor as well. The extra weight wouldn't help as they ran out along the wall.

Sheva looked ahead and started walking toward the front of the pack. She would be the one who needed to find the door.

"Sheva, what's the code?" Hunter asked. "Just in case one of us makes it there first." He was stretching to prepare for the run. Part of Ashton was upset that Hunter would ask that. She knew exactly what he was thinking and didn't like it. Since Byron had thought about turning them in, Ashton had felt like the group was trying to get away from them. Ashton did see the logic, though. Whoever made it to the door first should be able to open the door, and there was no way Sheva was fast enough to get there before Hunter.

Sheva looked at Ashton, asking with her eyes if she should say something. Ashton could tell the same thing was running through her friend's mind—she didn't want to be left behind and that number was the only leverage Sheva had.

Ashton just nodded to her. For now, they would have to trust that Hunter, Byron, Pais, and Versal had their best interests at heart.

"It's 3590242," she said.

"3590242, got it. All right, let's get this over with. One, two, three . . ." Hunter darted in front followed by Byron, Versal, and Pais. Ashton quickly grabbed Sheva's arm and pulled as they ran into the sun and into full exposure on the grassy battleground.

CHAPTER 19

Ashton

Ashton and Sheva were not running fast. Sheva's frail body limited her ability to move as swiftly as Ashton could. The others were far ahead of them, palming the wall as they searched for a door that could be their freedom to another park. The Land of Legends park was at least a mile long, so it could be a while until they found the door if it wasn't near the battlefield.

Sheva put her hand on the wall between them to see if she could feel anything. While Sheva looked for the door, Ashton kept a lookout. Ashton looked ahead and then back toward the castle again, and that's when she saw them.

Augland security was in pursuit. Three figures, led by Wolfe, came rolling around a corner in a full sprint in their direction. Voices in the distance began yelling. Wolfe had found them sooner than any of them had expected. Sheva and Ashton were now far behind Hunter and the rest of the group. While they could still see them, which was promising, they would be the first ones caught. Ashton pulled Sheva closer and dug into the ground below her, needing them both to go much faster.

Sheva let out a small groan as she could feel her legs start to go. Ashton pulled her up more to alleviate her struggle, but that just slowed them down.

"Just keep running!" Ashton called back to her. As she turned ahead, the security team gained several yards on them and were catching up fast.

"I can't go any faster," Sheva replied with the little breath she could muster while trying to suck in enough air to fuel her run.

"Keep trying," Ashton urged. "I'm not leaving you." Ashton tried to calm her down. She was almost dragging Sheva at this point. While Ashton was in the best shape of her life due to all her running in the past few weeks, Sheva's extra weight was slowing her down.

Then it happened. Versal, Hunter, Byron, and Pais stopped suddenly and looked behind to see where Ashton and Sheva were.

"They found it!" Ashton smiled, gasping in air. It would be their only reason to stop. Ashton's heart leaped out of her chest, bursting with hope they could get out of here. She had new energy and pushed harder to get to the door. It was a race. Wolfe and his security team versus Ashton and Sheva. Hunter was shouting. They were going as fast as they could.

Wolfe's security men were getting close, and as Ashton looked back she could make out faces. Wolfe, looking very determined. She knew he was fast too.

Ashton's eyes turned back to the group in front of them and saw that Hunter had just punched the code into the keypad, and everything froze for a moment. If the code didn't work, this was it. All their running would have been for nothing. The door swung open.

Ashton and Sheva were getting closer, and she could feel the heat of Wolfe and his crew gaining on them. Ashton refused to take her eyes off that door. She wasn't sure this was going to work and feared that Hunter would selfishly walk through the door and shut it behind him. If he did, there would be no way they would have time to punch the code in again and get through the door.

Ashton couldn't feel her legs anymore, running as fast as she could with Sheva right beside her. Even if she wanted to stop, she wasn't sure she could.

We are so close! Ashton dared to look back, and Wolfe was only steps behind her.

"Stop! Ashton, stop!" he yelled.

She didn't listen. They were so close and so was he.

"Wait!" Ashton yelled to Hunter, who was looking through the door and back at Ashton. She could tell he was thinking they wouldn't make it in time. Ashton thought the same, but she needed him to try.

Ashton and Sheva were only a few yards away when she saw Hunter look at them with a flustered gaze. He took a long stare at them and then darted through the door. Ashton's heart sank. She couldn't believe it. He had left them. The door was slowly starting to close behind him, and Ashton pushed herself forward and ran as fast as she could, essentially lifting Sheva's full body weight behind her, resting it on her back. Ashton saw the door closing much faster than she expected. *Stay open*, she willed.

"Don't do this, Ashton!" Wolfe's voice broke her train of thought, but she wasn't going to listen. "Stop!"

They were so close, so close—she just prayed they would make it before the door closed. The burning in her legs turned to cramping, and she was about to collapse. *Just a little farther, come on, we can do this.*

Then it happened—they were right there, and the door was still open, just a crack!

Sheva screamed, and Ashton briefly looked back to see Wolfe reaching out for her. This would come down to the second. Ashton reached out for the door and put her hand out to catch it. She did. But she was going too fast to just whip it open; instead, she swung Sheva through the opening and ran right into the wall to the side.

Wolfe was only a few feet away, and their eyes met briefly. He looked astonished. With one swoop, she went through the door and closed it as fast as she could. It took her a second to realize that she had done it. The men were on the other side of the door.

She heard their frustrated pounding. It wouldn't take them long to figure out a code to get through, and she and the others would need to be gone. Ashton looked over at Sheva, who was lying on the ground dry heaving. As she lay there, Ashton looked around to see if she could see the others, but they were nowhere. Ashton put her hands on her knees, catching her breath, and heard muffled voices on the other side of the door.

The world around her looked like nothing she had ever seen. Black skies above were littered with white dots, each bright and twinkling.

"This must be Venus." It looked like they had traveled to another dimension. "Beautiful," she said out loud. Grey dust surrounded them and lifted as the wind changed direction and swirled around them.

131

Wolfe's stern voice seemed to vibrate through the door, and it brought her back to what was on the other side, back in the Land of Legends. "Code! Who has a code for this?" he yelled.

"Get me through that door, now!" Wolfe shouted and Ashton panicked. She could hear a different voice shout out numbers and could hear beeping sounds as they attempted a code for the door.

"Ashton," Sheva said, but Ashton was momentarily distracted by her new surroundings.

It was black outside, but the small stars above helped with visibility. Moments before, it had been daylight and their eyes were still adjusting to the change. Maybe a mile ahead of them was a large city, with bright neon lights and tall buildings. That would be the only place to go and most likely where the others had headed too.

Just then, another pound came from the other side of the wall. Ashton looked over at Sheva, lying on the ground next to her.

"Come on, we have to move." Sheva resisted and Ashton bent down to pull her arm up. "I know you're tired, Sheva, but we have to get going." They would have to move fast if they were going to put any distance between them and Wolfe. Once they made it through, they were sure to catch up quickly.

Sheva was hobbling now. She wasn't used to this much exercise, and her age didn't help the situation. Ashton wasn't sure what exactly they were going to do once they arrived at Venus Park, but it would be easier to sit and rest with Suits around. Each step pushed dust toward them and Ashton could feel the small dirt particles in her lungs. Sheva coughed loudly and often. Ashton looked back; if Wolfe had come through the door, she hadn't seen him. Most likely, it would be hard to notice them in the surrounding darkness. Their only navigation tool was the large vibrant structures that grew closer with each step.

From the noises in the distance, it sounded like the city was packed with people. Ashton took her mind off her aching bones and sore lungs to admire the scenery, which was breathtaking. The night sky shone, and the city dazzled like a bright festival. She smiled through her heavy breathing. While the situation was not ideal, the calming effect of the stars above her almost elevated her above the chaos and away from the constant throbbing in her body.

"There's music; we're getting close!" Sheva wheezed. She was right. There were rolling hills before the city, but as they came closer, the pounding beats of music rattled the ground below them. Ashton took one last glance up at the stars before putting her attention back on their dash.

Sheva was starting to slow down, and her coughing didn't make it easier. Ashton looked back and saw tiny dots moving toward them. At least they weren't too close, but they would soon catch up. Ashton was sure Wolfe was more determined now that they had bested him at the door.

"Sheva, come on, we're close," Ashton said, pleading with her.

"I can't make it." Sheva slowed her running.

"Please, we just need to get to the city to hide." Sheva couldn't actually think that Ashton was going to leave her. "You can make it; come on, you just need to push a little farther. See? We are almost there." Ashton pointed to the bright lights that were so close.

"Please, Ash, I can't—"

Ashton stopped her. "Get up. I am not leaving without you." With that, Ashton pulled Sheva up and hoisted the older woman onto her back. Nothing was going to stop her from bringing Sheva with her. Ashton couldn't let herself panic. She knew she needed to be strong, and that Sheva needed her right now. Sheva had always been her rock, and this was her time to take care of Sheva. She pushed harder, even though her legs screamed for her to stop.

CHAPTER 20

Wolfe

After the interaction with his father and Senator Chandler in the conference room, Wolfe had made his way to the office. His brain was still reeling from Ashton's violent actions against the Suit. It would take her and her cohort a few hours to make it out of the park if that was their plan. Wolfe knew they must be still wandering the forest, most likely making their way to the Land of Legends train station. He would catch them there; he would not let Ashton slip through his grasp.

Wolfe had glossed over the short list of individuals he trusted on his security detail. He found it hard to concentrate. He couldn't wrap his mind around what just happened. Ashton had dismantled a Suit—not just any Suit, a valued member of the Augland elite—and now she was on the run. While his mind told him it was an accident, he couldn't help but think: *Had he been so blind to who she truly was? Could she be part of a resistance? The Colony? NeuroEnergy?*

Wolfe held her file in his shaking hands. It was a flimsy, soft, blue folder with only a few papers stapled together. It outlined everything, every infraction, every misstep. There was a guy named Niall she had been close to back when she worked at Maya Bay, but nothing out of the ordinary to make Wolfe think she had any affiliation to the outside organizations. His fingers grazed over her picture. She smiled brightly and her tousled brown hair looked more unruly than he remembered. A small smile crept to the side of his mouth and then disappeared. She was no longer innocent. Ashton with a head full of disheveled curls. They had shaved her head and worn down her heart. She looked different now.

Wolfe's thoughts were interrupted by a knock at the door. His security men, the few he trusted and had summoned, barreled into his office. They were prompt, exactly how he had trained them. He had worked alongside these five men for most of his adult life and had learned to trust them unconditionally—and them him. Being a security manager was something he enjoyed. It was structured and planned, and people did what they were told.

Wolfe's office was not large, but it was efficient, with a picture window facing out toward Augland, covered by a drawn shade. Unlike the rest of the Executives who preferred to view Augland from the top of their needle-like structure, Wolfe chose to keep his lair more secluded. He didn't care to look at the world outside of his four walls.

"We have a security breach." Wolfe was direct, almost robotic as he spoke to his men. "There is a rogue group of workers trying to escape. We need to catch them before they make it out of the park."

"Yes, sir," the five men said, almost in unison. They dressed in all black and their bodies were in peak condition. They had to be: they were not Suits. Their bodies were mortal.

"They are somewhere in Land of Legends. I'll need at least two men at the train station. The others will go with me to search the grounds. We have some security already out there searching, but they've come up with nothing. I expect more from you all."

Wolfe was stern, but he knew his men well enough to know they were up for the challenge. They thrived on exceeding expectations. Just like him. He was asking them to hunt their own. It wasn't fair and he knew that. It wouldn't have been his first idea.

Wolfe had mixed feelings. He had trained his men for anything: any rebellion, any fight, to die for his command. These workers received special privileges, and in return, absolute loyalty to Augland 54, Augland, and the AEC was expected. If he was going to fulfill his role as the someday CEO of Augland 54, he needed to have those who would do anything for him. He would need to gain their trust and, in turn, be able to trust them as well. Now, he found himself asking something of them he didn't believe in. He knew Ashton wasn't a threat. She was kind, caring, and above all, she had a good heart. But he was now talking about her as if she were defined otherwise, using words like "rebellious," "threat," "renegade."

An image of Warren's angry face flashed across Wolfe's psyche. Wolfe flinched, even though his father wasn't physically in the room. Warren needed to see results and depended on Wolfe to deliver. If Wolfe didn't succeed, who knew what would come of him. He was already on the last straw with Warren, who tended to act irrationally. As a child, Wolfe knew the only way to get approval was to play Warren's manipulation game.

His men would need to apprehend Ashton and bring her to the cages. Wolfe still had no idea what would happen after she was found. But he knew she would be, and before that happened he needed to figure out what he would do when it did.

Before Wolfe could dismiss his security team, his interconnect buzzed. It was a message from Jorgeon, big bold letters on the screen that said, "Workers are in the dorm." That was exactly what he needed Jorgeon to do: take care of the workers so there wasn't a full-blown rebellion amongst them all. It seemed that Jorgeon could take charge when given direction.

"Dismissed," Wolfe said to his men. "Radio me if you find anything and I'll join you shortly. Do nothing with the workers until I get there." They nodded and marched out of his office.

Wolfe looked around his now-empty office to make sure he had grabbed everything he needed. Interconnect and handcuffs were essential for this operation, and his handgun in case things spiraled out of control. He truly believed they wouldn't. If he found Ashton first, he would just need to explain to her how it needed to be. If only he could find the words.

Wolfe entered a large room filled top to bottom with small screens displaying all of Augland 54. The screens were an overwhelming blur of movement, but Wolfe knew every camera angle and went straight for Land of Legends.

"Any movement behind the castle?" Wolfe asked as he quickly scanned for anything out of place. A man sat on a chair in front of the wall of cameras, selecting one after the other and zooming in.

136

"None. They made their way far into the forest, beyond the cameras, so we lost them. We have two men scouring the northeast side," the man replied, pointing at a camera shot.

Wolfe furrowed his brow. That didn't make sense to him. There was no way out for them near the forest. To get to the train station, they would need to run to the opposite end of the castle, adjacent to the Viking camp. Wolfe almost chuckled. There was no way they would be able to get to the train station unseen.

"All right, thanks. Let me know if you see anything."

Wolfe exited the camera room and headed down the long hall toward his office and elevator. It would be a waiting game until Ashton and her group emerged from the forest.

Wolfe made his way to the castle in Land of Legends where his men would be scouting out the forest area. He rarely spent any time within the walls of the small castle township because customers typically wanted to play the Viking chieftain. The castle and town mirrored the intense attention to detail of the Viking camp. Cobblestone walkways, wheelbarrows full of hay, steel mills, and small market carts lined the town. Jorgeon had done his research and knew exactly how to make this place feel realistic.

Wolfe looked out of place, dressed all in black and walking the silent streets up toward the large castle entrance. His men would be on the patio deck looking out toward the forest in anticipation of the defectors exiting the thick forest line.

"Any sign of them?" Wolfe asked as he approached three of the security men stationed along the large castle deck. It had a panorama view of the entire forest line, which made it impossible for anyone to emerge without being seen. Two of his men were stationed at the train entrance to ensure the refugees didn't slip past.

The view was beautiful. Abundant evergreen trees, native to what had once been known as the Seattle region, swayed high above them. The breeze seemed stronger as they stood far above the ground below them. The silence was deafening as Wolfe and his security team stood still, ready to pounce at a moment's notice.

He wasn't nervous. No, he knew they would be found. She couldn't stay in the forest forever. But there was still the matter of what would happen when they were found. Warren was not known for his cool and collective demeanor. Wolfe thought about hiding Ashton and the others away until his father had cooled down. He would say he was interrogating them to find out more information about the Colony and NeuroEnergy. Warren would want to know of anything going on outside the Augland walls. Warren was paranoid. He knew Augland stood on uneven ground.

"Wolfe!" A security man on the left side of the castle deck pointed out toward the left outer wall of the forest. Wolfe quickly made his way toward the man. Wolfe scoured the left side of the castle toward the forest and back, trying desperately to see what his security man saw.

He then saw her: an older woman just above some of the shrubs between the forest and the towering Augland boundary. Then she vanished below the brush. Wolfe gave an approving smile. He had found them.

"Let's go get them." Wolfe turned around and jogged toward the stairway, down toward the lower level of the castle, his men behind him.

By the time Wolfe and his men turned the corner toward the forest, he saw Ashton and the older women running along the border. Without notice, he bolted forward toward them. Wolfe breathed heavily as he sprinted, feeling the power surge from his legs. His men trailed behind him again.

Wolfe looked on as Ashton dragged the poor old woman behind her, dangling like a rag doll being pulled by a toddler. Ashton was fast, but the extra weight made her typically strong stride look more like a hobble.

As Wolfe came closer, he shifted his eyes to the other individuals running ahead of Ashton. From the distance, he could make out Hunter leading the pack, followed by Byron, Pais, and finally Versal. They were running alongside the wall and it perplexed Wolfe. It would have been easier to go diagonally, a straight shot to the train station. To be against the wall only hindered their progress and would eventually make it easier for Wolfe to trap them. There was something he was missing.

Ashton kept looking back at Wolfe and with each stride, he drew closer and closer. It wouldn't be long now. Her fear showed on her face as she turned and looked at them—at him. Hunter had suddenly stopped. Wolfe turned his head to see what he was doing. He was facing the Land of Legends perimeter wall, looking down at something. Wolfe tilted his head and narrowed his eyes to adjust to the distance. Panic overcame him as the realization of what was happening. They weren't heading toward the train station at all. Ashton and her friends must have found out about the door system between the parks. *But how?* This wasn't good and Wolfe knew it. Wolfe screamed into the interconnect for the door password. *Why had he not known this? How had he missed this?*

"Stop! Ashton, stop!" Wolfe yelled. She didn't listen. Instead, she stared straight ahead and quickened her step, her red hair flowing majestically behind her.

"Wait!" Ashton yelled at Hunter, who was now holding the door to Venus Park open for them. Wolfe set his sights on Ashton and the woman she was with. He would catch whomever he could.

"Don't do this, Ashton!" Wolfe pleaded. "Stop!"

Ashton didn't listen and instead looked intently at the door as Hunter bolted through it, leaving Ashton and her companion behind. This gave Wolfe the chance to catch up. There was no way she would get through the door in time. Wolfe was now full sprinting and gaining with each step he took. Ashton was fast, but he was faster and would collide with her if he didn't slow down.

Then the impossible happened. Ashton reached out and grabbed the door, swinging it open and catapulting her feeble friend through. For a moment, she faced him, and Wolfe couldn't help but look, wide-eyed, as their gazes met. Her power seemed to paralyze him in the moment and all he could do was watch as she slipped past him through the door. Then she was gone.

Wolfe pounded his fists against the door.

"Code! Who has a code for this?" Wolfe shouted at the three men behind him. One of them took out their interconnect and asked whoever was on the other end to find a code for the exit doors.

"We almost had her, Wolfe," said one man, who was still trying to catch his breath. "She's in Venus now. Call their security. She is still in our hands!"

"No. We are the only people to know about this. We must keep as few people as possible involved," Wolfe snapped back. "And why do they have a code to this door?!" he shouted at the men behind him, who seemed frozen in place. He turned around with an angry look, ready to take his frustration out on his men.

"Get me through that door, now!" Wolfe shouted through gritted teeth. Not only did he let them slip through his fingers, but how was he going to explain this to Warren? A sliver of doubt surfaced as he thought about Ashton. No way a worker of her status would know of a secret door. *Could he really have been so blind? Could she truly be from outside Augland?*

By the time Wolfe and his men had made it through the door, Ashton was long gone. The wind howled as it flung dust left to right, and they walked along the grey ground of Venus in utter darkness. Wolfe was at a loss for words as he stared across the valley and stepped toward the blaring lights of Constellation City. He couldn't believe that they had made it right past them. The dark world had embraced Ashton's chase and Wolfe had lost her in the abyss. He knew where she would go; the city was the only place to hide here.

Warren was going to be furious. The last thing he wanted was for Ashton and her friends to make it outside Land of Legends. Wolfe had been naïve and thought it impossible. He had tried to think of every angle, obviously missing the engineers' door.

"Walk around the city; search every worker but stay discrete." Wolfe's men would do what they could, but time was of the essence and they would need to move quickly. Maybe if he apprehended them soon, Warren wouldn't find out they had made it to Venus. But Wolfe knew Constellation City. Here, workers and Suits mixed with each other in vibrant chaos. It would be like finding a needle in a haystack.

CHAPTER 21

Ashton

As soon as they entered the city, they were surrounded by crowds. Every color of Suit, clothing, and lights exploded around them. Each individual was seemingly in a more outrageous outfit, skin color, and appearance than the next Suit; it truly was an alien world.

Bubble-like glass balls slowly moved above them, casting a shadow over the Suits below. As the music pulsed, so did the lights inside glass spheres. Ashton stood staring at half-human, half-animal Suits who swam around within them. The sky above mesmerized Ashton with its contortionist show of bubbles.

Next to her, a tall Suit with high heels and a cone-shaped headdress wrapped into her braids bumped into them. Sheva and Ashton just stared. The Suit had dark green skin and large bug-like eyes. As they walked toward the large crowd, they thought their best bet was to get in the middle of it all.

"So this is Venus?" Ashton whispered to Sheva.

"We are in Constellation, the city inside Venus Park," Sheva whispered back. "It's an entire park modeled after life in space. Aliens and stuff."

Lining the streets were carts and stands selling souvenirs, squishy-looking creatures in water, pink jelly foods, and blue cocktails. Workers screamed at the crowd to come look at their tiny trinkets and unique food choices. This place was like nothing Ashton had ever seen. There were curly tree branches with thick winding trunks. They were not like the ones from Land of Legend's forest or Maya Bay. Most had deep blue trunks and bright yellow leaves with ladders going up toward tiny huts. Workers hung around them.

Behind the trees were buildings, balconies with circular white windows and neon colors spotting the entire building. Signs flashed off every empty surface. The night sky was strikingly dark compared to the streets that lit up this park.

Ashton and Sheva continued through the city, trying to move more quickly now that the awe of the city had worn off. This wasn't the time to admire. They needed to hide.

Something touched Ashton's arm and yanked her to the side. Defensively, Ashton whipped to the side and crouched into a fighting stance, ready to protect herself and Sheva.

"Come on!" the voice yelled, and it was familiar.

"Hunter!" Ashton almost yelled and relaxed. "Get off me," Ashton said, more animated than she intended.

"Don't do this now. Just come on," Hunter said, giving Ashton a darting look as he glanced around to make sure Ashton and Sheva weren't being followed.

He dragged them across the main street toward one of the tall, dark-brown buildings with neon lights rotating around it. Ashton hadn't seen Wolfe since they had reached the city, but her bet was that he was heading her way and that Hunter was right to hurry them along.

"Thank goodness you guys made it!" Versal hugged Ashton as they entered a small alley where the group was hiding. "We were so worried." She squeezed Ashton tighter.

Ashton's response was not warm, but she suppressed her resentment. They had left her and Sheva behind. But she restrained her anger; if this was going to work, she still needed them. Ashton had no idea how she was going to get Sheva out safely, and a part of her was actually relieved that they had found the rest of the group.

"Stay low." Hunter guided them all the way to the side of a diamond-like mirrored building. If it had been daytime, she was sure the reflection from the building would have exposed them; however, at nighttime, it seemed to darken their hiding spot to give them complete coverage.

Moments later, they saw men dressed all in black, searching the streets. Wolfe was taking off hats and turning around workers, trying to locate the fugitives. Hunter turned to Versal, who was shaking and holding back tears. He gave her a look that told her to pull herself together and keep quiet. Ashton brought Sheva, who was still trying to catch her breath, closer.

Wolfe tore through the crowd, looking for them. Ashton didn't recognize the other men with him, but they were conducting a search of the area. They kept moving past their position and Ashton felt her chest relax as the threat slowly moved away from them. The rest of the group must have been feeling the same because Ashton heard Byron and Hunter let out a sigh.

"How did you guys make it through?" Byron turned to Sheva and Ashton.

There was a long pause. Ashton didn't answer and instead just rolled her eyes away from the group, still scanning the area for more security guards.

"Well, you are welcome. I knew you'd make it. That's why we waited at the entrance," Hunter chimed in with a smug look on his face.

Ashton wasn't surprised by his narcissistic reaction. Was he actually going to pretend like he hadn't just left them, had taken the chance that they would somehow make it through the door? It was typical though, acting like he had done them some sort of favor. Sheva stiffened and Ashton was sure she felt the same way. Hunter had been going to leave them there to save himself. Out of everyone who could have run after her, she really wished it hadn't been him and his posse.

Ashton thought that Pais and Byron had liked her at one point, but that was before they'd become friends with Hunter. She didn't really have a choice, though; all she knew was that from this point on, she was going to be looking out for herself and Sheva, no matter what.

"We need to get out of the street; it's too dangerous for us to be out in the open like this," Ashton said. The anxiety from being so exposed was brewing panic inside her. It wouldn't take long for Wolfe to circle back through the city and maybe even the alley where they hid.

"Ashton is right; it's too dangerous to walk through with them out here," Hunter said, repeating what she had said.

All of them looked around to see what else was in Constellation City. Bright lights caught their attention at every location, but one stood out among the rest. It was a blaring sign with hordes of Suits standing outside.

"Cyclops looks packed with Suits," Sheva said. Ashton nodded. If anything, it was close enough and seemed to be the perfect place to hide.

Ashton brought up the back with Sheva in front of her and Byron, Pais, and Versal following Hunter. They crept through the Suits and quickly made their way across the street. While it was easy to tell the difference between the Suits and Suit-less workers, no one seemed to pay any mind to their behavior; instead, everyone just ignored them.

The Cyclops had two large black doors in front of it, with little circles for windows built into it. Alternating colorful lights shone through the cracks. Hunter slowly opened the door and peered inside. From where Ashton was, she could already tell that this was some sort of party.

Slowly, they made their way through Suits who were all laughing, drinking, and dancing to the loud music. Ashton could barely hear herself think. She saw a few waitresses too. They were dressed in colorful outfits and bright, crazy makeup that made them look less than human. The Suits inside were just as peculiar as they were out in the streets. Here though, some still looked human, just dressed in colorful outfits. Ashton blended in with her bright red wig. As she looked up, she saw workers in cages above, also dancing, some contorting their bodies wildly to the beat of the music.

A young girl with frizzy black hair, bright blue lipstick, and orange clothing walked around the bar with a tray. Ashton recognized the tray as the exact same type she'd used at the restaurant at Maya Bay. The waitress went toward the back and disappeared, which could only mean that they had a service quarter somewhere in the back of the restaurant. If the services quarters had an exit, maybe there was a way out of the city.

"Stay here," Ashton whispered to Sheva. "Whatever you do, don't leave. I'll be right back."

"Where are you going?" Sheva looked at her with concern.

"Don't worry. I'm going to find a way out the back; maybe they have a back door through the city." Ashton smiled at Sheva, hoping it would give her reassurance. Sheva was nervous and didn't want Ashton to leave her. Ashton didn't want to leave Sheva either, but if Sheva stayed where she was, she wouldn't get caught, even if Ashton did.

"Good thinking," Hunter chimed in. "You go do some research; it's mostly you they are after anyway, so at least if you get caught, we might be able to get away." Ashton didn't necessarily like him saying it out loud, but it was true.

Sheva stayed in a dark corner of the room. The rest followed and watched Ashton as she wove her way through the maze of people gathered and laughing around her. Maybe the back would be a safe bet. There were so many people around that it made it difficult to go through each of them. She maneuvered her way through the crowd, getting bumped left and right by the many Suits who were packed into the club. The waitresses looked busy, and most of them didn't even take notice that a strange worker was in their establishment. She knew if this were Maya Bay, she would be able to tell in a heartbeat that someone didn't belong. These workers were clearly not so alert.

All Ashton needed to do was find the service entrance that might lead them on a safe path out of the city. If they waited too long, this place might be swarming with people looking for them. She was sure Wolfe had figured he needed more resources. If he didn't, he wasn't as smart as she thought.

"Darling. You the new recruit?" Ashton turned to look at a girl with curly blue hair and blue goo that looked as though it was melting from her red eyes and down her cheeks. Ashton jumped, startled at being noticed.

"Um." Ashton froze. She was sure this was the end for her. The girl would surely know that Ashton was not supposed to be there and that someone would know what they had done. She couldn't let that happen.

"Hello? I don't have all day," the girl demanded. Ashton just stared at her.

"Y-Yes!" Ashton said finally. She was not sure where she was going with this, but it came out before she even could think about it.

"Well, that took you a long time," the girl said sharply, grabbing glasses from the nearby table. Then she softened and added, "No problem, I know how it feels the first time you see this place. It can be a lot."

"Yeah, that it is," Ashton said, giving a sigh of relief.

"Huh? You are going to have to talk louder here. I'm Clary." The girl picked up a few glasses from a backlit standing table.

Before Ashton knew it, Clary had led her to a dark door that almost blended in with the walls. As they walked through the door, bright lights buzzed above them, and it took a moment for Ashton's eyes to adjust.

"Did they give you makeup? Outfit?" Clary asked as she laid the tray of glasses down at a dish pit to the right of the door out to the club.

"Uh, no," Ashton said. Seeing her in the light was much different. Clary's face clearly looked painted on with different colors, but the bright bleeding blue from her eyes looked clear. Her red eyes remained just as off-putting.

"Figures. Tonight you can pick from the wardrobe we keep for extras, and I'll let you borrow some of my makeup. Just know, the brighter the better. There is glow-in-the-dark purple and red in my bag. You are going to be thrown into the mix here; we are super busy tonight. So just come find me at the bar when you're all done up. Go crazy, use your imagination—with that red hair, people will love you." Clary walked briskly toward the hall where interesting-looking workers dashed left and right past them. Much like Clary, they all wore intricate and colorful outfits. This was a much faster pace than the restaurant at Maya Bay.

"Have you done this before? Or am I going to have to start from the ground up?" Clary asked as they went down one long hallway dodging waitress after waiter, to the next.

"Uh, no, I've—I—just came from Maya Bay. So I've done this before." Ashton caught herself. She didn't want to admit she'd come from Land of Legends. She thought her red wig would be suspicious, but thankfully, she had shed her Viking fur long ago. Clary didn't seem to notice.

"Thank goodness!" Clary sighed in relief. "All right; I've got to go, but here is my makeup. Don't lose it and get ready and come find me. And don't take too long."

As quickly as Clary had come, she was gone.

Ashton looked at a room full of outfits and then down at the small bag of brightly colored paint. As slyly as she could, she looked around to see if there were any cameras. There were. Of course, that's what she was trying to avoid. It wouldn't take them long to figure out where she was.

Think, Ash.

CHAPTER 22

Ashton

The workers' changing room in the service quarters of the Cyclops bar was small but packed with colorful and absurd costumes. Ashton knew she had to change; in their Viking and Saxon black and leather undergarments, she and Sheva and the others stuck out like sore thumbs amongst the colorful and futuristic styles of Constellation City.

Excitement bubbled inside her as she grabbed handfuls of festive-looking items: pink socks, purple gloves, sashes, skin-tight shiny pants, and blinding, shimmery jackets. Ashton still had the makeup bag Clary had given her. She removed her leather and quickly changed, throwing together the most clashing outfit she could muster. Long fur swayed as she swung a vivid red jacket across her shoulders. She almost lost her balance as she shimmied to fit into tight, reflective black pants. Finally, she finished off her exotic look with a bright blue tutu. It wasn't the best-looking outfit, but it would do.

She looked around to find something in which she could hide costumes for Sheva, Hunter, Byron, Pais, and Versal. Nothing. Instead, her gaze shifted to a long piece of fabric hanging on the wall, bearing a variety of colorful wigs. Ripping it from its tall corner, she folded it and took the four corners in toward each other, creating a bag. Ashton put all she could quickly grab and placed it in her makeshift tote.

As she slyly followed a worker out of the service quarters, she thanked the darkness for its cover. With her costume, she blended in, but she knew if anyone took too close of a look they would spot her as out of place. The music blared and the lights danced to the beat in a dizzying display. *Boom. Boom. Boom.* The sound mimicked the beating of her heart against her chest.

She wove through dancing Suits. She twisted through the crowd, smiling at the servers she passed, trying to look purposeful as she navigated through the chaos. Ashton squeezed through the last person on the dance floor and back toward where she had left Sheva.

Ashton was out of breath and full of nervous adrenaline.

Ashton searched left to right, the blaring lights impacting her line of sight. This had been where she had left Sheva. Her eyes widened as she searched until she saw feet shuffling behind a large bench in the corner of the restaurant. Soon, Hunter's head popped out from the side and met Ashton's gaze. Sighing with relief, she headed toward him. "We don't have much time." Ashton opened up her homemade bag and started displaying the outfits. Not necessarily something she would have picked if given more of an opportunity, but this was the best they had.

"What is this?" Hunter picked up one of the blue jackets and made a face.

"Our disguise."

Seeing his distaste, she went on encouragingly, "They are probably looking for us based on what we are wearing, so this is our way to go through the city undetected."

Seeing there weren't better options, Hunter soon started digging through the clothing Ashton had provided. Versal followed and quickly rummaged through in search of the best outfit she could find. *Classic Versal.*

"You could have picked better," Versal half-joked.

Ashton ignored her. "They had cameras everywhere in there. We need to move quickly because I'm sure they saw me. We can't move through the service quarters. It's a maze in there. So I suggest we take the streets."

Sheva, Hunter, Byron, Pais, Versal, and Ashton walked out of the bar and back near the alleyway they had just come from before they had made their way into the Cyclops. Ashton led the way. Once out of sight and hidden, Sheva took a white top and started shedding some of her Saxon gear. It was more sheer than Sheva would have liked, but it looked good against her dark skin.

Ashton picked up Clary's makeup bag from inside her tote and started imitating Clary's look. She put big red circles around her cheeks and smeared dark blue paint on her eyelids. Sheva looked at Ashton and started laughing. Sheva finished her look by putting on black pants and a bright oversized pink jean jacket. The two of them giggled as their looks became more outrageous with each new addition. It was a welcome moment of levity in their grave situation.

They would still need to be careful, even though their new outfits would protect them from being spotted right away. If they were identified on the cameras, it would not take long for security to find them, and the road was still packed with Suits.

Looking around cautiously, the group slowly made their way through the city.

"We should split up, Ash," Hunter whispered to Ashton. "It's our best chance. We will meet at the end of the city. Near the trains."

Although she didn't like the idea of splitting up, she knew he was right. Their best chance was not to be seen as a group. Ashton still didn't trust Hunter after the last stunt he'd pulled, leaving Sheva and her behind at the doorway between the parks.

"I won't leave without you, okay?" Hunter read her mind.

Ashton nodded, quickly grabbed Sheva's hand, and made her way to the right side of the street while Hunter and Versal made their way to the left of the large crowd of Suits on the main street of Constellation City. Byron and Pais headed straight ahead, weaving in out of the patrons on the road. Ashton could feel Sheva's heartbeat through their interlaced fingers. It mimicked her own as she guided them away. She looked confident, but inside Ashton was afraid she was leading them to their doom. There were times she felt as confident as the warrior she portrayed in Land of Legends. Other times, her anxiety made her crumble as if she would shrivel away and turn to dust. This was one of those moments.

The night sky was illuminated by the brightness of the city dazzling around them. There was a slight breeze that felt divine after the run they just had and the stuffiness of the Cyclops Club. Out of the corner of her eye, Ashton saw what she had dreaded: A group of men dressed all in black who were looking at each individual as they walked by. Ashton pulled Sheva closer. It was Wolfe's security men heading their way, and they were taking up almost the entire street looking in between people as they approached. Ashton looked down and pulled Sheva behind her. A sharp pain took Ashton's breath. She had hoped that their new attire would help. *Please let them pass.*

"Stay calm," Ashton said. "Just breathe." She spoke to Sheva, but she was really talking to herself. "Walk normally with your head toward me, like we are talking," Ashton said. Once Sheva's gaze met Ashton's, she seemed to relax. "We've got this; we really do. All we need to do is get past them," Ashton said.

They couldn't shift their direction because the security men were coming from the center of the large crowd, out toward the end of the street. Toward them. Ashton stepped in behind a pair of long-legged, lime-green Suits. The thick crowd reminded Ashton of the cramped trains she had ridden every day when she worked at Maya Bay. *How had that only been such a short time ago?*

A tall, thin guard was only about fifteen feet away and Ashton started shoving Sheva to the left to get as much distance between him and them as she could, hoping he wouldn't see them.

"Whatever happens, I want you to run," Ashton whispered. She took a deep breath in. Ashton's mind raced at all possible scenarios. Wolfe's security men were trained. They knew what they were doing, and it would be next to impossible to outsmart them.

I'll push her, push her ahead and throw myself on him. I've fake fought people his size; I can do this. Just follow through. Her internal hype didn't help her fears.

He was getting closer; with each step Ashton prepared herself. Her palms filled with sweat and she was starting to shake. Ashton looked ahead, sizing him up. He looked as though his knees might be weak. He was tall and dangly. She just couldn't give him the chance to trap her in his long-limbed web. Ashton tensed. Ready to fight.

"Hey!" a voice rang out in the distance. "Hey, you! Stop!"

Ashton froze, and then spun into action. She shoved Sheva away and prepared herself for the attack. But as the moment grew closer she could feel her memory fly away as if she needed to relearn to walk. Her knees buckled.

The man was now only a few feet in front of them.

"I found them! I found them!" a voice on the interconnect located at the guard's hip shouted. "Central street near the Satellite Café!"

The security man ran and grazed Ashton's shoulder as he pushed past them toward where the man on the interconnect had directed. It took Ashton a moment to unclench her fists. They had just narrowly escaped certain exposure. Ashton looked in front of her to see if she could see any more of Wolfe's men. They were gone.

Ashton picked up their pace, weaving in between the hoard of Suits. They weren't going to get lucky again if another one of Wolfe's men came strolling by them. Ashton pulled Sheva behind her and they darted in between Suits, trying to stay as close to the wall as they possibly could. All she could hope now was that it wouldn't take long for them to find the end of the city.

She didn't know if Wolfe and his men were behind them—at least from what she could see in front of her. Ashton wasn't sure if they would figure out she wasn't where they thought she was, and start coming after her and Sheva again, but it felt good to be ahead of them at this point, especially after the close encounter.

The red synthetic material of Ashton's jacket stuck to her as she glistened with sweat. It wasn't warm out, but between the running and the layers of clothes she was wearing, she started to feel the material grip her skin.

"I, I need a break . . ." Sheva whispered. Ashton looked behind her for the first time since they had avoided getting caught. Immediately she could tell Sheva was struggling. Her face was flushed and drops of sweat trickled down her forehead. Voices could be heard only a few yards behind them. The city was getting less crowded. The shops lining the streets had disappeared, leaving only street lamps casting shadows between them.

"Okay, we can jog slightly; we just need to get to the end of the city and out of sight," Ashton said, pleading with Sheva to carry on just a little farther. Ashton wasn't frustrated; she understood what she was putting Sheva through, but now wasn't the time to give up. They didn't have the luxury to rest.

As packed full of Suits as the city limits were, the moment Sheva and Ashton made it out of the city, stillness hit. The tall, round buildings were behind them and only tiny, circular white huts stacked on top of each other lined the perimeter of the city. The building lights and signs were turned off, which helped them stay mostly out of sight.

"I don't see them; do you think they all got caught?" Sheva sounded worried, as if she had known them longer than the twelve hours they had been together.

That broke Ashton's gaze away from the city and toward the street they had just come from. She pulled Sheva out of the center of the street and toward the town's tiny homes.

"I don't know," Ashton said. "We will wait a little while longer." Ashton moved closer to the wall and out of the lights' brightness.

It was silent and Ashton felt her senses heighten as she listened intently for anything around them.

Scared and white-faced, Versal and Hunter soon appeared on the road, looking haggard but relieved. Ashton came toward the street.

"You made it!" Ashton said with relief as Versal and Hunter tried to catch their breath.

"Yes, barely," Hunter said panting.

"Where are Byron and Pais?" Ashton asked, already knowing the answer. There had to have been something that drew Wolfe's men away, and it couldn't have been just luck.

"They got caught. Both of them." Hunter looked down and shook his head. "Versal and I were only a short distance from them and didn't even see Wolfe before it was too late. I think it took them by surprise as well. Byron tried to run away, but Wolfe caught up to him so quick."

"Now we know it isn't just Ashton that they are after; it's all of us," Hunter admitted. "We have to keep going." It was what Ashton had been saying since she saw the cameras in Cyclops.

"You don't think we should wait to see if they got away? Maybe they just caught one," Versal suggested hopefully.

"There were too many men. There is no way they are getting out of this one," Hunter said harshly and Versal recoiled.

"Hunter is right, Versal. If anything, they know our plan, and if they knew we were heading to the small town outside the main area, that is where his men are heading now," Ashton said.

The four of them all stayed low between the building and street lamps.

"Sheva, where would the train station be?" Hunter asked.

"Right there." Ashton could see Sheva point to a rolling hill, where they saw workers coming and going. It wasn't far.

"Great, we head there now, and cross the tracks," Hunter said.

"Cross the tracks?" Ashton asked.

"Yeah, it's still too dangerous to take the train. Wolfe's men will be able to catch up to us, no problem."

Ashton hadn't thought of that and couldn't mask her disappointment. She just nodded as Hunter grabbed Versal and started walking toward the open dusty field that led down to the train station. They walked slowly and with confidence. They needed to look like the other workers getting off their shift heading toward the train station. If they ran, it would make them look guilty and out of place.

"I'm sorry, by the way," Hunter said to Ashton. That took Ashton by surprise.

"For what?" Ashton asked.

"For leaving you guys," Hunter said sheepishly.

"I get why you did it. I wasn't sure we were going to make it either," Ashton sighed. While she didn't like what Hunter had done, she understood why he had done it. It wasn't just him he had been looking after; it was Versal, Byron, and Pais.

"We are almost there; we just need to get to the other side," Hunter whispered. "But Sheva won't last much longer, and I think you know it." Ashton looked over at Sheva, who was busy talking to Versal. Sheva smiled widely as they joked about something, but Ashton could still see the pain the older woman had with each step. Versal had that effect on people. She could light a room with just her presence. Sheva was kindhearted, which made them a perfect positive duo.

"She will make it. You don't know how strong she is." Ashton looked him straight in the eye.

"You'll do better once you figure out that you need to only look out for yourself. She is pulling you down and is the reason we almost got caught back there. If it hadn't been for her, we would have had enough time to get through the city without having to wait."

Ashton disagreed. She would have never done any of this if it hadn't been for Sheva. Sheva was what kept her going.

"I don't care; she stays. And we will get through this together," Ashton said. That was the end of the conversation. While Ashton knew what he said was true, she would not leave Sheva. Sheva was the only family Ashton had left.

CHAPTER 23

Wolfe

Wolfe had spotted Byron and Pais almost immediately. Even without their Viking and Saxon costumes, they stood out, awkward and confused amidst the fast-paced city that surrounded them. He knew the group would have to head down the main street of Constellation to get out of the city and make their way to the train station. His sole focus was on making it impossible for them to pass.

They grabbed Byron and Pais and dragged the two young men into a nearby shop, which Wolfe cleared with a command. Wolfe was determined to get as much information out of the captives as he could.

"Tell us where she is!" a man in black shouted. Byron looked frightened as the imposing figure above him engulfed his personal space. "Where are they?" Their captor raised his voice again.

Both Byron and Pais were sitting on the ground next to each other with their hands cuffed behind their backs. Looking away, Wolfe could almost hear their hearts beating out of their chests. Wolfe walked up to the man screaming in Byron and Pais's faces and tapped him on the shoulder. It took the guard by surprise and he quickly rose and let Wolfe take his place.

The small parlor was dark, with only a couple of lamps burning dimly. Wolfe's shadow crossed the boys first, then he softened his gaze, remembering how he'd

155

worked and even become close with them over the previous few weeks of training. He might be disappointed with their actions, but Wolfe knew better than to
scream at them. His father led with fear. He did not.

Wolfe squatted so he was eye level with them.

"Give them some space, guys," Wolfe said to his security team without taking
his eyes off the two captures. The two security men backed up toward the exit but
stayed just out of arm's length from the two prisoners.

"You both know we aren't after *you*—you technically didn't do anything
wrong, did you?" Wolfe asked. He tried to look sympathetic. Wolfe didn't know if
they would take the bait or not. But first thing was to gain some trust, give them
a way out to get more information.

They both took a moment and soon shook their heads no. Wolfe smiled. He
knew he had them.

"I mean, if anything, she convinced you to help her escape . . . what threatened *your* lives?"

Pais and Byron looked confused.

"What I'm saying is that I can spin this however I want to. Let's say you tell
me where she—they—are and what the plan may be, and I go back and tell the
Executives that you both didn't want to go—that you were forced." Wolfe stood
and started pacing around the room. "Or, I could tell them that you two were the
masterminds behind this whole endeavor. That you knew Ashton would get close
enough to the customer to be able to destroy his Suit. That you two told her how
to do it and created this whole plan yourselves." Wolfe came closer to them. "That
you two are NeuroEnergy spies. Or maybe even working for the Colony?" *Give
them two options. Make one more appealing than the other.*

"What? No, no!" Pais shouted. "That's not what happened!"

"Then, tell me what I want. Tell me where they are going next."

There was silence for just a few seconds until Pais spoke. Wolfe knew he
just needed to be patient. He knew Byron and Pais well enough. They weren't
the brightest. Many people would have seen this mind game a mile away, but
not them.

"They are . . ."

"Pais, no!" Byron shouted.

"It's them or us, Byron." Pais looked over at Byron, who looked panicked. "They are going to the train station," Pais confessed.

"Then?" Wolfe bent down again. "I want to know the plan."

"There isn't one really. They just want to go out to the woods. We heard, we heard there might be people out there." Pais stopped.

Byron looked away. Wolfe didn't seem surprised at all by what they were saying.

"Go on," Wolfe said as he kept his focus on Pais.

"We heard rumors that there are people outside who have built a society. The whole point was to get away and go there. I don't know anything more than that, man, I really don't." Pais wiped his forehead nervously and continued, "You have to believe me, we don't know anything about Ne—the energy thing. I mean I've heard of it, but that's all!" Panic was painted all over Pais's face as he looked at Wolfe for sympathy. Wolfe just nodded up and down as he thought over the plan Pais had just told him.

"All right, thank you, Pais. It was good that you told me." Wolfe patted him on the shoulder. "And Ashton, she is the one that leads the group?" Wolfe added.

Pais knew that the plan was all Hunter's, but it didn't make sense to implicate him. "Yes, it was all Ashton; she's been planning this the whole time." Pais was wide-eyed, looking intently at Wolfe.

"You've done well, Pais. I'll be sure to tell the Executives and I'm sure they will understand the position you were put in." He smiled, but it was forced. He wanted so badly to think that Ashton hadn't planned this. That this had been an accident. Wolfe took pride in the fact he could read people, know what they were thinking. He never once thought Ashton was capable of this. *If this is true, she's a much better actress than I gave her credit for.*

"Take them back to the cages. Make sure they talk to no one and hold them there until I get back," Wolfe instructed his men who stood behind him. "The rest of you, they are heading toward the train station. We will cut them off before they can get on the train. Let's take the back way through the city, so they don't see us coming." Wolfe walked off, leaving Byron and Pais. He needed to update Warren.

"What do you mean she got away?!" Warren screamed into the interconnect. Wolfe reflexively moved the hardware away from his ear. He was now in one of the back streets of Constellation City.

He pressed the side button of the interconnect to speak. "We were able to detain two of the individuals with her," Wolfe said.

"But she's still out there?! You are incompetent! How is it that she has gotten not one, but two parks away from us? This is unacceptable! Do we even know where they are now?" Warren argued.

"We know that they are heading to the train station, but we haven't obtained the camera footage to identify where they have gone specifically," Wolfe said honestly. He then closed his eyes, waiting for the backlash from his father.

There was silence.

"We didn't get much information from the two we did get," he started.

"Well!" Warren was getting impatient.

"They are trying to find a way out of Augland." Wolfe had decided he wasn't going to say exactly what Pais had told him. He still needed to keep Warren calm.

"You think she was working for NeuroEnergy? Did they send her here?" Warren added.

"No, the two we caught had no idea about NeuroEnergy; they are going out to look for the Colony."

"How did she even know about them?" Warren was frustrated, and it wasn't a question he wanted to be answered. "We have strategies in place for this kind of disobedience and this will be resolved, you hear me?" Warren sounded stern over the receiver.

"Yes, sir."

"It is now more important that you get to her before she gets out of another park. Once we have her, we will be able to fix the damage she has done." Warren clicked off. Frustrated, Wolfe hit the side of the wall with his open hand, then leaned against it.

"Sir?" A man came toward Wolfe.

"Yes."

"We were wondering what the course of action will be." Wolfe turned to look at his right-hand man, who had succeeded in catching Byron and Pais with him. He paused, shaking his head in frustration.

"They won't get away this time. We will be ready for them. They are heading toward the train station. Might even be there. Get down there now. Don't let them get on that train." Wolfe headed toward the busy streets of Constellation, in the direction of the train station. He knew their plan now. Sooner than later, he would outsmart them, outmaneuver Ashton. It was who he was.

CHAPTER 24

Ashton

The streets had faded to the same grey dirt that greeted them coming into Venus, and the small white bubble-shaped structures disappeared behind them. They were getting close to the end of the park. As they joined other workers heading toward the train station, they felt the tension of going into the proverbial lion's den. The train station would be the first place Wolfe looked for them. It was the obvious choice, the only way to make it out of the park.

They arrived at a large opening to the train station just as the train was coming in and people were both boarding and leaving.

"All right, once it leaves, we go across the tracks to the main terminal and onto the other side, then cross those train tracks to the other park," Hunter said. He sounded as if he were trying to convince himself. The train station had two trains, each going in different directions. On the other side of the tracks was the entrance to a new park.

Hunter and Ashton walked only a few feet ahead of Sheva, who had now latched onto Versal for support. "You think Byron and Pais will be okay?" Ashton asked. She hoped Hunter had some positive outlook that would help her feel better about their companions being caught. While their capture had saved her and Sheva, she couldn't help but feel some guilt for what had happened to them.

She didn't like Hunter and they had followed his every word, but Byron and Pais weren't too bad themselves.

"I don't know," Hunter said with no expression. Ashton took in a deep breath and exhaled her sadness.

"I thought we would have at least seen Wolfe and his team by now," Ashton said. There was no response from Hunter, Versal, or Sheva.

It made Ashton uneasy that they had come this far without even seeing security. It seemed unlikely that they had thrown their pursuers off by going toward the train station instead of trying to find the next door outside of this park.

"Unless Byron and Pais ratted us out. If they did, we might be screwed," Hunter said tersely, paying attention to how many cars were left from the train that sped up in front of them. "All right, we only have a couple of minutes until the next train after this one." Hunter was guessing, but he would be right. The trains always came five minutes apart, no matter which park they were in.

Ashton headed over to Sheva and took her hand. The train was reaching the end of its serpentine body.

"You ready?" Ashton asked.

"Yes," Sheva replied.

"All right. Let's go." Hunter motioned them all toward the end of the track, and Ashton looked down. The jump to the tracks was only a few feet, but it felt like a cliff's edge. The trains didn't stop. They would come regardless of who stood down there. Ashton had never witnessed a suicide by train but had heard of it countless times. Those who couldn't take the constant fear and overwhelming sense of hopelessness found the easy way out.

The wind blew down the long, pitch-black hole that disappeared on either side of them. The darkness in the tunnels sent shivers down Ashton's spine. The echo of the out-of-sight train bounced off the tunnel walls. She dropped to where the bulkhead of the train station dipped down to the steel tracks. Sheva put her feet down first and reached out toward Ashton, who helped glide her down to the uneven ground. Ashton and Sheva crossed with little effort. It was only a few yards to the other side.

Versal struggled to pull her weight up onto the middle platform between the two trains. She hadn't received the same training Hunter and Ashton had with Wolfe.

161

It took some effort to pull Sheva up, but Ashton was able to do it. Versal and Hunter started walking along the middle divider, ready to repeat the crossing to make it to the other side before the train coming from the tunnels appeared.

"Just saw two cameras," Hunter said. Ashton looked around the large grey room. He was right. There were cameras in each corner of the train station.

"Over there!" a man suddenly shouted. "It's her!"

Ashton's heart stopped. She grabbed Sheva and ran toward the second track.

Ashton jumped down and almost took Sheva with her, but Sheva was able to catch herself before slowly making her way down onto the second set of tracks. The horn of the train blared and Ashton looked to see a glaring light heading straight toward them.

"The train!" Sheva shouted. Ashton grabbed her arm to help her down. Two security guards were closing in on them. They jumped the first track easily and were only feet away. One of the men in black put his hand out to grab Sheva and caught her by her coat, yanking Ashton back in the process. Sheva screamed.

Ashton pulled with everything she had to get her away from him. The train was coming. If she didn't get Sheva free and across the tracks, they would be hit.

"Let her go!" Ashton screamed, tugging hard at Sheva's arm. Sweat formed on Ashton's brow. She used the side of the bulkhead to pull Sheva. The train was seconds away, racing down the tracks, fast and loud.

Sheva pulled her arm out of the first arm of her pink jacket and then the next. The oversized material made it easy for her to navigate her way out of the man's grasp. Within seconds, she was free as they stumbled down on the hard metal tracks and scrambled to make it to the other side of the platform. The train was almost upon them; Ashton wasn't sure if they were going to make it.

She quickly hoisted herself onto the platform and put her hand out, down toward Sheva. A wide-eyed Sheva reached out in a desperate attempt to save herself. Ashton couldn't breathe. Her sole focus was pulling Sheva up, but her hands slipped. She was so sweaty. She couldn't keep her grasp on Sheva. *C'mon, c'mon!* Ashton was desperate. This couldn't end with Sheva getting hit by the train, it just couldn't.

"Pull up!" Ashton shouted. She wouldn't be able to bring Sheva up in time. This was it. She wouldn't be able to move fast enough.

A hand came out of nowhere and grabbed the back of Sheva's shirt and threw her onto the platform, seconds before the train nicked her foot.

Ashton finally remembered to breathe, and she sucked in air, her hands shaking uncontrollably. Sheva started to sob as the reality of what could have happened shook her to the bone. It shook Ashton too.

Ashton sat up and pulled Sheva into her grasp, wrapping her arms around her and squeezing just enough to not crush any bones. For a moment, she thought she had lost Sheva and it scared her more than anything.

Ashton suddenly realized that the person toward whom she had built such resentment had been the one to come back and save Sheva. Hunter could have left, but he'd stayed.

"We have to go!" Hunter shouted at them against the shrieking of the train brakes.

Ashton quickly grabbed Sheva and ran with Hunter and Versal toward the opening of the next park. The large platform echoed as they ran to a large banner around a cement opening labeled "Victorian." Strangely, Ashton was filled with emotion. This felt like a homecoming. Momentarily, her mind filled with memories of her childhood. And of Niall.

The train disappeared as Ashton walked through the opening to Victorian and turned to look back at her near death. There, standing on the middle platform between the two tracks stood Wolfe.

Ashton's eyes met Wolfe's. So much was said in just one glance. In less than twenty-four hours, everything had changed. *What time was it? Had to be evening.*

They had gone from—what was it? Friends? More than friends?—to fugitive and captor. Where once there had been a chance for a relationship, now they were enemies. With the swing of her ax, Ashton had changed everything.

Wolfe shook his head. Ashton wished there was a way she could tell him she hadn't meant all this to happen. But if it all were to happen again, Ashton didn't think she would act any differently, if she were honest. This was the first time in a long time that she actually felt free. Ashton's life wasn't tied to someone else's agenda, only hers—and for that, she wouldn't apologize.

But Ashton had never wanted him to look at her this way. If anything, all she ever wanted was for him to be proud. For what she did to him, she felt terrible, and in a way, his anger was justified. But so was hers.

Holding his gaze for one more second, Ashton turned and ran through the small crowd that had gathered, passengers on their way into the park. It was sundown. The fugitives had been on the run a full day. The sun came down over Victorian Park, sparkling off the windows of the mansions and parasol umbrellas of Suits out for an evening stroll.

Ashton, Sheva, Hunter, and Versal stood out much more here than they had when they first arrived in Venus Park. They were dressed in bright neon colors with red and blue paint smeared across their eyes, cheeks, and lips. The workers passing them were dressed in long, thick, puffy skirts with billowy white blouses. The men's high-waisted pants paired nicely with the women's dark grey and white attire. Ashton remembered her childhood in these clothes, every day overheating in the thick heavy skirt and tight corset.

The sun came down below the large plantations that lined the countryside beyond the town. Victorian was by far the largest park in the entire Augland 54. It spanned miles, with the Old Town in the center. When Ashton worked here as a child, she had spent most of her time in the stables and barns on the various plantations of wealthy Suits. It had been typical to see politicians and retired Executives living out their endless days in one of the Victorian mansions. Each home came with several live-in workers. A colonial paradise.

Ashton, Hunter, Versal, and Sheva didn't stop to gather their thoughts or put together a game plan. They just ran. Hunter and Versal had run ahead of Sheva and Ashton, but that was to be expected. Sheva was again struggling with all the running they were doing.

Sheva pulled on Ashton's arm as they hobbled along the cobblestone path between properties. She turned to find her sinking to the ground, holding her knee.

"I think I twisted it." Sheva looked down at her already swollen knee cap.

No, no, no, no, no. "Shev, you need—" Ashton was at a loss for words. It seemed at every turn they were dealing with another problem, another obstacle. "Okay, it's fine. We will just, we will go . . ." Ashton looked around at the world around her. They needed to get out of sight. Workers around them were already giving them strange looks. Hunter and Versal had turned and slowed down, wondering what Sheva and Ashton were doing. Ashton picked up Sheva and put her arm around the woman's shoulder to take off any pressure on her knee. Sheva winced in pain as she walked.

Off in the distance was a large home with a nearby barn. It was all black and cast a shadow as the sun slightly touched the top floor of the three-story Victorian home. "Let's head over there." While it wasn't ideal to stop while Wolfe was so close, they didn't have much of a choice. If they headed into the Victorian city, looking as they did, and with Sheva's condition, Wolfe would be able to catch them, no problem. At this point, they needed to hide.

"Ashton . . ." Sheva started.

"Stop, I don't want to hear it," Ashton said. She really didn't, because every part of her thought about it. This would be easier without Sheva, easier to worry only about herself and find a way out of here by herself. If Ashton thought about it, she knew she would be able to get far away from Wolfe more quickly than he would suspect.

"I won't leave you." Ashton could feel her body starting to get tired. She had burned more calories today than she had in an entire week training for Vikings, and with very little food.

Ashton motioned to Hunter and Versal that she and Sheva were heading in the direction of the large mansion and they looked confused. She didn't have time to worry about their thoughts.

"What happened?" Versal asked. They reached the small barn and crept inside. Miraculously, it was empty, only barn animals chewing their food. As they caught their breath, Versal looked around the small barn, disgusted.

Ashton pulled Sheva's arm from her shoulder. "Shev is hurt," Ashton said calmly, laying Sheva down on a soft patch of hay. The barn was small, but it had four walls and shielded them from the view of the countryside of Victorian. Behind them, a goat and cow had migrated to the stalls just adjacent to where Ashton had set Sheva down. It wasn't surprising that Versal found it repulsive; the smell of barn animals and manure filled the air.

"Now what are we going to do?" Hunter questioned out loud, pacing back and forth.

"You do what you want, Hunter!" Ashton was quick to respond. Her reaction surprised both of them. Hunter looked at her, bewildered. She didn't normally lash out like that, but then again, her actions the last day hadn't been normal. "I'm sick of you giving me this treatment like we are holding you back from something. If it really is that big of an inconvenience for you, then just go!" Ashton turned toward Sheva, who was still preoccupied with her knee. Ashton's heart was pounding, but it felt good to finally say what was on her mind. Hunter had helped her and Sheva back at the train station and for that, she would be grateful. But Hunter had done more damage than that. She had built up so much resentment over the last month that even a look from him in her direction would set her off. Getting farther away from Land of Legends, away from the certain death, had cleared her head. She was strong and wouldn't let Hunter, or anyone, walk over her again. Still, she hoped he wouldn't leave. She needed help to get out of Augland. She had made up her mind that getting out of Augland altogether was their only option.

Hunter didn't speak for a while and Ashton was okay with that. The only thing Ashton cared about was getting a place where Sheva could rest and they could regroup, with a game plan for going forward.

"It's late; not many people are out. We will have until at least five o'clock in the morning until we start seeing more people around here," Ashton said.

"Right, which would be the reason we should go now," Hunter said.

"How far do you think we'll get, Hunter. Huh?" Ashton was being combative.

"Oh, so sitting here waiting to be found is a better idea? C'mon Ashton, you aren't that naïve."

Ashton saw red. She stood up and walked right up to Hunter, not taking her eyes off him.

"All right, that is enough you two," Sheva demanded and Ashton stopped dead in her tracks, still searing with anger. "You're no good on no sleep, so might as well get some shut-eye."

Hunter blinked and looked away, but Ashton still burrowed her gaze through the side of his head, envisioning clocking him a couple of times.

"Up there, then." Hunter pointed to a large loft above the hay on the floor of the barn. Ashton stormed off to the other end of the barn, which wasn't far, but she needed to get away from Hunter. She instead put her gaze out a small window, toward the sun setting over the pastures. Reaching down, she grabbed the makeshift necklace that Sheva had given her. She had never taken it off, and never would. It was the only material thing she had left.

Calmness quickly washed over her and she felt a new sense of relief. The last light hit right above her eye level as it sat peacefully just above the hill. It reminded her of Maya Bay and a deep sadness washed over her. So many mixed emotions. Wolfe had told her that fear brought out the worst in people. *Could that be true about her too?*

Ashton didn't find sleeping on hay as bad as she'd thought it would be. They were able to find some straw and a nice, sheltered area above the stables. She nestled up against Sheva, digging her face into the older woman's underarm. She fit perfectly there, like a small bird under a wing.

"Thank you, darling," Sheva whispered. Ashton looked up at her. She hadn't seen Sheva from this angle before. More wrinkles had formed around her mouth and her cheeks were sunken, but her deep brown eyes looked as beautiful as ever. "Sleep; it's time for you to rest."

Ashton's eyes became heavy and instantly, she was asleep.

CHAPTER 25

Wolfe

Wolfe stood at the top of a small hill, peering down toward the opening to the Venus train station. There were so many workers moving to and from the platforms. He knew now that Ashton, Hunter, Versal, and the older woman wouldn't be in the same outfits they had worn in Land of Legends. He noticed that Byron and Pais had changed to something more in line with Venus Park. It was smart; he would give them credit for creativity.

Wolfe scanned the opening from left to right.

"There," he said, pointing to the middle of the train station. He saw the four individuals he was looking for. Ashton had made one big mistake. She kept her red wig on, and it was a dead giveaway.

Running fast, he went straight for the station, keeping the bright red dot in his vision. If he knew what car they boarded, it would be easy to catch them, even if he didn't make it to the train in time. He would have security waiting for them at the next station. They couldn't escape.

The train doors opened and workers scurried in and out. To Wolfe's surprise, the four of them didn't move. They stood there. Waiting. For what, though, Wolfe didn't know.

The doors closed and the train took off. Then it hit him. They weren't going to the train station to catch the train. They were crossing the tracks.

Wolfe's fury surfaced. He had been outsmarted, again. He had underestimated them at every turn, and he was getting tired of it.

The four of them separated into groups of two, each stepping down to the tracks.

"Catch them!" Wolfe shouted out to his men. "They're going to cross!"

Wolfe didn't have much time. The next train would be coming any minute.

One of Wolfe's men quickened his pace, going for Versal and Hunter. Another headed for Ashton and the older woman. As the pursuers drew closer, the two groups of fugitives made it to the platform between the two trains going opposite directions.

One of Wolfe's men jumped down and reached out, catching the older woman by her bright pink jacket.

Wolfe saw Ashton get pulled back, her hand wrapped around the older woman. She tried to pull away. Wolfe finally made it to the platform and hopped down onto the tracks.

The horn for the next train sounded. They only had seconds to get out of the way. As his attention came back toward Ashton, his heart almost leaped out of his chest. She needed to get off the tracks or she would be hit.

The older woman shed her clothing, and she and Ashton sprinted to the other side of the track. His guard wouldn't have enough time to get to them before the train arrived.

Wolfe made it to the center platform and helped his security man up.

"I'm sorry, sir. I thought I had her," he said as the train came fast in front of them. The screeching of the braking cars drowned out the man's continued apology. Wolfe wasn't listening. He hadn't seen if Ashton and the woman had made it across. He peered through the windows as they sped by him, hoping to see any sign that they were safe. The train seemed to go on forever.

The train departed and Wolfe took his first breath. He looked up to see Ashton, staring back at him from the large entrance to Victorian. Her eyes met his and he shook his head.

How had it become so difficult for him to catch her? He prided himself on how good he was at his job, the time and effort he had put into this career. *Did he want her to get away? Was he subconsciously letting her slip out of his grasp?* He needed to pull himself together and remember his path in this world.

She pulled her gaze away from him, and he swore this would be the last time he would let her walk away. Next time, he'd be ready.

CHAPTER 26

Ashton

Ashton blinked. For a moment, she forgot where she was. It was clearly morning, and she was in a barn. She heard people in the distance outside and sat up. Ashton looked around to see Sheva, Hunter, and Versal all sleeping on the hay beside her. Versal was huddled close to Hunter's neck.

Ashton stood up, moving slowly to not wake Sheva. The old ladder made creaking sounds as she slowly stepped down one after the other. She walked around the barn animals: horses, cows, and a goat, which had found its way to the top of a mound of hay in the corner of the barn. She went over to pet the cow, hovering her hand between the black and white of its face down to the soft, almost fuzzy nose. The cow pushed its nose toward her hand, allowing Ashton to pet it. Something that she missed about the Victorian days was taking care of the animals.

Ashton took off her coat and red wig, just to free her head of the itchiness. Her wig was balled up in knots from rolling around in hay all night.

"Hey there," Ashton said while she patted the cow, prompting a couple of sniffs. "Shh, it's okay."

Ashton walked around to the front of the barn and peered through a glass window, out toward the cobblestone street. Suits walked around in the distance—not many but a few, likely those who liked to take a stroll in the early morning.

While she couldn't say exactly where she was, this was like the peaceful mornings she'd enjoyed as a child. Victorian Park brought back so many memories. She had met Niall in this park.

The women wore long dresses with lace designs starting from the top of their hats down to the puffy frills at the bottom of their dresses. The men wore suits, black with two slits in their coats. People in Victorian seemed more poised and sophisticated, nodding politely at others while they walked upright. Men on horses trotted down the road. So much less intense than Venus.

Rustling on the second floor brought Ashton's attention back to the tiny barn. Ashton made her way to a bowl of water that sat dripping on the edge of the barn, most likely for the barn animals. Thirst overcame her and she bent down to the grassy, stale water. She sniffed it and her stomach lurched at the thought of drinking it, but her overwhelming need to quench her throat took over. She dipped her hands in and brought it to her mouth, and the cool water seeped down her throat. Ashton closed her eyes, taking gulp after gulp. She opened them again and stared at her reflection in the rippling water. Her shaven head and clown-like makeup shocked her. She dipped her hands back into the lukewarm water, disturbing her reflection. She cupped water to her face to wipe off the stale makeup. Then, she set her attention on the outrageous attire. She shimmied off her tutu. Black would be best. The neon colors would draw too much attention as they walked the streets. *There*, she thought. She picked up her red wig that dangled on the ground beside her. It was time to get moving. Ashton could hear the others starting to wake up.

They had been walking for what felt like forever. Ashton turned at every twig snapping. She didn't want Wolfe and his team to sneak up on them again. They hadn't come across anyone in hours. Not when they walked through town, trying to act like workers on a mission. Not when they entered the outer fields. Not for hours. While at first, they had all thought it strange, a sense of relaxation eventually started to wash over them.

"You are being paranoid. I bet they figured we'd get out and they should just forget it," Versal said.

Ashton knew there was no way they had escaped.

"They probably searched the whole place while we slept and couldn't find us. It would explain how we lost them. I mean, that barn was a great idea," Versal continued. Hunter scoffed beside her.

Ashton should have probably said something, but to see everyone, even Sheva, more relaxed made her feel relieved. But in the back of her mind, she knew they weren't safe, not in the slightest.

"Do you mind if I hang onto Hunter for a minute?" Sheva broke Ashton's chain of thought.

"What? Why?" That didn't come out right, but Sheva didn't seem to mind.

"Just to give you a rest; it would be good to let you walk straight for a while," Sheva said. Ashton couldn't necessarily argue with her logic. Her shoulder ached, but she was determined not to mention it.

"Hunter, mind if I hang onto you for a while?" Sheva turned toward Hunter, who walked just a few steps ahead of them.

"Uh, yeah, I guess."

Ashton shifted Sheva over to Hunter, who took her arm, ducking down as he was significantly taller than her.

"You should go hang out with Versal," Sheva said, and Ashton glared at her. *What was her deal?* Ashton was a little hurt that Sheva wanted to be with Hunter and was pushing her off to Versal.

"Just be careful with her; her knee needs to rest," Ashton said.

"All right, boss," Hunter retorted, making Ashton both embarrassed and angry.

Ashton quickened her pace and caught up with Versal, who turned and gave her a warm grin.

"What's the story with you two, anyway?" Versal asked, motioning behind her toward Sheva. Ashton realized she had never really opened up about how her relationship with Sheva had begun, to either Versal or with Hunter.

"I've just known her a long time. We used to ride the train together." Ashton guessed Versal was hoping for more of a captivating story, but that was it. Sheva was just someone Ashton had met on the train, whom she told stories to and laughed with. While it may have seemed insignificant, sometimes Ashton had thought that Sheva was the only person who cared about her. She'd had Niall, but he could be self-centered. Sheva was always looking out for others. The older woman taking Ashton under her wing had been the best thing that had ever happened to Ashton.

"I can tell that you both care for each other. It's cute." Versal broke Ashton's thought. She had a genuine smile.

"Yeah, I guess," Ashton said.

"I think Sheva needs a break," Hunter shouted to Versal and Ashton.

Ashton stopped and looked back at Sheva, whose beet-red and squinting face indicated she was in pain. A lot of it.

The end of Victorian Park was at least a few miles ahead of them. It would take time to walk there.

"Yes, let's find somewhere we can hide out for a little."

They were walking through the forest that surrounded Victorian Park. Ashton had led them away from the main path behind the mansions and out of the main streets of Victorian. While they had rid themselves of most of their funky attire, they would still stand out amongst the other workers and Suits.

Hunter, Versal, Sheva, and Ashton looked both ways down the path. It was still relatively early, so there weren't many Suits roaming around. They drew closer to a cobblestone road, which spanned a few yards. To cross it would put them out in the open. They had escaped notice by dodging between the large homes lining the streets. As they went deeper into the city, the alleyways between homes grew farther apart.

The building directly in front of them was on the outskirts of town and seemed abandoned. Wooden planks covered the windows. Nothing stirred, but they heard upbeat piano music. While Ashton's first instinct was to stay away, part of her wondered why something would be open this early in the morning. Scanning the buildings around them, Ashton saw a dimly lit and battered wooden saloon building. Curiosity stung her like a bee. As kids, they hadn't been allowed to go into these areas—only the older workers could.

"I guess in there," Ashton said, nodding toward the saloon. The loose planks of the walls were clattering against the building with the wind.

"Seems secluded enough. Probably too early for drinking," Versal said.

"It's not a bar," Hunter said, looking away. "It's a brothel."

Versal gasped.

Niall used to scare Ashton with the whole "if you don't get your act together, they'll send you to the brothel" routine, but she had always thought it was a myth.

"Let's go in, I'm so thirsty," Versal said. Ashton thought she was most likely mimicking Ashton's own need to see for herself.

Ashton stepped closer to the swinging doors that hid the interior enough to keep prying eyes away. "I'm going in to see if I can find some water. Versal, can you keep an eye on Shev?" Versal had backed away as Ashton approached the doors.

"I'll be fine, Ash," Sheva snapped. Ashton looked over at Sheva as she slowly tried to rock her knee back and forth. Ashton built the courage to push the door. As she entered, she saw Suits dozing in chairs in the dim light. She looked up and saw a young girl, probably not much older than herself, on a stage. She danced around to the music playing in the background while some Suits stood beside and watched. Her long legs dangled on the dance floor as she swayed from side to side. Her blonde hair was frazzled, and her eyes were dazed and staring ahead. Slowly she raised her hands and twirled around, causing her already short skirt to lift. Ashton looked away.

"Excuse me, what are you doing in here?!" called a nearby voice. A worker came at her with such energy that Ashton almost fell onto a nearby chair. Ashton hadn't realized she was standing in the center of the entrance, just steps away from the swinging door.

"I didn't hear we were getting any girls today; who sent you?" the barmaid asked, her dark eyes drilling into Ashton.

"I uh, I'm new to the park. I was just looking around," Ashton replied.

"You should have been told that this part of the city is off-limits to you; this is strictly for workers of the bar. You'll be in trouble if they find you here." She was a tall girl with messy brown hair and a ratty old corset with a white and brown marbled skirt.

"I—I was just looking for some water. I'm not used to the heat," Ashton stuttered.

The barmaid looked perplexed.

"Please, just a cup of water and I'll go," Ashton said, hoping that begging would help.

175

There was a long pause before the woman just exhaled and said, "Fine, then you go—but I catch you here again and I'll call security." With that, she turned and headed toward a long, high bar with bottles lining the back.

"What is this place?" Ashton asked as she followed her.

"What do you think? It's what they call a 'brothel.'" She poured a glass.

"I didn't know that was an actual thing; I thought they were just to scare—" Ashton stopped as she realized she was talking to a worker at a brothel.

"You can say it—scare you into behaving—well, it's true. This is one area you don't want to be sent to. People here, they don't leave. You come here; you stay here until you . . ." She paused.

Ashton's gaze went straight to the girl on that stage. The poor girl looked already dead inside. Pale, skinny, with skin that looked paper-thin. Her hair, like the barmaid's, was messy, dirty, and unkempt.

"What did you do to get here?" Ashton pried.

"None of your business," the woman snapped. She took the tall glass, now filled with murky water, and slid it across the bar toward Ashton.

"I'm sorry," Ashton said.

"Don't mind it; it doesn't matter anyway. Now go. Suits will start leaving their homes and coming here pretty soon, and you can't be here when that happens. They'll think you work here."

"What do they do?" Ashton had to ask.

The barmaid looked at Ashton then away. "Dance, sing, drink, flirt. You name it. There aren't rules here," she said.

Ashton looked down at her cup of water. Her heart went out to these poor women. Suits treated workers as toys. It was awful. To be doing this for life . . . she couldn't imagine.

"All right, what are you really doing here? And don't give me any crap about working here. You don't work in Victorian." Ashton's head jolted up and the woman was now on her elbows, squinting her eyes at her.

"I—I don't know what—" Ashton couldn't even finish.

"All right, then, let me just call up to management and I'm sure they would be happy to help you get where you need to go." Ashton's eyes went wide at the young woman.

"No! Please no!"

The young woman smiled slightly. "All right then, spill." She crossed her arms as she stared intently at Ashton.

Ashton's mind raced faster than the upbeat piano music that danced around the rickety old two-story building. She knew if she did say what they were doing there, the woman could call it in, let "them" know they were here. *Think of something else, anything else.*

"C'mon. I don't have all day." The young woman grew impatient.

It came out before Ashton could think. "I ran away. I'm from Land of Legends and we—I—I mean, there are a few of us—are being hunted now by security. I—I'm just trying to get to the train station . . ." Ashton stumbled over her words but hoped that telling the truth would help her cause. The woman furrowed her brow and then scoffed.

"You, you are joking, right?" She had a hard time getting that out.

"No. If they catch us now . . . I think they will kill us."

"You're as good as dead now," she laughed. "Stupid choice, but I can't say I don't respect your efforts. Wish I would've when I had the chance." The woman's hair loosened as she shook her head back and forth. Ashton was stunned. She knew it hadn't been a well-thought-out plan, but not laughable.

"Thanks for that. I needed a little laugh in my life." The woman at the bar turned behind her and grabbed a glass bottle out of a small refrigerator behind her. She pushed it across the bar at Ashton.

"Here, it's the clean water. And you can't go back out there looking like that. It's at least another two miles to the train station." She gave Ashton a once over, starting from her tattered red hair down to the black shoes she wore.

"I'll grab you clothes. It won't be much, but you'll look less noticeable. Trust me, if one of 'em politicians sees you, they will for sure report you."

Ashton's jaw dropped slightly open, stunned by the sudden hospitality this woman was showing her.

"Thank you! I mean, I can't begin."

"Don't, or you're done for sure. There is no way out of this place. Take what you need but you didn't get it from me, you hear?"

Gratitude poured through Ashton like water rushing down a river, but then was overrun with empathy. The poor women here. This was no life. What did they have to lose?

"Come with us," Ashton said before she even thought about it. The more people, the less likely they would be successful. Ashton didn't care, though.

The woman laughed again, this time glancing down at her feet.

"You don't get it. I can't leave. I'll never leave this place. Augland won't let me. Once I was assigned here, they put something in me. I tried to go twenty feet out that door," she motioned toward the swinging boards. "They caught me within two seconds. You're deader than dead if I follow you. I'm too valuable. They can't let me get out. Better to keep this place a scare tactic and the customers happy."

The woman walked away from Ashton, heading toward the back room behind the bar. Ashton felt the darkness creeping into her bones. Augland was worse than she'd ever imagined. It was a true prison.

CHAPTER 27

Ashton

The woman rounded the corner of the bar only moments later, carrying a dusty pile of neatly folded clothes. She placed the pile on the table in the back of the bar where Ashton was waiting.

"It's not much. Honestly, these are from almost ten years ago, so the dress code has changed since. I wouldn't let anyone get too close because they'll notice."

Ashton looked over the pile at the woman. Again, she looked at the striking features, sunken eyes, pale complexion. This woman was trapped. Every worker in Augland was trapped. How had she not noticed this before? How had it all seemed normal?

"Thank you. I'm . . ." Ashton didn't know what to say. The woman waited, but only awkwardness filled the air around them. It felt suffocating. There was nothing Ashton could say.

"I'll say it again: I don't think you'll make it. Your best bet is to use one of the supply delivery routes."

Ashton knew of a delivery route; it was in Maya Bay. But it would be next to impossible to use as it was highly visible. Large ships came in and out of the bay every couple of weeks, delivering and taking supplies. Each Augland provided specific supplies that supported the other Auglands. Augland 54 was known for fish and timber.

Ashton thought about this option. It would be difficult. There was no way to know when a shipment would be coming. Besides, each ship and vehicle was searched before it departed.

"You should go now. It's getting late and we have customers coming soon."

The woman looked down at the pile of clothes and then down at her feet. Ashton could see that she had already thought of escaping and this was the way she would have done it. If she could. Augland had made sure she could not. The idea that Augland Executives were tracking her infuriated Ashton. Why? To keep her from spreading information about the mistreatment of workers?

Then it hit Ashton: this was how they had done it at Land of Legends. They'd had to stay in the dormitories; they couldn't leave or take the train to any other park. They just moved the workers from one prison to the next, keeping them in fear of what would come if they didn't do as they were told.

Ashton reached out for the stack of dusty clothes, brushed them off, and hugged them to her chest before turning and heading toward the swinging doors.

"I didn't get your name." Ashton looked over her shoulder.

"Bez," the woman said. She was already wiping down the counter where the clothes had left a small dust imprint.

"Thank you, Bez. I hope I see you again someday."

Bez gave a half-smile toward Ashton. They both knew it was unlikely. More than unlikely.

"These clothes smell terrible."

Versal was the only one speaking up about the musty odor; the others realized the luck of getting something that took them out of their Venus clothing. Ashton cringed at her grey-stained, short-sleeved blouse and brown corset paired with a short plaid skirt. It was shorter and much more revealing than the normal attire of Victorian, which would be glaringly obvious to Suits and other workers. These were clothes meant for brothel workers.

Ashton tied her red wig in a similar bun to Bez's. She needed the long locks out of her face and off her neck. After changing their clothes in their hiding spot behind an abandoned building, Sheva, Versal, Hunter, and Ashton headed down the long cobblestone street toward the vast mountainside. They stayed in the shadows of the buildings when they could. Sheva knew which direction they would need to head to make it to the train station, which, according to Bez, was only a couple of miles away.

As they walked, Ashton pondered Bez's suggestion of using the delivery route to escape Augland. She had been right; that seemed the only way out of the park. If they made it to Maya Bay, they would then have to hide until a boat came, somehow make it onto the boat, and then not be detected. While she knew it was a long shot, it seemed like the only way out. The walls of the park were too high and covered in cameras; they would never make it over.

"You kept it." Sheva's voice broke Ashton's thought process.

"What?" Ashton asked.

Pointing toward the small, wired moon rock that laid just below Ashton's collarbone, Sheva said with a smile, "The necklace."

"Of course I did," Ashton said, putting her hand up to the small treasure around her neck. "I thought about you, every day since . . ." Ashton and Sheva still hadn't had a chance to talk about that dreadful day Sheva had been torn from Ashton's arms on the train.

"I thought about you too. Seeing you lying on the train floor that day almost broke me."

"What happened to you?" Ashton had to ask. It had been eating at her since they had been reunited.

Sheva's smile faded and her eyes became almost grey in despair.

"They put me in some dark, underground, cage. It was cold. I didn't know where I was, what day or time. It was awful. I thought I was going to die there."

At this revelation, hatred dug deeply into Ashton's heart. Her sorrow and anger almost pushed her over the edge. She could only imagine Sheva's mistreatment as she lay on the cold ground with bars around her.

"I hate this place," Ashton whispered emphatically, moving closer to Sheva. "And I'm so sorry that happened to you. We are going to get you out of here."

Ashton hoisted Sheva's arm over her shoulder more to give her more stability as they headed up a hill. Hunter and Versal were only a few feet in front of them.

"There it is!" Versal let out a hoarse whisper.

They had reached the top of the hill just past the last barn and farmland and could see the train station. Sheva hobbled next to Ashton as they walked on top of the small hill. Both Ashton and Sheva were out of breath, but relieved. Other workers came beside them as they all shuffled toward the station. If it weren't for their disguises, it would have been easy to recognize them. Even so, they needed to be cautious as their wardrobe was vastly different from the typical attire. They hadn't seen any security guards or run into Wolfe since crossing the tracks and they were all feeling a little lighter.

Ashton didn't share in the group's optimism; she was sure Wolfe was still hunting them. If she knew Wolfe, he would not be one to give up. She also knew he was too clever to just keep chasing them blindly. If they hadn't seen him in a while, it meant he was up to something.

"Try to relax," Sheva whispered as Ashton looked around the top of the mount. Small rolling hills lined their sight. Each blade of grass swayed in the wind. The sun hovered above and cast a purple haze across the horizon. Farm animals grazed below, appearing like moving dots in the distance. Victorian, from this vantage point, looked as though she could squish it with her fingers. If only she could. While Augland had created a supposed paradise, all she saw was Bez and that brothel.

"What do you mean? I am relaxed," Ashton said defensively.

"I know you, Ashton; you are predictable," Sheva replied as she looked over at Versal, who was smiling about something with Hunter.

"What do you mean?" Ashton tried to keep the hurt out of her voice.

"You play things safe because you prefer consistency. Things that ripple around you make you panic." Ashton had never thought about herself like that. "It just means you are a cautious person. Not bad, but sometimes just going with things and letting things happen isn't the worst. You'll never find any joy in life if you constantly worry about what is going to happen."

"It's getting harder to see the good in this world at all, Shev. I saw, I saw a young girl in that brothel who looked like she was on the verge of death. This place is killing her slowly. It isn't a place to live; it's a prison where we go to die."

"That's why we are doing this," Sheva insisted. "Can't you feel the hope? Well then, you finally see why you are doing this. Your life back there isn't your path. I knew the world before Augland and this isn't it."

Ashton considered Sheva's words. She hadn't realized what this place was about until she messed with the system and became a fugitive.

"Promise me something, Ash. Promise me that you will get out no matter what. Don't give up." Sheva was serious, and she looked straight into Ashton's eyes. Her eyes were pale and her face wet with dripping sweat.

"Shev, what are you talking about? Don't talk like that."

"You promise me, or I stop right now," Sheva threatened.

"We are so close to getting out of Victorian, and the train station is right there . . . if we get out of here. We are going to make it, Shev." Ashton hadn't yet disclosed the information that Bez had shared because she wasn't sure it could work.

"I know, but just in case, you promise me that you'll leave if I can't make it," Sheva said as they briskly walked down the last hill to the train station.

"Okay, I promise, but you have to promise to try and make it, okay?"

"I promise." Sheva smiled, getting what she wanted out of Ashton.

Ashton looked back periodically as they walked to the train station, joining workers on their way to and from the heart of Victorian or its surrounding plantations and farms. The sun was in front of her and she could see the dark shadows fall on the small hill they were descending. She kept her eyes peeled for the tall shadow of Wolfe.

The large opening into the train station was only a few feet in front of them now, and Ashton could feel a much cooler breeze come toward them from the train station, which felt refreshing. The city architects had hidden the station well and built it into the hillside, leaving only a gaping hole for workers to walk through. It blended in with the hills and was covered by tall grass as if nature had built land around the concrete opening.

"Train is coming," Hunter whispered to them. At first, the train sounded like only a whisper, until the horns blared, notifying workers of its arrival. It looked like their timing was perfect.

Hunter was looking around; Ashton guessed he didn't trust how easy it was for them to escape either. Versal bounced up and down nervously beside Hunter, holding his hand.

Wolfe and his men were on the chase. Ashton wouldn't fool herself for one moment. She sensed it as the hair on the back of her neck stood up. There was danger in the air. It suffocated her as her heart pounded hard against her rib cage.

The train grew louder as it approached.

"We have to move forward." She pulled Sheva up toward Hunter and Versal. Ashton couldn't see anyone, but she knew this wasn't safe. Workers looked dazed as they exited long shifts of working in Victorian. While many lived in Victorian, there were still those who only worked shifts there and took the train home to other parks when done.

The train started to approach. The people around them started to work their way up toward the front line.

Hunter leaned toward Ashton and said, "We need to split up."

Ashton looked across his shoulder to see a guard coming toward him. Behind Sheva's shoulder, she saw another guard pushing his way toward the center of the worker crowd.

"They are coming at us from both angles," Ashton said nervously.

"It's that or we just wait for them to take us," Hunter said. "Let's hope they haven't seen us yet, and we can get away with the crowd."

Ashton thought about where to run. The train couldn't come fast enough, and even if it did, they weren't going to make it without Wolfe and his men getting to them first. They would be caught either way.

Ashton took a step back and ran into something behind her. Not something, someone.

"Don't even think about it. Don't run; just stand still." Ashton froze at the sound of Wolfe's voice. Her heart beat quickly: this was it. She had thought they had escaped, and they hadn't. He'd been one step ahead of them this whole time. *How stupid, we should have seen this coming.*

Two men in black stood behind Hunter and Versal, and Ashton could tell Versal hadn't noticed them yet, but Hunter had. He pressed his arm around Versal, pulling her closer to him. His sudden movement took her by surprise, but then she too saw what he had.

"Wait until the train passes; don't get on. We are going to do this without an audience, understood?" Wolfe continued. "Nod, if you understand."

Ashton nodded.

Sheva grabbed Ashton's hand and squeezed. The train was approaching now, and Ashton knew that the moment it passed, they were done for.

"What's going to happen to us?" Ashton asked Wolfe quietly without looking back to face him.

Wolfe didn't respond.

The train seemed to be moving in slow motion as it screeched to a halt in front of them and opened its metal doors to let workers pile in.

"Let them go. I did this. They had nothing to do with it." Ashton doubted begging would help at this point, but she had to try.

"That can't happen, Ash, and you know that," Wolfe muttered grimly. "They did this too, and there are consequences. This is out of my hands." Ashton could tell she wasn't talking to the same Wolfe she had grown to know, even liked. There had always been two sides to him. This was the one she didn't care for.

"I know you don't have any reason to believe me, but I did this because they were hurting us! You weren't doing anything to help us. I had to save Shev; he was going to kill her." There was no response, so she pressed on. She knew there was another side to him, a softer, caring, and empathetic side to Wolfe. If she could just pull that side out, maybe she would be able to convince him to let them go. "C'mon, Wolfe, even you know it was getting out of hand. You knew it was wrong. You can't blame us for trying to get away. You shared with me; you struggle, I know you do. I—"

"Stop. Just stop!" Wolfe raised his voice and one of the security men actually looked toward him and then back to Hunter and Versal.

Wolfe lowered his head to right above Ashton's ear. "Don't stand there and try to manipulate this situation because I confided in you on some small level. It won't work."

Ashton stopped talking. Wolfe was angry, but she couldn't let this happen. All she could think to do was hit Wolfe and try to get Sheva on that train somehow. Ashton knew it was her they wanted. He may be frustrated, but her fury burned around her like red fire. She had done this. Maybe, if they could get on the train, Sheva, Versal, and Hunter could escape.

CHAPTER 28

Wolfe

After Wolfe had watched Ashton and her group escape his grasp into Victorian, he had decided to switch tactics. Instead of chasing them through the entire town and its surrounding farmland, he would have his detail of guards block every exit as quietly as possible. If general security was recruited for the search, word would get out that there had been an escape attempt and that so far, it had succeeded. News like this could lead to rebellion among the workers of Augland 54, or even worse, have a detrimental effect on the reputation of Augland 54 to the AEC.

Wolfe had gone to sleep for only a couple of hours. The adrenaline from the chase kept him up, and he knew rest was going to be impossible, so he might as well get back on the chase. He didn't want to miss the opportunity to capture the fugitives. He knew Ashton and her friends would need to rest—to sleep, even, which gave him hope that he wouldn't miss their escape.

It had been some time since he had heard from his men in the camera room. One thing Ashton didn't know was that Victorian was the most heavily monitored park. It was the park in Augland 54 most frequented by high-profile politicians and so had the most cameras and security. As soon as the fugitives had emerged in the morning and crept onto the streets of Victorian, they were spotted. Wolfe was now watching them creep through the outskirts of the town as he plotted his next move.

He had watched Ashton enter the brothel. He could have called his men to go after her there, but he knew Suits would be there and he didn't need Ashton and her group to run in different directions. No, he needed to trap them together, and all at once. He needed to get them all out of the park and end this business altogether.

Wolfe left the camera room, grabbed coffee and toast, took the elevator down the needle-shaped building, and headed to the train. He was going to join his security team and cut off Ashton and her group at the Victorian train station. He was confident this time. Until then, he had some time.

Wolfe walked through the creaky swinging doors of the brothel. It had been almost two years since he had had any contact with Bez, but he knew her well.

"Well, look what we have here. A VIP guest." Bez leaned up against the bar where she had been pouring drinks for Suits drooling over the girl onstage. None of the Suits moved or even glanced in Wolfe's direction. The Suits were programmed to feel drunk and in a stupor. The drinks Bez poured were only colored water. It was busier than Wolfe would have liked but he didn't have time to wait for the Suits to leave.

"Hello, Bez. Been a while. You look awful." He grinned and so did she. He wasn't kidding. Her hair looked frazzled like she hadn't brushed it in days, her dress was in shambles as it slid off her slim body. She had given up and Wolfe knew it. Bez had fallen for a Suit, hoping he would take her away. The Suit was married and when their affair became public, she was reprimanded. Actually, Wolfe had saved her from the cages more than a couple of times. Bez knew this, which was why she felt so comfortable around him. Wolfe walked along the bar and toward one of the back bedrooms. Bez followed.

He shut the door behind him. "You helped them. Why would you go and do that? You know you make it harder and harder to keep you here and not the cages." He wasn't angry; he knew why she had done it.

"Oh, you know, Wolfy, I saw something in the girl. She's a fighter. Maybe she will actually beat you at your own game." She was patronizing him, and he deserved it.

Wolfe sighed. "I can't keep protecting you."

Bez did a half-grin and shrugged her shoulder.

"Protecting me from what, Wolfy? From certain death? I think I've already cashed in my ticket on that one." He thought he had done her a favor but, like with the Ashton situation, he realized he hadn't done any of the workers any favors. Bez plopped on her quilted bed in the small bedroom.

"Why are you here?" Bez asked.

Wolfe looked confused. Why wouldn't he be here? He couldn't check in on someone he considered a friend? To be fair, he wanted to know about Ashton and Bez's conversation. What she had told her. It was killing two birds with one stone.

"Are you going to take me to the cages then? What? Take me away from managing this crapshoot? I don't think so. Hard to keep good talent, am I right?"

Wolfe chuckled, but what she said hit home. She understood Augland more than he had given her credit for.

"Either that or you're losing your touch. I would have thought for sure you would have swooped in and grabbed them the moment they stepped foot inside these walls."

Wolfe didn't appreciate her pointing out that he hadn't caught Ashton yet. He had a plan, and he didn't need to explain himself to her.

"Oh my . . ." she said, and Wolfe brought his gaze back to Bez. She stood up from where she had been sitting on the bed and took a step toward him.

"Wolfy!" she continued.

"What?"

"You . . . you don't want to catch her." Bez came closer as she narrowed in on his darkening blue eyes and blushing face. He took a step back.

Bez laughed hard.

"Well, if I knew that's all it would have taken for you to fall for me, I would have tried a little harder. Or maybe it's the opposite, and I need you to despise me to chase me toward the exit. Which one is it?"

"I don't know what you are talking about. I'm going to catch her—them. All of them."

Wolfe stumbled over his words. Bez was smart and didn't believe him for a second. He was off his game. He wasn't sure if he wanted them to escape or to catch them.

"Either way. You're wasting your time. I'm not giving you any information." Bez turned and walked back to the bed. "Unless . . . there's something in it for me." Bez put her hand on the headboard that rose above the mattress a few feet.

"I can't give you freedom, Bez. I can't get you a Suit. You know I can't." Wolfe shook his head. There was no way he could spin promoting a brothel worker, even if his father was the CEO. Even if she wanted to go to the cages, his father would dismiss the notion at a moment's notice. She was too valuable a worker where she was.

"I want to know what you two talked about. Why would you help her, Bez?"

Bez looked out the dusty window on the wall in front of Wolfe. He felt for Bez. She had been working at the brothel for years and it was no life to live. She was young too; it would be many more years of this.

"Worth a shot, huh, Wolfy. Guess you and I are destined for greatness, and with that comes the price of our freedom." Bez ignored Wolfe's question. She understood, and accepted, the system in a way that broke Wolfe's heart. His interconnect beeped and brought his attention to his side.

"Sir, cameras have seen them, about a mile out," a static voice said over the interconnect.

"Thanks, be right there," Wolfe answered. He turned toward Bez, who still looked away from him toward the lit window. Wolfe didn't know what to expect. Bez wouldn't help him. While they were friendly, she still knew he was part of Augland.

"As always, Bez. Good to see you."

"Yeah, let's pray this is the last," Bez said. There was no humor in her voice anymore. Wolfe wanted to say more. To say something that would give her hope to hold on further. He couldn't and wouldn't. He turned and left.

Walking past the last cobblestone and onto the grassy rolling hills toward the train station, Wolfe had a direct view of the entire field the workers used. They were small hills that, once the street ended, curved down toward an opening—the train station. It was covered in grass and dirt to hide its wide opening amongst the hills and help it blend in with the Victorian aesthetic. Perched on the hill above the train station, he surveyed the area. He was able to see anyone coming and would easily identify them as they approached.

He was going to catch them. This was their only way out and he wouldn't let them slip through his fingers again.

"Sir, no sign of them near the exit." Joao, his right-hand man and best security guard, stood beside Wolfe.

Wolfe just nodded. "Thanks, Joao."

Wolfe's eyes were fixed on the entrance. The last time they had been spotted, Ashton was still wearing her red wig. If she still wore it, she would be easy to spot. If not, her bald head would be a dead giveaway. Wolfe focused on a group heading toward the entrance to the train station. As he predicted, the red hair and crippled woman were a dead giveaway.

Wolfe nodded to Joao, who was still by his side.

"Red hair?" Joao asked.

"Yes, it's her," Wolfe said with satisfaction. "Now we wait . . . we want them closer and to grab them by surprise. I don't want to cause any unneeded attention. This is supposed to be discreet, and I plan to keep it that way," Wolfe said.

The train would come in exactly five minutes. It would only take him two minutes to get down there from the top of the hill and another two to sneak up close enough to them. This was about to end.

"Don't even think about it. Don't run; just stand still."

Wolfe was inches away from Ashton. He could feel his adrenaline pumping. He knew his frustration was close to getting the better of him; it was hard to shut off once he shifted his mind to business.

But Ashton confused everything. He wanted to tell her everything would be all right. He wanted to comfort her. But his men were watching his every move, looking to him for direction. He felt like he was playing a character he could not break. Wolfe, Head of Security for Augland 54. Wolfe, son of the CEO. Wolfe, though Suit-less, on the side of the Suits.

Wolfe wanted to turn her around and shake her. He was still angry with her decision to run. It had only made things worse. Now she had put him in a position he didn't want to be in.

Wolfe looked off to the side to where Joao and two other security guards stood behind Hunter and Versal. Hunter looked nervous as his eyes darted between Wolfe and Joao standing behind him.

"Wait until the train passes; don't get on. We are going to do this without an audience, understood? Nod, if you understand." *Don't make this harder on me or you* was what he really wanted to say.

Ashton nodded. She was scared. He could see it as her body shook in front of him. He hated that he made her fear him.

The train was approaching. Wolfe needed this moment to pass as quickly as possible.

"What's going to happen to us?"

He didn't respond.

"Let them go. I did this. They had nothing to do with it." It pained him she resorted to begging him to let them go.

"That can't happen, Ash, and you know that," Wolfe said, looking down at his feet as he stood behind her. "They did this too, and there are consequences. This is out of my hands." It took Wolfe only a moment to turn off his emotions. It was too much to try and speak to her as himself. He needed to mask his emotions and become the man he had trained so many years to become. *And I thought the Suits were the only robots.*

"I know you don't have any reason to believe me, but I did this because they were hurting us! You weren't doing anything to help us. I had to save Shev; he was going to kill her . . ."

Wolfe wasn't listening to her. He distracted himself with any thought he could find to keep her words from digging deep at his soul. He knew how unfair this was to her, to all of them. She reached deep to find that softer side he had shown her, but Wolfe couldn't let him out. Not in front of his men, not with what was at stake. He needed her to stop.

"Stop. Just stop!" Wolfe raised his voice and one of his security men looked back toward him and then in front toward Hunter and Versal.

He lowered down to right above Ashton's ear. "Don't stand there and try to manipulate this situation because I confided in you on some small level. It won't work," Wolfe lied. He knew what they had between them, or at least how he felt about her. But if this had been her plan all along, she had manipulated him; she had played him this entire time.

Ashton stopped talking. He knew his words had hurt her, or at least silenced her for some time.

CHAPTER 29

Ashton

Ashton's eyes shifted from side to side. It was only a matter of moments before the train doors would close—and their chance of escaping along with it. She gripped Sheva's hand tighter, the sweaty palms making Sheva's bony hand feel slippery.

Wolfe's presence was overwhelming. He had still not grabbed Ashton, but she knew if they tried to move, he would stop them with little effort.

"AHHH! AHHH! Stop, please, sir, stop!" Sheva's voice pierced the stale air of the train station.

Sheva let go of Ashton's hand and fell to the ground yelling. Workers around them turned to look, glancing from the old woman to the security guards surrounding them. Sheva's performance grew louder and more dramatic as she rolled on the ground at Ashton's feet. She raised her hand toward Wolfe in self-defense.

"My knee! You broke my knee!" Sheva began crying hysterically on the floor. Ashton bent down, confused and concerned.

"Go," Sheva whispered.

Ashton glanced toward the men in front of Hunter and Versal heading toward Sheva, who was still rolling on the ground screaming in apparently inconceivable pain.

"No! No! Go away! Don't touch me!" Sheva, impossibly, was getting louder and louder. In a split second, Ashton saw the look of surprise on Wolfe's face as he looked around at the workers now all looking in their direction. Wolfe hadn't wanted a scene, but he was getting one anyway. Sheva stuck out her leg. It was swollen and black and blue under her short Victorian dress. Even Ashton hadn't realized how bad Sheva's legs had become. Maybe it was not as much of an act as it seemed.

"Please stop hurting me!" Sheva screamed.

Ashton stood up, seizing the moment of distraction, as the security men tried to stop Sheva from yelling. A hand pulled Ashton, and she rolled back on her heels. Ashton jumped, thinking Wolfe had finally laid a hand on her. But then Hunter's other hand came down across Ashton's side and around her waist. He half pulled, half hoisted Ashton through train doors that had just started to close.

As she was flung into the train, Ashton's eyes never left Sheva. Looking frailer than ever, she gave Ashton a quick smile. She was sacrificing herself to help them escape.

"Shev!" Ashton yelled. She wiggled against Hunter's tight grip around her, thrashing to free herself.

"Stop, Ashton. We have to go." Hunter grabbed Ashton's hand and yanked her toward the next car where they opened the door and made their way through.

Wolfe had realized what was happening and ran past Sheva to get on the train. He was not going to let her go. Wolfe darted through the train doors and began his pursuit on the moving train.

"We need to keep going!" Ashton yelled as Hunter and Versal kept looking back toward the men chasing them. Each train car was connected to the other with a sliding door that opened and closed.

They ran through three cars, pushing past the standing crowds, and were heading toward the fourth. The cars were becoming less crowded with workers, which made it easier for them to dodge left and right, but it also made it easier for Wolfe to get past them and catch up.

Hunter and Versal trailed closely behind Ashton. She was pushing people aside and guiding them through the train.

Wolfe dodged left and right. Ashton saw that two of his men also managed to get on the train and were struggling to catch up.

Ashton could feel Wolfe coming. She tried to weave between people to slow him down. It wasn't as easy for him to get through people as it was for her, thanks to her size and her many years riding packed trains with Sheva.

Ashton grabbed a pole and swung right into Wolfe, pushing him to the side of the car. Wolfe put up his arm in defense, but she had swung lower than he had anticipated. It stopped him in his tracks, and Ashton used the force of it to project herself forward. But Wolfe quickly regained his footing.

He reached out and grabbed Ashton's plaid skirt that swayed behind her, which made Ashton lose balance and fall hard to the ground. She looked back and quickly kicked her foot toward his face.

"Ashton, please stop. You don't want to do this!" Wolfe almost whispered while her foot connected with his face.

Ashton didn't listen and scrambled to get back on her feet and make her way through the car to catch up to Versal and Hunter.

Ashton crossed through the sliding door into the fourth car and saw Versal struggling with one man while Hunter was fighting the other. Ashton catapulted full force into the man grabbing Versal, putting her arm around his neck and spider crawling up his back. He let go of Versal, who scrambled forward and out of his grasp.

The guard pulled Ashton forward, and she slammed him into the pole in front of her.

He let go of Ashton and reached behind to help support his back: Ashton knew she had caused him pain. She used the moment to get up and went straight to Hunter to help with his fight. Hunter wasn't losing, but he wasn't winning either, taking a couple of hits before swinging wildly back at the man.

Then, two arms came up around Ashton and took her by surprise.

Wolfe had wrapped his arms around her from behind, and she was stuck. Versal sprang into action. Like a charging animal, she targeted Wolfe. She picked up the bag that Hunter had left on the ground full of clothing and shoes and started swinging it at Wolfe while Ashton struggled to gain control.

Wolfe took one arm off Ashton to defend himself against the pack Versal swung at his face. That was all Ashton needed to quickly take his arm and twist it back to get him to let go of her left hand. He released her.

"Run, Versal!" Versal took one more targeted strike before running after Ashton.

She took the bag and, seeing as it had worked on Wolfe, she swung it right at the man fighting with Hunter, who put up his arm in defense. Hunter threw one gut punch before following Versal and Ashton through one more car. The train was finally coming to a stop, which was good because they were running out of cars to go through.

"Hunter, we get out of the next car!" Ashton yelled, out of breath.

"Okay," he said. Blood streamed down his face.

They ran through the last door into a storage car and locked the sliding door behind them. The train was slowing down; they had one more chance to make a run for it.

Ashton braced herself against one of the poles coming from the ground to the top of the car. The brakes halted the train and Ashton now noticed where they were. Her breath caught. They were at the Maya Bay train stop.

The doors opened and the three of them bolted out the door, into the train station, and toward the entrance Ashton knew well. Ashton led the pack with Hunter and Versal behind her and Wolfe and his security men close in tow.

Ashton jumped down from the train platform to the sand that lined the beach entrance. The restaurant at Maya Bay lay straight ahead. She wanted so badly to go in, find Niall, and enlist his protection from the security men. The sight of the familiar restaurant sent a wave of impending hopelessness.

The sand made it impossible to keep speed, as her feet sank deeper the harder she pushed against it. Versal and Hunter struggled beside her.

It was a clear day, and the crashing waves hitting the sand vibrated around them. The sea air filled her lungs as her muscles burned. She could feel the strain on her limbs with each movement. Ashton didn't know where to go. She headed toward the restaurant because it was the only thing she could think to do. *What are we going to do?*

Ashton had no plan, nothing. She was hoping they would get to this point and be able to hide away until the ships came in. It wasn't foolproof, but it was all they had.

She passed the restaurant and headed toward the sandy beach. She glanced back and saw Niall, standing wide-eyed on the restaurant terrace.

What is he thinking? The last time he saw me I was washing dishes, and now here I am running for my life with security only seconds behind. Does he even recognize me?

Ashton yearned to go back in time. Back to when she was standing there next to Niall on the terrace, joking about something, him making her laugh and feel safe.

Her feet kept moving until she felt the sand harden under her feet. The water had created a much more secure footing. She stopped. She was hitting the end of the road.

"What are we doing?" Hunter panted. Ashton didn't answer; instead, she looked off into the deep blue water in front of her. She wished she could fly toward the sunset. Get lost amongst the waves.

"Ashton!" Hunter yelled.

"This is it; there's nowhere to go," Ashton confessed. She had led them here. She knew there was no way out of Augland. To be back in Maya Bay was all she had wanted, and now she was here, at the end of it all. *Would they just run forever?*

"No, I won't take that answer. We can't. You can't just give up." Hunter pulled her away from the open water back to himself and he looked intently down at her, squeezing hard at her forearms. "We can do this, Ash, we can. Don't give up."

It was no use. Her mind was numb, and her body felt hopelessness slowly poison her. Hunter bent down so he was eye level with Ashton.

"We can do this. Don't let Shev's sacrifice be in vain."

Ashton met his gaze and for a moment was furious to hear Sheva's name coming from him. Even worse, he was right. This isn't what Sheva would have wanted. She would have been angry with Ashton. Breaking her promise.

"I—"

Ashton's eyes adjusted to the water behind Hunter. Ashton tore away from Hunter and raced toward a small boat that was capsized near a rocky cove on the beach. Hunter and Versal followed. The boat was small, but it would float and that was what she needed.

"Help me flip it over."

Hunter quickly used his strength and turned the small white-and-blue boat over. Suits sometimes used these small recreational boats for water sports. Many times, workers had to come to gather them at the end of the day and return them to the boatshed near the resorts.

"Push! And get in," Ashton yelled, standing on the far-left corner with Hunter taking the right. Versal hopped inside and almost fell over as she tried to keep her balance on the swaying boat.

Ashton's feet touched the water as she pushed hard. The boat loosened under the sand and soon glided over the rippling waves. The water was freezing but felt refreshing since her body temperature was heightened. She put both of her hands against the sandy edge of the boat and pulled herself in. Hunter did the same.

Ashton turned to see several security men coming to the edge of the water, stunned as they watched the small boat float away from them on the water. This might be a suicide mission, but it at least bought them time to think.

Without oars, rowing the boat was difficult. Hunter, Versal, and Ashton used their hands to propel themselves against the current. It felt like they were moving slower than molasses.

Ashton's arms burned, both from the cold saltwater and the constant need to push against it. The farther they fled the Maya Bay shores, the faster the tide took them out. It was much needed after the initial struggle to go against the riptide.

Wolfe and his men still stood on the beach, staring as they put distance between them.

"What now?" Hunter asked as he dipped his hand deep into the cold water.

"I don't know," Ashton replied. Fear overwhelmed her, but she had to keep going. What Hunter had said haunted her. Sheva wanted her to keep going, so Ashton would. *But soon they would run into the wall. Soon, they would have no choice but to give up.* Ashton's inner thoughts cast doubt in her mind.

"Why aren't they following us?" Versal asked, looking behind her at the men on the beach.

"Because they don't have a boat," Hunter said as if it had bothered him she had asked such a stupid question.

Or they know there is no way out.

They fell silent, the only sound the rhythm of their hands pulling out and back into the water. The beach was almost out of view. Ashton and Versal kept switching sides to give their arms a break.

Thud. Their boat suddenly stopped. They'd hit a wall, the edge of Maya Bay. Its mirrored surface had hidden it from view as it reflected the water and sky around it. Hunter began to pound his hand against the wall.

Ashton leaned over the edge of the boat and reached down under the water.

"It goes underwater."

"How deep?"

Ashton looked down at the semi-clear water. It was deep. She couldn't see the bottom. She heard a splash and looked behind her to see Hunter diving into the water.

"Hunter!" Versal shouted and looked down trying to see him, but he had disappeared.

Ashton and Versal watched in silence as the water moved their boat, bouncing it against the mirrored wall.

"I don't see him," Versal screeched. Her face was so close to the water, it was almost submerged.

Ashton looked down as well, hoping to see Hunter. Then she heard something in the distance, almost like a buzzing sound, and she turned her head toward Maya Bay. A fast-moving black object targeted them, and Ashton knew instantly what and who it was. Wolfe and his men had found a boat and were coming quickly toward them.

"What do we do? What do we do?" Versal repeated. Ashton didn't know what to do. She looked frantically around the water.

Bubbles came from the right side of Ashton and with relief, she saw Hunter's rippled face rising toward the surface. He gasped for air as the water separated around him.

"What did you find?!" Ashton couldn't wait.

"They're there, they're coming!" Versal hyperventilated.

Hunter rested on the side of the boat as he inhaled deeply.

"It's . . . it's . . ." He breathed heavily. "It's about fifteen feet down. We can do it." He smiled and began to laugh.

Ashton sat back on the boat. They had found it. He had found it. The way out of Augland. The sound of crashing metal against water brought her back to her senses. That was all the push Ashton needed to bounce up and look down at the dark water below her. She had never dove so deep before and she was tired, but she couldn't give up. She wouldn't give up. Sheva wouldn't let her. She dove.

CHAPTER 30

Wolfe

Wolfe had them. The train was approaching and it would soon be gone, leaving Ashton in his grasp at last. He thought he would have caught them before, but he would settle for a victory in Victorian.

Ashton and Sheva stood only inches away from Wolfe. To be this close to her, after all that had happened, was agonizing. He wanted to say something, anything, to her. He could only imagine what she was thinking—that he was a monster, at the very least. How could he tell her that he was working on how he would protect her? That he didn't want to hurt her?

A scream ripped through the air.

"My knee! You broke my knee!"

Sheva had thrown herself onto the ground and was thrashing and yelling at Wolfe's feet. He took a step back, looking at her swollen leg. For a moment, Wolfe thought he had really hurt her, brushed into her somehow to cause such pain. He looked from side to side. Workers stared, looking down at Sheva and back up toward Wolfe.

Ashton knelt to help her friend, but the woman's cries grew louder. Wolfe was taken aback. He didn't need this attention. Her howling had even his security guards wondering what he was doing to a poor elderly woman. She stuck out her leg, making the swollen, black-and-blue limb more visible to others.

"Please stop hurting me!" Sheva begged. Wolfe glanced down and thought for a moment to help her up.

A red blur darted quickly out of his vision. Something had pulled Ashton away from Sheva.

"No!" Wolfe shifted his eyes toward Ashton.

The older woman put her hand out and grabbed Wolfe's leg, wrapping her fragile hands around him. He looked down at her and almost kicked his leg away, but he didn't want to hurt her. Instead, he used his strength to shimmy his way out of her grasp.

It was too late. Ashton had already made it onto the train. He didn't need to tell his men what to do; they knew they needed to go after them. In a panic, Wolfe darted toward the doors and squeezed through just as they shut behind him.

Wolfe looked above the heads of the workers and saw Ashton's red hair disappearing toward the next train car. He started swimming toward them through the sea of workers.

They bolted through three cars and were heading toward the fourth. The cars were becoming less crowded with workers, which made it easier for Ashton and her crew to dodge their way through, but it also made it easier for Wolfe to catch up.

Just as he reached her, Ashton glanced behind her, and then back in front of her. She quickly grabbed the pole in front of her and swung around, taking Wolfe by surprise.

Oof. As her weight barreled into his rib cage, he stumbled back.

He saw her scramble to her feet and he reached out to grab her and caught the thick fabric of her Victorian dress. She was quick. He would give her that. For a brief moment, he regretted training her. She was using his techniques against him.

He tugged on her dress and Ashton stumbled and lost her footing. Ashton wasn't the only one who was quick. He reached out with his other hand to get a better grasp.

"Ashton, please stop. You don't want to do this!" Before he could finish, her foot collided with his face.

Wolfe shook his head a couple of times, but by the time he was coherent, Ashton had already made her way to the other train car. Wolfe grunted in frustration as he jumped to his feet. This was getting out of hand and it needed to end. To be honest, it was becoming embarrassing.

He flung the sliding doors opened and saw Ashton battling with Joao. She was occupied and this would be the perfect moment to subdue her. There were no other workers in the car except for his men, Ashton, Versal, and Hunter. One by one they could pin them down and keep them in this car.

Wolfe enveloped Ashton, picking her up and squeezing her to stop her tense muscles from fighting him. Her body wiggled in his grasp, but he had too good of a grip on her. *Just stop, Ashton. Please.*

Something hit him on the side of his head and for a moment the world went black.

Wolfe took one arm off Ashton to defend himself and he saw Versal's lengthy figure swinging something hard at him. That was all Ashton needed to quickly take his arm and twist it back to get him to let go of her left hand.

The ringing in his head faded. Versal and Ashton had run ahead and through to the next car.

Wolfe stood by the sliding glass door, holding it, but they had locked it behind them. Wolfe had to watch as the sliding doors of the train opened and the three of them darted out toward the bright lights of Maya Bay.

Wolfe's frustration boiled over.

"What are you doing? Go get them!" he yelled at Joao, who stood still behind him. Falling over himself, he ran past Wolfe and out the train doors. The other security men followed.

The cameras would show everything. They would show how these workers kept slipping out of his grasp and getting the best of him. Warren would do his worst. He wasn't opposed to punishing his son, degrading him as if he were a small boy getting caught lying.

Even if he wanted to fight back, Warren's Suit was too powerful. He had an unfair advantage. It was the games he had played with his mother that bothered him the most, and Warren exploited it. He would destroy her self-esteem right in front of Wolfe. She was such a fragile woman and Warren had had a twisted hold on her.

Wolfe had to give it to Ashton. She was smart to head out toward the water. There was no way out of Augland except through the Puget Sound—at least, that she could access.

He kept chasing and saw the boat at the same time as Ashton. *Of course, there was a boat*, Wolfe thought. Everything was against him.

Wolfe sat at the bow of the small motorboat speeding across the water. The waves crashed against it and he bobbed up and down. He was surprised to see how far Ashton, Hunter, and Versal had made it on the small dinghy they had commandeered.

"Go faster!" Wolfe yelled, not taking his eyes off the white-and-blue boat. It wouldn't be long until they made it to the end of Augland's glass bubble.

Each second felt like forever as he traveled against the strong salty current, but each second brought him closer to Ashton's boat. He was close enough to make out faces; Hunter was gone and only Versal and Ashton sat in the boat. *C'mon, c'mon, c'mon!* Wolfe's eyes burned from the salt and wind, but he wouldn't take his eyes off them.

They dove. Ashton's boat swayed left and right from the momentum of Ashton and Versal diving into the dark abyss of the blue water. Wolfe ground his teeth in frustration.

CHAPTER 31

Ashton

Ashton's fingers hit the cold water first, then the top of her head, and then finally her body. The freezing water sent stinging ripples through her stomach and her muscles tensed. She opened her eyes and the salt stung. The silence was deafening as she reached down and pulled her body deep into the water. While the water was dark and deep, it would be much worse if she didn't make it down to the end of the glass. Wolfe would be nearby by now and could still come after them.

The deep blue contrasted against her light skin. Ashton struggled to move fast enough. The water slowed her movements and she wrestled with it, turning and kicking. The deeper she went, the darker it became and the more she struggled. She looked to the right to see Hunter pass her. He looked graceful as he danced through the water, kicking and using his hands to navigate. Ashton mimicked him. Her hands reached out, she pulled back, and, as if it were innate, she found her rhythm.

Ashton's lungs began to burn. Terror set in as she tried to hold her breath longer. Thoughts raced through her mind. She wasn't sure how much farther down she could go without a breath. She kept her eyes on Hunter.

Hunter's body shifted and then disappeared. Ashton's eyes widened as he seemed to fade into the darkness. Then she saw it. The end of the wall. Ashton put her hand out, brushing up against the glass, then down to nothing. She had made it. Made it to the end of Augland 54.

The other side of this would be real freedom. The freedom she had been looking for. The only thing she needed to do was last long enough to make it to the other side. Leveraging herself on the glass, she pulled herself across and set her eyes on the bright shining light on the other side. In the excitement, Ashton's mouth opened against her will, and her body instinctively pulled in water as if it were air. She pulled at the light, hoping if she reached out it would grab her and take her to the surface. She couldn't give up now, not this close.

Her muscles cramped, twisting and making her body stiffen only feet below the surface. She reached out and her fingertips cleared the water's surface.

Her periphery started to go dark as the world around her centered around the small white light above her. Then she felt a pull and she rose above the surface. The moment her lips were out of the water, she pulled in air, and it quenched her. As if life had been given back to her, she sucked in deeply and exhaled, throwing up the water she had taken into her lungs.

The sun shone brightly down on her, warming her skin. Her eyes remained shut as she took another deep breath in and a tear rolled down her face. Certain death—again, she had escaped it. Then she laughed as she felt the real wind and sun for the first time. The wind had a different smell, earthy and sweet. She inhaled through her nose as she bounced on top of the water.

"Where's Versal?" Hunter screamed, searching the water below her.

Ashton turned her focus to Hunter, then to the water below. It didn't stir. She couldn't see anything below them.

"We have to go get her!" Hunter said, his eyes swimming with fear as he pushed the water around him.

Ashton swam to him. "No, Hunter, we can't go down there." She pulled his arm. "We can't go back." It was no use; he ducked down below the water. It didn't take long for him to resurface; his lungs were tired and he couldn't hold his breath. Ashton looked through the hazy thick glass where the silhouette of Wolfe on his boat swayed.

Ashton knew this would break his heart, to leave Versal. It would hurt Ashton as well, but that swim had been tough for them and they had been training for a month now. Hunter began to cry soft tears of exhaustion. Ashton began to cry too, for the first time feeling the impact of losing Sheva.

Hunter and Ashton bobbed in the water, waiting for Versal and knowing she wouldn't come. The time passed and their bodies were weak. They would need to swim to shore and begin their journey before Wolfe and his team came after them, if they did at all.

Ashton lay on the ground, resting and letting her body shake off the water and adrenaline. The tightness in her chest was still there.

She took a deep breath in. "You think we lost them?" she asked Hunter, who was on his knees, breathing heavily.

"Yeah," Hunter said through a strained breath.

They both tried to hear others coming toward them, but all they heard was the crashing waves and swaying of trees.

Ashton turned to look at the cement walls and glass dome of Augland 54. She had never seen it from the outside.

"We should move, up this way," Hunter said. Ashton turned to him; he pointed above a tree line and away from Augland 54.

She pushed herself up and followed behind Hunter, who seemed to know exactly where he was going.

"What now?" Ashton asked as she struggled to take in air. She shivered as the wind blew on her wet face. Her skirt and hair were dripping with seawater. The air here was cooler than inside Augland. The greenery and thick forest were similar to Land of Legends. Same trees, same bird sounds, but still . . . different. As if Augland was a dream and this was reality. Which it was.

"Should be up this way, maybe another mile or so."

"How do you know?" Ashton questioned. He seemed to be the only person in Augland to know about this place.

Hunter didn't answer, leaping from one rock to another across a small stream.

"Hunter, how do you know?" Ashton's exhaustion made her temper flare. She didn't want to be ignored. Part of her resented him. Out of all the people—Sheva, Versal, Byron, and Pais—it had to be him.

She wasn't sure what she had expected. The world outside Augland felt so different, but not different at all. She thought the moment she escaped, everything would change. But she couldn't feel anything at all.

The forest was thick and Ashton pulled tree branch after tree branch from her way. She had no idea where Hunter was taking her or if they were going in the right direction. Trusting Hunter was not something she liked.

"We have been walking for an hour, Hunter. I think we should stop and rest for a while. We've put enough distance between us and Augland." Ashton was exhausted. She felt her knees buckle after each step. The terrain didn't make it any easier. Small rocks and squishy dirt made for uneven terrain.

"We just need to find an area where we will be well hidden," Hunter responded with annoyance. He let out a big sigh as he stopped walking. "You know, I think we could camp here, right under that large brush. If anyone comes, we would be able to hear them down the hill. What do you think?" Hunter looked down the steep cliff to their right. Augland was still in the distance, a giant bubble among the trees. From the hill where they stood, they could see the beach, the wall to the Predator's Biome, and all the way to the needle that rose above it all: the Executive Office.

The moment Ashton set her head down on a bed of moss, she closed her eyes. She huddled next to Hunter for warmth as they both shivered uncontrollably. Exhaustion finally took its toll.

Ashton was shaken awake.

"Ashton," Hunter whispered. "Shhh." He put his finger up to his mouth. Orange light surrounded them as the sun appeared above the mountain. A beautiful sunrise. A real sunrise. A true orange that gave heat to her cold face.

The sound was getting closer. Ashton didn't think they would find them so quickly, or at least she had hoped they would have more time. *At least I saw the outside world.*

Ashton crept slowly along the hard ground, sticks poking into her arms and legs. They hadn't yet changed out of their Victorian attire and her skirt kept getting stuck on the vegetation around her. She found herself reaching back to pull it forward.

"Who's there?!" A voice radiated through the forest.

"Run!" Hunter flew to his feet and ran up the hill. Ashton jumped to her feet quickly, followed Hunter's lead, and tried to dodge the trees that stood in their path. She looked around and couldn't see who was following them. For all she knew, she and Hunter could be running right toward them.

Hunter stopped. Ashton caught up to him and froze. Right in front of them were two men. Not Augland security men. These men were dressed in green and white with branches and trees stuck to their shirts. If it weren't for Hunter, she may have run right into them.

"On the ground!" one man yelled.

Both Hunter and Ashton slowly made their way down to the ground.

"Tie them up; we will take them back to the village," the man ordered.

Hunter and Ashton were restrained. A rope was laced tightly around Ashton's arms and she could feel the coarse material rub against her soft skin. The men didn't say anything to them while they walked.

"Where are you taking us?!" Hunter yelled. The men didn't respond.

They made it to the top of the hill and then down through the brush. The ground below them began to change. Fewer rocks and less dirt to a manmade path; smooth and blackened concrete. Ashton looked ahead and found there were roads weaving left and right just beyond the mountainside. Roads with houses, all overgrown. *This must be a neighborhood*, Ashton thought. She was reminded of how Sheva had described her home before Auglands had taken over. She had described the white, one-level home she'd shared with her husband. Sheva had described white roses and wooden fences, just like the ones in front of her. Of course, she'd never talked about the tall grass or broken windows. A tug at Ashton's restraints pulled her forward and she almost stumbled.

The men followed the road, pulling at Hunter and Ashton.

Ashton's mind began to race. *Where were they going?* It was in the opposite direction of Augland 54. They were taking them farther away.

They turned left into what must have been another old neighborhood. Each house was hung with wildlife and overgrown brush. They were nothing like Victorian homes, or even the Maya Bay resorts. These homes were small, old, and unkempt.

Home after home lined both sides of the small road. After a while, the road ended in a circle of hard pavement. The men pulled them toward a house. It was dark brown with two wood pillars on either side. People began appearing in the homes, staring at the captives as they made their way toward the brown house. Ashton stared at a small child standing with two adults to her left. Their home was white, with a broken white fence dividing it from the pavement.

This was it, the place Hunter had heard about: the Colony. All the rumors were true: people lived outside of Augland. Hunter and Ashton looked at each other and smiled as the realization hit them both at once. They laughed with a joy that exploded their entire worldview.

"We came from Augland. We have come to join the Colony!" Hunter explained to the two men. "We escaped Augland!" He almost laughed as he was in pure excitement now. The two men didn't respond, just pushed them toward the home.

"Did you hear me? We are here to join you," Hunter continued.

Hunter's excitement faded. Ashton wasn't sure what she had expected, but a warm welcome would have been nice.

Ashton looked over at Hunter and panicked.

"You'll first have to see Cahya," said one of the men.

"Great! Yes, take us to Cahya," Hunter said. He sounded oddly optimistic as if he knew who she was.

"Who is Cahya?" Ashton whispered.

"She is the leader of camp; she will know what to do," the man said.

Steps led up to a porch that wrapped around the front of the home. Ashton was confused; this didn't seem like a home of a leader. It was just as run-down and derelict as the others around it.

One of the men opened the front door and shoved Hunter and Ashton into a candlelit room. A woman stood near a fireplace.

"Cahya, we found some wanderers in the foothills."

"Bring them in," said the woman. The home was filled with the smell of burning wood and sap.

"Welcome, you two; we've been expecting you." Cahya walked toward Hunter and Ashton and stood right in front of them.

"You were?"

She nodded to the two men who then untied them both. Cahya wore a long, flowing dark dress that almost matched her skin tone. Her hair was braided and twisted to the top of her head.

"Please, sit." She gestured toward the brick fireplace at two chairs on the other side of the room.

Hunter and Ashton made their way toward the fire. Ashton suddenly realized how cold she was. Her clothes were still damp. She rubbed her hands together as they started to prickle from the combination of the heat and cold.

"You said you were expecting us?" Ashton said as she turned to Cahya. "How did you know we were coming?"

Cahya looked down and walked toward them. Ashton began to sense that this wasn't right.

"Hello, Ashton," a familiar voice said behind her.

She turned to look at the door frame: it was Wolfe.

CHAPTER 32

Wolfe

He slowed the small motorboat as he approached the now-empty dinghy. Wolfe looked down into the water. He could see figures deep below; they glowed against the inky darkness. Ashton's red hair swayed in the water.

Something caught his eye, and he shifted his focus to another figure rising in the water. Seconds later, the brown-haired Versal gulped in air as she made it to the surface. She coughed hard, and Wolfe put out his hand to bring her up. Her instincts kicked in, and she pulled away and started to swim toward her small boat.

"Stop, Versal. C'mon, get in the boat; it's over." Wolfe tried reaching for her again.

"No!" she said through her coughs. She hung on the side of the small boat, trying to pull herself up. Her long arms reached forward for any leverage she could get. Wolfe let her struggle; deep down, he was saddened at how visibly frightened she was of him. He just needed to remember she was afraid of Augland, not him. He wouldn't hurt her. But she didn't know that.

Versal began to sob as she clung to the side of the small boat. She didn't have the strength to pull herself up or dive deep enough to make it beneath the glass. Wolfe's boat came right beside her, and he bent down to pull her frail body out of the water.

211

"Come on, Versal. It will be all right." He tried to talk to her as her body convulsed with cold and fear. Wolfe took off his jacket and put it around her. The water in the Puget Sound was freezing, and he could see the cold seeping into her bones.

Versal looked confused as she gripped Wolfe's coat and wrapped it around herself, her sobs not subsiding. "Come on, let's turn around," Wolfe said to the man driving the boat.

"But they could still come up!" the man said.

Wolfe looked back at him and glared. Ashton and Hunter had made it to the other side. If not, they drowned trying. It wasn't impossible to make it beneath the glass, but it would take some strength, something he wasn't sure Ashton or Hunter had much of by now. He wished he could see it. Make sure they both made it. Unfortunately, Augland's walls distorted any view of the outside world with their simulation and were only transparent from the outside in. The breeze was picking up, and Versal's shivering nearly vibrated the boat. Besides, if they did make it, he knew where they were going. *Thanks, Byron and Pais.*

The man turned the boat around and Wolfe sat down next to Versal. He brought her close to him and shielded her from the breeze. She shivered and leaned close to him.

"What is going to happen to me?" she asked, not looking at him.

Wolfe didn't answer, and that was all that Versal needed to break down crying again. He hugged her tightly, hoping it would console her in some small way.

Versal would be placed in the cages next to Sheva. Wolfe hated doing it, but there was nowhere else he could put them. There would be no way Warren would let them go work in another park, not with their escape narrative. Warren was a paranoid man and feared the masses. Instead, he hid workers away, casting them from the surface and from the lives they knew.

Wolfe headed down the long tunnels of the old Seattle Underground. It was dark, but he had been down in the tunnels so many times, he didn't need light to know where he was going. His hands brushed up against the rough, brick walls that helped guide him along the path.

Versal had been locked away, and he had made sure she received clean, dry clothes. His father would view this small action as a sign of weakness, but Wolfe took the risk. Versal wouldn't last long down here in the cages drenched in Puget Sound water.

Wolfe walked slowly, appreciating the time to himself. It had been a long two days, and his anxious mind needed to rest. With each step he took, he found ease. He used his key card to open a tunnel door, and bright light enveloped the dark space. The real sun shone brightly on his face, exposing the light stubble that covered his chin and cheeks. It had been some time since he had visited Cahya.

PART 3

CHAPTER 33

Ashton

I t was a trap. Ashton glanced furiously from Hunter to Wolfe, to Cahya. All of this, all her running, Byron, Pais, Sheva, and Versal lost, for nothing. For a moment, Ashton had grasped freedom. She had breathed air outside of Augland. Seen the sky. Felt her heart begin to release the weight of fear. She had trusted Hunter. She had believed there was a colony of free people outside the walls of Augland. *How could I have been so naïve?*

There was no exit. Cahya and Wolfe stood in front of them, and the Colony men who had brought them in stood guard behind, blocking the door.

It was getting harder to breathe. Ashton looked around the shabby living room, smoky from the fire, and felt the tattered flower wallpaper closing in on her. She didn't understand. The Colony was supposed to save them. She had thought they would welcome Augland escapees with open arms.

"Sit down." Cahya motioned to a set of chairs facing her before the fire. Hunter and Ashton ignored her request and remained standing, frozen in place. Cahya turned to Wolfe, who stood stoically next to her with his arms crossed. He shook his head.

"We expected some setbacks, Wolfe," Cahya said calmly. Wolfe's posture grew agitated, and he started to pace.

Ashton stared at Wolfe, wide-eyed, trying to read him. Why hadn't he grabbed Hunter and Ashton and dragged them back to Augland? He even seemed upset about finding them. Ashton could not figure out what was going on. *Was Wolfe a Colony spy?*

Wolfe pointed at Ashton and Hunter. "We have no park anymore, thanks to these two! Land of Legends is done for. That was the entire foundation of the plan! I don't see how you think this is anything but bad."

Plan? Ashton furrowed her brow. "What plan?"

Wolfe didn't acknowledge her.

"We just need to rethink and find a solution. That's all," Cahya said.

"You're not the one risking everything. I am the one actually in there. Nothing is going to change if I don't become CEO. Setbacks like this are not helping!"

Cahya remained collected in the face of Wolfe's outburst.

"Wolfe, your obtuseness won't do us any good. We can still find a way to our goal. You need to consider what we have done so far and where we need to go. Just because things haven't gone according to your plan doesn't mean we give up." Wolfe was quiet. Then, after avoiding her gaze, Wolfe finally glanced over at Ashton.

"And you didn't know about this . . ." Wolfe eyed Cahya carefully.

"You know I didn't, Wolfe." Cahya was stern and seemed hurt by the accusation.

"What's going on?!" Hunter shouted. He looked at Wolfe, full of rage. Wolfe had been hunting them like animals for days, and now, he thought he could just switch sides? From where Ashton and Hunter were standing, he was still the enemy.

Cahya turned to Wolfe and said quietly, "You might as well tell them."

Wolfe sighed. "Augland 54 has a treaty with the Colony," he said, nodding toward Cahya, "to bring back any workers who try to escape. If they find and return escapees, we leave the Colony alone." Wolfe crossed his arms across his chest. Cahya put her hand on his shoulder.

"Our children started to go missing a few years ago. They were going into the woods and disappearing." Cahya walked toward the stone fireplace. "Wolfe came to us almost a year ago. He came clean about Augland breaking our treaty and taking our children without our knowledge. My son was one of them." Tears started to well up in Cahya's eyes. "If we revolted, there was no way our Colony would survive. They could tear us apart with their Suits."

Ashton looked around and realized there were no Suits. In fact, there was hardly any technology or electricity.

"I came to them when I was working security. I had seen so many young children being ripped away from the Colony and forced into Augland and the cages below. When I met Cahya, I knew I couldn't let it happen anymore, but we had to be smart about it," Wolfe said. His stance had softened, lightened. He looked more relaxed as he continued to explain—but sad. "Cahya spoke with NeuroEnergy, who had their own suspicions of what the AEC was doing in their Augland parks. Augland 54 is finding ways to generate energy and put the Northwest division of NeuroEnergy out of business."

Cahya stepped in. "NeuroEnergy won't help us until we know for sure. They don't want to risk their relationship with the AEC. But if we confirm that Augland 54 is going against the treaty that ended the war, they will have the ammunition they need to . . ."

Wolfe reached across his chest and put his hand over Cahya's, which was still resting on his shoulder. Ashton's stomach lurched.

"That's true," Hunter broke in, looking straight at Wolfe. Ashton turned to him, shocked. Hunter avoided her eyes. "They won't hurt their relationship with Augland until they know for sure."

"Wait, what? How do you know?" Ashton's head felt ready to explode. She could hear her heartbeat swishing in her ears. Nothing made sense anymore. She felt betrayed by everything and everyone she thought she knew.

Hunter sighed. "Because I am—well, was—their spy."

Ashton didn't know anything about NeuroEnergy. But apparently, Hunter knew all about it; he was part of NeuroEnergy!

It was all Ashton could do to process this revelation and continue to follow Hunter's story. She glanced at Cahya and Wolfe. Had they known about this, or was it news to them too?

"NeuroEnergy knew that Augland was up to something, so they sent me to work as an engineer. Once I was in there, though, NeuroEnergy had no way to get me out, especially since I didn't have any intel for them. They abandoned me in there." Cahya and Wolfe both looked surprised, but nothing compared to Ashton's confusion as Hunter continued to explain that NeuroEnergy had never forced people to work for them. Therefore, many people who lived in the Colony had once come from NeuroEnergy. Auglands and NeuroEnergy always had their disputes. Auglands tried to generate their own energy to dispose of the needs of NeuroEnergy, which created tension between the two entities.

"All information is kept amongst the board members," Wolfe said, glossing over the fact that Hunter had been a spy within Augland. "Our best shot, and the plan I had been working on for months, was to be successful enough at the Land of Legends park that my father would promote me to the Executive Board, as head of Security, and give me a seat at the table. It was a long con. If I were to take over Augland 54 when he retired, I could demolish it from the inside. That was until you ruined any shot of that happening by killing a Suit and running away." Wolfe almost spat out the last words in frustration, glaring at Ashton.

"Wolfe. I . . ." Ashton started but didn't know what to say. She wasn't sorry. She hadn't known. *But why didn't he tell me? Why didn't he trust me? I could have helped.*

"How were you going to do that?" Hunter said before Ashton could gather her thoughts enough to get another word out. "How were you going to destroy it from the inside? By enjoying the privileges of CEO while workers suffered and died?" Hunter was more accusing than asking.

"For so many years, I tried to lay low and stay out of the Executive Office. I couldn't stomach how far Augland was taking this." Wolfe looked pained as he spoke. "If you could see what I've seen, down in the cages, where they keep the old, the hurt, and those captured from the Colony . . . They don't survive long there."

"Why are they even keeping people below?" Ashton asked Wolfe in an anguished voice.

"Everything is kept so secret. If I can get on the Board and gain their trust, I might be able to find out and get NeuroEnergy's support. If I can just help them see that the AEC is planning to dissolve them and take their energy assets into Augland . . ." He sounded desperate.

This was the side of Wolfe Ashton had seen on the rock, the real Wolfe. He'd tried to hide in Augland, but he had almost let the charade drop in front of her. Ashton finally understood all that was going on inside him. She saw the enormity of his internal struggle. She knew what that felt like. For so long, Ashton had kept a mask on, submitting to Augland, but deep down, she had been bursting to be free of the Augland chains.

All of a sudden, it was like her life was passing before her eyes, memories rushing past. Niall had tried to tame her, and for a long time, he was successful. It wasn't until she took on the character of Freya that she began to break out of her shell, for the first time seeing an inner strength she never knew she had. Augland had tried to bury her further in Land of Legends, but she had used their plans to unmask herself. She was free, confused, and angry.

"Where is Sheva?" Ashton demanded. She already knew the answer. Wolfe hung his head.

"Ashton, I had no choice; we had to take her down to the cages." Ashton's heart stopped as her worst fear was confirmed.

"You left her there, in the cages?" Ashton shouted. She needed to be angry, and Wolfe was the perfect target. Her fists balled, and she narrowed in on Wolfe.

"I had no choice. The men I was with, they work for Augland and so do I. If I had freed her, they would have known something was going on."

"Versal too?" Hunter added bitterly.

Wolfe stood tall as he looked over at Hunter. "Yes, Versal too."

Hunter sighed in relief. Versal was alive, at least, even if she was in the cages of Augland 54.

"Calm down." Cahya stepped between Ashton and Wolfe. "We don't have time to think of what we've lost. We have to focus on how we can regain our strength from here."

"Cahya is right. We can't fight amongst ourselves. We need to figure out how we fix this if we can." Wolfe backed away.

"We?" Ashton scoffed, "I'm going to get Sheva."

"How?" Hunter asked. He felt the same about Versal.

Ashton didn't know. All she knew was that Sheva was suffering, and she wasn't about to team up with Wolfe. But she couldn't just walk into Augland, find Sheva, and then walk right out. She had never seen the inside of the cages; she didn't even know where to begin.

"What if you just went back and said you couldn't find us?" Hunter suggested. "That might give us time to find a way back into Augland to get Versal and Sheva. If you truly want the cages to end, you'll find a way to get them out." Hunter was testing Wolfe.

"I can't come back without something; there will be more to pay in trying to find her than the Colony can handle. They will think that Cahya is hiding you."

"You are full of excuses! You could let them out!" Ashton was desperate.

"I can't just walk in there and walk out—" Wolfe stopped midsentence, an idea forming in his head. He turned and walked away from the large fireplace. "Cahya, I need something to write on."

Cahya looked toward the two guards who quickly left the room, pushing the door open, presumably to grab what Wolfe needed.

"What is it?" Ashton asked. She wasn't ready to forgive him or trust the Colony that held them prisoner, but she didn't see any other options.

"I think I have an idea; it will be difficult and may not work, but it's all I've got for now." Cahya's men returned with a charcoal pencil and paper, and Wolfe snatched them, slamming them down on the table in the middle of the room and then furiously sketched something.

Ashton looked down at a drawing Wolfe was creating: small winding parallel lines through a large circle.

"Back when I was in cage security, people would die in the cages almost daily. We didn't dispose of the bodies up on the surface because they didn't want any of the Suits or workers to see them. Instead, we used a tunnel system that was part of the old Seattle Underground. It's covered with cameras and monitored, but if we could somehow get there and disable them, I may be able to sneak Sheva and Versal out of that tunnel."

Wolfe shook his head, already seeing holes in the plan he had just developed. Wolfe looked at Ashton and continued, "They are underground, and the tunnel, here, goes around the perimeter. If I can get them through the security system, that's where they could make a run to the shores, and the Colony's boat could take them here." Wolfe dropped the pencil in frustration. "The problem is, even if I turned off the cameras, they would be up again in no time. I know because I helped create the system. It would take disabling alarms, cameras, and having key cards. And they would need a guide to get through the tunnels. You'd need everything to be perfect to get this plan to work. I wouldn't be able to do it without being noticed. If they took one wrong turn or took too long it would be over."

Wolfe leaned on the table and pinched the bridge of his nose. Ashton looked down at the piece of paper where Wolfe had drawn the tunnel directions. The problem wasn't that he wouldn't be able to do it—it was that he needed help. Ashton's help.

"You said that you can't do it by yourself, but what if I helped?" Ashton said. "I could go down in the cages and let them out. You can show me which direction to go, and I could lead them. All I would need is for you to disable the cameras and get me that key card."

"Absolutely not. I'm not trying to put you in the cages; I'm trying to save people, Ash."

"She's right," Hunter added. "You could bring her back to Augland and put her in the cages. From there she could save Shev and Versal while you distract the people up in the Executive Office. Besides, wouldn't it look good if you were able to bring in Ashton like you were supposed to?"

Wolfe gave Hunter a long stare as he considered what he said. "No, this isn't a good plan; we will think of something else," Wolfe said.

"We don't have time to think of something else, Wolfe!" Ashton yelled. She felt her anger rising as she thought of both Sheva and Versal lying in cages. "We don't have another choice, and this gives us what we both want."

Cahya finally stepped in. "This plan gets you what you want, but not what we need. This doesn't help the bigger picture. Think clearly, Wolfe; we are playing the long game here." Ashton was about to butt in, but Cahya put up her hand and continued. "We've all lost people. Don't think your loss is more than any of ours. We can't risk the plan for a few people."

Cahya looked around at Wolfe, Hunter, and Ashton, her commanding presence keeping them quiet. "What happens when Executives find out that prisoners escaped from Augland? Do you think they aren't going to come to the Colony first? What, no one thought of that? There is a treaty that is protecting this Colony right now. How many more people do you think will die if they come for us? I have to protect my people."

Wolfe's face burned red, and the veins on the side of his neck protruded visibly. Cahya was right; this could start a war. By coming to the Colony, Ashton had put them all in danger. They all stood in silence, frozen by the gravity of the situation.

Ashton didn't necessarily like the plan of turning herself into Augland, but if there was any chance of getting Sheva out of the situation, she was going to take it, no matter the consequence. Wolfe would just have to accept it.

"I'm doing this, whether you like it or not. What other choice do we have? We don't have time to stand here. Do any of you have a better idea?" Ashton stared daggers into Cahya and Wolfe, trying to look more confident than she felt.

Wolfe let out a sigh. "I don't like this plan, but you're right. If I'm going to stay close to Warren, I'll need something to bring back to him, and our time is running out. I'm sorry, Cahya, the Colony is in danger no matter what."

CHAPTER 34

Ashton

Wolfe and Cahya went into the back room, which Ashton guessed was the kitchen, to discuss plans and information Hunter and Ashton were not privy to. Ashton and Hunter were left with the guards who had escorted them through the forest. While they no longer felt like prisoners, they weren't free either.

Ashton found her anxiety eating away at her. She was going to let Wolfe take her back into Augland 54, into the hands of the AEC. Anger and dismay burned with the ashes of hope and fear.

"Hey, you okay?" Hunter pulled his chair close to her and sat down. She was staring into the fire lit just inside Cahya's home. The heat made her skin glow brightly and sent prickles along her cheeks.

"Not really, no." Ashton was too tired to lie. While she and Hunter weren't necessarily friends, they had been through a lot together over the past few days. He took Ashton's hand. Ashton flinched. It wasn't normal for him to be this nice to her, but she had to admit it felt good to be consoled. He pretended like she hadn't reacted and held her hand, tightening his grip.

Ashton relaxed. "I can't help but think about what will happen to me." She threw a stick she had been fiddling with into the fire.

"You can't think like that; what you are doing is brave. What you have done is brave, more than I can say I would be willing to do if I'm honest." Ashton looked at Hunter. She hadn't thought of it as being brave. Stupid, yes. Necessary to save Sheva, yes. But brave never crossed her mind. "I'm sorry for being such a jerk to you all this time," Hunter said more kindly than she had ever heard him speak. "You didn't deserve it."

Ashton didn't know what to say to that. She couldn't tell him he wasn't that bad because he had been a jerk to her. And he had been a spy. She smiled at the irony of it all and chuckled.

"What's so funny?" Hunter smiled back at her.

Ashton shook her head. "I wouldn't have thought that you and I would become friends through all this."

"Whoa, I wouldn't go that far," Hunter laughed, and she just shoved him on the shoulder.

"Hey!"

She smiled at him. Who would have thought that after only a few days of adventure, Ashton and Hunter would be sitting in a home in the Colony, having a friendly conversation? Overnight, Ashton's world had changed drastically. Augland now felt like a suffocating cocoon. She had escaped into the woods and sprouted wings. She was shaky and unsure, but at least she was free. And now, she was volunteering to be caged in the Augland sheath.

Someone cleared their throat behind them, and Ashton and Hunter turned to see Wolfe. "Sorry to interrupt you two, but Ashton, we need to go. We'll be leaving Hunter here." Wolfe didn't look at them. Instead, he turned and headed for the door.

Ashton looked at Hunter, who gave her a sympathetic look before smiling reassuringly. "Take care of yourself, okay? And go get our girls." Ashton nodded, then followed Wolfe. She took one last look at Hunter, knowing that if she was not successful, it would be her last.

Wolfe and Ashton walked away from the house that served as Cahya's headquarters, out of the cul-de-sac, and down the street. They came to the end of the street and turned the opposite direction from which Ashton had entered with the guards. This route took them down another long street lined with homes, all similar in size, with variations in color and dilapidation.

The Colony was close to Augland 54; Ashton guessed it couldn't be more than a few miles away. It was on the other side of a large hill just across Puget Sound. The Colony was well hidden amongst the tall green trees and hills.

Wolfe had a remarkably keen understanding of the landscape outside Augland 54. He had been exploring it since he was a child, when his father had realized that Wolfe's boundless energy could be expended by letting him roam outside the bubble.

Augland 54 had been created around the major cities of Seattle and Bellevue in former Washington State and had expanded over the years to the countryside of what used to be known as North Bend. The dome stretched from the forests of North Bend to the edge of Bainbridge Island. The old Seattle downtown had been converted into Hollywood Boulevard, and the Executives and AEC politicians had turned the skyscrapers of old Seattle into the Executive Offices, with the CEO's offices housed in the giant Space Needle, overlooking it all.

Ashton and Hunter had taken their boat to the barrier right outside Bainbridge Island. The Colony had the island; it was their territory. Wolfe frequently made his way there, climbing up the large hill on the island. This was the last point from which he could still see the bubble of Augland. It spanned for miles.

Under the bubble, each park sustained its own virtual weather system. Here on Bainbridge, they experienced the natural rainy weather of the region. Inside Augland, the dome's multiple glass screens displayed the atmosphere each park needed for its unique environment. The rainy, gray weather of the Pacific Northwest didn't fit the aesthetics of Maya Bay or Victorian. There, sunny skies and warm temperatures were in order. All the screens had to do was show the weather, and the Suits could program what that weather felt like. Not everyone could enjoy the benefits of virtual reality, however. For the workers of Augland 54, it might look sunny, but they could still feel the real cold.

Wolfe saw Augland like a snow globe. It trapped him inside a false reality. Out in the real world, he felt at peace, as if freedom could take his problems away.

The cul-de-sac the Colony occupied was hidden by trees, but the neighborhood had been cleared of the overgrowth and was slowly becoming a place that mimicked its prewar appearance. Wolfe led Ashton along the street, where some Colony members worked in their gardens and others stared at them from the steps of their houses.

"Hey, Wolfe!" someone shouted. Wolfe looked up to see a young boy swinging his arm back and forth to get his attention. On a previous visit, Wolfe had brought the boy a warm coat and a basketball. Wolfe smiled and nodded at him. Every time Wolfe visited, he wished he could stay, wished he didn't have to go back to Augland. It made it harder and harder for him to come out each time. The people here didn't live great lives, but they were free and happy—something he hadn't felt in a long time.

"Keep up; we will need to make it back to Augland before sundown," Wolfe said, a few feet ahead of Ashton. The sun was coming down in front of them, and Ashton could make out Wolfe's tall and muscular silhouette in front of her. To be alone with him after so much had happened made her nervous. He had been her superior and her ally, her friend with whom she had shared a kiss, her hunter, and her enemy. What was he to her now?

Ashton jogged slightly to catch up with Wolfe. Now that they were alone, there were so many things she wanted to talk about with him. Her heart was beating quickly as she approached him. Wolfe made her feel so many emotions. What had happened between them the last few days was a lot to process. She was fond of Wolfe, then scared, then angry, and now, knowing what he had been trying to do for the workers, she almost felt guilty for the chase she had led him on.

"Wolfe?"

"When we get down there, in the . . . try and get warm, your skirt should work fine. It will get cold. And it's damp." Wolfe stared ahead. Ashton nodded.

"Wolfe?" she tried again.

"And there isn't much for food. Or water, but I can see what I can do to get you something."

"Okay, but Wolfe . . ." She didn't like this side of Wolfe. Although he wasn't a Suit, he was robotic, able to turn his emotions on and off at will. Ashton found herself getting flustered.

"And don't say anything to anyone. No matter what. There are cameras and audio recorders. They could use it against you. I don't know, maybe—"

"All right, Wolfe, I get it. But we should talk," Ashton interrupted him. So much had happened since they had last spoken. She needed some answers.

Wolfe didn't respond and instead just kept walking in front of her.

"Don't do that; don't just walk away. If you have a problem . . ." Ashton started and then almost ran into Wolfe. He had stopped and turned toward her.

"If I have a problem? Yes, Ashton, I have a major problem. I opened up to you that day on the rock and told you things, even kissed you, and I thought that meant something. Then you messed everything up and ran away. No regard for anything but yourself. And now . . . now there is nothing I can do to protect you."

Wolfe threw his hands up. Ashton took a step back. She could see the frustration boiling within him.

"You ruined everything, my plan, all my work. I cared for you, and I got . . . careless. I had everything under control, and it was going to work. Now, I'm here walking with the one person I've grown to truly care about, back to what will most likely be her death."

Ashton saw his frustration turn to sorrow. She hadn't seen the situation from Wolfe's point of view before. He had so much pressure on his shoulders from his father, from the Colony, from the workers he was trying to save. He was playing double agent and was close to failing both sides. So much depended on what they did now and how selfless they could be. She finally saw the bigger picture, and it was greater than her or Sheva or Wolfe.

Ashton didn't know what to say. She'd been consumed with her feelings, her hurt, and her destiny. She hadn't been like Hunter, who was working for NeuroEnergy, or Wolfe, who was trying to gain control and change Augland from the inside out, or Cahya, who was looking after her Colony. She had only been thinking of herself and her freedom.

Ashton looked at Wolfe and could see the vulnerability he felt around her. She realized she was probably the only person with whom he could let his guard down. She reached out and touched his arm. Wolfe immediately tensed. He looked down at her hand and, without hesitation she wrapped her other hand around his waist, pulling him close to her.

Ashton must have taken him by surprise because his entire body tensed as she wrapped herself around him. But after a moment, his body began to loosen, and he swathed his arms around her. At that moment, something deeper between them connected. Ashton laid her head on his chest and closed her eyes. She could feel his heart beating next to hers. They both had that in common. They had both been hiding their true selves for so long. The masks they had been forced to wear seemed to fall and clatter on the ground. Ashton was done hiding.

Ashton didn't know how long they held each other or which one of them needed it more. It felt good to hold each other, and with each moment that passed, she could feel their sky-high walls melting down.

Ashton pulled away slightly, only enough to stare up at his face. She looked deeply into Wolfe's marbled, sky-blue eyes. The world became hazy around her with comfort and happiness. For a moment, her anxiety disappeared; her anger, hurt, and sorrow became dust.

Wolfe bent in and kissed her. It felt like they fit, like they somehow completed each other. Their imperfection was each other's perfection. When they pulled apart, Wolfe lightly kissed the top of her forehead. Any doubt in Ashton toward Wolfe or his mission disappeared at that moment. She had peeled back his layers and seen the real him. He had done the same to her.

"Well, this doesn't make it any easier," Wolfe said as Ashton closed her eyes, snapping back to reality.

Wolfe was taking Ashton back into captivity and would be her captor. It felt like Ashton's heart was being ripped out of her body. These were too many emotions to feel in one day.

"I wish we could just run away, right now, and not look back," Ashton said. If it weren't for Sheva and Versal, she wouldn't think twice about it.

"You know we can't. We both are committed to our causes and have our reasons." They broke apart and started walking side by side, slowly intertwining their fingers. For the moment, they could pretend.

The sun hovered over the tree line, and Ashton rested her head against Wolfe's arm. He smelled of pine. She took a deep breath in.

"What was your childhood like?" Ashton asked after they had walked a while in silence.

"Mine?" Wolfe seemed surprised by the question. "Not much to it. I grew up in the Executive Offices, Warren was an aspiring CEO, and my mother . . ." Wolfe paused, "my mother was—is—a beautiful woman. Strong, nurturing, caring." Wolfe sighed. "I didn't know what life was like for the workers, for the Suit-less, but everything seemed to be running smoothly. My grandfather was appointed CEO and followed AEC law right down to the last letter. We even worked well with NeuroEnergy, and we partnered to bring energy and resources to the outside Colony."

"Then you went into security?" Ashton asked.

"When Warren was appointed CEO of Augland 54, he put me in with security because he wanted me to be stronger." Ashton noticed that when Wolfe spoke, he used his father's first name.

"I was put in charge of the cages; there were more people than we had room to employ. I saw the reality, the brutality, of Augland then. Yes, they were looking to expand the parks, but until then, the extras were thrown into the cages. Partly to keep numbers down, partly to keep the workers above in a state of unknown fear." Ashton could tell Wolfe was finding it difficult to talk about this. "We had a meeting to discuss the cages. I brought up the idea to Warren that we could let the extra workers, especially the old, go to the Colony to live out the remainder of their lives. That was how we had it for many years."

Wolfe paused as he helped Ashton up on top of a rock and down to the other side. They took a turn from the street and toward a forested area. Wolfe helped Ashton over a rock wall that divided the street from the forest.

"Warren feared the Colony would get too large, feared they would rise up against Augland 54. The Colony had developed a good relationship with NeuroEnergy, and that didn't sit well with him either. They had a powerful ally, and Warren was not about to be the CEO who slipped up and started another war between NeuroEnergy and the AEC. While NeuroEnergy is still part of the AEC, they act independently." Ashton was finally beginning to understand it all. She had had a vague idea that there were two powers in the world—the AEC, now the parent company of Augland parks, and NeuroEnergy—and that there had been a war, but now, the reality of it all was being pieced together in her head.

"So I revamped the cages. Ashton, I didn't know what else to do. I didn't know how to disobey Warren. The cages kill so many people. It's damp and cold, and we don't spare much food for them." While it surprised Ashton what Wolfe told her, it didn't at the same time.

"But Warren grew power-hungry. Neutrality wasn't enough; he had to show the Colony who was in charge. That was when we began stealing kids from the Colony."

Wolfe was silent for a while. They walked through the damp, overgrown forest, and Ashton took deep breaths of fresh air, trying to savor every moment outside of the Augland bubble.

"I'm not proud of my role in this, Ash; I am ashamed of what I did to contribute to the Executives' reign, to Warren." He looked down at Ashton beside him. Ashton could see how much this hurt him, and she could only imagine how he must feel. She looked down at his hand and squeezed it tighter. She wanted to comfort him and let him know she wasn't judging him.

"You were doing what your father told you. You're doing the right thing now, and that should count for something," Ashton said.

"That's no excuse. I only hope that I can somehow correct the mistakes I've made in the past. I know that I won't be forgiven, but I can do my best." He looked down at their entangled hands. "Ashton, are you sure you want to go back to Augland? I wouldn't blame you if you wanted to run."

Ashton had asked herself the same question multiple times.

"It was my choice. I wouldn't be able to live with myself if I just ignored my friends and let them die."

"You are different from the shy girl I saw on the stage the first day of Land of Legends," Wolfe said as he smiled at her.

The sun shone through the forest at an angle, beginning to set. Wolfe sighed. "We are close."

Ashton was surprised; she had imagined Augland 54 to be farther away. She wanted more time. Anxiety rose within her like a cold front. Ashton stopped in her tracks as she saw Augland's glass dome come into sight from the top of the hill. She didn't know what was going to happen after this point. She wished they could keep walking forever.

"I'm scared, Wolfe. I'm not strong like this."

Wolfe scooped her toward him and hugged her tightly. She took a deep breath in and shut her eyes, tears escaping as she let go. She always needed to be so strong; for once, she just wanted to feel safe. And she felt safe in Wolfe's embrace. She didn't want to let go.

"Yes, you are. You are the strongest woman I know." He looked down at her as if to drink in the sight of her.

"I won't let anything happen to you, Ashton. I promise."

Ashton looked up at Wolfe and could see in his eyes that he was telling the truth. He would not let anything happen to her if he could, but Ashton wondered how much control he actually had. Augland was powerful, too powerful.

They both watched in silence as the sun came down across the large domed wall of Augland 54. This was it, and all she could do was hope their plan would work.

CHAPTER 35

Wolfe

Wolfe tried to slow his pace when he realized how close they were to the boat that would take them to the Seattle side, right near the entrance to the tunnels.

"I'm scared, Wolfe. I'm not strong like this." Ashton stopped in her tracks as she saw Augland's glass dome come into sight at the top of the hill. Wolfe felt her hand shaking, and he wanted nothing more than to grab her and run away. Instead, he pulled her toward him and hugged her tightly. He could feel her tears as she buried herself into him.

"Yes, you are. You are the strongest woman I know. I won't let anything happen to you, Ashton. I promise," Wolfe said.

Wolfe knew he shouldn't make a promise he didn't know he could keep. But he was going to try.

CHAPTER 36

Ashton

Wolfe and Ashton spent the boat ride from Bainbridge Island back to the mainland in silence. Ashton sat at the front of the boat, shivering from the wind and slashes of ice-cold water. Her heart grew cold as they came closer and closer to the suffocating globe of Augland.

They landed on the Seattle shore and were only steps away from the towering fake world of Augland 54. Ashton could see no way in but trusted that Wolfe knew what he was doing. He seemed to move in and out of Augland with ease, something Ashton had thought impossible until a few days ago.

"I have to put these on you now that we are getting close." Wolfe showed Ashton a pair of cuffs he had taken from his pocket. His blue eyes showed his sadness. Their time together as friends was over. In a moment, he would become her enemy again.

Ashton put her hands out as he placed the cuffs carefully around her small wrists. They were heavier than she thought they would be.

"You'll see the worst side of me soon. Ashton, I don't know how else to change things but to get to the top." His eyes looked desperate. Wolfe had been in the resistance for years, a world Ashton had just entered. She didn't have any solutions, but she hated what Wolfe had to do. Every time he had to hurt someone, it took away a little bit more of his humanity. This was going to be a much harder goodbye for Ashton than she'd thought it would be.

"I understand." Ashton couldn't say more. It would make this moment too difficult for both of them. They had to go back to Augland.

Wolfe took out his key card and brought his interconnect up to his mouth. The old Seattle Underground was just on the other side of the door. These tunnels would lead her back into Augland and into the cages.

"This is Wolfe. I have Ashton with me, and we are entering the underground tunnels now, southwest wing."

Wolfe opened the door and took in a deep breath as he looked at the long hallway that led underneath Augland. They stepped down, beneath the city. They walked down an old, underground city street. Pipes and wooden beams lined the tunnel. Ashton could somewhat make out the shapes of doors and old buildings; at times, the space narrowed into a tunnel of debris, and they had to step over piles of bricks and wood. It was dark, and Ashton couldn't see more than a few feet in front of her. She relied only on Wolfe's guiding hands as they walked.

"This used to be Seattle, a long time ago, way before the war. I think there was a fire. The city was built on top of all this." There was so much Ashton didn't know.

Ashton and Wolfe walked in silence as they made their way through the tunnel. Wolfe led the way as Ashton followed him through the dark abyss.

"I'm sorry," Wolfe whispered to Ashton. All she could do was look at him, tears in her eyes. There was too much to bear: the Colony, Sheva, Versal, and Wolfe. He felt it too. On top of it all was the fear of not knowing Warren's intentions.

Wolfe took the center of the chain that connected Ashton's cuffs and pulled her forward. Ashton looked behind her, but Wolfe didn't look at her. Two men came toward Wolfe. Ashton winced in pain as the cuffs chafed against her wrists with the pressure of being jerked forward.

"Good work, sir!" said Joao. He was clearly one of Wolfe's most trusted security team members, and he smiled admiringly as Wolfe pushed Ashton out in front of them. Ashton remembered the security guard as the man who had stood behind Hunter and Versal at the Victorian train station.

"Take her to cage 515, Joao; I'll be back down in a moment to give further instructions," Wolfe said in a tone that made him seem so foreign to her now.

"Yes, sir."

They had come to a crossroad within the tunnel, and Ashton could see that Wolfe was headed one way, and she would go the other way. She looked one more time and saw Wolfe glance back and nod before he disappeared into the darkness.

Joao reached out for Ashton, and instinctively, she recoiled. He grew angry and grabbed her elbow, shoving her in front of him.

While the tunnels were dark, Ashton's eyes had adjusted. She tried to watch the tunnel in front of her as she was roughly pushed along. Ashton was just able to make out details of the space around her. Pipes lined the short ceiling. The wood planks beneath her creaked under the heavy weight of the men behind her. There were doors and signs, nothing that Ashton could make out, but she could glimpse what looked like small, long-empty shops. Dust floated in the light from the guard's flashlight.

Joao and two other men from Wolfe's security detail walked in silence as they made their way toward the end of the underground streets and through a large steel door. Like Wolfe, they used a key card to enter. As they entered, Ashton was instantly hit with a horrendous smell. Feces, sweat, and then something that took her mind back to Land of Legends: death.

"This way," Joao told Ashton and forced her to the right. She looked back and glared at him. He reminded her a lot of Wolfe. They had a similarly tall build and rough facial features with forward-facing foreheads and bushy eyebrows. His eyes were dark, though, which was a contrast to Wolfe's icy blue eyes. His beard was longer, too, but groomed so that not a hair seemed out of place.

She turned away from him, and all she could see were the horrible conditions of this dungeon. Sheva had described this place well. It was cold and dark, with just enough light to see the skin and bones of the people hanging onto life by a thread. Ashton wanted to vomit and cry at the same time. Long bars lined the corridor; each person had maybe three feet of room before they were closed off from the next prisoner. Ashton didn't even look at their faces; she couldn't bear how much they had suffered or the fear that engulfed this dark place.

"Come on! Keep moving." Ashton was pushed again. She was getting tired of it, but she held back. She needed to lie low and not make waves. Just like Niall had taught her.

"Here we go." Joao opened one of the small empty cages and shoved Ashton inside. She stumbled in and fell. He followed her in and undid her cuffs.

"Welcome home," he snarled as he turned and closed the door.

The room was small, and the floor felt slimy as she lifted her hands. There weren't any windows, so while she knew it was night, she wouldn't have been able to tell otherwise.

The darkness took her in, swallowing Ashton until she couldn't tell how much time had passed or even if she was awake or in a nightmare. She couldn't help but feel a part of her wishing she hadn't agreed to return. This place was inhumane. Ashton's feet kept sliding on the damp ground as she paced back and forth, one step forward, one step back.

She turned to her right as she heard coughing.

"Hello?"

There was no response.

"Hello," she said again as she crept closer to the front of her cage and wrapped her hands around the cold metal bars. She could barely see into the cell next to her. The cement walls divided them, but the metal bars allowed some view of the dingy hallway and the side-by-side cells. Ashton could see the silhouette of a small person huddled near the bars of the adjacent cell.

"Hi," Ashton said again in a softer tone. There was a slight movement.

"Who are you?" the voice asked, the terrified, high-pitched sound of a small child.

Ashton's blood ran cold. *What is a child doing in this dungeon?* She spoke softly. "My name is Ashton. Are you all right?"

The small figure crawled closer toward her, and soon, Ashton was able to make out details of her face and figure. She was skinny and had bright golden eyes with jet-black hair. She was covered in dirt from head to toe. Her tiny fingers wrapped around the metal bars, and she pushed her face between them to get a closer view of Ashton.

"No." She began to sob. "I'm so hungry and cold."

"What's your name?" Ashton asked. It was all she could do.

"Jagatha," the small girl responded. "Why'd they put you in here?"

"Don't tell anyone, okay? But I hit a Suit with an ax," Ashton whispered conspiratorially. Jagatha let out a small giggle.

"Really?" she asked. Instantly, the tiny figure seemed to move even closer, and her golden eyes became a little browner.

"Yep. I had to hit it a few times before it just fell on the floor twitching, like this." Ashton wriggled her body, imitating the Suit. Jagatha let out another laugh. Then Ashton heard another voice.

"Did that happen? You really killed one?" a man in the cage across from them asked.

"Well, it wasn't moving after I left it."

"Left?" he asked, pressing his face against the bars.

"Yeah, well, I was able to get out of Augland with my friends; two of them are here now, though."

"You got out? How did they catch you?" Jagatha asked.

"It's a long story. I made it as far as the Colony." Ashton stopped talking. She realized this information would be new to them and something she probably shouldn't talk about. Wolfe had warned her not to say anything to the workers, and now here she was talking when she should have been keeping her mouth shut.

"It's real then? There is a place outside of here?" The man sounded hopeful. "How did you end up back here?"

"I got caught by Augland security," Ashton said. She thought about telling them the truth but couldn't risk putting Wolfe's life at risk if word went around that someone had helped her.

"How did you survive out there?" Jagatha peered at Ashton through the darkness.

"Well, that part wasn't hard. There wasn't anything scary or dangerous. It was beautiful. There were green trees everywhere and houses where people lived." Jagatha's eyes sparkled as she tried to picture what Ashton was talking about.

"Too bad we'll never see that," said the man as he leaned his head against the bars. "People only leave here in body bags."

His words sliced through Ashton. These people were just waiting to die, maybe even praying for it. She hadn't been here a full day and already couldn't wait to get out.

"Quiet!" a voice rang through the cage walls and down the long hall. Jagatha quickly scurried away from the bars and back toward the wall of her cell. Ashton looked around desperately to see if anyone was coming but saw nothing. The man and the young girl remained quiet. Ashton could hear the small sobs coming back from Jagatha's direction, but she could no longer see her.

Ashton sat down on her heels, pulling her skirt down and around her legs. The air felt stale as she inhaled, and she thought she could see her breath as she exhaled. Coughs echoed from one end of the hall to the other, alternating with cries as if the walls were singing the prisoner blues.

Ashton put her hands up to her ears and slowly slumped down to the fetal position. She shivered as the cold, damp ground touched her bare skin. She had seen death, felt heartache, smelled decay. Augland had hardened her, and now, she was back to where the only safe place was—her dreams.

"Come."

A voice woke Ashton from her sleep, and for a moment, she had to remember where she was. She shivered as she looked, wide-eyed, around her. A guard she hadn't seen before came into her cage and grabbed her hands, cuffing them.

"What are you doing? Where are we going?" Ashton asked, confused and scared. The guard didn't say anything as he started dragging her toward the door. The fight in her took over, and she started to push back as the guard pulled at her.

"No!" Ashton shouted as she fought against him. *Where was Wolfe?* He said he would come the next day. *What day was it?*

The guard yelled as he pulled Ashton toward him and picked her up. Ashton started thrashing her legs back and forth. Suddenly, a soreness she hadn't felt since her training in Land of Legends stopped her full-force attack on the guard. She didn't know how much fight she had left in her.

"Stop!" He squeezed Ashton's body, and she quickly became limp. The guard dropped her to the ground and dragged her down the hallway. Ashton scrabbled along and tried to breathe, but each breath felt like daggers in her lungs.

She was thrown into a room with no windows. It was empty except for two chairs facing each other. She was forced into a chair.

The door opened, and she saw a shadow of a tall man walk through and shut the door. They were alone. The man came into view. It wasn't Wolfe.

CHAPTER 37

Ashton

He didn't speak. Ashton's breath was shaky as she stared at him. Everything had gone wrong. She wouldn't get the chance to see Wolfe again. She wouldn't be able to save Sheva. Wolfe was right—this was not a good idea. She had entered the lion's den, and now she was face-to-face with a lion. What had she expected?

The Suit-less man in front of her grinned. If it were darker, she would have assumed it was Wolfe, but his red beard and blond hair told her differently. He was dressed in black, just like the security men and workers in Augland. *How many security men are there here? Does he know Wolfe?*

Ashton tried to remain still and stoic, but her body shook, not from cold but from terror.

"Why are you here?" the man asked.

Ashton was taken aback. *Didn't he know?*

The man smacked his hands on either side of the arms of her chair and was only inches away from her face.

"Why. Are. You. Here?" he asked again.

Ashton pushed up against the back of the chair, trying to pull away from his face.

"I hit a Suit," Ashton confessed, smirking back at him in defiance. She didn't want him to see her fear.

"No. I am going to ask you again. Why are you here?" He stood up and grabbed a glove from his pocket.

"I—I ran away?"

His hand connected with Ashton's face, and she felt a sharp pain across her jaw. Her eyes rolled as the pain seared through her.

"Who sent you?"

"No—" This time the blow came on the other side of her face. Again, Ashton's eyes rolled; her body tensed, trying to pass the pain. A metallic taste lined her cheeks, and she spit. Every ounce of her wanted to get up and hit him. The cuffs around her wrists prevented that. Instead, she pulled herself up and stood tall. Her eyes narrowed in on him. He wouldn't get far with her. She would make sure he didn't see anything but strength. He pushed her back down on the chair. It rocked, and for a moment, Ashton thought it would tip over.

"Do you know Cahya?" he asked. Ashton just looked at him, searching the darkness to make out his eyes.

"No." He hit her again. Ashton could feel her face swelling and heat radiating off her sensitive skin. While she could not pull away from the man physically, she pulled away mentally, trying to detach herself.

He leaned in close to her.

"I don't want to do this. Just tell me why you are here," the man whispered. Ashton could feel the desperation in his voice. She turned toward him and stared directly into his eyes, sneering. He looked away and backed up, glancing at the far-right corner of the small room, then back at her. She now understood. The Executives were watching. They were waiting for her to slip up and implicate the Colony. Why? She still didn't know.

"Is NeuroEnergy working with Cahya?"

Ashton raised her head and braced herself.

"No," she repeated. This was the only answer she would give.

Each time he hit her it became easier for Ashton to remove herself. The wall that had come down with Wolfe was quickly rebuilt, and she could feel herself slipping away into her mind. It was safer there.

No more. Ashton was done letting Augland bully her. She was going to take control. The worst they could do was kill her. What was life for a worker, condemned for not having enough money to live in a Suit? She hoped there was a bigger plan, but her part in it was done. Still, she would not give them the satisfaction of seeing any weakness. She had power. They wanted her to admit something. To doom the Colony. Well, she wouldn't let them do it. The power felt great. It gave her freedom. It gave her all she needed. More importantly, it gave her purpose.

At some point, Ashton passed out.

Ashton woke up in her cage, her face throbbing. She put her hand up to her cheeks, and she could feel the red swollen areas. She smiled. She was still alive and knew their tactics hadn't worked. She had stayed silent.

"You okay?" Jagatha asked in the darkness.

"I'm fine." Ashton sighed and leaned against the wall, closing her eyes. She heard a scratching sound and opened her eyes again.

"What are you doing?" She pulled herself up and dragged herself to the prison bars.

Jagatha didn't turn toward Ashton.

"I'm scratching my name in the ground. I want the next person to know who was here. Maybe they will do the same. Maybe it will start a list of people who lived here. I want to write my name before—"

She pushed the small rock she was holding harder into the ground. Up and down. She didn't finish what she was going to say. Ashton's bruised body didn't compare to the hopelessness she felt in Jagatha.

"Jagatha, you can't give up," Ashton said, trying her hardest to think of something better to say. Anything. Jagatha was too young to feel this hopeless. "Come here."

Jagatha turned around, and Ashton motioned for her to come closer. She came as close as she could and reached her tiny arms through the bars as Ashton did the same. Ashton winced in pain, but she let the young girl sob as she rested her head against the bars.

Ashton hadn't been in the cages long, but she could feel all their pain like it was her own. She was drowning in it as if each person was pulling her down into deep water, suffocating her.

"I thought you weren't going to return," Jagatha whispered.

Ashton wanted to cradle the girl's small frame in her arms. "Jagatha, I'm going to get you out of here," Ashton whispered.

Jagatha jolted her head so quickly that it pulled Ashton's arm farther between the bars.

"How?" Jagatha looked intently at Ashton.

"I—I can't tell you how; all I can say is I promise to help you out of here. I promise. I need you to promise not to say anything, though."

The small girl nodded and leaned against the bars, smiling. *What have I done? I don't even know if I can get Sheva and Versal out.*

Right now, Ashton just needed to wait and survive long enough for Wolfe to come.

CHAPTER 38

Wolfe

After leaving Ashton in the hands of Joao, Wolfe had made his way through the Seattle Underground to the Executive Offices. The skyscrapers and impossibly tall needle seemed so unreal under the dome of the Augland sky. Every time he returned to Augland, he felt the unnaturalness of the repurposed city filled with nonhuman Suits when he knew a real sky rained down far above him and floating bodies in pods controlled the machines he considered his colleagues. Or at least, they would become his colleagues if he received his promotion to head of Security.

Just as he arrived at the elevator entrance, the doors opened to reveal his father. Wolfe was caught off guard. *Does he know what I've done? Has he come down to arrest me?*

"Wolfgang, my boy," Warren greeted him, stepping out of the elevator doors. Something was off; his father was not generally a welcoming man.

"Hello, sir," Wolfe responded.

"I heard the good news; you got the girl!" Warren said with a smile on his face.

"Yes, she had made it to the Colony, and they turned her over when I arrived. The other one drowned while diving."

"Good, so the treaty is still intact," Warren said. Wolfe held his tongue. He knew Augland 54 had broken the treaty years ago when they started taking children from the Colony.

"What's your intel on them? I want to see it."

Wolfe looked down at a folder that he'd grabbed off his desk before heading to the elevator to Warren's office. One thing Wolfe had learned about his father was to be prepared. He knew Warren would want to know everything about the escape attempt and the people close to Ashton.

Warren took the folder and began glancing through it.

"Sheva, Versal, Byron, Pais," Warren mumbled as he read. "Niall and Bez, those people are her friends. Get rid of them. All of them." He shoved the papers back toward Wolfe, hitting him in the chest.

"Sir?" Wolfe asked as his father started to step away. He didn't understand why Niall and Bez.

"You know," Warren waved his hand, "get rid of them. We don't need them; just do something. I don't want people to think we let criminals get away. We don't know who else she conspired with. There has to be more than just consequences for crimes committed." Warren let out a sly smile. "Do it in front of her—that should send a message. They should have come forward and turned her in. Should give that girl, whatever her name was, a reason to not sleep at night."

There was a long pause.

"Wolfgang, you know, I've found through my years that people care less about what will happen to them, but more about what will happen to the people they love. It's a good technique."

He wore a devilish smirk as he smiled at Wolfe.

"We haven't had any revolt since her stunt, but that doesn't mean something won't happen. It has gotten around that she escaped."

"Let me figure out what to do with her," Wolfe said, desperately thinking of a way to save Ashton; to save them all.

"What did you have in mind?"

Wolfe looked over at him, thinking hard about it. "We—" Wolfe didn't want to stammer in front of his father.

"We do like the Saxons did: we publicly hang her," Warren said, interrupting Wolfe. Warren clapped his hands in excitement.

"No," Wolfe said too quickly. Warren raised an eyebrow. He was always on the lookout to catch Wolfe in weakness.

"No?" Warren said. "We must show why they need to stay obedient, Wolfgang."

"That would make her a martyr." Wolfe knew he was scrambling, and he knew that his father could tell. Warren paused as he considered what Wolfe had said.

"You're right, we can't have that. Yes . . . we could make her into a symbol, though. Beatings and shaming . . . and we will make it part of Land of Legend's show. She will watch her friends die, and we will watch her pain. Then we send her to the brothel."

Wolfe's face went white. He took in a deep breath.

"This is what I expect from my new head of Security." Warren grabbed Wolfe by the shoulder. Wolfe took a long pause before looking at Warren. His father's mechanical eyes shone bright blue.

"Yes, you heard that right. I announced it today, once we found the girl. I think it's time you take on a new role here. You proved to me you won't give up, and you are willing to control those Colony people. I need that. And now you have an opportunity to take ownership of the way we deal with these kinds of situations."

This was a test.

Warren was making sure that Wolfe hadn't gone soft. He was testing his son's loyalty. Wolfe had known Warren was suspicious of him. The new park was what started it. Warren had given Wolfe control, all the while ready to bait him. He hadn't been creating a park to rehabilitate workers. He had been creating a park where workers came to die for the enjoyment of the customers. In so many ways, Wolfe had underestimated his father, but then again, there were ways his father had underestimated him.

"Thank you for the opportunity." Wolfe smiled. He had his own plans and getting higher on the corporate ladder meant he was that much closer to his goal. Wolfe turned to leave, but his father stopped him.

"Oh, and Wolfe. Review the interrogation tapes of that girl. Brock couldn't get anything out of her, but I know you will do what's needed." Wolfe stopped in his tracks. *Interrogation?* Wolfe's stomach lurched. He could not imagine what Ashton was going through, and he hated himself for not suspecting his father of undermining his control.

"Of course."

"Good, schedule it for tomorrow." Warren patted his son on the shoulder, squeezing hard and coming close to his ear. "I have a meeting, but you are welcome to go up to my office and help yourself to some whiskey. I know how much you like it."

Wolfe went into Warren's office and looked around. Sitting on his father's desk was a screen. It showed a small dark room, the interrogation room. Wolfe finally understood. The interrogation of Ashton was not to learn more information. It was to see how far Wolfe would take it. Warren was going to use Ashton against him.

Wolfe poured himself a glass of whiskey and downed it in one gulp. His plan would need to happen today.

"Sir, welcome back and good to hear you got the runaways."

A security guard sat at a small desk looking over an array of screens, each one showing a dark cell and a frightened prisoner.

Wolfe just nodded and looked over her shoulders at the screens.

"I need to see the schedule for this week," Wolfe demanded.

"Oh, yes, sir, of course. I've got that here." The woman shuffled through papers and soon picked up a paper with the names of workers on it. "Here you are, sir."

Wolfe took the piece of paper and looked it up and down.

"I'll be making edits to this, but your shift will end at 10:30 tonight."

"Oh, but, sir, that's not when the shift change starts."

"And I am telling you your shift ends at 10:30 because I need you somewhere else." Wolfe was frustrated. "Are we going to have a problem?"

"Oh, uh, no, sir, I will leave then." The woman shifted her weight, embarrassed.

"I will return with the updated work schedule. That is all," Wolfe said as he turned, but then he changed his mind. "Why don't you take a break. I need to review something."

The guard immediately rolled her chair back and exited the room without a word. Wolfe turned his attention to the screen that showed the interrogation room and began scrolling back in time. He wondered if he wanted to see this or not. He could only imagine what they would have done to her. He pressed play.

Ashton's hunched body came into view. Her red hair was disheveled, her face smeared with dirt. Brock came into view. Wolfe had known him for a long time; he was a great interrogator, but he was his father's pet.

He watched as Ashton stood her ground, not betraying any information about him or the Colony. Each blow sickened him as her face grew bloodier and more swollen. He could tell she was in bad shape even through the dark screen showcasing the even darker room. The blows came over and over again.

Wolfe wanted it to end, but he also needed to see what had happened. He needed to know what information Warren had and how he was going to use it against Wolfe. After the tape finished, he saw Ashton's limp body being taken out of the dark room.

The next step in Wolfe's plan was to get a key card with the name of one of the security guards on shift that night. That was his only way of making sure he wasn't implicated when it all went down. He wanted to cover all of his bases in case they were caught. He used his key to enter a small computer room and grabbed a blank key card. He sat down at the computer and put in his credentials. Next, he needed to consider who would take the fall for this. Whom could he sacrifice for the greater good? He knew who it would be, and while it didn't feel good, he felt confident in his decision. It didn't take long for the key card to print. Wolfe grabbed it and started heading toward his office.

Wolfe sat down in his sparse office. He took a deep breath in as he put together the pieces he needed for his plan.

I hope this works, he thought to himself.

The key card, coordinates, set of keys, and watch felt heavy in his pockets. He knew the cameras were always watching, so he picked up a folder and pretended to read it. He had to be careful. Warren was suspicious, and he knew his every action was being monitored.

There was a knock at the door.

"Hi there," a familiar face said.

Wolfe looked up, surprised. "Jorgeon, how are you?"

"Well, all things considered. It was strange to go from seeing you every day to not having you around at all. I took over the project; I'm not sure if you heard or not," Jorgeon confessed—or maybe he was bragging.

"I figured as much when I didn't go back to the park," Wolfe said. "It looks like security is where I belong. I wasn't any good at the park stuff anyways. Glad to hear it was given to you."

Jorgeon seemed surprised at Wolfe's sincerity.

"It was an honor working with you. I know we had our moments, but it was a very good show. I heard you caught Ashton. Well done!" he said as he took a couple of steps into the office, looking around.

Wolfe quickly stood up from his desk and set down the folder he had pretended to read.

"Yes, yes, you heard right. We were able to get her and two of the others who escaped."

"They need to be reprimanded for what they did to that customer. I was mortified. Any thoughts on what will happen to them?" Jorgeon asked. He was always eager for dramatics.

"Yes, the Executives and I, as head of Security now, are handling it. They will be punished for their involvement in the incident."

"Incident? That's what I would call a crime," Jorgeon chuckled sarcastically.

"Yes, crime."

Wolfe sat back down behind his desk. They both just stared at each other for a while.

Jorgeon broke the silence awkwardly. "Well, I think that's enough chit chat; there is much work to be done now that I'm managing the entire production. Busy, busy."

"Right. Same here," Wolfe said, looking over at his computer screen. "Have a good one, Jorgeon. I'm sure I'll be seeing you around."

"You as well." Jorgeon started to head out of the room and paused. "Oh, I meant to ask. It wasn't hard, was it?"

"What do you mean?"

"Well, you were so fond of Ashton. She was your star. You worked with her so much, and . . ." He said the next words with a smile: "I thought I saw you two sitting together, all cozy. I don't know, it just seems like it would be difficult to bring her in?" Jorgeon posed it as a question, but he said it with clearly malicious intentions.

"Ashton is a traitor. She committed a crime. I did my job. If you are insinuating that—"

Jorgeon raised his hands in defense. "Oh, no, Wolfe, you misunderstand. I was merely making an observation. I didn't mean to make you upset." He put his hand on his chest.

Wolfe remained sitting, stone-faced. He would not be goaded by the passive-aggressive questions of his former inferior.

"Got to go, but so good chatting with you." Jorgeon turned and walked out the door. Wolfe sat back in his chair, and his eyebrows tensed as he watched Jorgeon walk out.

I don't have time for this, Wolfe muttered to himself. He sat up and checked his watch: it was just past 10:15 p.m. He quickly left his office and locked the door, checking both directions before heading toward the elevators. Jorgeon's conversation had added fuel to the fire. People were growing suspicious, and things needed to happen quickly.

CHAPTER 39

Ashton

Ashton's conversation with Jagatha was interrupted by the sound of two guards walking down the hall. Ashton's cell was flung open, and she found herself face-to-face with Wolfe. Her sense of relief mingled with a sense of foreboding. It felt too soon to be seeing him again. It couldn't have been more than twenty-four hours since they had seen each other. *Something's wrong.*

"Sit!" Wolfe yelled, and it caught her off-guard. He threw down a chair and motioned for the guard next to him to do the same. They set up the chairs facing each other in the cell. Wolfe sat down, and the guard stayed out in the hallway. Reluctantly, Ashton sat down in the chair opposite Wolfe.

By the way Wolfe looked at her face, Ashton knew that he wasn't surprised by her swollen cheeks and purple sunken eyes. She didn't know what she looked like, but she knew it must be bad.

"How did you know about the Colony?" He gave her a look that told her she needed to play a part.

"I don't know what you are talking about." Ashton knew how to play this part. She had played it all morning in the interrogation room.

"Don't play dumb with me, Ashton." He moved his chair closer to her so their faces were only a few feet apart. Ashton tossed her head to move her red wig out of her face. In the dark light of her cell, Wolfe's large presence was intimidating. He had changed his clothes, or at least taken off his jacket from their trip from the Colony to Augland. His silhouette towered over her even as he sat on the chair. Darkness surrounded him until he came closer, and his ocean-blue eyes stood out against the chaos that surrounded them. For a moment, Ashton faltered. Half of her was terrified, but the other half wanted to wrap herself around him and hug him.

"Are you a spy for NeuroEnergy? Is that it?"

Ashton was about to respond, but she felt his hand move on top of her Victorian skirt, hovering before placing his hand down. Ashton flinched. *What was he doing?*

He left something on her lap and withdrew his hand. She understood.

"I'm not going to tell you anything!" Ashton screamed, trying to create a distraction. She saw a sparkle in Wolfe's eye, but it disappeared in an instant.

"You have two choices here, Ashton. You can tell me how you knew about the Colony, or we will go forward with your punishment. The choice is yours."

Wolfe tilted his head up and down as he spoke, signaling Ashton to keep going.

"I don't care what you do to me; I'm not going to say anything!" Ashton put as much emotion into her speech as she could muster. She wanted the guard to think she was frightened.

Wolfe gestured to her lap and mouthed, *Coordinates.*

"That's too bad, Ashton. You know we have your friends upstairs, and I'm not sure they would like to go without food for a week. You remember Sheva and Versal? What about Niall or your brothel friend, Bez?" The severity of the situation returned to her heart with a heavy thud. This scene she and Wolfe were acting out could mean life and death for the people she loved. Ashton had returned to save Sheva, but now she knew she wouldn't leave without the others. *Why is Wolfe giving me this information? Does he want me to save them all? Is he letting me know they will die? Is he trying to make sure my emotion is genuine?*

"What will it be, Ashton?" Wolfe's face formed into a sneer while his hand once again slid something over her dress. Ashton lifted her hands to cover it. Wolfe released it too soon. Ashton watched in horror as a set of keys fell to the floor with a loud clatter. Ashton met Wolfe's eyes in panic.

Without skipping a beat, Wolfe stood up, sending his chair flying. Ashton bent down and grabbed the keys off the cold floor. Wolfe grabbed her arm and pulled her up, slamming her back into the wall. The guard was watching now: Ashton could see his face over Wolfe's shoulder.

"You will give me the names of the people who told you about the Colony!" Wolfe shouted at her.

Shouting erupted from Ashton's prison friend, the caged girl next to her. "Stop it! Stop it! Don't hurt her." The guard with Wolfe turned toward Jagatha's cage cell to silence the disruption.

Wolfe came close to Ashton's ear and whispered, "You've got twenty minutes. No guards will be here, and I'll wipe the cameras. Versal and Sheva are on the second floor; the stairs are straight ahead and to the left. Come back down here and out the door we came through to the tunnel." Wolfe pulled away, taking Ashton with him, and then slammed her back against the wall.

"Are you working with them?!" Wolfe screamed. The charade was almost over. Wolfe would leave and Ashton had twenty minutes.

For a moment, Ashton considered nodding, playing the meek girl she was supposed to be. But Wolfe was about to leave, and he had all but told her she would be escaping to leave Niall and Bez behind to die.

Without thinking, Ashton whispered back, "I can't leave with them, not if Niall and Bez are in danger."

Wolfe was speechless. He looked both furious and confused as to why she would be so stupid and so bold. Ashton couldn't believe she had said it either, but she knew she could never live with herself if she didn't try to save all she could.

Wolfe sighed. "Jay, go." He paused. "Go get the stick."

The guard looked back, nodded, and disappeared to the right of the cage.

"What are you talking about?" Wolfe growled, still pushing Ashton up against the wall. "What are you doing?"

"I can't leave Bez . . . or Niall. Wolfe, you know I can't."

"Ashton, you have to. The things planned for you . . . please. We have a plan. I can only give you twenty minutes. Take Sheva and Versal and go."

"I can't leave and have them take my place, Wolfe. I'm sorry."

The guard returned, and Ashton knew that they wouldn't have another chance to speak.

"Here you are, sir." The guard handed Wolfe a long wooden stick with a spoon-like divot at the end. Ashton had never seen anything like it.

"Thank you, Jay," Wolfe said as he released Ashton and backed up. Ashton watched as he shook his head.

He raised the long stick above his head. Ashton realized what he was doing and nodded. She saw the pain in his eyes and wanted to let him know she understood he didn't have a choice. She shut her eyes and shook her head, putting her arm up over her face, and screamed. Wolfe struck. All that anticipation, and she felt nothing. But she heard the crack in the darkness of the wood hitting its mark. Ashton turned back to Wolfe, who was tense and gripping the wooden stick hard. The man behind him seemed unaware. Wolfe had struck his own leg to protect Ashton from the blow, but he remained stoic as if he had felt nothing.

"I'll let you think about this, Ashton, and will return tomorrow to see if you have changed your mind. Just think about it; it will get a lot worse." Wolfe was warning her.

He turned to leave and discreetly left something on the chair as he walked out: his watch. As soon as Wolfe and the guard disappeared, Ashton grabbed the watch. It was 10:40 p.m. Twenty minutes, maybe less, was all she had. Somehow, she had to get not only Sheva and Versal, but Bez, Niall, and Jagatha as well. She had no idea where Niall or Bez even were.

Ashton slipped the watch onto her wrist; it fit loosely on her small arm. She stuck both the key card and coordinates into her blouse, stuffed between her skin and corset. The flimsy plastic of the card stuck to her skin. *Why didn't the Victorian attire have pockets?* Using the keys she still held, she began fumbling with the cage door. She tried the first key. It didn't work. She tried the second one and cursed Wolfe for handing her so many keys. She fiddled as she tried each one with the rusty pit. Finally, with a click, one of them worked.

As she stepped out of the cell, she heard Jagatha whisper her name. The small girl was reaching for Ashton through her cage.

"I promise I'll be back. I won't leave without you," Ashton whispered. She didn't stay to hear Jagatha's response, but she saw the despair in the small girl's eyes. Without looking back, Ashton ran toward the stairs to get to Sheva and Versal.

Ashton hobbled along the dark walkway to a closed door. A key card hung on the ring of old, rusted keys, looking strangely modern. She swiped the card on the small black keypad next to the door and heard the inner mechanism unlock. A set of dark stairs spiraled up the top level. There must have been a light, but Ashton couldn't risk it.

After making it up the steep, dark staircase, Ashton ran the key card again to open the door at the top of the stairs. She cracked the door open. No guards were there, just another long hallway of cages. Ashton crept through the door and tiptoed out, looking into each cell as she passed.

"Sheva, Versal," she whispered, trying to be heard but quiet enough to not draw attention. There was no response. "Sheva, Versal," Ashton tried again, but again, nothing. Ashton went closer to the cages, peering into each as she went by. She passed cell after cell of sleeping workers.

"Ashton?" a weak voice said amongst the darkness, and she saw a hand reaching out a few cages ahead.

Ashton stumbled to the cage and grabbed the familiar old hand.

"Sheva, are you okay?" Sheva looked sick. Her skin looked like ash and her eyes were bloodshot. Her knee was wrapped up in cloth and it looked hurt. Sheva coughed.

"It's okay. I'm going to get you out of here." Ashton grabbed the keys and started trying each one again until the cage door opened. Sheva almost fell into Ashton's arms. Ashton wanted to hug Sheva forever, but there wasn't time for that.

"We have to go; do you know where Versal is?" Ashton asked and Sheva pointed down the hall. Ashton put Sheva's arm around her shoulders and pulled her along.

"There," Sheva said. Ashton quickly began trying the keys.

"Versal . . . Versal, it's Ashton."

"Ashton? Is that really you?" Versal shot up toward her cage's entrance with tears welling in her eyes. "You came back for us!"

"Shhh, we have to be quiet," Ashton hissed through her teeth as she finally found the key and swung open the door. "Come on, we don't have much time." Ashton looked down at Wolfe's watch. 10:46 p.m.

Ashton pulled Sheva toward her again, and they raced down the hallway. A few hollow eyes watched them, awake with curiosity. When they reached the end of the hallway, Versal helped Sheva down the stairs, and Ashton took one last look at the second-floor cages, at all the people she was leaving behind.

At 10:51 p.m., Ashton pointed Versal and Sheva toward the door to the tunnels while she sprinted in the opposite direction toward Jagatha's cell. She tried a key. Then another. Then the third and the fourth. *No, no, no, no, no.* Ashton understood: there was no key for Jagatha's cell.

"What's wrong?" Jagatha asked, panicked.

"Jagatha, where do they keep the keys?"

The small girl shook her head.

Ashton put her head against the bar. "Jagatha, I'm sorry. I—"

"You there! What are you doing out of your cell?" a voice boomed from the other end of the hall. Wolfe had said she had twenty minutes. It was 10:55; she should have had more time.

There was nothing else to do. Ashton ran toward Sheva and Versal. When she reached them, she shoved the key card against the door. The door opened and Ashton pushed them inside.

"Head to the tunnel, and when you reach the first split, go right and keep then going straight. Don't wait for me."

Sheva and Versal began to protest, but Ashton slammed the door in their face. She could hear the security guard closing in behind her.

Ashton's best chance was to somehow subdue the guard—if that was possible with her aching ribs and swollen face. She hadn't eaten in a day and already felt fatigued from her ordeal. Ashton took in one deep breath as she could hear his footsteps getting closer. She clenched her fist, preparing to make the first strike.

Ashton thought of Wolfe's training and the dances he had taught her. More importantly, the defense. The guard was seconds away from her. *Go!*

With all her strength, Ashton swung a high kick and hit the man right below the rib cage. He recoiled in both shock and pain. He had not expected such force from such a frail girl. With her unruly wig and sunken cheeks, Ashton was sure he had not seen her as a threat.

Using his hunch to her advantage, Ashton kicked him again, this time right in his kidney. He stumbled back. Ashton, feeling confident, went in with a full-body swing with her left hand, but he blocked it with his arm and came through with a full swing of his own, connecting with her right side.

Ashton tried hard to inhale, but it was all pain. The man regained his composure and came toward her, grabbing her blouse and pushing her into cage bars. He took her left arm and placed the cuff around her wrist, then reached for her right hand.

It was now or never. There were three lives, maybe four, depending on her right now. Ashton used her free arm and one leg and projected herself against him, pushing him again into the hallway wall behind them. Ashton quickly turned around and gave him a knee in his groin. He let out a cry and sank down to the concrete floor.

Ashton grabbed the other side of the cuffs hanging off her left hand, swung around behind him, and put the cuffs around his neck, blocking his airway.

"I want the keys! Where are they?!" Ashton screamed. "Where?"

Her voice cracked as she pulled a little tighter on the chain of the cuff. She had no idea where this strength had come from, but she felt powerful. The man tried to grab her, but she pulled tighter every time he reached out until his hands stopped reaching for her, and he grasped at his neck.

"Keys!" Ashton demanded.

CHAPTER 40

Ashton

The guard reached down into his pocket and produced a set of keys, a ring with what looked like a million keys on them. "Which one?!" Ashton asked. She pulled tighter and let the chain cut off his airway. It dug deep into his skin.

"Number 514," he said through strained speech. Ashton looked up to see that was Jagatha's cage number and nodded toward Jagatha, who was still staring at them. She looked at the keys. Attached was the same key card that Wolfe had given her. "Give the keys to her!" she yelled.

The guard did as Ashton asked and sent the keys flying toward Jagatha. Jagatha bent down, put her small hands through the bars, and brought the keys up toward the keyhole. "514, Jagatha, just look for 514."

Jagatha went through each one, desperately looking for the right key. She could hear the voices of other security guards in the distance. "Hurry," Ashton whispered.

"514, 514, I got it!" She brought the key up toward the keyhole and turned it. Jagatha leaped out of the cell and approached Ashton.

"All right, get in the cell," Ashton said to the guard as she started to drag his upper body in that direction. The chain must not have felt great because he was starting to choke with each pull, spitting up saliva. Ashton couldn't let up until he was in the cage and couldn't harm them as they left.

Ashton forced him into the cell and quickly turned while Jagatha closed the gate behind her. The guard coughed and massaged his neck. Ashton looked down at her watch: 10:57.

"Help! Down at 514! Workers are escaping," the guard yelled.

"Come on, Jagatha, we have to go!"

"They're escaping!" the guard yelled again right before coughing. "Down there, I see them."

Ashton pulled Jagatha toward the tunnel door and used the key card from the guard's key chain to gain access, but the first try didn't work. "Come on!" Ashton shouted. She tried again and again, but the light wouldn't turn green.

"Down there, by the tunnel door!" the man shouted and pointed toward them; the other guards must be getting close now. Finally, the key card worked and Jagatha darted through. Ashton paused. If she tried to get back into her cage the guard in Jagatha's cell would know she had everything to do with the escape. They would want information on who had helped them escape. Ashton was hoping she would get back in undetected, but to go back now would be suicide. She couldn't help her friends if she was dead.

Both Ashton and Jagatha went through the door, and Ashton quickly closed it behind her. It was dark, so Ashton took Jagatha's hand as they ran down the long tunnel, trusting that they wouldn't run into anything.

Ashton's heart was beating out of her chest, and she could feel the adrenaline coursing through her veins. Catching up to Sheva and Versal would be her new mission. Chances were if they could run fast enough, they would eventually run into them. Sheva was still hurt and wouldn't be moving fast.

Ashton tried to recollect exactly which way the guards had taken her when she'd first arrived with Wolfe. She remembered that there had been a wooden sign; it had something written on it and there was dust everywhere. Ashton dragged Jagatha behind her. The girl's tiny feet pounded on the floor, making the walls echo with sound. It made it difficult for Ashton to hear if the security men were far behind them or not. Ashton's eyes widened as she searched high and low for any sign.

"Ashton?" a voice called out from ahead.

"Sheva!"

Ashton reached her hand out to Sheva and Versal, who were hobbling down the tunnel in front of her.

"Thank goodness you are okay," Sheva burst out. Ashton put her arms around her and brought her up. Versal stood next to them.

"We have to keep moving. They know we are here," Ashton said. She grabbed Sheva and wrapped her arms around her again, holding Sheva by her waist.

"Come on, let's go; we need to go this way," Ashton said pointing to the right, remembering what Wolfe had said about the tunnel directions. When they made it to the first split tunnels, they were to take a right.

Ashton pushed them as fast as she could go, but all the girls were much weaker now and moving at a rapidly decreasing rate. Ashton kept looking back to make sure the guards weren't close, so they still had some time to make it out safely.

"Turn right here," Ashton said as they came to the fork in the tunnels.

Sheva said something but Ashton wasn't paying attention. She didn't want to lose focus, as she tried to discern how far the guards were behind them.

"We have to hurry! Go faster, we're almost there!" Ashton whispered to the group. She pulled Sheva closer to her and tried to catch up to where Jagatha and Versal were, but it was proving to be difficult.

"I need you to push hard, Sheva, please," Ashton said through a strained breath. There weren't any more voices, but she could hear the footsteps, and she was sure they could hear them as well. The echoing of their footsteps carried.

"There they are, just ahead!" a voice rang through the tunnel walls. Ashton turned to look and could see black figures shifting in the darkness with flashes of light.

The sound of a guard's interconnect echoed: "I want you to shoot them! They don't get away, you hear me!" Ashton heard screaming. "Yes, sir. Men, start firing!" a man yelled.

"Run!" Ashton yelled.

Sparks of lights from behind them sent lightning down the tunnel, and Ashton could almost feel the wind from bullets whizzing by. It made a large banging sound when they hit the end of the tunnel. They were close. As Ashton ran, she ducked her head down to protect herself. The bangs were loud, but all they could do was keep running, praying to miss them.

Versal and Jagatha were at the door before Ashton and Sheva. Versal used the key card and started opening the thick steel door. The bullets kept hitting the wall. Jagatha screamed. BANG, BANG, BANG. Each hit louder than the one before, and Ashton recoiled as sparks flew. The bullets had hit the steel door that kept them in the tunnel.

"I got it!" Versal shouted and pulled open the door. A bright light shone instantly as the crack between the door and the outside world became wider. Ashton pushed Sheva through, then Jagatha, and finally Versal. The bullets had stopped for the moment, but it didn't mean the guards weren't near. Ashton could feel their presence, and the danger felt so close, it made her shake in fear. Finally, Ashton pushed herself into the star-lit night sky and pulled the heavy steel door shut. Stunned, she glanced at the door she had just escaped from.

"I need something to hold this closed!" Ashton yelled. The guards would be at the door any minute, and they needed all the time they could get to make it out to the forest.

Versal and Jagatha ran toward the forest to see what they could find. The sound of muffled voices on the other side told her the guards were at the door. She pulled as hard as she could and put one leg up on the wall to give herself some support as she tried to keep the door shut and them in the tunnel.

"Here!" Versal came with a large branch that looked long and sturdy. It was perfect. The first tug at the door happened, and Ashton could tell that she wouldn't be able to hold them off. Jagatha came to help pull.

"Versal, put the branch through the door handle and make sure it goes on the door frame," Ashton told her. Versal took the direction well and shoved the branch through the small opening. It was long enough that it went over the frame of the door, and Ashton slowly let go to make sure it would hold. There was another pull at the door: the branch moved slightly but didn't let the guards come through.

"It worked!" Ashton yelled and turned to hug Versal. "It worked!" She laughed. Ashton glanced at the overgrown sidewalk that led up to the door. Sheva was on the ground lying motionless. "Sheva, we did it!" she shouted in pure excitement. There was a long pause as Ashton waited for Sheva. "Sheva?" Again, silence.

Ashton sprinted to her side and pulled her face toward her own, coming only inches away. She turned to assess her long-time friend's frail and old body.

She still wore the Victorian outfit, like Versal and Ashton. Like theirs, it was torn and dirty from the cages and pursuit out of Augland. Blood was coming down from her side, which covered some of the grass on the ground and spilled onto the concrete.

Ashton lost her breath as her heart skipped a beat. "No, no! No, Sheva, no!" *This can't be happening*, she thought to herself. All the work they had done, and they had escaped. She needed Sheva to make it to the Colony.

Sheva's eyes slightly opened, and Ashton could see it was difficult for her to breathe. "Ashton."

Ashton's heart surged, and her eyes widened as she felt the small amount of life left in her friend.

"Yes, Sheva, I'm here. You're going to be all right," Ashton said as tears started to roll down her dirty face. She put her hand near Sheva's face and started to stroke it with her open palm. "Stay with me, Shev. Stay with me, please," she begged.

Sheva tried to pull her head toward Ashton but ended up wincing in pain and put her head back against the hard ground.

"You'll make it. You're going to be fine." Ashton repeated but knew she was only convincing herself. In addition to her knee, a gunshot wound would be next to impossible for Sheva to recover from.

"Ashton, you need to go; get everyone out of here." Sheva's breath was less than a whisper.

"I'm not leaving you!"

"Sweetie . . . please."

"No, no, I'm not. I can't." Ashton tried to bring Sheva up to her feet. Sheva cried in pain.

"Come on, it's this way; Versal, I need your help." Versal and Jagatha came, and they pulled Sheva toward the water. Ashton couldn't look down at her. She just needed to keep moving. "We will go across the water; the boat is right up this way," Ashton directed.

Versal and Ashton stumbled out of the boat, which was harder with Sheva's weight. While the boat ride was easy, Sheva struggled through the harsh wind and crashing waves. She winced in pain with every movement. Ashton couldn't take her eyes off her while she guided the boat to the island across from Augland. She followed the same path Wolfe had taken with her.

"Ashton?" Hunter came out from behind a small brush area. He had a disheveled look, like he had been camping at the beach since she had left the Colony for Augland.

"Hunter!" Versal was excited to see him but didn't want to let go of their formation as Sheva might slip. He ran toward them and picked up Sheva in his arms. She had stopped speaking and her eyes remained closed as he cradled her.

"We have to hurry; they saw us leave," Ashton said as she turned with Hunter and Sheva toward the direction Hunter had just come from. Ashton touched Sheva, brushing the top of her stubbled head. During the transition, she had lost her wig.

"It's okay, Sheva, we are going to get you to safety," Ashton promised, whispering to her.

Sheva didn't say anything back to her, but had slightly opened her eyes and was looking out at the moon and smiling.

"Hunter, put me down," she said. Hunter did as Sheva asked, and Ashton looked at him, confused.

"What are you doing? We have to go!" Ashton yanked at Hunter's shirt. "Pick her up, we have to go, we don't have time!"

Hunter didn't say anything, and no one moved around Ashton.

"Fine, I'll do it," Ashton said. She bent down to pull Sheva up, but she couldn't take her full body weight.

"Ashton, please." Sheva's breath was shallow now, and she breathed heavily. Ashton bent down and put her head by her neck.

"No!" Ashton said, broken. "No, we can do this . . ." she pleaded. She needed Sheva to hold firm, but she could tell the older woman was giving up. After all that Ashton had done to save her. They had finally made it out of Augland, and they were so close to the Colony.

"Sheva?" she said, not hearing anything coming from her. "Sheva!" Ashton yelled again, but there was nothing in her eyes anymore, no movement, no life. Ashton took her friend's hand and squeezed it but felt nothing in return. Ashton burst into tears as she realized what had just happened. She had lost her.

Ashton put her head against Sheva's chest and sobbed. All she wanted was for her to get up and be okay. Sheva wasn't coming back, though, and Ashton knew it. Ashton pushed her face toward hers and just rocked back and forth.

The pain was like nothing she had felt before. It cut deeper than any cut and struck harder than any hit she had ever felt. It was gut-wrenching, twisting her insides as she sobbed uncontrollably. She could tell at that moment that nothing would ever be the same. She would never be the same. She thought Augland couldn't hurt her, but she was wrong. It had taken something more precious to her than anything. It had taken Sheva.

CHAPTER 41

Wolfe

Walking away from Ashton's cage was difficult. It was his fault for saying what would happen to Niall and Bez. If he had kept his mouth shut, she would have gone along with the rest of the group. He wanted to turn around and tell her she had to leave. He had put a lot of things in motion to help this escape, things that she just didn't know. Again, Ashton was determined to make things difficult.

He thought hard as he walked the long, dark, and damp corridors of the cages. If she wasn't going to go willingly, he would have to force her to leave.

"Brock, we have some men getting two new workers today," he said over the interconnect. Brock was one of Warren's men, the same man who had interrogated Ashton. Would you have one of your men do a quick round around 10:50 p.m.? I want to make sure we have security coverage."

Wolfe felt bad. He had told Ashton she had until 11:00 but knew if she was spotted, then she would have to go with Sheva and Versal. There was no way her plan would work if they knew she had helped the others escape. It was a risky move, but Ashton didn't understand what would happen to her if she stayed. She needed to leave.

"Yes, sir. No problem." Wolfe nodded as Brock responded over the interconnect. It was now time for the second part of his plan to commence.

Stepping into his office, he shut the door behind him and made his way to the leather chair behind his monitor screen that he rarely used. The same papers he had left previously were scattered on top of the wooden desk. He took a deep breath and reached around to grab the bottle of whiskey he had near his desk and the two glasses that were next to it.

Typically, he didn't change and try to look presentable when going up to the Executive Offices because it felt so foreign to him. This was going to be a special occasion, though. Getting up and heading toward his couch, which also happened to be his bed, he opened a large closet. All-black shirts and pants lined the reachable places, but back in the far corner were a black tie and white shirt that would go well with his black pants. He quickly put them on and looked at the time. It was 10:40 p.m. He would need to hurry.

"Knock, knock," Wolfe said as he knocked on his father's glass door.

"Ah, Wolfgang, happy you stopped by." He glanced up from behind his desk. "Oh, what's that?" Warren looked at the glasses and whiskey that Wolfe had brought with him. "And you're wearing a tie? Never thought I'd see the day." He smirked.

"I thought we should celebrate. I mean, this is a pretty big deal that I'm now officially head of Security of Augland 54. I wanted to thank you for the opportunity." Wolfe brought the glasses down in front of his father, who still sat in his office chair. He poured the caramel-colored liquid and passed a glass to his father. His father tapped his glass then took a big swig.

Wolfe sat down in one of the chairs in front of Warren's desk and brought his leg up to rest on his knee.

"I'm having one of the men get Niall and Bez today, but I am concerned about the brothel's productivity without Bez," Wolfe started. Warren shook his head.

"The blonde girl can take it over." That proved to Wolfe that Warren was more familiar with the brothel than he had thought. While Warren didn't know Cherise, he knew of her, and that was something Warren didn't normally know.

Wolfe just nodded. "You know, I did watch the tape." Wolfe started, taking a quick sip of his whiskey then placing it on the table.

"Oh?"

"I just thought that I've seen our interrogator do a better job than that. I'm surprised at how easy he was on the girl." Wolfe looked intently at Warren.

"You. You thought he was easy?" Warren was stunned.

"She's a young girl. I mean, a persuasive one, maybe even manipulative. You saw how she captured the customers' attention in Land of Legends. I just would have thought, from previous viewings of his ability, that he, of all people, would have been able to get information out of her." Wolfe hoped his small seeds of doubt would plant themselves in Warren's mind and blossom. While Warren was cunning and intelligent, he wasn't able to control his paranoia. "Just surprised, that's all."

"That's an interesting perspective. How do you plan to do it differently?" Warren asked.

"Well, you had a great point. People don't fear what will happen to them but what will happen to the people they love. I've already spoken to her. Told her about Niall and Bez. I've got my men getting them as we speak."

Warren smiled and nodded his head yes. "What did she say?" he asked.

"It's not what she said, it's what she did. She begged me not to hurt them. Tomorrow, we will torture them until she gives us what we want."

Warren leaned back in his chair. "I'm going to be honest, Wolfgang, I'm surprised by your shift in attitude."

"Well, I take my new position here at Augland seriously. You know I've wanted this for some time now." Wolfe took yet another sip of his drink. His father studied him, and Wolfe stared at him as if to challenge him.

"Well, I'll cheers to that." Warren brought his glass up. Wolfe mimicked.

"Sir!" The interconnect that Wolfe had taken with him rang.

"Yes?" Wolfe replied, knowing full well what his officer was about to mention.

"The girl, that girl that hit the customer. She . . . she's escaping." The man sounded as if he was running. Wolfe quickly stood up and pushed his chair behind him.

"What!" He shouted. Wolfe needed to sell his surprise.

There was silence over the interconnect. Wolfe spoke again, "Tell me what has happened!" he shouted.

Wolfe didn't look at his father, but he could sense that Warren was angry. In his periphery, he could see his father's fists clench as he sat on every word that came through on the interconnect.

"We are chasing them through the Old Seattle tunnels," the same voice said.

"Do not let them leave, or I—" Wolfe started but Warren stood up and snatched the interconnect from Wolfe's hand.

"This is CEO Warren! Do not let them leave Augland, no matter what! I want you to shoot them! They don't get away, you hear me!" Warren was angry, more so than Wolfe would have anticipated. Wolfe didn't think he cared so much about them escaping as much as he cared about someone outsmarting him. He prided himself on his ability to maintain control, and when that control was tested, he lost it.

Warren tossed the interconnect against his office walls, and it broke in two. Wolfe stared, as that was his line of communication with his team. He was now in the dark, and he had to maintain his composure.

"Wolfgang, so help me, if you had anything to do with this . . ." Warren breathed heavily.

"Sir, how could you think that?" Wolfe was being condescending, but he was hoping his father didn't notice.

"Oh, stop with the horse crap. I know you hate the cages; I know you liked that girl. I know it all because it is my business to know." Warren was accusing him, hoping that Wolfe would admit to his guilt. Warren had already shown his hand, though. Wolfe knew he had been tracking him and would come first to him as the person who'd let this happen.

But Wolfe had thought of every angle. There were no leads tying him to their escape. The key cards were of Warren's interrogator, Brock. The keys were his as well, which he would report missing at any moment. Brock was in charge of bringing men down to do a shift-change security sweep. His men would report that Wolfe had asked for coverage of the security detail from Brock, asking him to go through the cells. He had been celebrating with Warren when they escaped.

"You think that girl means more to me than Augland? I've lived and breathed this establishment since I was a child. I would never let anything come in the way of that. She was a pawn, entertainment, something shiny to look at while I degraded myself teaching fake fighting to a bunch of unappreciative workers."

Warren would have a tough time proving this and a worse time convincing the Board after making Wolfe head of Security. It was his decision to cast that vote, and he cared more about their impression of him than anything. Warren thought his son didn't know him well, but Wolfe had watched through the years and had learned how to be cunning and manipulative as well.

Warren shook with anger as they stared at each other but soon sank in his chair in defeat. "Just go find them," he said defeatedly, drinking the last bit of whiskey from his cup.

"Yes, sir," Wolfe said before turning to walk out. As he turned, a small smile crept to his face. For once, he had done it. He had outsmarted his father.

Walking down the halls, Wolfe headed to the camera room. He had lost visibility into whatever his guards were doing in the tunnels. He would need to see if Ashton had made it out or not. Wolfe barreled through the camera room doors and went straight to the tunnel camera footage. The halls were empty except for the entrance door to the tunnels. His men were pulling hard to open it, but it seemed blocked by something. Wolfe narrowed in. If they were trying to get out of the tunnel, it could only mean that Ashton had made it out, but he wanted to be sure.

"I need the cameras outside of the tunnel. Do we have that?" Wolfe asked the security man in the camera room.

"Yes, one moment, sir." The man changed the images on the screen in front of Wolfe. It was then that he saw it. The girl with red hair was walking away, holding an older woman. She had made it. Wolfe had to catch himself from sighing in relief. He watched her until they disappeared from his view, walking toward the boat he knew she would take to the Colony's island.

Hope you find peace, Ash, he said to himself as she slowly made her way out of the camera's view. He hadn't known what to say to her before taking her to the tunnels. He did only wish that Ashton found her freedom. She, like all the workers, had been mistreated, abused, manipulated, and lied to. He did hope she would find peace and happiness.

Ashton would take his note to Cahya, and they would all move to Hood Canal. It would be a hard trip to move the entire Colony, but it was a safe area with vast amounts of food options. It would keep them well hidden from Augland officials and less dependent on the supplies Augland received. It pained him that he wouldn't be able to visit, but he would be under great scrutiny from his father. If he were to take over, he would need to win over the Executives. His feelings toward the Colony could hurt his ability to gain that trust.

Here Wolfe was. He had completed what he had worked so hard to do and at a great cost, but for a good cause. He was now on his road to becoming CEO. Warren would fight him along the way, but Wolfe was confident he would prevail. He was stronger than that. He was a fighter.

CHAPTER 42

Ashton

Ashton cried as she pounded the ground beside Sheva.

"Ashton." Hunter knelt beside Ashton and touched her shoulder.

"She's gone." Tears were still rolling down Ashton's face and onto Sheva's lifeless body. To hear it out loud made it more real to Ashton.

"We need to go, Ashton. We can't stay." Versal was sympathetic. They didn't have enough time to stay there much longer.

"We will lay her to rest here on the island," Hunter said as he squeezed Ashton's shoulder. "At least she made it this far."

Ashton tried to hold back the tears as she responded. "Okay."

Hunter shoved his arms underneath Sheva's body and picked her up. Carefully, he walked toward the camp he'd made for himself. The rest of the group followed close behind him.

He laid her down in a shelter he had set up with tree branches, with a soft-looking bed inside. Twigs and greenery surrounded her. She fit perfectly there, like it was meant for her, Ashton thought. Hunter crawled out and came to stand next to Versal, Jagatha, and Ashton. She could see Sheva's hands folded around her blood-soaked Victorian blouse and the wrap around her bruised knee.

"Should we say something?" Versal said as she pulled Hunter closer to her.

"Ashton? You knew her best," Hunter said as he placed his hand on Ashton's shoulder.

She took in a deep breath. "Sheva, you deserved to live a great life," Ashton said as her blood boiled with both sadness and regret. To use Augland's slogan seemed fitting, as they didn't deserve this life, and Sheva didn't deserve this death. She sobbed as the trees swayed left and right from the wind. Jagatha wrapped her tiny body around Ashton, consoling her. Ashton looked up, refusing to look at Sheva again. She didn't want to remember her this way. She wanted to remember Sheva before the day she was taken, the woman who had laughed and joked with her. Who had taught her things and cared for her. That was the Sheva she was going to remember.

She felt Hunter get up from her side. "Come on, Ash, we need to go to the Colony," he urged. "There's still work to do. They can send someone to bury Sheva properly." Ashton knew he was right. It was the right thing to do for Sheva.

The time it took to make it back to the Colony seemed to go by much faster than when Wolfe and Ashton traveled from the Colony cul-de-sac to the Seattle Underground doors. As she made her way along with the others, she must have replayed every interaction she'd ever had with Shev. She missed her already, but those memories kept the pain at bay.

They were greeted by Cahya and several other Colony members as they took them in and fed them inside Cahya's home. Several kind women helped them bathe and change into clean clothes. Cahya herself sponged Ashton's wounds and gave her some soothing herbal tea for the pain. Ashton sunk into the soft bed that was offered to her and, for the first time in a long time, slept.

When she awoke, Ashton found herself thankfully alone. The silence was welcome. She slipped out behind Cahya's house toward the beachfront a few yards ahead of the house.

Ashton kept walking and, before she knew it, she had headed past several of the homes and down a path that led through a densely wooded area along the beach. It was quiet, which was a nice change from the cries and coughs of the cages. Ashton had made it far enough and stopped to admire the beautiful purple flowers surrounding her, along with the sound of crashing waves on the rocky beach of Bainbridge Island. She bent down and sat amongst them, picking a couple of blossoms and making a small bouquet. The flowers were beautiful—deep purple with white spots near the center. The sun was out, and she lifted her face toward the heat. She felt out of place, yet she felt she was somewhere she could stay forever.

Ashton brought her hand to the center of her chest, where the moonstone necklace Sheva gave her hung around her neck. She grabbed it and squeezed tightly, closing her eyes and taking a deep breath in. Now it was too quiet around her, suffocating. Sheva's lifeless body flashed in her head as if it were there to haunt her forever. Ashton cried out loud, letting all the air she had just sucked in release with such force that it rattled her voice box.

It came at her all at once: the hurt, the fear, the anxiety, and even the anger. She let it all out because she couldn't keep it in any longer. Ashton screamed again, and her voice cracked as the sobs strained her vocal cords.

Ashton needed to cope with Sheva's death in her own way, away from everyone, but there were still things that needed to be done. There was so much to process. Bez and Niall were still in danger, as was Wolfe. Ashton tried to inhale and exhale, telling herself to breathe, but it wasn't working. This was too much for her to take. The anxiety was crippling, and she collapsed into a fetal position, still holding the stone in her hand. There was nothing Ashton could do about the past now. All she could do was focus on the future: the Colony. Ashton pulled herself up, still hurting from the exhausting run and her interrogation. It didn't compare to the loneliness she felt. Her heart had broken.

She wasn't sure how much time had passed. Her salty tears dried out her eyes and fair skin.

Ashton suddenly remembered that she needed to give the coordinates from Wolfe to Cahya so Cahya could get the people of the Colony away from Bainbridge. It was no longer safe for them there.

Her trip back to Cahya's house was brief, and she bypassed the now-chatty Jagatha and Versal on her way to Cahya's kitchen.

"I was wondering where you had gone, Ashton," Cahya said as she looked up from the stove where she boiled water. "Tea?"

Ashton nodded.

"Wolfe gave me new coordinates for a location for the Colony," Ashton croaked. The screams had reduced her voice to hoarseness.

Cahya passed Ashton a cup of tea. It burned her fingers as she wrapped her hands around the clay mug, but as she took a sip she felt the instant soothing effect on her tender throat.

"He gave me this." She handed Cahya the piece of paper that Wolfe had given her while visiting her in her cage.

Cahya read his note, which seemed to have more on it than Ashton had originally thought. She now wished she would have read it before handing it to her. Cahya smiled and nodded. She then turned her gaze toward Ashton, and her smile faded.

"Ashton, I know loss causes pain," she started. Ashton's eyes started swelling again with tears. She knew she was talking about Wolfe and Sheva. "It is how you live and remember them that truly heals."

"I can't. I just picture her face everywhere." Ashton could barely form the words. "And who I left behind. I keep thinking of them," Ashton confessed. Cahya nodded and set her tea down and wrapped her arms around her. Her long braided hair smelled like fire and lavender.

"You are born to live a life full of gratitude for all you've been given. Loss, loss of life is part of the process. It helps us identify life as something precious, worth being lived."

Ashton appreciated what Cahya was trying to do, but right now, she needed her space. She needed time to heal. If that were possible. She pulled away from her and walked toward the exit.

Before Ashton was out of earshot, Cahya had one last thing to say. "Ashton, please come to me if you ever need anything. I know pain and loss. Life can be positive if you let it."

Ashton just nodded and kept walking through the living room and toward Hunter, Versal, and Jagatha. She sat down with them, but their voices sounded muffled. So she stared off to the distance, leaving the present to drift away from her mind.

Cahya spoke in the direction of the exit to her home, enlisting the attention of one of the guards. "Powlen!" Her soft voice carried. Her guard came inside the door. "Tell everyone to grab their essentials, only what they can carry. We must leave this camp within the hour, and we have a long journey ahead of us."

"Yes, Cahya." Just as quickly, he disappeared to fulfill his orders.

The Colony moved swiftly to depart, just like Cahya had asked. It was astounding to Ashton how quickly they rallied. Soon the whole group had gathered in the cul-de-sac. Cahya made her way to the head of the large group of Colony folks and looked toward her people.

"Thank you for your swiftness, as we need to leave quickly." The crowd became quiet as Cahya spoke. "This place has sustained our houses, our hard work over the years, and our memories, but that doesn't make it home. Home is where we are all together and safe. We leave now to be safer, stronger, and better. We will go where our children can dwell and grow in security. We no longer will be bound by what Augland says or wants, as we are free people, and free people do not take threats lightly. We will persevere as we set our sights on our new futures. We will follow the stars and let them guide us through. Let us go and thank this village for all it has provided for us."

Cahya turned and raised her hands toward the empty street lined with homes. Some still had smoke coming up from the chimney tops. Each Colony member did the same as they turned toward their homes and thanked them. She started moving in the opposite direction of Augland, and the Colony followed.

Ashton let several people walk past her as she slowly picked up a small bag for the trip and walked alongside them.

"You okay?" Hunter came up to Ashton with Jagatha and Versal close behind.

Ashton looked at him and nodded. She didn't feel fine, but she didn't want to talk about it either. All Ashton wanted was to make sure no one else was going to get hurt for her actions. If Augland's guards made it to the Colony, they were sure to hurt people.

Hunter reached out quietly and laid his hand on Ashton's shoulder, understanding her pain. "It's not your fault, Ash."

She touched his hand appreciatively and trudged on. They had a long journey ahead of them.

Whew! I made it! Ashton thought to herself as she caught her breath, coming up on top of the hillside of the new Colony location. She headed down a few steps and stopped on a rock that she had now claimed as her safe haven. Ashton went there almost every day to watch the sun rise above the mountains and canal. It was her sanctuary first thing in the morning. It had been tough at first to start anew, but after a while, things started to come together, and they were able to develop and grow.

It had only been a few months since they moved, with no sign of Augland's men or Wolfe. It would be tough for the guards to find them since they were now much farther away from Augland than they had been. Their new camp was an abandoned resort, or that was what some of the older Colony folk had said. It had rooms for all of the Colony people, with homes lining the rich, rocky shores. People fished and gathered shellfish. The soil was perfect for crops. At first, it was difficult, but they had come so far in a short amount of time.

Ashton picked up a small blade of grass and started pulling it apart as she looked across the beautiful landscape. Hunter had told her she needed to forgive herself, even though he thought there was nothing to forgive. He had been angry with Augland when she had told him what they had planned for Bez and Niall. Ashton appreciated him listening to her and helping her get through it. They both held out hope that Wolfe had been able to do something to save them. They would likely never know.

She thought about Versal and Hunter, who had made their relationship official. Hunter had joined the Colony's engineering team and was putting his skills to work teaching them about new technology. They had started building different things, and Ashton was proud of him. He was preparing for a trip to NeuroEnergy to become the Colony's advocate.

Ashton looked down at the blades of grass on her new navy-blue dress that Versal made for her. Versal had started sewing clothing and was good at it. Ashton had never owned anything as pretty as this dress.

Jagatha had really opened up once she started at the Colony's school. She told Ashton all the time about her friends and what she was learning. She had come a long way from the shriveled shell Ashton had first met back in the cages.

Finally, Ashton thought about Wolfe and what he had sacrificed to help her. She felt inside that he was okay, and that brought her peace. He was smart and would have found a way to survive there. Still, she missed him.

The wind started to pick up, and it felt great as it swirled her short, messy, brown hair around. The soft curls were starting to form again. She put her hand up to push her hair back. The new cuff bracelet dangled from her wrist, along with Wolfe's watch. The Colony guards had said they could take the cuff off for her, but Ashton decided to keep it on as a reminder of what she had been through. At times, like now, Ashton felt at peace. Sheva's moonstone, Wolfe's watch, and Augland's chain were constant reminders of previous times.

The sun had almost risen above the mountains, and soon, the sky would shine brightly across the horizon. Ashton could feel the warmth. She liked feeling the first bit of sunshine before the cold night disappeared. She and the Colony were free for another day.

She knew she would one day meet Augland again. She had a purpose now, and that purpose was to break its walls and watch as its perfection crumbled. She no longer could rely on someone else being brave enough to change it. Ashton had already survived—and that was proof enough that anything could rise from the ashes.

ABOUT THE AUTHOR

Erin Carrougher is a Pacific Northwest-based author whose debut novel, *Augland*, is set in Seattle's not-too-distant future. While her day-to-day work is all business, working sales in the technology industry, she enjoys fantasizing about dystopian worlds in her spare time. When she's not writing on her comfy couch next to her dog, Griffen, Erin loves spending time with her husband, Joe, and their family and friends, and enjoying life outdoors as much as possible. She's the proud auntie of Annabelle and Wyatt, her two favorites until more come along. If Erin has any downtime, she fills it with cooking, reading, and binge-watching reality television shows. You can find her at www.erincarrougher.com.

A free ebook edition
is available with the
purchase of this book.

To claim your free ebook edition:

1. Visit MorganJamesBOGO.com
2. Sign your name CLEARLY in the space
3. Complete the form and submit a photo of the entire copyright page
4. You or your friend can download the ebook to your preferred device

Morgan James BOGO™

A **FREE** ebook edition is available for you or a friend with the purchase of this print book.

CLEARLY SIGN YOUR NAME ABOVE

Instructions to claim your free ebook edition:
1. Visit MorganJamesBOGO.com
2. Sign your name CLEARLY in the space above
3. Complete the form and submit a photo of this entire page
4. You or your friend can download the ebook to your preferred device

Print & Digital Together Forever.

Snap a photo   Free ebook   Read anywhere

Lightning Source UK Ltd.
Milton Keynes UK
UKHW011428160123
415435UK00020B/249

9 781631 959257